HORIZONS

A Novel by Jenny E. Shaw

This edition published 2019

ISBN 9-780648-482628

HardtHouse Publishing
www.hardthouse.com

Shield your aching eyes and gaze

At images that shimmer

And vanish through the haze

Of hot and endless summer.

Your eyes play tricks it seems,

Standing there – in the white-hot sun

Where nothing can be seen –

But the far horizon.

Jenny E Shaw

Chapter 1
THE ARRIVAL

A plane in trouble! Not easily forgotten that sound, and instantly recognizable - if you've heard it before.

Suddenly, out of the stillness of a desert afternoon, the cough of an engine - a sound that had persisted in Tammy's dreams for most of her childhood. She had thought that was all in the past... gone, like the life she barely remembered; her pink, frilly bedroom back home, the dog in the yard, and recently... Oh and much too soon - her parents...

But there it was, unmistakably a plane; unmistakably in trouble, and close.

As though transfixed, she stood there like a small animal caught in a sudden glare of light.

Slim, lithe and brown as a berry from years in the sun, the deep colour of her skin belied the depth of the blue in her eyes and the flaxen hue of her hair.

Untrimmed for years, it hung like a curtain down her slender back, gleaming almost white in the harsh Australian sun.

She was, for reasons she could not have explained coherently, very afraid, and she stood - frozen to the spot.

With all of her concentration she was willing the plane to stay in the air and pass her by. She did not want to be a witness to the horror of history repeating itself. It couldn't possibly be happening! Not here in the same place, after all these years.

But the plane had circled and the tone of the engine told it's own undeniable story. This plane was coming down; the pilot searching for a place clear enough of rocks or shrubs; an area large enough to take his little craft without tearing it to pieces.

Tammy knew this place well, she usually avoided it because of the memories it evoked. Why on earth had she come here today?

It had been a beastly day, with hot, gusting winds, dust-devils, eddies and willy-willies springing up unexpectedly all over the place. And although she had gone about her usual tasks, Tammy had been strangely unsettled all day; as if something beyond her understanding was terribly wrong.

She had been daydreaming as she'd walked along, and had wandered further in her search for food than she normally would have.

Most days, if she was searching for some wild fruits, she would have set off in other directions, because this path led to 'that place' – and let's face it, there was nothing here but dust, spinifex, a few spindly trees... and memories.

But here she was, and now, it was happening all over again. Was history to repeat its cruel joke, right before her eyes?

As she'd wandered along the trail, humming praise-songs to herself to chase away her melancholy mood, she had been vaguely aware of a soft droning sound, but it had merely been a backdrop to her daydream and had not impacted her conscious mind – until that unmistakable sound.

Another cough from just above her – this one had a kind of finality to it, and then, nothing but the silence of the bush. Everything it seemed, was holding it's breath and Tammy was no exception.

Then there was a rushing sound and the plane was right in front of her. It tore across the small clearing, going much too fast. Tammy couldn't watch, but even with her eyes closed she saw it all.

But the terrified young woman saw it all from a completely different perspective. In her mind, she was inside the plane, head buried in her mother's lap, screaming her fear as her father battled the controls of the small plane that was supposed to be taking them on their great adventure.

Chapter 2

GRAND ADVENTURE

They had been on the trip of a lifetime. Dan, a bush pilot for many years, had saved for ever it seemed to buy his own light plane. He and his little family would fly away on a round Australia trip.

He so wanted his wife and child to see the bush from the vantage point of the air – the bush he had worked in, loved and respected for most of his life.

He had assured his worried wife that it was perfectly safe. Hadn't he travelled miles across this country, in all sorts of planes? So off they'd set; dreams of adventure lighting up their eyes. That was until the dust storm hit out of nowhere, over a remote corner of the Northern Territory.

Blown about like a leaf, they had survived the initial blow, then to end up heaven only knew where, with compass and radio dead and every working part of the plane full of sand that was as fine as talcum powder. It was then that Tammy first heard that cough – a sound, it seemed, never to be forgotten; the engine's final gasp for air and fuel as the plane came down, in a clearing, of sorts – lost in the vastness of Central Australia.

Tammy never did find out exactly where she lived. A tribe of local aborigines had their own name for the place, but that had meant little to a child who was too young to have studied geography, even if such a name would ever be found on a map.

Tammy had been barely six years old when the grand adventure had ended in the wilds of Central Australia. Rescue had never come, and her family had made their lives as comfortable as possible in this harsh landscape.

For years, Tammy and her parents had survived. Dan had a good knowledge of bush craft and insisted that his family should learn from him all that he'd learned during his years of working at all sorts of jobs in the outback.

Finding a place to live had been his number one priority. For he reasoned, that even if rescuers were to eventually come, the family would still need somewhere to shelter from the extreme conditions as they waited.

With no idea of their location, and no way of alerting the outside world to their predicament, he had known that it wouldn't really matter much if they were missed, and they would be of course. For no one would have the slightest clue as to the fate of the little plane.

Regular flight paths would be a long way from where they'd come down, and not too many people ventured out here in light planes, fuel simply didn't stretch that far.

So Dan, ever the realist, decided they should make the best of things in their unforgiving new home. There was always the hope that some day, someone might come this way.

The aborigines who came by occasionally were nomadic. They would camp nearby for a while in a sheltered valley at the foot of a rock escarpment – a surprising fault-line, Dan supposed, in an otherwise quite barren landscape. A small stream surfaced there from under the ground and an oasis of sorts had developed. Dan, Betty, and their daughter Tammy had been befriended by these kind and noble people. They had learned their language and taught them their own.

It didn't take long for them to discover that their new friends had little idea of any kind of world outside of the vast interior that was their home. It seemed they were one of the last of a few tribes who had somehow never been found by white settlers, living their lives as their people had for generations before them.

They did not know if there were any other white folk nearby who could help the stranded travelers. It seemed they had seen white people occasionally, a long way off to the east, but had always kept their distance. Dan and his family soon realized that any contact with others of their own kind would be many days walk away, through difficult country.

The tribe, meanwhile, were more than happy to help their unexpected neighbours find food, to share their water, and to offer any other bits of information that might assist in surviving far from the nearest supermarket, but that seemed to be all they were able to offer.

So, the family enjoyed their company when they came by, learned all they could, and otherwise set about making a life for themselves. It soon became obvious that they would be here for some time.

So it was that the years had come and gone. Tammy had become independent in the bush. She had even traveled on occasions with the tribe, just to see where they went and what they did. They never went anywhere near any civilization as far as she could see, and though she'd enjoyed the experience, she had decided that it was much nicer in the new home that her father had found for them.

Several things had governed Dan's search for a 'home'. Shelter was the main priority, of course, plus ease of access, and availability of water. And that had to be all year round, not just now and then. So, firstly, he'd built a donga, similar to those built by their neighbours.

That would do, he had said, until something more substantial could be found.

He'd had a bit of a look around and decided that the rocky formations scattered about, and the underground creek, had to mean caverns somewhere. He was determined to find one that would make a safe and secure home for his wife and child.

One day, he'd found the very thing. He had been poking around rocks, cracks, fault-lines and fissures for so long he'd almost given up. The heat that radiated off the stark outcrops was stifling, but Dan diligently kept to his task.

Then, one day, quite without warning, he stumbled through a crumbling section of rock, onto which clung some stubborn greenery, (although more grey than green) and virtually fell into a dark hole of some kind. Scrambling to his feet, he gave his eyes a moment to adjust and looked about him. The sudden change in temperature was amazing and he stood there in the cool dark interior for a moment to catch his breath.

Then he turned on the torch he'd carried for days, just in case – blessing the fact that there was still some life in it.

He had known that the small store of batteries he'd carried in the plane would not last forever and had been experimenting to find the best way to make light without batteries or power.

In the fast dimming light of the torch he saw that a long dark tunnel sloped steeply downward ahead of him. He followed this tunnel down several feet, shaking the torch every few moments, hoping to get just a bit more light out of it. The floor of the tunnel seemed fairly smooth except for the occasional step down, but the going was pretty easy.

The passage eventually opened up to a smallish cave, dark and not very inviting, but further examination revealed a fairly wide fissure in the wall on the other side. Not prepared to quit having come this far, he had ventured further in, climbed and scrambled over a large boulder and was greeted by an amazing sight. There, in front of him and some distance below, was a huge cavern.

This larger cavern was bright as day with a soft sandy floor and a small stream actually flowing through it.

The water came trickling through a crack in the rock on the far side, splashed merrily down the few inches to the floor, where it then flowed along a creek-bed it had carved for itself through the centre of the cavern.

In the dry and seemingly waterless environment in which Dan and his family had found themselves, the tinkling sound of running water was music to this desperate father's ears. The stream flowed across to the rock wall beneath where he stood and when he leaned over the boulder and looked down, he saw that it then simply vanished underground once more, possibly to surface again to create the oasis where the aborigine tribe camped. Perhaps it continued on from there to eventually become part of the underground water that he'd heard lay beneath the Nullarbor Plain, far to the south.

Maybe, if you knew where to look, this dry and barren land was not quite so dry after all. The water flowed freely despite the barren land above him, so he was hopeful that it would continue to flow all year round.

He wondered briefly whether the stream actually flowed underground all the way from up north, where he assumed it would be fed by the wet season rains.

But wherever it came from, it was here, where he needed it and he was thankful. It would most certainly provide for his family.

As he stood there, amazed at the sight before him, the words of Genesis 7:11 came back to him.

He remembered the old Authorized version that spoke of the 'fountains of the great deep', how they'd 'broken up' and how the heavens had also opened, causing the great flood – known to all as 'Noah's flood'. He could almost see, in his mind's eye, the water bursting up from beneath the earth. The force of it would have carved out this cavern.

And as they'd receded, the rushing waters would have smoothed out the sides and also no doubt would have laid down the floor of silt that now made a soft, sandy floor to the cave. Now, all that remained of that tumultuous time in earth's history was this placid little stream, squeezing its way through a mere crack in the rock wall, and gurgling merrily down another hole to continue its journey under the ground again.

Dan looked up to see where the light was coming from and he noticed a number of jagged openings along the edges of the high vaulted ceiling. These were obviously where small rock falls had occurred at some time in the past and were now the sources of the light filtering in to the cavern.

The sunlight created a warm glow, and to Dan's eyes the overall result was a completely charming place. Dan knew that he had found his home.

So right there, he fell on his knees and gave thanks to God for this most miraculous discovery. Then, with a song in his heart he turned his attention to the immediate job at hand – that of moving his family and their few possessions into this amazing place. He decided to build some sort of low wall alongside the stream, to prevent the cavern from flooding if wet season conditions further north increased the flow of water, although the soft sand on the floor of the cavern did not seem to show any signs of heavy flooding, at least not for some considerable period of time.

Dan knew that only time would tell.

In the meantime he was just thankful for the provision of such an excellent shelter and for a ready source of fresh water.

In no time at all, the family had moved in, bringing with them every conceivable thing from the wreck of their plane.

Over the months that followed, they stripped the plane of everything that could possibly be used in any way, until virtually no sign was left that it had ever existed. Tammy's mother knew then that they would never go home, and something inside her began to die from that moment.

She tried to stay strong and she taught her daughter every trick she'd ever learned about sewing and cooking, but somehow, the inevitability of spending the rest of her life separated from all that she knew and understood took its toll, and she just slipped away a little at a time. Tammy remembered it well, and it always brought a tear to her eye.

She had been just fifteen, and a woman long before her time, when she and her father had stood by a lonely grave to say their goodbyes.

It was snakebite that had finally taken her father's life. He'd never been afraid of snakes and never killed them unless it was for food. But this one had reared up under his boot, striking his leg. Tammy had tried to save him, doing all that she knew. But the antidote from the plane's first-aid kit was long out of date. Dan had put up a valiant fight, but there was nothing anyone could do.

And so, Tammy stood again by a grave, alone this time. Eighteen years old, and a true beauty, she'd wondered how she'd cope on her own in this vast wilderness. Then with the toughness that her father had bred into her, she had set her small chin and determined to carry on, as her parents would have wished.

She'd informed the tribe of her father's death, when next they'd come around and they had expressed sympathy, even though they understood better than Tammy, that once death reaches out for you in this part of the world, you can't fight its inevitability.

The kindly tribal elder had offered for her to live with them, but she had declined with thanks, preferring her home deep inside the earth. He had understood and nodded wisely, promising that she need only call on them if there was anything they could do to help her.

The women made sure she knew how to signal with fire, so that if the tribe were anywhere reasonably close, they could come if she needed them.

Then, thanking them, she had turned away to begin what was to become a lonely existence. The nightmares of the plane crash had eventually faded, gone into the mists of a childhood now long behind her. She was too busy, just getting from day to day, to worry about such things.

Each day was its own battle for survival, and she was, or so she believed, better off than her black brothers and sisters, for she had all the bits and pieces from the plane to make her days a little more comfortable, as well as a secure, weather-proof home. She would manage; she owed it to the memory of her father, who had taught her so much about survival.

And she owed it to her mother, who had bequeathed her a quiet strength, willing it into her little girl, even as her own had left her.

Chapter 3

UN-NAMED FEARS

A sudden crashing sound jerked Tammy out of her almost trance-like state and she brushed away the tears that had blurred her eyes, as memories had flooded her mind for the first time in longer than she cared to remember.

She realized that the plane was on the ground and was not moving. It seemed that someone had kicked open the door, and it was this that had startled her.

As she watched, five people scrambled out of the damaged plane and stood looking at it in horror. It was painfully obvious that this craft was not going anywhere. One wing was hanging off after a brush with a ridiculously small shrub, inconveniently situated in what had appeared from the air to be an open clearing. The undercarriage, or what was left of it was a crumpled mess, thanks to some rocks scattered in the red dust. The fragile little machine had proved no match for them.

As the small group cast their eyes around the vast wilderness that surrounded them, they were no doubt wondering if their survival had been a mixed blessing.

Still, at least they were alive, for now, although there was no way of knowing how long they would last out here without the essentials of life. And there certainly didn't seem to be too many of those in the immediate neighbourhood.

Tammy watched them from her vantage point behind a scrubby little bush clinging precariously to the side of a jagged rock, and knew that she must go up to them and offer them her help. But she was unable to move.

It was as though she had somehow become rooted to the ground. Her heart was pounding and she was cold, despite the searing heat. Some unnamed fear held her in its thrall, and she crouched there, paralyzed.

Suddenly, adrenaline pumped through her and she turned and ran. Swiftly as a creature of the bush she ran, at first not knowing or caring where, so long as it took her away from her nameless fear. Then she headed instinctively for home. She found her way into the tunnel, feeling her way into the first cave, through the crack and over the rock. As agile as a cat, she ran down the stairs that her father had cut in the rock wall, and flew into the corner set aside as her bedroom.

Throwing herself down onto the bed made of wadding from the plane seats and animal skins, she lay there shivering and sobbing.

After a few moments, the sobs subsided, and Tammy sat up. What on earth had caused such a reaction? She scolded herself and stood up. She knew that she must go back there at once, those people needed her. Surely they would die if she left them out there alone.

But the going was not as easy as the thinking. And she continued to stand in the middle of her bedroom floor, held there by doubt and fear. Finally, reason overcame her fear and she fetched a skin bag and filled it with water. Grabbing some cups from her kitchen, she set off once again, down that path to the clearing. Sheer determination kept her going, for every step got harder, and the instinct to run back became stronger the closer she came to the crash site.

As she came near the clearing, she could hear voices. A woman's voice, tinged with panic was crying out that they were going to die in this awful place, and she knew she shouldn't have come on this crazy ride, and it was all Dave's fault.

If he'd been half the pilot he'd said he was, they never would have got lost in the first place and anyway, why couldn't he land that little bitty plane without crashing. Didn't they learn how to do that in pilot school, or wherever he'd learned to fly that useless piece of junk out there? A man's voice spoke soothingly through the tirade, trying to calm this woman's obvious hysteria.

Another man's voice yelled at her to shut up. Didn't they have enough trouble without her adding to it, fighting with the only person who had any chance of getting them out of this mess alive?

And so the voices continued, their fear and panic clearly overruling commonsense. Didn't they know that it was far too hot to be expending all that energy, and that they should be trying to find some shade and some water?

She compared all this mentally with her father's calm approach to their very similar predicament all those years ago, and marveled once again at his strength and courage, in what was after all a pretty desperate situation.

I must go to them, she thought. They need me; they obviously haven't got a clue what to do next. Then she heard a man's voice, cutting across the others. This was the voice she'd heard trying to soothe the hysterical woman just moments ago.

"Hush now, everybody," he said. "This is getting us nowhere. We must find shelter before we bake in this sun, and we must find water. The little we have won't last long. There's bound to be something in the plane we can use to rig up some sort of shelter. Then you can all get some rest while I look about a bit and see if I can find out where we are, or at least something to help us survive till rescuers find us.

"Rescue!" screamed a woman's voice again. "Rescue you say! Where on earth is help going to come from out here? We are at the end of the earth and I tell you that we are all going to die out here!"

"Nonsense, Vivian!" Another woman's voice chimed in. "You're allowing panic to overrule here. We must remain calm and do as Dave says. Come on, you and I will go out to the plane and see if we can find something to eat and drink. Then Dave can scout around and see what he can see."

Two women then came out of the sparse shade offered by the scattering of spindly gum trees that somehow persisted in surviving in almost impossible conditions, and headed out to the wrecked plane. Three men remained, talking softly together, a sort of council of war, Tammy supposed.

One of the men had a fawn coloured uniform on and she guessed that he would be the pilot, and probably the leader of this unhappy band of travelers.

One of the other men seemed to be injured slightly. Someone had wound a makeshift bandage around his head and a small amount of blood had soaked through. It didn't appear to be too serious though.

Two of the men then followed the ladies out to the plane and the pilot started to check out the few spindly trees. In an otherwise treeless desert, a few stunted gums had managed to grow to a size that at least provided some shade for a person sitting down, probably because of the water that wound its way under the ground nearby. He was wondering how they could be persuaded to offer more shade, trying out various ideas in his head.

But he was cut off mid-thought, for it was then, as he stood there scratching his head, that he looked around and spotted Tammy.

For a while he stood there stunned. Logic told him that a young woman with cascading white-gold hair and blue eyes simply could not be standing in front of him. But either she was there or he was dreaming.

"Are you for real?" he asked. "It was Bob that got the clout on the head, not me."

Tammy nodded slowly. "Yes," she said, "I'm real."

Slowly, she stepped forward, offering the skin full of water and the cups. "I brought water, it's very hot out here."

"Thank you," Dave answered, staring in amazement at the vision before his eyes.

He realized that he sounded awfully trite, and he wished he could say something profound, but it seemed as if his tongue was stuck to the roof of his mouth.

For what seemed like a lifetime, he simply stood there and stared at Tammy. She seemed afraid, trembling a little like a frightened fawn. He could not imagine where she had come from.

Her clothes were obviously hand-made from scraps of fabric and animal skins, yet, even without any of the trappings of modern fashion, she was, in his eyes, the most beautiful sight he'd ever seen.

Suddenly, he remembered his manners. "The name's Dave," this sticking his hand out awkwardly, "I'm the pilot, or at least I used to be," he added ruefully, indicating what was left of his aircraft. "The other two guys are Bob, that's the one with the bandage on his head, and Gary. The ladies are Viv, I guess you heard her yelling. Her sister is Marian. We came from a station property somewhere over there – Riverside it's called. Not that there's any water actually in the river."

He waved his hand in a roughly southeasterly direction. "Exactly how far over there, or where exactly there is, I'm not too sure. We'd been on a sightseeing trip when this dust storm came out of nowhere..."

Dave knew he was prattling and his words sort of faded away as he saw the rueful smile on Tammy's face. Thinking that he'd made a fool of himself, he hesitantly asked what it was that he'd said.

Tammy gave a little shrug of her slender shoulders, smiled again and then told him briefly, how she had come to be there. He was relieved, he supposed, that this vision standing before him did not seem to think he'd made a total goose of himself, but her words completely dashed any hopes he may have had of rescue. She told him that she had been living there for seventeen years and in all that time they were the first white people she had seen.

"And I have absolutely no idea where we are," Tammy added. "Dad used to say that he reckoned Alice Springs was over there, somewhere," she said. "But, he didn't know how far, just that it's sort of north," she finished with a little smile. Tammy had pointed in a direction that Dave guessed was north-west from where they stood in the middle of no-man's land. And as he looked around him, he realized that the few trees standing at head-height beside them, were the only ones for as far as the eye could see. The only sight to greet his searching eyes was red sand, spinifex, saltbush and rocky outcrops – several of which had put paid to his aircraft.

Refusing to be daunted, however, Dave insisted that he had a compass and that he was pretty sure he could get the radio working in the plane. Tammy quietly mentioned that the dust storm might well have damaged sensitive equipment. That is what had happened to them and no amount of persuasion had been able to get them working again.

Dave, however, insisted optimistically that he was sure it would be okay.

"We'll get out of here," he assured her, "and we'll take you with us."

Tammy stared at him. After all these years, she needed to think about the implications of that. Was going back what she wanted? Who did she know out there? And what was there to go 'back' to?

"I'll bring some food," she muttered. And off she went; running as fast as her legs would carry her. Dave called after her. The others, hearing his call, came out of the plane, but Tammy was gone. Indeed Dave was left wondering if she had even been there at all. Then he looked at the bag and the cups in his hand and realized that he had not dreamed it.

His fellow passengers gathered around him full of questions and he tried to explain what had happened.

"I'm sure she will come back," he said, "She'll want her cups and this bag. We sure could use her help and she said that she was going to bring us some food."

Dave took a deep breath and mentally shook himself. Why on earth was he mooning about this slip of a girl when he had all he could handle right in front of him? And so he turned his attention to the tarp the guys had found in the plane, helping them tie it to a couple of the spindly trees, where hopefully, it would offer some shade if not coolness. He hoped the weight of it wouldn't pull them over.

Settling his charges down for a makeshift meal of the now stale picnic remains the ladies had organized, he tried to sort out their situation, and how it was now somehow connected to a young woman that filled his senses and made scrambled egg out his brains.

Tammy, meantime was busying herself making a meal and trying not to think of the pilot of the crashed plane as anything more than another human being that needed her help.

But try as she might, images of his broad shoulders straining at the thin material of his shirt and those eyes, such a dark blue, piercing and yet gentle, would not leave her mind. A handsome face, she thought, in a rugged sort of way, with a strong jaw.

Deliberately she jerked herself out of her daydream and put the finishing touches to the food preparations. Rather than take it out to them, I'd best bring them here, she said to herself. It's way too hot out there, and besides it would be nice to have visitors. Her first, she realized.

The local aborigines would not go near her cavern. For reasons that they had never really shared with her, they were afraid of the place. Perhaps it was the sound of the water, it did echo a little. Perhaps it was a sacred place, although she doubted that, for if it were, surely they would have objected to her and her family living there.

All this daydreaming was not getting things done, she told herself impatiently and so making sure that all was ready, she set off again for the clearing; to invite her guests to dinner.

Arriving at the crash site, she found the five survivors, draped in an exhausted huddle. The little they'd had to drink was already dehydrating away and the stale picnic scraps had not been very satisfying.

Viv, Tammy thought of her as the noisy one, was already complaining of heatstroke, thirst and hunger.

In the midst of trying to reassure his little band, Dave looked up and saw Tammy approaching.

"Look," he said to the others," I told you she'd come back."

Climbing to his feet, he went out to meet Tammy. She smiled shyly at him and extended her invitation for them all to join her in her home. She had a meal prepared and she would manage somehow to provide a bed for each of them.

They must of course stay with her until something was settled one way or the other. They were welcome, she said, to make her home their own.

Somewhat stunned at the vision that stood before them, it was a moment or two before they could react. Then they all clambered awkwardly to their feet and clustered around her. She felt a little overwhelmed. Tammy was small in stature, not much over five feet tall, and she suddenly felt tiny in this circle of curious people.

Ducking her head and pushing through them, she called out over her shoulder. "Follow me."

Then she set off at a fairly fast clip, checking every now and then to see if they were following. Occasionally she would slow a little if she thought one or the other of them was lagging too far behind.

Viv complained loudly the whole way, declaring to anyone who would listen, and they were all trying not to, that she couldn't possibly keep up and where on earth was this savage taking them.

On and on she went and Tammy began to think of her as a blowfly, buzzing lazily about on a hot afternoon. Thankful that not too many of those found their way into her cool home, she wondered how she'd manage to put up with this woman's incessant whining. Oh well, her father had always taught her to be charitable and kind, not that she'd had a lot of practice, she mused. She'd cope somehow. She felt sorry for Dave, who seemed to cop a large measure of her abuse, and for poor wounded Bob, the sorry individual who had married her.

Soon the little group arrived at Tammy's home, and she shepherded them through the small opening and the passage.

Over the years, Tammy's father had widened the entrance a little bit, trying to make access to their home a little more convenient. The darkness frightened Viv, however, and she hesitated to enter. Tammy was amused to notice that for the first time she was actually quiet, but she gently reassured her that all she had to do was follow her voice as there was nothing to fall over.

She warned them that the passage did slope downwards, and there were a few small steps.

She assured them, again, that except for the steps, the floor was smooth, there was nothing to fall over, and the walls were close enough to touch with both hands.

"The distance is only a few feet, so just follow me. I will tell you as we come to each step," she told them.

Then, they were over the top of the rock and the cavern was spread out before them. For a moment they were silent as they took in the view, then Dave let out a long slow whistle.

"This is amazing," he said, "I've never seen anything like this, it's... beautiful!"

"Thank you," said Tammy shyly. "It's been my home for a lot of years now. I'm very comfortable here, and I hope you will be too. With somewhere to stay, you can take the time you need to work out your next move."

"Yes," said Dave, wondering just exactly what that next move could possibly be.

Tammy led her guests down the flight of stairs and invited them to wash and make themselves at home while she served up the lunch she had prepared. Soon they were all sitting around her homemade table eating a fine spread.

Kangaroo meat, prepared in the way she had been taught by the aborigines, with a few of her mother's refinements added, and some salad from her garden. The seeds for her garden had come from many of the bush tucker plants around about.

She had learned by trial and error to propagate some of these and so was able to grow them close by. This meant that she didn't have to hunt for them all over the bush, unless she wanted some variety. The project was assisted of course, by her ready source of water, which, as her father had hoped, had never let them down.

She had helped her father plant trees around their home and had planted a few more herself since, encouraging these to grow from seed pods from the trees near where the tribe camped. She had lovingly watered them and cared for them, until they offered shade to both her entrance-way and some of her garden.

Her guests were suitably impressed. Even Viv had settled down sufficiently to thank her hostess, and with food and drink in front of her was far too busy to talk further.

With the meal over, accommodation needs were seen to and a bed was found for each of them. The big bed that her parents had used, served for one couple, and it was not too difficult to find enough cushions, animal fur and grasses, to suit the other three.

With the practical needs seen to, they sat back around the table with a cool drink each, and began the enormous task of planning their escape. Tammy had little to offer. Her very presence here meant that escape had confounded her parents, and would, she reasoned, very likely do the same to the intrepid bunch sitting around her table.

Each of them was keen to hear Tammy's story, so slowly at first, reluctant to draw on painful memories, she began to relate her experiences. The group soon realized that her story offered little encouragement to people looking for a way out of here, so they decided that the first thing they had to do was return to the plane and see if anything was working. Each had a hat, so Tammy found her home-made sunscreen and offered it around. Then they set off again for the fateful landing spot and the wreck of Dave's little plane.

The little group made it to the plane without incident, even Viv had only complained once or twice about the heat and the flies. Tammy's sunscreen also contained an insect repellant, so if she'd put it on as everybody else had done, she'd have been a lot better off – but the others held their tongues.

The wreck of the plane was indeed a sorry sight. Dave knew that his pride and joy was never going to fly again and he sighed. Viv was making the most noise, but he realized that it was him who had sustained the greater loss.

Supposing they ever got out of here, it was doubtful he would ever be able to afford another plane. In fact, he doubted very much if he'd ever be able to pay for this sorry mess.

On arriving at the crash-site, the ladies went immediately to the plane and were already fossicking around inside even as Dave stood there mentally saying goodbye to his 'freedom machine.'

Shaking himself out of the doldrums he climbed into the plane and scrambled into the tiny cockpit. He began a routine test of its equipment and found to his joy that the radio did seem to be still operational.

Problem was, as it was only small, designed for local flights not too far from base, he doubted if there would be anyone within range. Still, he was a positive person, so not too perturbed he reasoned that once they got underway, they'd soon raise someone. Surely they were not all that far from a station property somewhere out there.

Calling to Bob and Gary to come and give him a hand, he began to undo the fixtures so that they could take the radio out of the plane. It wasn't very large and Dave was sure it would present no problem carrying it on their escape journey.

He thought he remembered seeing a rucksack stuffed in a compartment somewhere, and hoped it would be large enough. Dave had definitely made up his mind that they would be getting out of this mess. He sincerely hoped that Tammy would come with them. This was not merely because they would most certainly need her knowledge and expertise, but also because he knew, even though he couldn't put it into words, that there was something about this girl that had captivated him and he didn't intend letting her go if he could help it.

Soon they had gathered every useful thing they could find from the wreck and divided it all into bundles so each of them could carry a share. They headed back to Tammy's home. Darkness was approaching and they would need an evening meal and a good night's rest. Tomorrow would bring its own set of problems.

Chapter 4
A JOURNEY BEGINS

Sleep did not come easily for Tammy that night. Her exhausted companions had retired early and all appeared to be sleeping peacefully. But Tammy was unsettled. How could she leave all this?

Her parents were buried nearby. This place was the only home she could remember. There was no one that she knew back east. Oh, she was sure there was family somewhere. Her mother and her father both had sisters and her father had a brother somewhere. But she barely remembered them. Their faces were vague at best.

Quietly, she scrambled out of bed and tiptoed to her cupboard. Somewhere here was a pack of photos, taken at the last family gathering and packed at the last moment since they had not had time to look through them before the trip away.

There was also a book in which her mother had written all the family names and addresses, so Tammy would remember her family and hopefully be able to find them if she ever made it back home.

Carrying it back to her bed, she lit a small lamp and softly turned the pages; recommitting to memory the long forgotten names and faces. Then putting the book under her pillow and turning off her lamp, she tried again to sleep.

Dave saw her light come on and as he lay there he listened to her soft movements. He found himself wondering what she was thinking.

Exhausted, he had slipped off to sleep fairly easily, but for some reason had awakened soon after. He had been lying quietly, thinking about his plane and listening to the even breathing of his companions. He'd sensed rather than heard Tammy's soft movements at first. She is like a small cat, he thought.

Is she afraid of what the future holds? Is that what keeps her awake into the small hours of the night?

As morning sent its soft glow down through the 'windows' in the roof of Tammy's underground home, she was still trying to sort out the clutter of her mind. Leaving here would be hard, and yet, how could she stay? Surely her family deserved to know that she at least was alive, that their brother and sister rested peacefully in the arms of the Lord they had both served with all their hearts?

But could she cope with a world that would be beyond her comprehension? Would people, even her own, treat her like a freak?

And yet even as these and a million other questions flooded her tired mind, she knew that she would go. For how could she let these uninitiated novices go out into the bush without her?

And in the back of her mind, despite her efforts to stifle it was the thought... How could she let Dave go...?

This was a completely new and foreign feeling, but it could not be denied. Somehow, without any understanding of how and why, she was aware that Dave would be a big part of her future.

As she quietly climbed out of bed to begin a new day, she was finally at peace. She knelt beside her bed and committed her day and her future to the God that her parents had taught her to love and trust, and went out to her kitchen to prepare some food for her guests.

Soon, they joined her in a simple meal, and it was obvious that feelings were mixed as a certain tension hung in the air. Dave and the other two men were fairly excited, and keen to get going. The girls were each a little uncertain at the wisdom of such a venture, yet mixed in with that was the equally confusing certainty that they couldn't really stay where they were either. There didn't seem to be any hope that they would be rescued, after all hadn't Tammy herself been here all these years and not a glimpse of anyone, until their own unfortunate arrival?

And so, the decision was made. They would leave as soon as they could, planning to begin their epic journey in the evening, when the day would begin to cool a little. They had little idea how long it would take them to prepare, although Dave was anxious to organize things as quickly as possible.

The next few days would be spent in choosing, manufacturing and otherwise preparing provisions for the journey and making anything they could from available resources.

They were amazed at the array of gadgets and gizmos that Tammy, and her parents before her, had rescued, adapted or invented over the years.

Some of these ideas could be copied, using items from the recent wreck, so willing hands set to the tasks ahead. Many trips were made back and forth to the plane; to be sure that nothing of use was left behind.

Tammy had suggested that, despite the searing heat of the days, they should carry something warm.

"The nights can get very cold in the desert," she told them.

As the day-trippers had not all thought to bring a jacket of some kind, she rummaged around among her parents belongings and managed to find something to more or less fit each one.

Finally, all was completed. Surveying the equipment, and going over, yet again, all the plans they'd made, they made the decision that they were as ready as they could hope to be. Exhausted after yet another busy day, they retired to their beds. The next day would be 'departure day'.

So it was that mid afternoon, the following day, Tammy called a halt to all tasks and suggested they get some rest, informing her guests that they would spend most of that night walking. Grumbling a little at the thought of the miles ahead of them, Viv headed for her bed. The others followed suit, each with their own thoughts on how they would handle the journey ahead.

When it had become obvious that these people would not be put off – that they were determined, come what may, to walk out of there, Tammy had gently suggested that, being city folk, they may not be as fit as they thought.

So as part of the preparations for the journey, she had encouraged each of her guests to undertake some training. Dave, who had lived an outdoor life, mostly doing hard physical labour, except for the hours he spent in a plane, seemed to be the fittest of them all, but the others had let themselves go quite a bit.

"If you don't get your fitness levels up just a little, you won't make it out there," she had said, in her shy way.

So, despite a few initial complaints from her charges, she had dragged them out into the bush each evening before their evening meal, and walked them along her many trails. She took them on increasingly longer distances, finally getting them up to a gentle jog, for at least some of the way. She hoped that in this way, she might prepare them a little for the rigours of their journey.

Gradually, silence descended on Tammy's cavern home on that last afternoon, as her guests, more tired than they had realized dropped off to sleep one by one. Used to keeping all hours, Tammy had rested, but not slept. So she kept a watch on the time of day. She had developed a method of telling the time fairly accurately.

The watch that her father had left on the box beside his bed, had continued to tick away for quite some time. But she had known that eventually, the battery would die, and with no hope of a replacement, she would need to find another way to work out what time of the day it was.

So she got into the habit of watching a bar of light that fell on one wall of the cavern each day. She would watch as it moved diagonally upwards on the wall, as the sun set each day, taking notice that the early morning sun touched the top of the opposite rugged wall, its golden touch on the rock sliding down until the sun went out of reach of the 'window'. It was a simple enough procedure to make marks on the walls at regular intervals. She had also learned to gauge how much light was in her home at any given time of the day, so that, if she was inside, she had a reasonable idea whether it was early or getting on towards evening. It seldom rained, so cloudy days were not a common occurrence either.

So it was, that at an appropriate time, she was able to rouse her guests in time to make their final preparations. She had prepared a light meal before waking her charges, and thanking her, they tucked in. Tammy had observed no lack of healthy appetites, despite the rather different food.

Having eaten and cleared up, they gathered their loads together, checked each bundle to make sure they could be carried with some comfort, and prepared to leave.

Then, having made a last minute check around to make sure nothing essential had been overlooked, they stood for a moment looking at each other.

Tammy suggested softly, that perhaps they should pray. Dave agreed that it would be a good thing to do, the two women nodded slowly, each hoping they wouldn't have to do it – while Bob and Gary just shuffled their feet.

With a little smile, Tammy led them in a short and simple prayer, asking God to guide their feet and provide them with protection along the way. Then, taking a deep breath, Dave led them out through the tunnel into the fading light on the first leg of the journey they hoped would eventually lead them home. For the five castaways, each step would take them closer to their homes, for Tammy each step took her further away from hers.

Though the evening air was still quite hot, Tammy forbade them to drink until it became necessary to replace essential fluid.

"We must ration water," she said. "There is water out there, but it is some distance between springs, and not all of them can be guaranteed to deliver. Added to that, some underground water doesn't taste the best. It can be a bit of an acquired taste," she added. "We must drink only enough to sustain us," she insisted. "I cannot stress this firmly enough. We must not drink, just because we are thirsty. We must measure out just enough to sustain our bodies each day, and resist, at all costs, the urge to just quench thirst.

"If your mouth is dry, find a smooth stone and suck on that. Chew gum, if you have any in your bags, but don't drink unless I say it is time to drink. Does everybody understand that?" she asked.

Reluctantly, her charges nodded their heads. Viv was on the verge of voicing a protest when her sister jabbed her in the ribs.

"Yes, Tammy," said Marian.

"We understand, don't we Viv?" this directed, rather pointedly at her sister, who nodded and shuffled her feet, but, for a change kept her peace.

Along with water and food, Tammy had made sure that each of them carried plenty of her home-made sunscreen. She planned to mostly travel at night, but they would not always find effective shade and she knew that they would soon burn up without some protection. Her mother had always said that 'an ounce of prevention is worth a pound of cure.' The others had laughed at this.

It had been a while since any of them had heard the expression, and for a moment each of them thought wistfully about their own mothers. They were suddenly very aware that they were a long way from anywhere, with no guarantees that they would not perish out here in this forbidding and unforgiving land.

The first few hours passed uneventfully. No one had much to say as each one was busy with his or her own thoughts. What lay ahead? There was no way to know of course and each of them dealt with the uncertainty in the best way they could. Those who were unsure if there really was a God who cared, briefly envied Tammy her quiet faith.

Their first rest stop, after a few hours of walking in the chosen direction, was alongside a line of small trees. These seemed surprisingly healthy as they meandered off into the distance, despite the dry environment. So it seemed that they might have been marking a possible underground stream, or where one had been not so long ago. A dry creek-bed did not necessarily mean that the water had not just seeped through the top layer and was lying there beneath the sand.

Tammy was hopeful that such would be the case and she would find water. Certainly, she knew that her aborigine friends had, the last time she'd come this way with them.

She also knew that occasionally, they would find fish buried deep in the wet sand, waiting, in a sort of fishy hibernation, for the next good flow of water.

Her companions had looked around and of course, could see nothing. But Tammy hoped that under the sand she would find the liquid treasure. She soon had the guys digging and in no time they came upon wet sand. A bit more persistence and water began filtering up through the red sand.

Dave watched as the hollow they had made began to slowly fill up, and soon there was enough to top up everybody's water containers. A small piece of cloth filtered out the worst of the sand, and it would soon settle anyway.

They sat down for a rest and enjoyed a meal with the flat bread that Tammy had made out of wild wheat shown to her by her aboriginal friends. A piece of wild fruit and some kangaroo meat completed the meal. A bright moon provided adequate light for their needs.

After a short rest, Tammy suggested that they had best keep moving. Nothing would be gained if they spent the cool hours sitting around. And so they struggled to their feet, put the packs on their backs and set off once again, following Tammy's lead as they trudged endlessly on through the night. At least, by wearing their jackets that was one less thing they needed to carry.

As morning approached, the travelers were glad to see the daylight. Dawn was initially cool and particularly beautiful. Even in their somewhat desperate situation it was impossible to ignore a glorious sunrise. Tammy said that they would travel for a while yet and then stop for some breakfast.

The morning quickly became quite hot and so a rest stop was called.

"This will do for now," said Tammy. "We can rest here for a while, have something to eat and then decide if we want to go any further before stopping for the day. We should have enough water for now, if we are careful," she cautioned.

Her charges headed gratefully for whatever scrap of shade could be found, and fell on the ground, no longer caring if they had something to sit on or not. Just to be off their feet was heaven.

While the group sorted themselves out, Tammy took a couple of plastic bags from deep inside her kit, and placed them over the branches of a small, scrubby bush. She tied these firmly to the thin stems with strips of cloth torn from something. She had obviously brought these items for this specific purpose and her companions watched her as they sat about resting.

"What are you doing, Tammy?" asked Marian.

"Hopefully, I'm getting some water," answered Tammy.

"We should be able to do this each time we stop. The leaves on this shrub will sweat inside the bags. If I am very careful when I untie them, I should be able to collect the moisture, then we can pour it into one of our containers.

"In this way, we should be able to top up our water supplies each time we stop for the day. It doesn't produce a lot of water, but every bit helps and at least we know that it will be pure."

"Hey, I've seen this done on TV," said Gary. "Does anyone else have a plastic bag in their packs? The more bags we can utilize, the more water we can collect."

That sent the two ladies off to search their packs. Each found a bag that had been used to protect something. Viv had put a pair of shoes in hers and Marian had put her jacket in a bag before leaving on the joy flight. She decided that water to live on was far more important than keeping her jacket clean so she happily handed it over to her husband.

Gary took both bags, tore a couple of strips of cloth off the bottom of his shirt and tied both bags to the small branches, just as Tammy had done. Then with a satisfied nod, he went and sat down with the others.

Chapter 5

NEW ARRIVALS AND TROUBLE AHEAD

As they sat there resting before getting the food ready, Dave noticed movement on the shimmering horizon.

The little group watched for a while and then Tammy smiled with pleasure, as the tribe who had become her friends came slowly out of the haze. They greeted Tammy warmly and politely nodded as she introduced them to her fellow wayfarers.

They were on their way, Barda explained, to a place a little further along, where they regularly managed to get water as they journeyed. He told Tammy that he and his people had heard Dave's plane crash and had watched from a distance as Tammy had met the survivors. He had known in his heart that his little friend would leave with these people; as they were, after all, her own kind.

So, keeping a respectful distance, he and his tribe had followed. He was not sure what to do, but had simply intended to watch and make sure that all was well.

In the wavering heat haze, none of them had seen the small group of people flaked out on the ground, until they were too close to remain unnoticed themselves. So Barda had decided to put his fears to rest and join his young friend, even though it meant meeting new people.

He asked Tammy why she had tied bags to the bushes, and was intrigued by the idea of using condensation to gather water. As he had not ever even seen a plastic bag, this was new to him and he examined it all very carefully as Tammy explained the process to him. She told him that her father had used this method of finding water many times in his travels around the outback.

"Of course, the problem in this part of the country, is finding a decent bush or tree, with enough leaves on it to produce a decent amount of water. Still every bit helps.

"If you want to try this for yourself, then go to my cave when you return to the oasis," she told him, "You should find a couple of these bags. Please feel free to take one or two and show your people how to use them. I know that you do not like my cavern, but I can promise you that you will come to no harm, even though the tunnel is very dark. Just keep your hands on each wall and walk straight in. There is a bit of a slope downward and some steps, but nothing to fall over.

Then, when you get to the big rock, just climb over and go down the steps my father cut into the rock."

Barda was unsure, but promised he'd think about it when they got back to the area.

The conversation then turned to where each group was headed. Barda mentioned that he and his people would be heading mostly east at this time of year anyway, as was their habit.

So he invited them to join the tribe and, in the traditional aboriginal way, to share both their food and their vast knowledge of the country through which they would travel in the coming days.

Tammy knew that soon enough they would be travelling on past where her dark-skinned friends would care to go, but she was glad to have them with her for as long as they cared to stay.

What neither Tammy, nor any of her friends could know was that out in the desert, two dangers lurked. And their peaceful little band would be moving right into the path of both.

In a particularly hot indentation in the endless sand hills of the desert country around them, a sudden shift in atmospheric pressure began to swirl the sand in a vaguely circular motion. Gradually, it gathered strength as it sucked in the surrounding super-heated air. Soon a huge willy-willy, fed by heat and shifting pressures, and full of sand and debris from the desert floor, began its journey towards the track where Tammy and her friends would soon be heading.

And in another direction, three desperate men, running from the law and their own fears, were lost, hungry, thirsty and heading straight for the unsuspecting group of travellers. These three had started out weeks ago, going on a rampage, stealing from station properties along the way. Their last port of call had resulted in a huge haul of food and valuables.

They had been about to make their getaway in a truck stolen from a neighbouring station, when a woman had come out from one of the outbuildings and yelled at them. Reacting with unthinking violence, one of them had leapt from the truck and grabbed her. She had fought like a wildcat, kicking and biting.

Struggling to hold her he'd yelled out for the others to help and between them they'd brutally subdued her. Not content with that, their leader, if you could call him that, suddenly lost his temper and had proceeded to beat the woman to death.

In the silence that had followed, they had stood and looked at each other for a moment, then run to the truck and scrambling aboard, had sped down the road towards the gate.

Not really paying attention to direction, they'd just driven, pushing the truck to its limits. The only thought on their collective minds was to get as far from there as possible, fearful that someone might have heard the commotion and come to investigate.

A dust storm the next day disoriented them, and already lost, they had been driving around in circles wasting fuel, when an empty watercourse, hit at speeds unwise for either the rough track or the ancient vehicle, had put their truck out of commission. Now on foot, minus most of their supplies and all of their booty, they were shuffling along with no idea of where they were going, just hoping that soon they'd find water or help before they perished out here in this forsaken place.

Their aimless wanderings were bringing them into a collision course with one giant willy-willy, behaving for all the world like a tornado, and a group of travellers ill-equipped to cope with the disasters bearing down on them.

The morning was wearing on. With breakfast over, the group had decided to continue on to Barda's watering place before stopping for the day. The heat was building, however, and Tammy knew that they must stop soon, to preserve both energy and water. Barda's people may have been used to walking in all conditions, but her little group of city-dwellers would not survive if they did not find shelter to wait out the day's intense heat.

So for the sake of those less conditioned to the harsh climate, they straggled to a stop near some spiky little shrubs. Although not perfect, this would do for a short rest before, hopefully, they could continue on to a better place to spend the day.

As each person in the group tried to find sufficient shade to sit in, one of the aborigines looked up and saw three men approaching. They were obviously in some sort of trouble.

They carried nothing in the way of supplies and were tired and lame. Tammy and Dave ran out to meet them, sat them down in a square foot or so of shade each, and set about getting them something to drink.

As they all sat there, each one facing away from the sun, in their own small spot of shadow, Tammy thought how strange it was that in all her years out here, she'd never sighted another white person. Now, in the last few days, it seemed that people were everywhere. Barda and his people had never come across anyone out here, in all their years of travelling in the area.

Dave was wondering where these three had come from, and he became very suspicious when he noticed blood on one of the men. However, thinking that perhaps he was hurt, Dave asked if there was anything he could do, and was amazed at the abrupt manner of the man as he snarled at him to mind his own so and so business.

Doubly suspicious now of these unusual visitors, Dave decided to keep very close watch on them. However, he decided against saying anything to the others at this stage, preferring not to alarm anyone unnecessarily.

Tammy, though, had acquired a sort of antenna for danger over her years of coping in a wild and lonely place, and all her senses were tingling. She knew that trouble had come with their visitors, and she waited for an opportunity to mention it to Dave as soon as possible.

As these thoughts crossed her mind, she looked over at Dave and their eyes met across the tops of the spinifex clumps between them. Each instantly knew what the other was thinking, and a slight nod from Dave assured her that he knew something was wrong. She was relieved to realize that she did not need to carry that burden alone.

At the same time, as he moved slowly among his people speaking to this one and that, Barda casually stopped by Tammy's side, and in the language that she alone in the group of Europeans would have understood, softly told her that the presence of the three men made him and his people nervous. She agreed with him and as she smiled up at him, told him that Dave, the tall man in the uniform, understood this and she trusted him to know what to do for the best. The old man was satisfied for the present, but continued on his rounds, warning his young men to be ready for anything. In his quiet way, with no hint of concern on his gentle face, he told them to carefully watch the newcomers.

After a short rest, Barda gathered his people together and told Tammy that if they hoped to replenish their water and find a good place to spend the day, then they must move on. So, somewhat reluctantly, the group allowed themselves to be persuaded that a better camping place was only a short distance from there.

Apologizing to their three unexpected guests, Dave explained to them that they were welcome to travel with them if they wanted, but they must move on now to find water.

The man who seemed to be some sort of leader, nodded without speaking and signaled to his companions to get to their feet and follow. With a few grumbles they did as they were told and keeping very much to themselves, the three of them followed the group.

The walk only took about an hour, but in the building heat of the day, all were soon exhausted and very glad when Barda pointed ahead to a small, shady grove.

Here, in what was obviously an old watercourse, they did find some water, although Barda said it wasn't as plentiful as last time they had come by this way. There was enough to replenish supplies a little however, and to refresh tired and thirsty bodies.

Then, just as they were about to get a meal together before resting throughout the hot afternoon hours, someone yelled out that a willy-willy was coming.

Everybody looked up and the sight that greeted their eyes was enough to chill them to the bone, even in the searing heat. They saw a massive, swirling column of sand, dust and debris bearing down on them like an express train.

Dave called out to everybody to get into whatever shelter they could find and to dig in as best they could. There was a mad scramble as everyone dived for any meagre shelter, grabbing bags and bedrolls and anything else they could get their hands on. Pressing in against each other as they waited for the melee of wind and sand to descend on them, they hoped to somehow escape the worst of it.

Then, it was on them in all its fury. It whirled about them, tugging at their clothes and their hair. It clawed at the flimsy shelters they'd pulled around themselves like a creature possessed, and they held on for dear life. Each tried desperately to keep eyes and mouths closed against the cloying sand that seemed determined to find its way into any and every crevice.

Noses were soon full despite their best efforts, as were eyes and ears, while clothes provided no barrier at all to the powder-fine sand whipping around them. How they managed to avoid being injured by some of the larger pieces of debris, remained a miracle.

The screaming wind and sand-blasting effect of the fine dust, seemed to go on forever, as each one choked and gasped for air. In actual fact, it lasted only a minute or two before it raced past them and headed off into the sand-dunes and spinifex behind them. As it passed they watched it picking up everything in its path, adding it to the debris already flying around.

Soon enough, however, the willy-willy began to wear itself out and its tattered group of victims watched as it petered out just a few hundred yards from where they stood in the ruins of their clothes and what was left of their supplies.

Stamping around and shaking at their clothes, each attempted to remove the sand from clothes, eyes, mouths and ears. (The stuff, known as 'bull-dust' in the Territory, is as fine as talcum powder, and gets into absolutely everything.)

The tribesmen thought the antics were rather funny and laughed gaily. They were oblivious to the fact that the super-fine dust stuck to their eyebrows and coated their black hair. Their good humour in the face of a most unpleasant experience lightened the mood for everyone. Laughter suddenly seemed to be infectious, and a good antidote for the fear that had gripped them only moments before.

Joe, however, the blood-splattered leader of the trio of strangers, a tall gangly man with the meanest face Tammy had ever imagined she'd see, yelled at them to stop laughing.

Didn't they realize, he screamed at them, that all their supplies were gone and now they'd no doubt starve in this endless, useless desert?

Shocked into silence by the vehemence of this verbal onslaught, the group, both black and white, stood and gazed as he ranted and raved, seemingly out of control.

Feet shuffled as folk tried not to show their embarrassment, and that only seemed to make Joe angrier. The women were getting frightened, and the tribeswomen had silently disappeared into the scrub, heading for anywhere that would take them away from the 'crazy white man'.

Dave tried to calm him down, but that only seemed to make him worse. So, assuming that it was just a delayed reaction to the fear that had gripped them all, he decided to let it go, hoping that if he left well enough alone the man would calm down. No sooner had these thoughts entered his head, than Joe stopped his tirade as suddenly as it had begun. He looked about him and made a lunge for a bag of supplies that lay in the sand.

"Come on, you two useless wasters," he snapped at his companions. "Gather this stuff up and we're out of here! And grab that radio, I don't know if it works or not after the storm, but we can't have this lot using it."

"Wait a moment, there!" said Dave. "You can't just help yourselves to our stuff. You can't leave us with nothing out here."

"Oh, yeah? Just watch me!" snarled Joe. With that he produced a pistol from the back of his shorts and threatened the group.

"Just keep out of my way and nobody will get hurt." He snarled. Then he proceeded to order Ed and Lenny to gather up as much as they could carry, while he held Dave and his friends at bay with the pistol.

"Don't attempt to follow us!" he said to Dave. "If we get a sniff of anybody, we'll shoot to kill."

Dave was certain that the pistol would be full of the fine dust and be pretty useless, but with the lives of the others his responsibility, he could not risk doing anything to provoke Joe, just in case the gun worked.

So he watched in frustration as with a final warning, the three of them headed off into the desert afternoon.

By now Viv and Marian were in tears, and the men had their hands full trying to calm them down. As the two women quieted down to the occasional sniffle, the aboriginal women started to drift back from the various hiding places they had found in the scrub. Their babies on their hips and the older children hiding behind their legs, they rejoined their men folk and began a tribal conference.

Meanwhile, Dave was trying to assess the damage. Bedding seemed to have survived in reasonable condition, due largely to the fact that they'd pulled it around them in an attempt to build shelter. But very little else was immediately visible.

The women had brought some bits and pieces back with them that the wind had scattered all over the place. So Dave began to work in a kind of grid out from the rock, searching for anything that might prove useful. The others watched for a moment, and then also began the hunt. Excited cries would carry on the now breathlessly still air as one or the other found something that could be rescued.

But soon enough they came together again, and precious little had been rescued. The day was slipping away and it seemed pointless to waste further rest time looking any further. In any case, what could possibly be left?

The radio, on which Dave had pinned such hope, had not worked at all despite appearing to be okay. He assumed that either the sand had ruined it after all, or it just couldn't make the range. In any case, it was gone now. He supposed that Joe would just dump it out in the bush somewhere.

The travellers, both white and black, decided together that the best course of action was to get some rest and worry about their next move later. So exhausted from their ordeal, they all flopped down anywhere that offered a modicum of shade.

When everybody had found a spot to sit, Tammy suggested that perhaps they should remain there overnight. They would feel better tomorrow after a decent rest, and a new day might bring some renewed hope. Dave and the others agreed.

Later that evening, after a hasty meal made from whatever they could scrape together, Tammy settled into her gritty bed and offered up a prayer that her Lord would provide them a way. If there were any supplies still to be found further out there somewhere, they would need time to find them anyway. So, having committed her cares to the Lord with the simple trust of a child, she curled up and was instantly asleep.

The day had passed quickly enough with all the commotion and Dave too, was glad to try and get some sleep. Smiling to himself at the uncomplicated faith of this young girl, whose very presence continued to confuse and amaze him, Dave was touched beyond belief and as he eventually drifted off to sleep, he found himself wondering if maybe Tammy's God might just get them out of this mess after all.

The desert morning was chilly, but the sky was a clear blue. It would be another hot day. So the first order of business was to find a way to carry enough water to sustain them until they got to the next watering hole. Then they would need to check out how much of their food could be found, if indeed any had been left behind by their three unsavoury visitors.

A small group of tribesmen had already begun the hunt for food and the women were hunting around for the mysterious foods that they found in the most unlikely places. Some of the men began to skin a couple of small kangaroos they'd found, but Tammy knew that it would be a while before the skins were cured enough to carry water.

So she began to look through her bits and pieces for anything that she could press into service as a kind of bucket.

One of the bags she had brought along was one that her father had always carried in his plane. It had a divider in the middle of it. She cut this out with the knife that was always strapped to her side, thinking that if she could gather in the edges somehow, and fashion some kind of handle, maybe it would serve. She also had a canvas water bag that she'd kept since first arriving in the wilderness and somehow Joe and his unsavoury friends had missed finding in all the confusion.

Soon enough, the women had gathered a supply of bush tucker from around the camp area, and the men returned with a couple more kangaroos they had speared.

A quick breakfast was thrown together and eaten, then the leftovers were prepared for carrying. The group then set about organizing themselves to travel. The dry creek-bed managed to deliver another small amount of water and the plastic bags had a bit in them too. The cold night had caused some good condensation to form, and it all helped to top up supplies. Tammy knew they wouldn't get very far that day, but was wise enough to realize that the group needed to be moving. The further away they were from Joe and his friends the better she'd like it.

She was very grateful that her aboriginal friends were with them. Their hunting and bush skills made her job of protecting Dave and his group that much easier. She was very worried about Joe and his two shifty mates though. She had no doubt at all that they hadn't seen the last of them.

With no bush skills and absolutely no idea where they were, it was almost certain that they would be out there somewhere keeping tabs on them and waiting for a chance to take more of their supplies.

Tammy was also aware that if her group were to reach a property where they could receive the help they needed, then the people there would also be placed in danger.

Joe, Ed and Lenny would be looking for a method of transport to get them out of the desert and back to civilization. Back to a place where they could find a safe hideout. As she talked about these concerns quietly with Dave, he agreed with her and they decided to keep a very close watch.

"They won't have a clue where to find water," Tammy said.

"No, they won't," agreed Dave. "I wouldn't either. They'll be keeping pretty close, I'd imagine. As the days get hotter, they'll start to get desperate. They'll be okay for food for a day or two, I suppose; they took just about all we'd brought from your place. We'll be okay as long as your friends are with us. Or do you know some of their tricks at finding food out here in this wilderness?"

"Yes," said Tammy. "Before my father died he taught me a lot about surviving out here. And Barda and his people used to take me out hunting.

They seemed to think I'd surely die on my own if they didn't give me a few clues. They actually wanted me to live with the tribe, but I chose to stay in my own place. I visited them often, though, whenever they were camping nearby. They are wonderful people, very kind and generous. I consider myself to be truly blessed by their friendship and their concern for me."

"I can see that they are all very fond of you," said Dave, with a smile. "Yes, they are good people. I'm grateful to them for helping to keep you safe."

Tammy looked up at him, and he smiled at her and reached out to softly touch her cheek. She blushed and turned quickly away, not too sure how to handle the surge of emotions that flooded through her at his touch. How gentle he was, she thought, and yet so strong. Had it really only been a few days since she'd met him?

It seemed as if she had known him such a long time.

She was as sure as she could be that she could trust this man completely. It looked like she was going to have to trust him with her heart, she thought, because she was certain that he had stolen it from her anyway. Was this what her parents had felt for each other?

Her mother had always told her that she would 'know' when love came. But she hadn't completely prepared her for these tumbling emotions.

Does he feel the same, she wondered? She stole a quick glance up at his face, and found him gazing at her, his eyes soft and gentle. Tammy remembered that her father had looked at Mum in just the same way, and the heart she felt sure she'd lost, skipped another beat and then went tumbling about again all over her chest.

Afraid to speak of her feelings and suddenly unsure of herself, Tammy turned away and tried to get her thoughts back on the situation they were all in. There was a long journey still to make, with certain danger up ahead, and she felt responsible for this group.

I must keep my mind on the job at hand, she scolded herself. Enough of this mooning about like a love-struck schoolgirl. Tammy smiled a little to herself. She remembered the books that her mother had told her were waiting for her at 'home'; back in a time and place long forgotten.

Her mother had stretched her own memory to recall some of those stories; stories of schoolgirl heroines and strong, handsome heroes. Those she could no longer remember she had made up, to help her little girl enjoy some of the simple pleasures of growing up.

Tammy sighed a little at the memories of her parents, and she struggled to bring her thoughts back to the present. Other matters required her attention and she needed to concentrate; not be getting all misty and dwelling on a past that was gone forever.

The group walked on until the day became too hot. Then they found a place in the lee of a hill and camped for the day. There was no water and nothing to tie a bag to, so Tammy insisted on strict water rationing. For two more days they walked on; tired, hot, thirsty and sick to death of sand and shimmering mirages that promised water, but vanished as they approached. Each longed to drink from the meagre supplies that they carried, but Tammy's eyes were everywhere and she insisted on the basic ration per person.

The landscape changed a little again, and a few scattered shrubs were dotted about. They weren't much, but they did provide some scraps of shade, if a person could get in just the right place.

Barda's group carried some mats made out pieces of long grass, and by propping them up over anything high enough to sit under, they could make some shade for themselves when they stopped to rest.

They were always willing to share, of course, but space was a problem. The best shade came from the lee of hillocks and rocky outcrops that were dotted about in the landscape. Gary and Bob remarked to each other one day, as they staggered along after Tammy and Barda's people, that they might as well be walking on the moon.

On a timeless day, there had been a little breeze, so the group had opted to continue on for a while after the breakfast stop. Time had got away, and it was almost lunch time before they realized it. They would stop soon, Tammy told them and as usual reminded them all to be on their guard.

"Just because we haven't seen Joe and his mates doesn't mean that they are not close by. The need for water will be quite urgent by now, and they are sure that we know just where to find it," she told them.

Just then, Barda came to Tammy and told her that his scouts had found a good place for the travellers to stop for a meal.

"There's shade up there," he said, pointing to the way ahead. "We do not know where it comes from, but there is always plenty of water. Our young men say trouble near, though; 'crazy men' not far from here. They leave sign everywhere," he laughed. "They are not good at hiding. I think they will try to get water and food soon."

"Yes, Barda," said Tammy. "Dave and I felt certain that they would be around somewhere. What do you suggest that we do?"

Barda suggested that he and Tammy and Dave should join his tribesmen for a meeting to plan their defense strategies.

"I'm not sure what we should do," he said. "We have no enemies. We live at peace and white folks are far to the rising of the sun. When we see them far off, we wave, they wave, and we each go our way."

Dave was a little amused at Barda's explanation of his relationship with the property owners, but he was also encouraged, because it meant that before long they could expect to meet up with people who could help them get home.

Providing, of course that they could manage to survive what seemed like an inevitable encounter with Joe and his unsavoury friends. So, while the group gathered for a brief rest in what little shade could be found in an all but empty wasteland, Tammy and the men folk sat in a rough circle and discussed the best way to handle the situation that each felt sure was only an hour or so away at most.

Chapter 6
CAPTURE

In the normal way of things within the tribe, a woman would not have been privy to the plans of the menfolk, but Barda had learned that Tammy did not fit into his understanding of such things; besides which, he had also learned to value her opinions and input.

Barda informed them that the place his scouts had found for a lunch stop was so good that even Joe and the others would have chosen it.

"The water should be plentiful, there is a small pond." he said. "There are rocks and even some reasonably sized trees hanging over. There is good shade. The water rises up from beneath the ground, and it is very hot. Our people have dug out a second pond, with a narrow channel to connect them, so water flows from one to the other. The second one cools down enough so that we can use it. It tastes different to most water, but it does not make us sick, so we drink it.

"We are sure that the bad men will find us there and attack."

"Can your young men tell us exactly where these three are?" asked Dave. "It would be good if we knew how long it will take them to arrive at the waterhole."

Barda said that they would be able to do that, and immediately sent a small group of hunters out into the desert. They had orders to find the group, to make sure they were not seen, and to get word back straight away. They were to keep watch and be ready to alert Barda to every move the three of them made.

Tammy knew that Barda's men would move like shadows, and that Joe and his mates would never see them.

"As soon as we know how much time we've got, we'll have some idea of how to prepare," Dave said. "We should wait here until Barda's messenger returns and then we'll decide what to do next. Do we have any weapons?" he asked.

"Men have hunting spears and boomerangs," Barda said. "Women have digging sticks. That is all."

"I have a pistol," Dave revealed. "I always carry one in the plane. I've never used it except for practice at the pistol club. I'm a reasonable shot, but I've never fired at anything alive."

"Well," said Tammy. "That would seem to be it. I guess it will have to do. Here's hoping that we can scare them enough that they'll leave us alone."

She sounded a lot more confident than she felt, but it seemed better to be optimistic. Perhaps they would be able to make it to a more populated area before trouble came. As soon as that thought came into her mind, she knew it was a faint hope at best.

Within minutes, a lithe figure appeared beside Barda. He seemed hardly out of breath and yet he had obviously been running. He squatted in the sand and whispered to Barda, who nodded his thanks and sent the young man off again to continue his watch.

"We have seen them," Barda said. "They have further to walk than us. I say we hurry now and make a trap. Scouts will tell us when they come. They are going that way. Maybe a desperate man can smell water as the animal does," he added with a smile.

Reluctantly, the travellers got to their feet and headed out into the heat once more. A sense of urgency drove them on, even though they would all have preferred to stay in the shade, thin and scant though it was. But the need to arrive at a decent campsite, and to get there ahead of danger, was stronger than the desire for rest. So they gathered up their bits and pieces and set out for the oasis ahead.

Barda and his people took the lead, unerringly following the directions known from previous trips to this oasis, so Dave trotted up and walked with this quiet and dignified elder statesman of his tribe.

"Do you have any kind of plan in mind?" Dave asked. "I have to confess that I have very little experience in such matters."

Barda nodded wisely. "It is good to be a man of peace," he said quietly. "We too are a people who love peace. This was so, even before Tammy taught us of the God who died for us.

"At first we found this a hard teaching, for we must look to that which is best for the whole tribe.

"But then we realized that sometimes we have needed to make a choice to sacrifice a weaker one for the benefit of our group.

"Many times that one would choose this way for us. Perhaps this was the choice that Tammy's God made for all His people."

Dave was not very knowledgeable about such things, but he listened to the old man's seemingly wise words and pondered again on the things he'd been learning over the last few days.

"I too have learned much from Tammy," he said quietly, "My life has taken some strange turns in a very short time."

"Ah!" exclaimed Barda, softly, "I can see that our little friend has pierced your heart. It seems that her gentleness is like a spear that has found a crack in the shell you have wrapped about you, my new friend."

Dave found himself smiling at the old man's quaint way of expressing something that he had not yet been able to face, even though in his heart he had known the truth of Barda's words, almost from the moment he had met Tammy.

"How wisely you speak, Barda. I need to think long about your words, for I believe that Tammy will be a part of my life for a very long time indeed. However, my wise friend," Dave said as he drew a long slow breath, "We have a problem that we must face, before we are all sacrificed to the gods of greed, here in this desert."

"Indeed," answered Barda. "You say that you have little knowledge of the ways of such men as we have recently been unfortunate enough to meet. We ourselves know only those things that Tammy has taught us of white man's ways, although I fear she too knows very little. But I have lived long, and it would seem to me that such ways as greed are common enough to all men.

"Among our people we try to share that which we have, but sometimes there are those who think they need more. It is not always possible to please every man. But as for these three, who bring trouble like an angry spirit such as those my people have long feared, perhaps some of the ways we trap animals may also trap men."

"We will be guided by your knowledge," said Dave. "Could you or any of your men use a gun?"

"Tammy's father had a gun. Sometimes he would show us how it worked. Our people know that it is a very dangerous thing. We know that it sends its death much further than our spears. We know only that it is best to keep far away from such a thing. I am sorry, Dave. We will use those weapons with which our ancestors have hunted and use only those skills our fathers taught us. Did Tammy not bring her father's gun on your journey?"

"No", Dave answered, "I suppose there was no ammunition left for it." And then he muttered, half to himself, "I wonder if Joe is the only one of those three who...?"

Barda nodded, as though he too was following Dave's train of thought. Either he was well accustomed to people who only spoke half of what they thought, or else was too polite to make mention of Dave's musings, other than to comment. "We cannot know, but we must say that they have, until we see that they do not."

"Yes, you are right, of course," said Dave. He was mildly amused at how quickly the old man had picked up his rambling thoughts, although, not necessarily surprised. This elder statesman may have been lacking in knowledge concerning modern life, but he lacked nothing in intelligence and quick wit.

"Here's hoping they don't, though. We don't need to find ourselves in the middle of the gunfight at O.K. Corral."

Barda frowned and Dave smiled at his puzzled look. "It's a saying that comes from the title of a Western movie," he said, only to realize that his venerable companion had no more idea of what a movie was, than he himself would have known the names of the myriad plants used for food by these desert people.

So, as they continued on their way, Dave found himself trying to explain to Barda what a movie was. He suddenly began to see just how much is taken for granted by western civilization.

As he tried, without much success, to convey a meaningful explanation of a 'movie', he wondered if folk back home realized that people still exist whose view of life is vastly different to their own; whose priorities are not which material thing to acquire next, but rather, whether there would be water at the next spring. And will the food be plentiful enough to feed the tribe?

Dave felt humbled by these people with their simple needs, by their open handed generosity and their concern for each other as an integral part of the survival of the tribe.

It had taken a couple of hours of walking, and midday was well past as they came in sight of the scattered rocks and trees surrounding an obvious oasis.

Trees here were healthier looking, as their roots were able to sink deep into the water that lay far beneath the sandy soil, and the shade they offered was a welcome relief to the weary group.

The children began to run, seemingly invigorated by the scent of the water, but their parents quickly called them back, fearful that their little ones would forget that the water was hot.

Not to be deterred, however, they were soon gathered around the smaller hollow. They dug the channel out again, with sticks that the tribe always had with them, as the sand had filled it in since last they had passed this way. Then they all watched in delight as water from the bigger pond trickled slowly into it. The children danced around it, laughing with the sheer joy of living.

Dave smiled at the innocence of the children, marveling that kids were pretty much the same everywhere, especially where water was concerned. Children, he decided, just had a natural affinity for the stuff. How vital, he thought, is this life-giving substance to the very survival of these desert people. It was going to be difficult to restrain the urge to touch the water until it cooled – it looked so inviting in this parched landscape.

He turned away from the children for a moment and noticed that Tammy was on her knees, apparently praying.

He caught her eye as she stood to join the group at the waterhole, obviously relieved to find this place where water was bubbling its life-giving nectar to the surface.

"I thought it fit to thank God for his gift of water and shelter," she said shyly. "It seemed like a good time to ask also for His protection, as it seems danger is not too far away."

Dave smiled and nodded his agreement. Again, he was struck by her simple faith. And he certainly had to admit that so far Tammy's God had not let them down. Despite the heat, the disaster of the willy-willy, and Joe and his friends absconding with their supplies, they had not gone hungry or unduly thirsty, and no one had been hurt. And now this delightful place right here where they needed it. Food for thought indeed.

When we get through this, he thought, I really want to talk to Tammy about it, maybe she can teach me more.

However for now, more pressing matters required his attention. Eventually, the water was cool enough to allow everybody to drink at the spring, and to fill their water containers.

The water had tasted very strongly of mineral and it was still luke-warm, but out here water was water, and one could not afford the luxury of being picky about temperature or taste.

Dave went up to the hot pool, keen to examine it a bit closer. He felt certain that this had to be an artesian spring and he was keen to know if it was a natural spring or whether someone had put down a bore at some time. He could not be certain, for the water seemed to bubble up from the middle of the pond. It was deep and with the bubbles and all the steam, it was hard to be certain whether there was a pipe down there or not. Eventually he gave up and instead found himself, to his surprise, simply following Tammy's lead and thanking God for His providence. It was, as far as he could recall, the only time he had ever prayed.

The women and children were quickly directed by their men folk into safe hiding places among the rocks. They were instructed that they must stay hidden and quiet at all costs, for the danger would be very real. Tammy impressed upon the mothers that the children must not make any kind of sound.

So the ladies gathered their little ones together, and in no time at all it seemed that they had completely disappeared. Any casual observer would never have guessed that at least a dozen or so mothers, and their numerous children of varying ages, were hidden in that outcrop of rocks and trees.

The men of the tribe, and Tammy's group, gathered by the pool to plan their defense strategy.

It was suggested that Viv and her sister, Marian, should hide with the women from the tribe, but that they must make sure not to give any sign of their presence. Gladly, they made their way up into the rocks. They all had plenty of water now, so they joined the other women who found them a shady place. All settled down to wait.

No one knew how long it would be before the three criminals made their appearance, but everybody wanted to be ready.

Viv decided that as her services did not seem to be required, and she would need to be as quiet as the proverbial church mouse, she may as well take the opportunity to rest.

So she curled up on a patch of soft sand, threw a light shirt over her head and shoulders, as protection from flies and the sun, and was soon asleep. Marian sighed, and joined her. Why not? She thought.

As Tammy and the men planned what they hoped would be a successful ambush, Dave deferred to Barda and the men of his tribe. He recognized that they knew far more about hunting and trapping than he did, and Bob was only too happy to let the others tell him what he should do.

Gary had some experience with camouflage, having done a stint in the army. But he too, deferred to Barda's superior knowledge and only offered a suggestion or two as he saw fit.

Gradually, a plan of sorts came together, and each one hurried to attend to his or her assignment.

Tammy was fairly confident that it would all work out, because she had been on hunting trips with the men before and knew that they always managed to capture their prey. She offered a silent prayer that trapping men would not prove to be all that different to trapping animals – after all, despite the violent nature of their prey, surely superior numbers should win out in the end. At least they hoped to have the element of surprise.

Soon all was ready, and each one settled down to wait. The afternoon heat was oppressive, but the oasis was comparatively cool and shady. The biggest risk in the short-term was that of falling asleep.

Dave had to shake himself awake several times, but he noticed that Tammy was ever alert. Like a little bush creature, she waited, as much a part of Barda's people as any of his eager young men. The flaxen hair shone in the dapples of sunlight, and he wondered how she kept it so beautiful in such harsh conditions.

It seemed that his thoughts were consumed by this wisp of a girl and he marveled again at how she had captured his heart. He was as sure as any man could be that he had found the one with whom he wanted to spend the rest of his life, and he promised himself that nothing would separate them, if he could do anything about it.

He thought back over his bachelor life; of the years following first this dream and then the next. Never settling down or letting himself think about how lonely he was. He thought too of the dream of owning his own plane and how that had been about the only one he'd ever really followed through.

And now, that too was gone. It was insured, but, would that be enough to put another one back in the air? It had been far from new when he'd bought it, and he'd got it at a pretty good price. Bargains like that didn't just fall out of the sky. Well, figuratively speaking anyway, he thought ruefully, recalling the crumpled mess that lay on the desert floor, back near Tammy's home.

He looked again over at Tammy, and wondered how she felt about leaving her home. She had told him that she was six when her father had found that place, and it had been her home since then. Seventeen years, she'd said.

That made her 23. She was so young; so innocent of life.

Was he too old to hope that she would ever want him? Though only in his early thirties, he suddenly felt quite old, despite the fact that his youthful body was fit, trim and well muscled. But she seemed so young!

Dave's reverie was suddenly cut short, as a low hiss from one of Barda's lookouts, drew their attention to a shimmer on the horizon. As they watched, the shimmer materialized into three figures. They were ragged and dirty, limping on damaged shoes and obviously hungry and thirsty. They carried nothing.

Apparently all that they had stolen had been used up indiscriminately, and the carry-bags carelessly discarded somewhere out in the desert.

They would not have lasted much longer out there by the look of them, and if it hadn't been for the gun sticking out of Joe's belt, they'd have looked pretty harmless. Dave, however, knew not to take anything for granted, and waited patiently with the others until the three fugitives entered the oasis.

The first thing to catch their eyes was the water. Desperately thirsty and quite beyond any thought of possible danger, they rushed as one for the spring. However, hot water was not quite what they had been expecting, so there were a few moments of confusion, while they sorted themselves out.

Then Joe saw the second pond, where the water drained away from the hot spring, so he went over to it and carefully tested it to see if it was cool enough to drink.

He gingerly stuck a finger in and then indicated to his mates that it was okay. They fell down on their knees to drink the still luke-warm water.

So consumed were they by thirst, that it seemed they didn't even stop to wonder why a pool, in the middle of desert, had obviously been recently attended. Fresh sand still marked the place where the children had re-dug the channel for the water to flow from one pool to the other.

The watchers let them drink their fill. Then, with spears or long sticks in their hands, and a large net that they had fashioned from any bits and pieces that could be strung together, the tribesmen came rushing out of hiding, yelling a war cry guaranteed to chill a man's blood in his veins.

Surrounding their hapless victims, wrapping them up in a tangle, they continued to jab them with spears and sticks until they were quite satisfied that they were completely subdued. Dave was a little concerned that some of the spear jabs might prove fatal, but on closer examination, he realized that the canny tribesmen were not even drawing blood. It was all for show, however convincing.

Dave sat on Joe and quickly retrieved the gun from his belt. Standing up he handed it to Tammy, who was by his side in an instant. Dave demanded to know if either of the others was carrying guns. Thoroughly dejected and fearful of their lives they swore that they were not.

A quick search verified this and so Dave indicated to Barda that his men could carefully untangle the miscreants, and tie hands and feet together as they released each one from the net. Dave and Tammy held them at gunpoint throughout the procedure, warning each of the tribesmen not to get in the line of fire.

In a matter of minutes all three were firmly tied with a rope made of thin plaited branches and vines, so tough it was virtually impossible to break without a knife.

They were placed in a row with their backs against a rock; a bedraggled band of would-be villains, whose rampage through the outback had just come to a sudden and ignominious halt – thanks to a tribe of primitive hunters, two city guys, a bush pilot and a slip of a girl.

Bob and Gary couldn't help but marvel at the way their joy-flight in Dave's plane had turned out. Who would have imagined, when they'd decided to take their wives on an outback holiday, they would end up marooned in the desert, miles from civilization, tracking through the desert with a tribe of aborigines and capturing a gang of thieves.

They looked at each other and smiled a victor's smile. Then, seeing how dirty and disheveled each looked, they burst out laughing.

Suddenly, it seemed, it was time for celebration. The women came out of hiding and there was much laughing and dancing and rejoicing.

The afternoon was now far gone so the decision was made to once again make an overnight camp. What better place could be found anyway?

The days ahead could be difficult, so it would be good to make the most of this almost unbelievable oasis in such a harsh and inhospitable place. And despite their desperate need to find civilization, perhaps a day of rest here would not go astray.

The desert nights were cold, even though the days were so hot, and so after a meal of whatever they could put together, the group of adventurers found sheltered spots among the rocks, using the sand and each other to keep warm. Tomorrow would again be hot, so before retiring they re-filled water containers. That way, the water should cool somewhat overnight and taste a little more pleasant.

Then, each tucked up as best they could and tried to put aside their busy thoughts and prepare for sleep. How much longer would they be out here, and how much further must they go until they came upon some sign of human habitation?

A roster had been worked out and a guard set, so that at all times during the night, someone would be watching the prisoners. Each of the volunteers hoped that it would not be them to drop off to sleep and so lose these three again.

These fears proved groundless, however, as the rostered times had been kept as short as practicable, for that very reason.

The next day dawned as usual with clear blue skies and all the signs that it would be as hot and airless as the days before it. Viv complained softly to herself, muttering as she set about organizing herself. Tammy was pleased that as time had passed, she had become less tiresome. Overwhelmed, she supposed by the enormity of their situation.

Hot, tired, and scared half out of her wits by their encounters with Joe's unsavoury crew, not to mention nearly being blown to pieces by the willy-willy, she had become most subdued, satisfying herself with a few mutters under her breath when confronted with yet another difficulty.

Chapter 7
MOVING ON ALONE

As the group came together after their morning meal, to decide whether to move on or stay for the day, Barda softly spoke up. He and his people would not be going on any further; this was as far east as they had ever travelled.

It was not too far past here that they had seen evidence of 'white folks', and so assuming that ahead lay the places where they lived, had always turned back, usually heading north or south, depending on availability of water.

Tammy was very disappointed, even though she had half expected it, and wept as she said goodbye to her friends.

She knew that it was very likely she would never see them again and she extracted a promise from Dave and his group that they would not divulge the whereabouts, or even the very existence of this tribe of desert-dwellers. She earnestly believed that they should all respect the wishes of folk who desired nothing more than to be left alone, free from the trappings of civilized society. Each gave their promise, and sad farewells were said.

Viv and Marian were more than a little fearful of going on alone, having become used to the comforting presence of people who were so obviously at home in this hostile environment, but Tammy assured them that she knew how to look for water, and how to recognize the signs.

"In any case," she reminded them, "We can always use our plastic water gatherers again if we need to."

Over the time since this adventure had begun, Dave had become quite adept at hunting too, so he also assured the ladies that between them they would manage okay.

Dave's biggest concern was keeping tabs on Joe, Ed and Lenny, and that thought reminded him to quickly check their bonds.

While he was sorry to see Barda and his little group of families leave them, in a way Dave was encouraged, because surely this meant that there were people up ahead who could help them get home and take Joe and his boys off their hands.

So, their good-byes all said, Tammy's group watched as their newfound friends headed off into a glaring sun that was getting hotter by the hour. Barda and his tribe were travelling south for a short while, before heading west again later in the year, finally returning to their camping place near Tammy's cavern. Their nomadic lives seemed pointless in many ways, but they were happy and contented. They cared for each other and seemed to have all they needed.

Tammy and her parents had made quite sure they knew who God was and that they knew everything He had done in creating their world and in coming to earth to die on the cross for all of mankind. Many of them had chosen to believe and were teaching their children also. Perhaps one day, Barda had said, they would venture out of the desert and see what lay beyond the oasis of the rocks.

"When I am gone," he had confided to Tammy, "The young ones will want to find a different world to the one we have shown them. They will want to know what your world looks like.

"Be brave my little one," he had said to Tammy. "It is right that you find the world you belong in, and it is right that you find it with this man who flew out of the sky and into your heart." This said with a smile and a twinkle in his eye.

The wise old man had not missed the looks that had passed between Tammy and Dave and he had known, even before Tammy herself, that whatever it is that happens between a man and a woman was happening between these two. Before he left, he held Tammy's hand in his and urged her to find her happiness.

"The future you must go into is a good one. Trust the Lord you have taught me is good, and trust this man too, for my heart tells me he also is good."

Tammy reached her arms about Barda's slender shoulders and hugged him. It was not his way, but he patted her shoulder and smiled his gentle smile.

Tears again filled Tammy's eyes as the tribe walked away, and she was not sure whether it was the shimmer of the desert light, or her tears that blurred her vision.

She watched as they gradually disappeared into the haze on the horizon and then, taking a deep breath, turned to her charges. Soon, their journey would be over and hers would be just beginning.

The decision was made to spend the remainder of the day resting and sorting out gear. Dave was anxious to be on his way, but he knew that the women were very tired.

Emotionally drained from all the excitement of the last couple of days, they really needed some time to recuperate. Viv's feet were swollen so Tammy ran some water off the main pond at the spring and made a little pool for her to soak her feet in. It soon cooled off enough for Viv to put her feet in and bathe them.

She actually smiled at Tammy properly for the first time and thanked her for her kindness. With her feet soothed by the water, she dried them, then found a shady spot and lay down. Dave found some bags to rest her feet on and she stayed there for some time with her feet elevated to reduce the swelling. Her exhausted body soon succumbed and she was asleep in moments.

The rest of the day passed slowly. Dave was a little bit restless but he tried hard to relax. He was wise enough to realize that he needed the rest as much as the others did. He poured over the charts that he'd brought from the plane and tried to work out where they were. But he had no idea how far they'd traveled and in any case, how far from where?

Meals were light during the day, both to conserve food while they were not burning up so much energy, and also because in the oppressive heat they were not really hungry. A sort of lethargy had gripped them and they lay about in the shade reluctant to make a move for any reason.

Lenny whined endlessly, and Tammy decided that she had preferred Viv's strident complaints to this pathetic creature, whose own greed and stupidity had led him to this situation. Tempted to yell at him to stop it for goodness sake, she held her tongue, and was amused when it was Viv who finally told him in no uncertain terms, to shut-up.

"No one wants to listen to you," she snapped at him.

"We've all had just about enough of you and your friends, so don't try our patience or someone will knock your block off!"

Joe lunged at her and would have inflicted harm if he had been able to reach her. However, Dave was alert and yanked at the vine holding the three of them tethered together. At the same moment, Bob, usually the quiet, inoffensive one, stuck his foot out and tripped Joe. So, consequently, his attempt to get to his feet failed. He spread his length and got a mouth full of sand for his trouble. This managed to drag Ed and Lenny and they yelled out as the vines cut into them. For a moment there was a tangle of bodies and vine. The disentangling process was accompanied by much swearing and cursing by the three of them. They abused each other and their captors, threatening violence on Dave and the others, not to mention their children and their children's children.

Dave patiently waited for them to get themselves upright and sorted out and then quietly suggested that they had better get some rest if they wanted to be fit enough to travel that night.

Breathing curses under their breath, the three recalcitrants settled down again. They were definitely rueing the day they had ever thought that travelling out the back of beyond, 'grabbing everything they could from those dumb country bumpkins' was the idea that would make them rich, with no chance whatever of ever being caught.

Any camaraderie or friendship that might have existed between them had long gone, and it seemed they hated each other now, as much as they hated the people who had been, in their opinion at least, their downfall.

Viv and Marian were worrying that they might not find water again once they left this oasis, so taking pity on them for their fears and doubts, Tammy informed them that the hot water meant that the Great Artesian Basin was beneath them now, and that finding water really shouldn't be that hard any more.

"My Dad knew this country as well as any white man could." Tammy assured them. "And I remember him telling me about this vast underground water system.

"When Barda led us to this place, I realized then that we had found where it begins."

At that point, Tammy paused, as she remembered... "My family and I probably could have walked out," she said softly, "Only, Mum wasn't much good at walking, and I was too small. Dad wouldn't leave us, so somehow, the years went by, and then they were gone. I didn't really want to try by then."

Each of them nodded, afraid to say anything. They were trying to imagine what it must have been like all those years ago. Viv and Marian were both in total agreement; they would never have ventured out here without her.

"How brave your father was, my dear," said Marian finally. "Thank you for all that you have done for us. We would have been lost without you. No doubt we would have perished out here. I am sure we all agree, don't we, that we owe Tammy our very lives?"

The others all nodded their agreement, and Dave reached over to touch her arm, smiling at her. The look in his eyes left Tammy in no doubt that he was glad he'd found her, even if he did believe that he might have survived, for a while at least.

The other four exchanged knowing glances, and they hoped that these two would have the opportunity to spend many years together. Marian, being a bit of a romantic, was quite sure that they were made for each other, and that this meeting was somehow ordained.

As evening approached, and the desert air began to cool, Dave called everybody together and suggested that they prepare a meal and get ready to leave.

"As Tammy suggested days ago, and even though it hasn't always worked out that way, it's still better to travel at night if we can," he said. "If we leave soon we can get a few miles under our belt before morning. Is everyone feeling rested enough to give it another go?"

There were reluctant nods from around the group and surly silence from the prisoners. But ignoring them, they busied themselves putting some food together. The activity was enough to wake them up and in no time they were ready and anxious to get going. A quick consultation with Tammy and they were on their way.

The night's march was quiet and uneventful. The flat country was almost featureless and the occasional stunted tree was ghostly in the moonlight.

Like orienteering, thought Gary, who'd done a bit of that in his time. If he'd had any idea where they'd started from he was sure that he would have been able to get this group to civilization in no time flat.

Chapter 8
CIVILIZATION?

And so they walked, on and on through the endless bush, only tired muscles and sore feet were proof that they'd travelled any distance at all. Very little changed in the bush around them, as days blurred into nights and into days once again.

Mornings dawned with breathtaking beauty, and sunsets were like fire lighting the sky but the tired travelers were not in the mood to enjoy it. Tammy did her best to keep spirits up with her positive attitude and her conviction that soon they'd find a nice place to stop and rest.

A nice place to Viv and her sister, however, did not mean a patch of spindly desert scrub and a sandy waterhole. To them it meant that lovely little coffee shop where they had so often sat and sipped coffee and eaten cheesecake, while resting their tired feet after a morning's shopping.

And speaking of tired feet, nothing in their memory had ever come close to the way this journey had damaged their feet.

No, nothing they could see out here in the grey morning light even remotely looked like a 'nice place'.

Sighing, they looked at each other, shrugged and tramped slowly on, following Tammy wherever she led, hoping against hope that soon she would lead them to a five-star hotel with all the trimmings.

Some of the places Tammy led them to had a spring of some sort, some did not deliver. But Tammy always made sure they carried as much as they could whenever they found good water and constantly reinforced her orders to drink only what was absolutely necessary.

Whenever they dry-camped, which was often, they would put bags over leafy branches of any convenient bush or shrub, emptying the gathered water into their containers several times during the day and resetting them again. In this way, even a dry camp would provide some water for the next night's journey. Even though their supplies were low at times, and thirst was a constant companion, they never actually ran out, and for this they knew they had Tammy to thank.

Joe, Ed and Lenny trudged along with the rest of them, totally dispirited now and convinced of their imminent death.

They had given up any hope of escape after a few initial attempts and almost welcomed the thought of rescue.

At least in jail they'd be fed real food, get to drink something more appetizing than water that tasted like dirt, and get to sleep in a bed they didn't have to share with half a desert of sand, not to mention a assortment of creeping and crawling nasties, many of which were quite happy to take a taste of salty human flesh.

(The city-dwellers among them were very glad that the only sign they'd seen of snakes had been the occasional track in the sand, and the dead ones that, reluctantly, they'd eaten. Each had been surprised, when having been persuaded to taste the cooked meat, that it hadn't tasted too bad at all. For Viv and Marian, it had been the thought of it more than anything.)

Dave had proved to be a taskmaster and he drove the prisoners on mercilessly. He had figured that if they were tired enough they'd cause less trouble, and his reasoning had seemed to be sound.

On one occasion, the vine, manufactured from the twisted tendrils of whatever green plant had been conveniently nearby, and worn from constant chafing, had given way.

Suddenly free from their bondages, they had made a half-hearted dash for freedom. Unplanned and with nowhere to run, the attempt was futile at best and Dave, Bob and Gary had been on them in moments. Secured this time with the rope off the tarp they'd brought along and used only as ground cover, or to throw over clumps of spinifex to provide a temporary shelter, any hope of further attempts seemed pointless.

About an hour or so after dawn, on one timeless day in a timeless land, Tammy called a halt for breakfast.

She hoped that the rather miserable little clump of bushes they'd come across would provide sufficient condensation, so she set about tying the bags over the leafy branches, while the other ladies prepared some food.

Footsore and weary, they all longed to sit and rest, but were hungry and thirsty, so they set to with as much will as they could muster.

By the time a meal was prepared, the bags were delivering a small trickle of water, which they poured into their containers. Then they quickly tied them back onto fresh branches in the hope of gathering more.

Viv really wanted a cup of tea, but there was no such luxury, so she had to content herself with the meagre sips of water that were the daily entitlement. It was barely enough to wash down the meal of kangaroo meat and assorted desert fruits, but at least the fruit provided small amounts of juice, which helped a little.

It was a quiet meal, devoid of any conversation. The only sound was the slight clatter of utensils and the usual desultory mutterings coming from the direction of Joe and his mates. No one even had the energy to shut them up.

So it was then, as each of them sat immersed in their own thoughts, they became aware of a sound that had not been there before.

"It's a motor!" yelled Dave. "There's a vehicle out there!"

"Is it coming or going?" asked Viv.

"I don't know," replied Dave. "Just wait a moment."

Each one sat there, waiting. The sound grew louder, and suddenly they were all on their feet.

"Where's it coming from?" asked Gary, rushing over to where Dave was standing, shading his eyes as he tried to penetrate the desert haze for any sign of a vehicle moving.

"Over there!" said Dave excitedly, pointing to a small cloud of dust on the horizon. "It's so far away, I don't know how we'll ever let them know where we are."

Suddenly everybody was running, yelling at the top of their voices and waving frantically. But the dust trail kept right on and was soon out of sight.

"East!" yelled Gary. "He came from the east. No way we're gonna catch him, but at least we know that someone is out there!"

"Okay!" said Dave. "But first let's just get over there, it's obviously a road of some sort." Suddenly, he remembered the prisoners, and swung back to the camp. But the three of them were bound tight and going nowhere, despite a half-hearted effort.

"Settle down, you lot," Dave said. "You'll be taken care of soon enough. Okay, troops," he said to the others. "Let's hit the road!"

Excitement energized them all and they hurried to pack up the gear. A rushed job, it lacked the usual care to get everything in the right pack. Haste, it seemed, was far more important, for the first time since leaving Tammy's home.

Heading off in the direction of the dust plume that still hung in the breathless air, they walked with a spring in their step that they hadn't felt since they'd begun this seemingly endless expedition. With the hope of human contact just ahead, they each began to visualize the things that they had been dreaming of since they'd found themselves stranded in the middle of the desert. A bath filled to the top with cool water. A drink so long it would take a week to get through it. Air-conditioning! A home cooked meal. All these things suddenly seemed to be a reality once again and steps were quickened at the very thought of them. Civilization was just ahead and nothing was going to stop them getting there.

Tammy was caught up in their excitement for a while, but as they rushed off into the heat of the day, she began to feel those old fears returning, and her steps began to slow. Dave noticed her falling behind, and dropped back to encourage her.

"Hey, guys, wait up!" he called. "You'll use up all your energy. It's hot out here."

Turning to Tammy, he looked into her eyes, and smiled at her. "It will be okay," he said softly. "I will look after you, there is nothing to fear."

She smiled at him, and tried to put on a brave face. But the reality of actually finding other people had scared her more than she had thought.

Since leaving 'home' the days had either been filled with danger and adventure, or with the mind-numbing boredom of trudging endlessly through heat and dust. So she hadn't had a lot of time to think about what would actually happen when they found that elusive homestead. But now, with the vehicle being so close, the inevitability of their rescue did not fill Tammy with the joy it did the others.

For her it would all be new and strange, for them it would be a return to their homes and their daily lives.

Bravely she set her face to the east and followed the others. She called out to them, that it could be some distance yet, and that they must conserve their energy. But they were wasted words. There was no stopping them.

Soon, they were standing right in the dust cloud, between the wheel tracks of what was obviously a four-wheel drive vehicle. The road, although road was a bit of an exaggeration, appeared to be well-traveled.

"Now," said Gary enthusiastically, "All we have to do is follow these tracks in the direction that vehicle came from, and we're as good as home!"

"What if the car was going home, not leaving it?" queried Marian. "If we follow the tracks that way we might be going further from rescue, not towards it."

Once voiced, the question hung in the air. Of course she was right. They could follow the tracks for miles and end up nowhere. Still, a choice had to be made. They could not stand here in the middle of the track, expecting to hitch a ride. That may well be the only vehicle to come this way for a week or more.

Dave knew that it was time for him to make a decision. He turned to Tammy and raised an eyebrow. The unspoken question was greeted by a small shrug of her shoulders.

"I do not know," she said at last. "We came from the east somewhere, as

I'm sure you did also?"

"Yes, we did, of course." he answered. "Riverside station. The homestead is about a hundred and five kilometers north-west from Tumberrumba station homestead. Tumberrumba's the biggest one around these parts. The co-ordinates for both are on the chart, but what use is that if we don't know where we are. We have no point of reference."

"Yes, we do!" said Tammy, slapping her hand to her forehead. "Of course we do. The water! Why didn't I think of this before? Dave, where's your chart?"

Not immediately comprehending, but responding to the urgency in her voice, Dave dug it out of his bag. He squatted down in the dust of the track and spread the chart out on the ground. They all gathered around him, anxious to see what Tammy was so excited about.

She pointed out a dotted line which marked the boundaries of the Artesian Basin.

"That spring, where we captured Joe and his mates, it was hot. That means it's Artesian." she said.

Dave nodded his agreement, and as he followed her pointing finger he realized what he should have picked up on ages ago. Hadn't he examined that waterhole, trying to work out where the water had come from? Hadn't he been looking to see if there was a bore? He berated himself, wondering where on earth his brains had been, as he'd totally missed the obvious.

As he looked at the map, noting the location of the Artesian water, he noticed where he'd put an X on the map ages ago – marking the position of the station where he lived; and from where he flew his plane, or used to, on sight-seeing trips for tourists all the time. From where they had all flown away... was it a life-time ago?

"So finally," said Tammy, "We have a starting point. See?" she said, pointing to a waterhole marked near the westward boundary of the Artesian Basin, "This has to be the oasis, and that means that even if the distance is still enormous, at least we have a direction and something to aim for.

"We must be either just north of the Territory border, or somewhere close to the far North East corner of Queensland," said Tammy, stabbing her finger at the place on the map that showed the corner where three states met. "At least, it's not far as the crow flies, as my Dad used to say."

"Or by plane – if you had one that wasn't a wreck somewhere in the wilderness," Dave added ruefully.

As the travellers leaned over each other's shoulders to look at the chart, it didn't look such a large area, on paper, until they looked up again at the vast emptiness that met their searching eyes.

Well, at least they knew roughly where they were, on a map at least, and although the area they'd have to cover was far from small, at least they felt that they might soon come across another human being and that thought helped them to feel just a little less 'lost'.

As Dave studied the map in front of him he also realized that they had not passed over a highway or a railway line in their travels, so they must have started east of the Stuart Highway and the Ghan. This, he figured, helped to narrow the area a little further.

"Surely, we must find a station property soon?" said Viv, looking hopefully at Dave. He smiled at her encouragingly, put his hand on her shoulder and, as positively as he could, told her that he was sure she was right.

As Tammy squatted there on the road, looking at the chart, she was interested to realize that the area where she had lived for so long seemed to be either very close to or even within the boundaries of an Aboriginal Reserve. How far into the reserve, she had no idea of course. She was amused to read that it was required by law, to have a permit to enter there. She wondered briefly where her father was supposed to have applied for one. Government departments had been a little thin on the ground, she had noticed. She wondered too, whether Barda and his people knew that at least some of the area they called home was a reserve, set aside for them.

Her mother had tried to teach her something of the geography of their home, but they'd been just names or squiggles on her father's chart from the plane. With no real understanding of space and distance, she had been unable to see the relationship between where she lived and the vast emptiness around her.

And it was only since leaving her home that she had begun to really understand how far her family had lived from any kind of civilization. Or for that matter, how close to Alice Springs they may actually have been. If only they'd known that, perhaps they could have walked out. Still... what was the use of speculation now?

Dave looked at the map again, noticed how stark and barren so much of it appeared to be.

"Did you and your parents fly over a highway or a railway line?" he asked Tammy.

"I don't remember," she replied. "I recall Dad saying we were actually heading south. He had decided to go south first, to Victoria and then Tasmania. Then he wanted to fly across the Great Australian Bight and show us the cliffs.

"From there, the plan was to fly across to Western Australia, up the west coast, across the Top End, then down the Queensland coast and back home to the Station.

"Of course, we never got anywhere near Victoria. In fact we hardly got anywhere at all before the storm hit us.

It would seem, on looking at where we are now, and the rough direction we've been travelling, that the storm must have blown us north-west. Did you pass over that highway – the Stuart?"

"Yes, the Stuart. It was originally built during the war years, to transport troops and equipment to Darwin, to protect our northern-most city. But, no, I didn't see the highway, or the railway – not before the storm hit. Looks like we both got clobbered in much the same area," he said, smiling at Tammy and shrugging his shoulders.

"Of course, once the storm took hold of the plane, I was flat out just keeping her in the air. Even though I tried to get some idea of where we were being taken, it was impossible to see with the dust being so thick. I don't recall seeing any visible landmarks until the storm spat us out and we ended up over your home."

This conversation did little to encourage their listeners and Viv flopped down in the dust where they stood, and wept. The high excitement of seeing the vehicle, seeing it vanish in a cloud of dust, then to hear Dave and Tammy speak of how lost they really were, just hit her. And in an emotional mess, she just felt that she couldn't go on.

Tammy rushed to her side and did her best to comfort her.

"Don't be afraid, Viv," she told her. "We'll find our way, honest. We know where the water-hole was, and Dave knows where Riverside Station is. Yes, it's a long way off, but we're not lost now, just a long way from home. Please don't give up now. Not when we are almost there," she added confidently – more confidently that she actually felt, she knew. But it seemed important to make Viv see that all was not lost.

Viv sat in the dust of the road and sobbed for a while, as Tammy sat beside her, holding her gently. But soon, as she sat there, staring at the tyre tracks on the road, she began to see that if someone had passed this way today, then sooner or later, someone else would come. So encouraged, she wiped her face, streaking the dust even more, and climbed to her feet. She gave Tammy a quick hug and thanked her for her understanding, promising everybody that she was fine now.

So, the group turned their attention to the task at hand. Which way to go. The consensus of opinion seemed to be that going west would only take them back into the desert.

Even if the Alice was to the west, it was surely too far to the north of them now. So home and safety must be toward the east.

No one in the group, including Tammy, could remember how many days they'd tramped through empty bush, scrub and desert, as one day had blurred into the next. It felt as if they had been walking for half their lives. They had no idea how far they'd travelled as they'd walked the lonely miles.

But, to this weary bunch nothing mattered except the possibility of human habitation at the end of this dusty track.

As they poured over the chart together, Dave marked the place where, he was fairly sure, the storm had hit. He knew, from the direction in which the sun had risen and set each endless day since then, that the frenzied wind had driven them west at least, and maybe a bit north, as Tammy seemed to think had happened to her father also. Problem was that he had no idea how far. But for now, he tried to plot a course from where they were at this point, to where they hoped a station property and homestead waited, and worry about where they'd come from later.

He knew that it would be pure guesswork, trying to figure out just where they had ended up, a half-hour walk from Tammy's place in the bush, almost exactly where Tammy's family had ended up all those years before. He reckoned there'd be plenty of time to figure that out once they were all safely home – wherever home was for each of them.

Tammy remarked that she had remembered her father pointing out a homestead as they had flown over it, commenting that it was a near neighbour to the one where they had been living, but couldn't remember if he had given it a name. She couldn't even remember the name of the one they'd lived at for several months.

She'd been so young, and it was so many years ago. And, even if she could have remembered, it might be different after all these years. Dave commented that although most properties stayed in the same family for generations, sometimes they were sold and renamed.

"Especially these days," he added. "Times are hard out here, and sons don't always follow their dads onto the land any more. University degrees and city life offer a life that's far more attractive than struggling out here trying to eke out a living.

Only a deep love for the land keeps people out here generation after generation. Riverside had been sold just a half-dozen years before I arrived there to work and run charter flights.

"Tumberrumba, on the other hand, has been in the same family for at least a century, so I've been told," he added. "Real pioneers, that lot. Whole extended family lives there – the father is mostly retired but his sons run it now; a number of brothers and their families. I think the eldest brother actually runs it, I know that he certainly has a fair bit of responsibility. I've dealt with him a bit – organizing charter flights and so on. Danny's his name – wife's name is Natalie. Nice couple. But I think that they all have a hand in running things; everybody's got their own area of responsibility. Pretty amazing, when you think about it. Still, I guess it's big enough to support them all. Just as well, I'd reckon."

There was a bit more discussion about direction of travel, as the question posed by Marian had caused some concern. But Tammy finally said that she was still sure that east from where they were, seemed the best way to go.

"Look, why don't we pray and ask God for guidance?" she suggested.

So, once again, a small band of people, far from home, formed a circle and held hands to pray.

The three criminals, standing in an untidy group, tied together with a weathered vine and a length of rope, laughed harshly at such foolishness. But by this time, everyone was well aware of just how well they'd been kept and guided, and no one had any complaints about joining in prayer. So ignoring the sneering of Joe and his mates, they bowed their heads and asked the Lord for guidance.

Then, taking a deep breath, Dave led them off down the road. The sun beat mercilessly down on their heads, as tattered hats offered meagre protection.

Each longed for shade and a cool drink. But by now they could almost smell rescue and the anticipation kept them going. The idea of sitting out the daylight somewhere and waiting until the cool evening to travel, didn't even rate a second thought. Rescue was in sight and a little discomfort seemed worth the trouble.

Soon enough though, the initial burst of energy faded, as indeed it must, and they trudged slowly on. It seemed like hours that they walked; apparently no closer to anywhere than when they had first set out on this fool's errand.

The afternoon wore on and as evening finally approached and their shadows ahead of them lengthened, they realized that they'd have to start looking for a place to stop for a meal. This would mean leaving the road to look for a suitable spot but the reluctance to do so was stamped on every face. This dusty track, with its tyre tracks was the only sign of civilization they'd seen since leaving Tammy's place, with the single exception of a bore at a water-hole – which apparently no one except Barda and his people had been near for some time.

Chapter 9

RESCUE!

Dave and Tammy didn't even consider asking if anyone wanted to head off back into the desert, so they said nothing and just hoped that soon they'd find something near enough to the road to make a suitable campsite, at least for a meal and a rest, if not for the night.

Just as all this was going through Dave's mind, a new sound – a very familiar sound, suddenly interrupted the flow of his thoughts. He looked up in amazement, as a plane appeared overhead. It was heading north-east, in the general direction of the track they were following.

Viv and Marian suddenly found their lost energy and ran around in circles, yelling and waving. Although not as quick to respond, in no time their husbands had thrown dignity to the wind and joined the women as they desperately tried to attract the pilot's attention.

The plane seemed as if it would go right over them, and had begun swinging off slightly more to the north, when suddenly, it tipped its wing, waggled a bit, and then began a slow banking turn. Coming right at them, it began to descend, obviously intending to land.

Quickly the group ran off the road, giving the plane room to maneuver. All four of Dave's passengers were jumping up and down with excitement, while Dave stood with his hands on his hips and smiled with great amusement. The three bound prisoners just stood and shuffled their feet in the dust.

Tammy stood still, suddenly interested in the red dust at her feet. They'd been found! Her task was complete. She struggled with her emotions. There was happiness of course, for her little group. Their quest was almost over. But for her there were more questions than answers. How would people treat her? Would they look on her as some kind of freak? Would she have to answer a myriad of questions about her life lost in the bush?

All at once she wanted to run; to turn from there and head back to her bush land home. After all, hadn't she been happy enough there? The security of the life she knew was suddenly far more attractive than the completely unknown life ahead of her.

Then, without a word, Dave was standing beside her. Taking her small hand in his, he gently squeezed and looking down at her, he smiled. He always seems to know, she thought. And the love shining in his face was unmistakable. Tammy remembered again how her father had looked at her mother, and she knew that this was the love her mother had told her she would 'know'.

Valiantly trying to put on a brave face, she looked up at Dave and tremulously smiled back at him.

She was still very much afraid of what lay ahead, but she was sure now that Dave would always be there for her, and that somehow he'd be able to help her through whatever came to pass.

The plane had touched down and dust was blowing everywhere as it taxied along the rough bush track. Enveloped in a cloud of dust as fine as powder, they all turned away from the plane, coughing and choking and trying to fan the stuff away with their hands. But even this small discomfort could not spoil the moment. Help had arrived and they were going home!

As soon as the little plane drew to a halt, the group ran over to it, greeting the rather stunned pilot as though he were a long lost friend.

For a moment or two pandemonium reigned as everybody tried to speak at once. Then Dave walked calmly up to the pilot and reached out to shake him by the hand.

"Hello, Roger. How are you?" he said.

"Dave? Dave Wilson? Where on earth did you come from?" asked a stunned Roger.

"It's a long story Roger, but we sure are glad to see you. How far are we from civilization, in fact, where on earth are we?"

"Tumberrumba homestead is about 20 minutes flying time thataway, close to the Queensland border," said Roger, waving his hand vaguely in the direction Dave and the others had been heading.

You are, in fact, actually on Tumberrumba property. There's an old artesian bore about a hundred kilometres back that way," - this with a wave of his hand in the direction they had just travelled, "And right near that is one of our western markers. We do cover a fairly big chunk of real estate," he added, in response to somebody's 'Wow!'

As he took all this in, Dave was quick to note that if they had not been following a road it would have been very easy to miss their target. He realized again how vast and empty this land really was, even if they were on Tumberrumba's property, it was still a long way to the homestead.

"It's truly a blessing that you came along when you did, Roger," he said. "We'd begun to believe that we might never find our way out of this mess.

"We noticed a dust cloud some distance from where we were camped, not too long ago, and could just make out a vehicle. So we rushed over as quickly as we could, but needless to say the car was long gone. So we started walking along this road anyway, in the hope we'd come across someone sooner or later. It was proving to be a long hot walk though, and we were hoping we wouldn't have to leave the road too far to find a half decent place to set up for a meal and a rest. We could have missed you if we'd gone too far off the road. You might not have seen us, especially if we had found some shade to sit under."

"Yep, I wasn't really looking down at the road. Getting on to home time, you know, end of a long day and all that. But with everyone jumping up and down and rushing about the way you were, the movement caught my eye. Thought it was just a bunch of 'roos at first. Last thing I expected to see was people out here, I'll tell you.

"That vehicle you saw would have been a couple of the boys going to check a pump out by one of the far bores. He'll be gone two days, minimum, so you'd have had a long wait for him to come back.

Boss reckons we need to cap that artesian bore out there too. They tell us now that the water down there isn't renewable, like we always thought, so can't have it just going to waste, can we? So, I reckon there's a chance they'll be doing that before they get back home. They'll have gear with them for a few days in case they come across something that takes awhile to fix. If they need extra stuff, that's where I come in, they just radio back to base and I fly out whatever they need.

"How on earth did you get out here on foot old son?" he asked, obviously bursting with curiosity. Finding a group of people wandering around the far reaches of Tumberrumba's grazing leases was not something he would expect to find on a normal day on the job. "Thought you were flying charters from Riverside these days?

"Have you come across any cattle?" he added, as an after-thought. "I've been out searching for strays."

"No mate, we've seen nothing but 'roos, emus and lizards for days.

"As for us being out here? Well, I'd love to tell you all about it mate, but can we get something organized first? We really need to get these ladies off to the homestead. We've been on the trail for days now.

"We've sort of lost track of time, but it would have to be a couple of weeks at the least, I'd guess; probably closer to three or four. We are all pretty well had it. Sufficient to say that my kite is no more. I'll fill you in on the details when we get out of this dust bowl. Tell you what though, we sure are glad that those fellas didn't cap that bore last week, it sure as heck saved our bacon out there. I hadn't realized that we were far enough east to actually be on Tumberrumba Station."

"Yeah, reckon if you folks came from further out past that bore, you'd have been right glad to see some water, even if it was hot." said Roger with a grin.

Okay, then," he added, all business. "Let's see now, three ladies, two seats. That's a bit of a problem."

"Take Viv and Marian," said Tammy quickly. "I'll be fine."

"Okay, pretty lady," said Roger, casting an appreciative eye over Tammy's lithe figure.

"Where, in this forsaken place, did you find this little beauty?" he whispered in an aside to Dave.

"Never you mind, you old scoundrel," said Dave with a playful punch to Roger's arm. "Just get these ladies back to the station and send a car for the rest of us. Oh, and call the police and tell them to come and pick up these three." he added, indicating Lenny and his unsavoury companions.

"Yeah, okay," said Roger, obviously confused by the strange assortment of people he had found wandering around in the vastness of his employer's property. Dave smiled to himself, thinking he'd have thought it a lot stranger if he could have seen the tribe of aborigines that had been with them when they captured the three crooks.

But for now, urged on by Dave, Roger set about helping Viv and her sister into his little plane. Promising to send transport and the police, he climbed on board, gunned the motor and with a final cheery wave rushed down the dusty road and took off. A final banking turn and he was headed off in the direction that they now knew to be where civilization and some home comforts waited. A little waggle of the wings and in no time at all he was just a speck on the shimmering horizon.

The seven remaining adventurers stood in the slowly settling dust cloud, watching as Roger and his chariot in the sky disappeared from sight. In the sudden quiet there was an almost surreal atmosphere and for a few moments no one was prepared to break the silence.

Then Dave said, "Come along, troops, let's get moving. We might as well keep walking. Not much point in just standing here. Home is that way." Dave pointed in the direction taken by Roger just moments before and the others sort of took a deep breath and shook themselves out of an almost trance like state.

Was it a dream? Had they really seen a plane? Was rescue actually coming? Suddenly galvanized, they let out a sort of ragged cheer and set off up the road with renewed vigour.

Only Tammy seemed reluctant. She had not missed Roger's look. She didn't need to be familiar with the ways of men to recognize that look. He had undressed her with his eyes and she'd hated it. There was no way she'd have climbed into that plane with him.

In that moment she realized how God had blessed her.

What if the pilot who'd crashed into her world had been a man like Roger, instead of the kind and gentle man who had encouraged and supported her from the moment they had met? A small shudder passed through her slim body at the thought.

Grave misgivings filled her mind. Should she have stayed back there in the desert, in her cavern home? Was she going to regret coming on this journey?

Then, even as these thoughts crowded her mind, Dave was once more at her side. It seemed as if he always knew when she felt confused or troubled.

"Not all blokes are like that," he said gently, as if he'd read her troubled thoughts. "There are a few, but most folk are pretty nice. Roger isn't really a bad person, he just doesn't have much in the way of social skills. He wouldn't harm you. Please try not to be afraid; I will be with you every step of the way. You will let me do that, won't you?"

Dave sort of hesitated and then he took her hand. Looking into her eyes, he said, "I really don't think I could live without you, Tammy. I've fallen in love with you and I want to spend the rest of my life with you. Do you think you could learn to love me too?"

"Dave," said Tammy softly. "I think I've loved you since we first met. I know that I could never have made this journey without you. Indeed, it was because of you that I finally decided to come. I was so afraid when I first saw all of you that I was almost paralyzed. It was only your gentle ways, and the way you looked at me that reassured me that somehow everything would be okay. Yes, Dave, I do love you and yes, I could not imagine the rest of my life without you."

And so, with the hearts of two feeling a little lighter, the now slightly smaller group, kept their backs to the setting sun and just kept on walking. With the sun getting lower finding a place to settle for a rest and a meal was a matter of urgency.

A small clump of scrub and bushes came into view, just ahead, and as they got closer, they could even see there were a few scattered rocks to sit on. So they decided that it would do. Unfortunately there was no chance that it would yield any water, but they were content to make do with what they still had left. Replenishing food supplies would normally have been the main task before leaving their last camp.

But the sudden appearance of the vehicle in the distance had totally distracted them, which meant that they also had to make do with whatever scraps of food were still in their packs.

Not that anyone really paid much attention to what they ate, as thoughts were definitely on the meal they could look forward to when rescue finally arrived. A little hunger now, suddenly seemed of no account – rescue was immanent, and that was all that mattered.

"I wonder how the girls are getting on," said Bob for the third or fourth time, munching on a mouthful of some tasteless berry, that Tammy had assured him would keep him alive, even if it wasn't the best thing he'd ever tasted. "How long has it been since they left? Would they be there yet?"

"I guess they'd be pretty close," answered Dave. "If I recall rightly, the airstrip is some distance from the homestead, so it would probably take half an hour to drive at least. I suspect that Roger would have called ahead on the radio, so someone might possibly have been waiting for them at the strip."

This seemed to satisfy Bob for a few minutes, but in no time he was up on his feet and pacing back and forth, looking up the road in the direction he hoped a vehicle would soon appear.

Time passed and soon the sun had set. Dave suggested they get some rest, as it could be some time before folk got organized to come and get them. But rest did not seem to be a priority. So, reluctantly, he and Tammy agreed that they should just pack up again and keep moving.

They walked on for about fifteen minutes. Darkness had fallen and a bright moon was throwing her silver light over the stark landscape. With nothing to spoil their night vision, eyes had soon adjusted to the pale light. But Tammy kept a close watch, to make sure they did not lose sight of the tyre tracks in the sand.

The cool night air had begun to replace the energy-sapping heat of the day and for a while it was a pleasant relief. But as the breeze strengthened the desert cold started to bite, so they stopped for a bit as each one scrambled into the warmer jackets that they'd brought from Tammy's home and had managed to hang onto for just this purpose.

Of course, there had been nothing to give Joe's lot, so they simply had to fend for themselves. They'd shivered each night without gaining much sympathy, for their discomfort was largely of their own making. Any spare clothing they might have had, they'd lost with all their stolen goods, somewhere out in the vastness of the desert.

With coats on, the group gathered up their bags once more and continued along the dusty trail, ignoring the plaintive whining emanating from the prisoners.

Finally Dave handed one of them the tarp, suggesting that they walk together and wrap it around their shoulders. If they couldn't co-operate with each other, too bad.

Then, as they straggled along, they suddenly all looked up as one. In the desert stillness, they could clearly hear the drone of a plane's engine approaching.

Looking up, they could just make out the lights on Roger's small plane as he flew over them once again. Dropping down until he was just above them, he waggled his wings and then, rising again, circled them slowly. Dave realized that he was marking their position for someone on the ground.

"Looks like help is on its way." he said.

As Roger circled lazily above them they watched almost as one for the first hint of a vehicle approaching. Soon enough they were rewarded as a pinpoint of light appeared on the horizon. As though transfixed they watched it draw nearer. It seemed to take such a long time, but Dave explained that because it was so flat here they would be able to see the light for miles. This was small consolation for Bob and Gary and they waited with very little patience. Joe and his unsavoury friends, however, were not at all keen.

They were well aware that rescue meant a certain jail term for them, but, all the same, as they stamped their feet and slapped their arms in a vain attempt to keep warm, the idea of a warm place, even if it was a cell, had a certain appeal.

Joe hoped that no one had linked him to the murder of the woman on that last property they'd hit. However, he knew in his heart that it would be hard to avoid the police putting two and two together, especially as Dave and the others would be certain to mention the blood, now dried, faded and caked with dust, on what was left of his clothes.

He wished that there was some way he could have discarded them, but a clean change of clothes was a bit hard to come by out here. Perhaps if he stripped off his shirt, but then he realized that he was securely bound and even though he struggled, he knew it was a vain hope at best.

Chapter 10
REST FOR WEARY FEET

Then, quite suddenly it seemed the big 4x4 was right beside them, as it pulled up amidst a cloud of dust. With the arrival of the car, Roger gave a final waggle of wings, a low swoop overhead, a banking turn, and he was gone, heading off back to the bunkhouse, an evening meal and bed.

On the ground an excited group was crowding around the rather bemused driver.

He had been wondering what on earth he'd find when he arrived, and hoping that he wouldn't miss them in the dark. Not that he'd needed to worry, they'd seen him coming and there was no way were they going to let another vehicle get away.

There was some confusion as everybody tried to talk at once and it took a while to sort it all out. Finally, Dave managed to quiet everybody down and was able to explain in part at least, how this motley assortment of travellers happened to be wandering around in the Australian bush.

Their rescuer had been given only the barest information. All he knew was to head off down the road and watch for the pilot to waggle his wings. He'd been told that he'd find some people there waiting for him. Dave asked him if he'd been told whether the police were coming, and he replied that as far as he knew they were on their way and he was to wait.

"I've got some food and drink on board, if anyone is interested," he said.

He then introduced himself as a roustabout on Tumberrumba station. He said that he loved his job because he never knew what he'd be doing day by day.

"But, this! This is something new." he said with a grin. "My name is Ray, and I'm pleased to meet you." This added with an even wider grin.

With the headlights of the vehicle illuminating the area, Ray pulled out a battered red esky and produced sandwiches and hot tea and coffee. The travellers had almost given up hope of ever tasting coffee again and they breathed in its heady aroma, as if it was the very air they needed to live.

Ray was rather amused at their reactions to what he considered pretty plain fare. But then he had not been wandering for days in the bush, eating food of a very different kind.

Tammy had never, to her recollection, even tasted coffee. She was quite sure her mother would never have allowed her to taste it at home, and of course such luxuries simply did not follow them into their bush land home.

If there had been any at all it would have been long gone before she would have been considered old enough to drink it. And come to think of it, she did vaguely recall her mother bewailing the lack of coffee. She remembered hearing her say sometimes, especially when she was tired, "A coffee. Oh, my kingdom for a coffee."

In her mind's eye, she could see her father laughing at her, offering her a drink of water with a flourish, a mock bow and the words, "Your coffee, Ma'am!"

So for her, this first taste of a drink that most people take for granted every day of their lives was a totally new and quite strange experience. At first she screwed up her nose and was not at all sure if she liked it, but after a bit of experimenting with milk and sugar, she decided that it wasn't so bad after all and quite enjoyed a cup.

The others were amused at her antics and a mood of great good humour soon had everybody laughing and joking as they sat around the gas lantern that Ray had also dragged out of the back of his car. It was impossible to tell what colour the vehicle was meant to be. It appeared to be much the same colour as the ground, a dusty red, as far as they could see in the light of the lantern. They supposed that they too were pretty much the same, as indeed everything soon would be after being out here in this wilderness for any length of time.

Joe, Ed and Lenny sat off to one side as the others laughed and talked, sullenly sipping their coffee with bound hands and wishing themselves anywhere but where they had landed themselves.

Anger and resentment had caused them to lay all blame for their predicament at the feet of their captors, totally blind to the fact that they had brought it all on themselves by their anti-social behaviour. Still, such is the attitude of crooks the world over; unfortunate circumstances are always the fault of someone else, never their own responsibility.

After half an hour or so of enjoying thick beef and pickle sandwiches and steaming mugs of hot coffee, they noticed the lights of an approaching vehicle off in the distance.

"This'll be the cops," said Ray. "They told me at the homestead that they'd not be far behind me. What have this lot done then?" he asked, indicating Joe and his mates slumped against the side of the vehicle.

As they waited for the police to arrive, Dave tried to explain all he knew about the three villains that he and his friends had captured.

"I have no idea what they've been up to," said Dave. "But one thing is for sure, it's no good. There is blood on Joe's clothing, and he is obviously a very vicious man.

He's tried a couple of times to kill us and they took all our supplies at one stage and left us for dead with no food. So we set a trap for them and managed to catch them."

He almost added that they'd had the help of some very capable friends, but caught himself just in time, remembering his promise to Tammy not to mention the tribe to anyone.

Just then, another four-wheel drive pulled up along side them. This one had the words POLICE emblazoned along the side and two burly officers, dressed in the kaki uniform of the NT Police, stepped out into the cloud of dust stirred up by their arrival.

Introductions were made all round and the sergeant was most interested in the three captives.

"Someone has been through a whole bunch of station properties, pinching all manner of stuff," he explained. "And a lady is dead, beaten to death by some cowardly so-and-so. I'll bet you anything you like that her blood matches this," he said pointing to the dried blood on Joe's shirt.

"We've seen these guys before. Haven't we boys?" This directed at the three dirty, bedraggled crooks being bundled unceremoniously into the cage in the back of the wagon.

"Accept the grateful thanks of the Police Service, and the family of the dead woman," the sergeant added as he stepped back into his vehicle. "We'd appreciate it if you could call into a Police Station somewhere and give us a statement as soon as you can see your way clear. I'm sure you'll be busy for a day or two, sorting yourselves out. When you're ready will do, it won't hurt these three to rot in the lockup for a few days."

"Thanks," replied Dave. "We'll get ourselves sorted somehow over the next day or so and call in as soon as we can to tell you what we know. It's good to hand them over to you. We've had a gut full of them, I can tell you."

So with a cheery wave and a honk of the horn, the vehicle pulled away and headed off into the darkness.

"Well, that's us done here," said Ray. "Let's clear up this stuff and head off back to the homestead, eh? Bet you guys, especially you little lady, are looking forward to a hot shower and a soft bed."

Tammy smiled shyly. She really had very little idea what he meant, bathing for her had been a simple matter of splashing around in her own stream. But she'd heard the other ladies wailing about hot showers for so long that she was sure it had to be the most wonderful experience life could offer.

Besides, she was as bone weary as her companions and any kind of place to lay her head had tremendous appeal right now. Physically and emotionally exhausted, she was sure she'd sleep for a week.

The travellers set to with a will and in moments had the esky, stove and lamp packed up into the car. A few moments more and their meagre possessions followed. Then they climbed up into the cabin, sank into the comfy seats and Ray headed for home.

Tammy couldn't remember if she'd ever been in a car. She supposed that she must have, but it was a memory that eluded her.

A little frightened at first, she soon began to enjoy the reasonably smooth ride that the big wagon offered. And although she was keen to see where they went, it seemed as if everything simply faded into some kind of dream.

The rest of the journey to the homestead was lost on her as exhaustion and the motion of the car drifted her off to sleep.

For the first time since leaving her cavern home, she didn't need to keep watch, ever alert for any kind of danger to herself or her charges. Suddenly, someone else was in charge, danger was a dim memory and Dave smiled down at her as he cradled her head against his chest. This was what he wanted to do for the rest of his life, look after her and care for her, for as long as they lived.

Chapter 11

JOURNEY'S END

The journey that only took twenty minutes in the plane took a generous two and a half hours on the ground. So it was five weary travellers who arrived at the homestead sometime around midnight on what had been a most eventful day. Dave gently shook Tammy awake, softly telling her that they had arrived. She awoke with a start, and was very embarrassed that she had allowed herself to just drop off like that. But Dave quickly reassured her that it was quite okay.

"It was a long boring drive and there was nothing to see anyway. Besides, you needed it I'm sure. You've had the burden of responsibility for all of us for this entire journey and a wonderful job you've done too in looking after us and keeping us safe. We'll always be indebted to you, won't we fellows?" This to the other members of their party, who agreed readily, that indeed they owed her far more than they could ever hope to repay.

Then suddenly, the vehicle was surrounded. Vivian and Marian were clamouring to greet their husbands and to hug a tired and bewildered Tammy.

The members of the homestead family, which seemed to include a kindergarten of children, were all eager to meet the rest of the adventurers and especially the little girl who had disappeared with her family all those years ago.

Never had they imagined that she would be still alive, and her hosts were eager to hear of her adventures in the wilds of the outback.

However, they remembered their manners, and outback hospitality insisted that these unexpected guests be made welcome and comfortable before all else.

There would be plenty of time in the morning to talk over the circumstances that had brought them here. For now, a bath, some supper and a comfy bed were of the highest priority.

Tammy was happy just to cling to Dave and be told where to go and what to do. No longer the one in charge, she was glad to relinquish that role. In a kind of daze, she followed her hosts into their huge home. She could just barely remember the house she and her parents had left so long ago, but she was certain that it was not anything like this one.

Big, airy rooms with high ceilings, surrounded by wide, covered verandahs, welcomed the visitors. Tammy could imagine that in the heat of the day, this house would be a cool oasis. Fans circled lazily from the ceiling of each room and soft mats underfoot covered floors that were polished so brightly, she could actually see her reflection in them. They were a warm golden colour in the lamplight and added to the pleasant feel of a comfortable home. A soft burbling noise in the background added to a totally soothing effect.

The next day, she was to discover that a generator to power the property's electricity needs had been the source of the gentle rhythm that had lulled her off to sleep – like a baby in its mother's arms is lulled by the soft beating of her heart.

After a bath in luke-warm water up to her neck, with some sort of sweet smelling froth and bubble that eased her aches and pains away, Tammy had sipped a cup of soothing herbal tea, refused any food as politely as she could, and finally, after a final lingering look at Dave for reassurance, she had followed her kind hostess, to a large airy room, in the centre of which was an enormous bed.

She had climbed into the bed, made up with snowy white sheets that felt cool and soft beneath her, and with one last whispered prayer of thanks, she'd surrendered to the pull of sleep. So exhausted was she, that she slept hours past the first blush of dawn, when normally, she would have been out hunting for her day's food supply.

A rather embarrassed Tammy emerged from her room the next morning. She had found a set of clothes draped over a chair in her room, and as all her tattered and torn rags had disappeared after her bath the night before, she assumed that she was expected to put these on.

They were cool and comfortable and when she caught a glimpse of herself in the mirror on the wardrobe door, she was astounded at her appearance. For one thing, she had never seen herself, except in pools of water, since she was a tiny child. So she didn't really know what to expect.

For some moments, she had stood in front of the mirror, trying to understand who this image was that was looking back at her. Common sense told her it was her own image, but she had no idea that her skin was so dark, her hair so white and her eyes so blue.

She had gazed at herself critically, trying to understand why Dave had been instantly infatuated with her. Was it the eyes? Or was it the flaxen hair? Perhaps it was the shapely body that she saw in the mirror?

She had realized, of course, as she grew up that breasts had formed and that slowly, over a period of years, she had grown a woman's body. But she had never seen the whole package before, and she was more than a little embarrassed, especially when she had caught a glimpse of herself without any clothes. Would Dave eventually see her this way? A sudden hot flush, crept up her body to her face as the thought went through her mind.

"Tammy!" she heard her mother say, "Put those notions out of your head, girl!"

She smiled to herself a little. "Yes, Mum," she said softly. "I will wait until we are married, I promise."

And with that, despite her embarrassment at the late hour, she had gone out to greet her friends with a certain spring in her step.

There was a definite glow about her, they noticed, and each of them caught their breath at the beauty of the young woman they had found in the bush; a woman certainly full grown, and to whom each of them owed their very lives.

Dave had been waiting for her and was quickly at her side. He led her gently to the huge sideboard where breakfast was laid out. A bewildering selection of foods were offered to choose from, so accepting his advice, she made her choices and went with him to sit at the table with the others, who had also risen late. But of course, none of them had intended to rise early, so they were not troubled.

The station owners had already gone about their day, not expecting their guests to show their faces too early.

So orders had gone to the housekeeper, provide them with breakfast and see to their needs.

The lady of the house breezed into the room as they were enjoying the plentiful array of food.

"I hope you all slept well," she said. "Is breakfast to your liking? Perhaps Lilly could get you something more?"

"Goodness me no!" chorused the group as one. "You've done us proud," said Dave, "I'm sure we couldn't eat another thing." The others agreed and thanked her most heartily for her generosity and hospitality.

"It's the way of the bush," she said. "We don't get many visitors out here. It's so nice to have the company. Though, having said that, I suppose you'll all be keen to be heading back to civilization as soon as possible."

"Yes, we certainly will. The city is calling me," said Viv. "Not to say that I haven't truly appreciated all that you've done. What with the bath, the bed and the food, you've made me feel human again. I'd begun to believe I'd never be clean again. Thank you so much."

"You are welcome, Viv," answered her hostess. "It has been entirely my pleasure. I'm sure we'd all but given you all up for dead. And as for this young lady..." She hesitated as a lump came to her throat. "I was a new bride out here when we heard the news of your family's disappearance, I can't tell you what a thrill it is to see you here, dear child." This last directed to Tammy, who smiled shyly at her host.

"I was not at all sure that leaving my home to come with Dave and his group was a wise thing," said Tammy, "I felt sure that there would not be anybody who would remember me or even care if I existed. I guess I really misjudged people and I am very sorry.

"You have all made me so welcome here, and even though I know it will be difficult to adjust, my new family, (and here she indicated Dave, Viv,

Marian, Bob and Gary) have become so dear to me over the last few weeks. We have been through a great deal together and not once has anyone made me feel like a freak.

"I must frankly admit that I am terrified of what is ahead, but know this at least, thank you for finding me, thank you for being such good friends.

And to you, my hosts, thank you most sincerely for opening your home and your hearts to me and my companions."

Natalie, the lady of the house, crossed the room in a couple of steps and took Tammy in her arms.

"Dear child," she said, "Even as we speak, my husband Danny is making calls to track down your family. Soon we will have information for you, people you can go and live with, who will take care of you until you find your feet, so to speak.

"You must try to be patient with folk, obviously they will be curious and no doubt the press will be anxious to interview you. I expect you will be quite a celebrity when reporters get wind of your 'rescue'. However, I am sure that Dave will be by your side every moment, making sure that no one is able to upset you or crowd you."

"You bet!" Dave chipped in. "There is no way I'm letting you out of my sight. If, as you've told me, there is a reason for everything that happens, and I'm being more persuaded each day that you may be right about that, then certainly there was a reason why I fell out of the sky right at your doorstep.

And there's a reason too, why you were walking along that path, on that particular day for the first time in years. We were meant to meet Tammy, my love, and I'm never going to let anything bad happen to you.

"You finish your breakfast now, and I will go and see how Danny's going. If he isn't doing too well on the phone, we should try the internet. Don't worry sweetheart," he said to Tammy, as he noticed her puzzled look, "I'll explain all about that soon – we've got years to teach each other all we need to know."

With that, Dave was up and out of the room. Each person in the room looked at the other and smiles were exchanged.

"Finally," said Viv in her blunt way, "These two have decided to stop dancing around each other, each pretending not to notice the other."

"Why, Viv," said Tammy, with a hint of mischief in her voice, "How can you say such a thing?"

The room filled with laughter and suddenly, Tammy realized that she really was among family. People who genuinely cared about her, and even more, were comfortable enough with her to joke and even have a little fun at her expense.

The dining room was, all at once, a friendly, welcoming place, and as Tammy and the others finished breakfast they gathered up the dishes and carried them into the kitchen where an aboriginal girl was preparing to clear up the last of the pots and pans and start on the plates and bowls.

Tammy offered to help. No one had ever served her since she was old enough to do for herself, and clearing up after a meal was second nature to her. However, the young girl shyly thanked her, but refused her help. Looking up at Tammy from under dark lashes that brushed her equally dark cheeks, she mentioned in a voice so soft Tammy had to bend close to hear her, that she had accidentally overheard two of them speaking quietly about the tribe they'd left behind in the desert.

"I believe that they are my relatives," she said softly. "My mother used to speak of a tribe that had never come near the homestead.

"She told me once that her grandfather had come in from the bush one day many years ago. He had said that he'd become separated from his people during a big storm and had lost his way.

He knew that the tribe would not wander about looking for him and that he must survive on his own.

"Unsure of direction he had just kept walking, until, nearly dead he'd been found by a white man who had brought him here to this homestead where he had been nursed back to health. With nowhere else to go he had stayed here and worked on the station. Eventually he married a local girl. Folk wanted to find his people and bring them in, but Mother said that her grandfather would not tell them where to look.

"They did not want to meet up with the white folk. So, no one really talks about them. It was a very long time ago, and I have not heard anything much since I was a little girl. Do you know where they are?" she asked.

"No, dear, I do not," said Tammy. "I'm not even sure I could find my own home. Well... I suppose I could track my way back if I chose, but, I'm not sure I want to do that, and I know that my friends do not want to be found yet." said Tammy. "The time will come, but until then, let's leave them alone."

"Yes, I'm sure you are right. Are they well?" asked the girl.

"Oh, yes, indeed they are." answered Tammy. "They were so good to me, and to my parents, while they were alive. I promised their leader, Barda, that I would never betray them.

They know that eventually the young ones will need to explore further. They already know that a whole world exists out here. But we must let them come in their own time."

"It is good, as you say," the lass replied. "Thank you for sharing with me. Now, I must get on, or madam will be cross."

"Don't worry, dear, I'll tell her that it was me who delayed you. I'm sure she'll understand. Thank you for telling me about your grandfather. Be assured that your people are all well and Barda looks after them very well indeed. He is a fine leader and very wise. Good bye, little one, perhaps we'll talk again."

The girl smiled shyly at Tammy and turned back to her chores. Tammy touched her lightly on the arm as she sighed a little and then went back to the living room to join her friends.

Dave smiled as she walked into the room and nodded ever so slightly, as if he understood her natural desire to spend time with someone she was familiar with.

For so many years Tammy had seen only black faces about her and so she was, at least for a while most likely to be more comfortable in the presence of aboriginal people than with her own.

But Dave had news for Tammy. "We've tracked down some relatives of yours, Tammy," he said with a smile.

Tammy drew in a short, sharp breath and her hand flew to her mouth as a tiny semi-strangled cry was quickly stifled. She couldn't fully understand what her feelings were at that moment. She just stood and looked at Dave with eyes wide and he was instantly reminded of the frightened fawn he had first glimpsed in the wilderness. Was it only a few weeks ago? It seemed like years, so much had happened since he had left Riverside Station on a joy flight.

(And that reminded him that he really needed to refund the fares they had paid him before leaving the neighbouring station, which in fact was over a hundred kilometres from here. He made a mental note to attend to that ASAP)

"Oh, Dave," Tammy whispered. "What do I do?"

"Well," said Viv, always the one to speak her mind, "You could arrange to meet them. That would be good."

"Viv!" said her sister, impatiently. "For goodness sake let the girl find her land legs before you have her rushing off to meet people she barely remembers."

Tammy sent Marian a grateful glance from across the room and the older woman smiled warmly at her.

"We've got some sorting out to do before we can head down south and cope with all that," said Marian. "I guess the police will want statements or some such from us so they can deal with Joe and his creepy mates. And I suppose they'll want to straighten out some old records that probably have you listed as dead, love." This last to Tammy, who put her hands over her face and sank into a chair as if it was all too much to take in.

"Yes," said Dave. "We must do all that as soon as we can, if that is okay with everyone?"

Each one nodded. They were keen to get this matter put away, so they could get back to the lives they'd all but forgotten were waiting for them, back in a city that seemed, at the moment, to be a million miles away.

The vastness of the country they had so recently traversed, and the many kilometres they had travelled to get here from their point of rescue, had completely overwhelmed them, to the extent where each was hard pressed to even remember what their own homes looked like; let alone the streets and the rather mundane jobs each had left behind.

"Oh my," started Viv. "The kids! Has anyone let them know we are okay?"

"Viv, they don't even know we went missing." said her sister. "As far as they know, we are still out here enjoying our outback farm stay holiday."

"Oh, of course." Said Viv, with a bit of a giggle. "It all seems so long ago, I was thinking that the whole world was out looking for us."

Just at that moment their hostess came back through the room with an armful of fresh linen from the laundry.

"Well," she chipped in, "We had been alerted by Riverside that you were overdue, and that they hadn't been able to raise Dave on the radio. So we'd all been out scouting round for you. We still had a fair bit of ground to cover before bringing in the troops.

We'd pretty much given up though and had decided that a full-scale search was in order. We'd been trying to gather a few more recruits for the search. The Police don't have too many people out here, but station hands make pretty good scouts," she added, obviously proud of the lads who worked on Tumberrumba.

"Mind you, some news may have reached down south. We were careful not to release names until we were sure what had happened, though we know what reporters are like – never let the facts get in the way of a good story, and if you need some you don't have, well make some up.

"But, here you all are, safe and well, and a bonus, to boot." She smiled at Tammy, from the doorway to the hall, as she headed off to the bedrooms. "No doubt the press will be on to that pretty soon." Her voice came floating back to them, as she bustled about her tasks.

"Yes indeed." Gary added, to no one in particular, as he sauntered in from the verandah. He had been out to have a smoke for the first time in longer than he could recall.

"I'd sort of hoped you'd give those away, after being without for such a long time," commented his wife.

"Well, maybe I will," he said. "I thought at first it was the thing I wanted most, but they don't actually taste as good as I thought they would.

"Of course they might be a bit stale, sitting around in my luggage all this time. But maybe, just maybe, this is a good time to make a whole new start anyway. In fact," he said expansively, "I'm also going to make a new start with work.

"This whole episode has shown me that life is too short to waste it doing something you hate. So when we get back, I'm going to tell my boss to shove his job and we are going into that little business you've always wanted, Marian. I should get a fairly decent payout from that wretched job I've poured my heart and soul into for far too many years."

Marian gave a little squeal of delight and dashed across the room to give him a great big hug.

Then, turning to her sister, she said, "Well, that's us all sorted out, what about you and Bob, Viv? Will you guys come in and join us?"

Then turning to her husband, "It's what we wanted, isn't it Gary?"

"You bet, come on Bob, you know we've talked about it for years."

"Yeah, I know," Bob, said slowly. "Well, maybe this would be a good time. What do you reckon Hon?"

"You know what I think," Viv answered. "Marian and I have dreamed of this for years. Let's make the break and do it now, darlin'. Like Gary said, life's way too short to waste, isn't it?"

So, while Dave and Tammy watched with bewildered smiles on their faces, the four of them went off to plan their great new adventure.

Chapter 12

NEW BEGINNINGS AND A PROPOSAL

"Well, Tammy," said Dave, "That leaves us. If I go back to flying, it'll have to be in someone else's plane, because mine... well... I can't seem to remember where I parked it..." He grinned at his own rather corny joke. "And I'm not even sure if that's what I want." he continued.

"Anything you do will be okay with me, Dave." said Tammy, quietly. "I have no idea where I go from here, but I surely hope that wherever it is, it will be the same place you go."

"Oh, yes, indeed," said Dave. "I won't be going anywhere much without you. I do not intend letting you get too far away, sweet girl. And that's another reason why I'm not all that keen on going back to flying.

"It would mean taking me away from you for too long at a time. And I simply do not want that. This flyboy thing is okay for a bachelor, but with your kind permission, I don't intend to be a bachelor for very much longer."

"Excuse me, Sir," said Tammy, half shyly and half teasing. "Was that meant to be a proposal?"

"It most certainly was," answered Dave. Then realizing what he'd just done, he stopped short and said softly, "I'm sorry, darling Tammy, how discourteous of me!"

Rushing to her side, he knelt down on the floor before her chair, gently took her hand, and with old-world charm, requested her hand in marriage.

With a little squeal, she threw herself off the chair into his arms, sending them both in a laughing, tangled heap onto the polished floorboards.

The others ran back into the room to see what all the racket was about, and as they watched the pair of them rolling about laughing in glee, their hostess, who had come back into the room just in time to hear it all, explained that Dave had just proposed to Tammy, "And I think she said, 'Yes!'" she added with a huge smile on her face.

When some sort of order was finally restored and the two of them were back in their chairs, Dave shared his joyful news with his passengers; although now, much more than that – recently become best friends.

"I realize that Tammy and I have only known each other for a short time, but I feel that I have known her all my life, and we've been through such a lot together. I know we will be right for each other.

"Oh, and by the way, Tammy," he added, "I'll be speaking to you later about God. I'm as sure as I can be that He is going to be right for me too. Will you show me how I go about seeing to that?"

"Indeed, I will!" said Tammy with joy shining in her eyes. "It will be my joy and my privilege."

Tammy knew that she loved Dave very much, in fact had known that she loved him even before they'd had left her wilderness home. It had taken a while for her to understand the strange feelings, but they had become clearer with each passing day. She knew also that he loved her.

She realized that she had accepted his proposal of marriage almost instinctively, as if every moment since they'd met had been leading up to that moment. Yet, deep down she'd known – could almost hear her mother saying, 'But he's not a Christian, dear.'

Now, in the twinkling of an eye, that nagging little worry she'd tried to ignore was suddenly, joyously swept aside – the one piece of the puzzle that had been missing from her perfect picture had suddenly dropped into place. Joy and relief flooded her heart and, as she whispered a prayer of thanks, she leaped up from her chair again, ran across to him and hugged him.

As the others had listened to this little exchange, and witnessed Tammy's obvious joy, they'd looked at each other and each one sort of smiled and nodded. Gary, acting as spokesman for the family, said softly,

"Umm, Tammy, we'd sort of like to do that too, if that's okay. We've seen how He has carried us through this little lot and brought us to safe haven, so to speak. So I guess we're going to have, um, church. Yeah?"

Their hostess who in the manner of most outback folk, had a deep faith in God, quickly went to the sideboard and took down a much-used and well-loved Bible.

"Come and join me at the table," she said. "Let's look at the Word of God together."

So each one went to the table and found a seat. Quietly, they sat around the table, as the lady of the house, read to them from John's Gospel.

The well-known but long-forgotten verse of John 3:16 had never sounded sweeter to these weary travelers and as Tammy quietly told them all she'd learned of God's love and care for her, one by one, each of them made their confession to God and asked Jesus to come into their lives, to forgive them and renew them. Very soon, each one was aware of a new, warm glow inside.

Tammy was so happy she wanted to jump for joy. Tears flowed freely as five newborn children danced around the room, celebrating.

As, one by one, they fell laughing into their chairs again, they spent some time reading from the Bible and singing any old hymn that they could remember from their childhood days in Sunday school.

By this time the man of the house had returned from his chores and was greeted by the happiest bunch of guests he'd had stay in his home for many a long year.

And so they passed the rest of the day in happy conversation as they planned their futures; futures that would have a completely different direction to the lives they had left behind.

The next morning dawned bright and clear and the guests of the house were up early and full of plans. Telephone calls were made and adventures related to families back home. Some of the calls got a bit complicated; as it appeared that some word of their sudden disappearance had filtered back to the news media in the cities.

The children, some teenagers in the care of aunts and uncles, some old enough to be off making their own way, were either just relieved that the 'olds' were okay, or completely stunned to discover that the lost folk had actually been their parents.

There was much explaining and reassuring, with promises to tell all when they got home. Then there was the organizing and sorting of their few possessions.

Riverside Station had been notified of course, the moment news of their rescue had been radioed back to Tumberrumba from Roger's plane. So all that was required was to arrange transport to return them to home base. Bob's vehicle, in which all four had travelled together, would still be waiting for them where they'd left it. And with precious few possessions left after their adventures, they would only need to pack the bags still sitting in their rooms, waiting for their return.

Then, would begin the long journey home to Sydney.

For Dave, all he'd carried with him was the bag he had taken on board the plane with some lunch and a drink, although he had got into the habit of keeping a change of clothes and some shaving gear in the plane, 'just in case'. And in this case he mused, it had been just as well.

Home for him had once been Brisbane, and that seemed a long time ago. He'd been a gypsy for too many years, most recently camping in the hangar of the home-stay station property where he had kept his little plane, operated his 'joy-flights', and dossed down on a cot in the corner.

He had helped out around the property wherever needed, if no guests required his services. And although he had some primitive cooking gear, most days he ate his meals with the station hands and roustabouts.

For a guy with nowhere to go and no one to answer to, it had seemed like a good life, if you ignored the many empty hours and the hole in your heart where a family had once held pride of place. That, he recalled, was before his wanderlust had sent a wife expecting his child, back home to civilization and some creature comforts.

Divorce had followed all too soon, when she had found someone with his feet on the ground and a steady job. He supposed, one day, he'd find her again and maybe meet his child – if she agreed to that.

But now, he had a warm glow in that empty heart that felt very different to the hasty relationships of his youth – back in the days when he hadn't asked for much from a woman, because he didn't have much to give. Oh, there were days when he'd wondered if he and Donna could have made a go of it, if he'd tried. When he thought about it, he reckoned that she had tried, and maybe if he had too...

They'd only got married because she was pregnant and she'd hoped, maybe, that he'd leave his wandering life and take her back home. She'd met him when he had come back to Brisbane for some 'city living', before heading off on the next crazy venture.

She had flown out west with him, captivated at first by his romantic, devil-may-care attitude to life. She had hoped for some adventure in her dull and predictable life, but had soon become heartily sick of the heat and the dust and the flies. Not to mention a husband who was always off somewhere, flying in that silly little plane of his, leaving her to amuse herself – and in a place where everyone seemed to have a purpose in life except for her.

Her constant nagging and his seeming disregard for her or her problems had soon taken the gloss off a marriage destined to failure.

And so, she had packed her meagre possessions and headed back home to her friends and family. Her parting words had left him in no doubt that he needn't bother looking her up, because she never wanted to see him again. And if he thought he'd ever see his kid, "Forget it!"

The divorce papers had followed, and with just the smallest pang of regret, he had signed them and sent them back to the solicitors, thus closing a difficult period of his life and, it had seemed, also closing the door of his heart. That was until Tammy appeared in the midst of the worst crisis he could have imagined, and turned his world completely upside down in the space of a second.

So with the past behind him, Dave figured he'd go back to Riverside, the station that had been his home, if you could call it that, for the last half a dozen years or so, say his goodbyes and pack anything he thought might be worth saving. Ahead of him now, thanks to Tammy, was a life that offered everything he'd long given up hope would ever be possible again.

He knew he'd miss the friends he'd made there, but no power on earth could have made him choose them over the future he hoped that he and Tammy would forge together.

Riverside, Dave knew, looked pretty much like Tumberrumba, saltbush, spinifex, some tough native grasses and a few gums, with vistas that went on forever – endless, empty kilometres of red dirt, rocky outcrops and not much else. The homestead, almost a carbon copy of the one in which they were currently guests, overlooked the river that a once optimistic pioneer had hoped would provide life-giving water for both humans and stock alike.

But, as it is with most just like it out here, it was more often an empty watercourse – home to creatures that slithered, crept and crawled, and had only actually flowed with water two or three times in the last two decades or more, as far as anyone could remember.

For a while after a good flow, water could be found underneath the river bed, but never in quantities worth the effort of digging for.

If it had not been for the discovery of Artesian water, beneath the farthest, south-eastern reaches of the property, Riverside would have died, right along with the dreams and hopes of its original owner.

However, Dave had to admit, that despite the harshness of the land, and his own lonely existence, there was a certain grandeur about the landscape, and if he was truly honest with himself, he had to admit also, that in truth, he had learned to love the place, in all its moods.

Snapping himself out of his mood of reflection, he became aware that people were bustling about and he was being asked if he was going with Roger in the plane, or driving over to the neighbouring property with Ray.

Quite content to fit in with the others, he suggested that maybe, as before, the ladies should go with Roger, and the guys drive over in the vehicle.

Tammy, once again, shyly refused a seat on the plane and opted to go with Dave. So goodbyes were said and promises to keep in touch were made. Their hostess smiled and nodded, knowing full well that once they touched home soil, Tumberrumba Station would fast become a fading memory.

But that was fine, she was just so happy to see them all working out their lives, bursting with enthusiasm for all the plans they'd made.

Soon they would be reunited with their families and that was the most important thing, except, of course, their newfound love for the Lord.

She offered up a silent prayer for their safety and for a long and joyful life walking alongside the One who had kept her and her family through all the changes of their lives; and who, she was equally sure, would do the same for her recent guests.

Finally, they were all bundled into the wagon, and they headed out to the airstrip. Marian and Viv climbed aboard with Roger and waved goodbye to the men and to Tammy, as the plane sped off down the strip and took off in the direction of Riverside. Tammy and Dave, Bob and Gary climbed back into the big 4x4, able now to spread themselves out a bit in the vehicle.

Bob waved his hand in an expansive gesture and with a ridiculously pompous air, said to Ray, "Forward Ho! My good man!"

There was much laughter and ribbing, as the happy bunch set off for the journey that would take at least two or three hours, even if they were not delayed for some reason.

One never knew what sand drifts or other unexpected things they could find out there. Sometimes you might find an animal in trouble and there was no way Ray could be expected to continue on until the problem, whatever it might be was taken care of.

Nothing could dampen the spirits of these intrepid travellers, however, and they were not at all worried about the time it would take, or about anything that they might come across along the way.

Chapter 13

BACK TO WHERE IT BEGAN

As it turned out, there were no more than a few short delays. Ray had to take a couple of detours as his favourite track had disappeared under sand drifts in a few places. But the big Toyota had handled worse and it was simply a matter of finding the best way through or around.

His passengers had no idea where one station property ended and the other began. But Ray knew every washout and every marker like the back of his hand.

By the time they arrived at Riverside, the ladies had been inside, had a joyous reunion with the hosts who had all but given up hope of seeing them again, and enjoyed a refreshing cuppa while they waited for Tammy and the fellows to turn up.

These four, well five if poor old Ray got a mention, arrived a little less rested than the girls and Roger. Even though the old bus was air-conditioned, there was no vehicle manufactured that could keep out Northern Territory bull dust!

So, after a bit of a dust off and a wash, everybody met on the deep shady verandah of the homestead for some much appreciated refreshments and a full and complete re-telling of all that had happened to them. Then after a cool drink and a bit of spell, Roger and Ray finally said their goodbyes.

Offering their thanks to their hosts for the refreshments, they excused themselves and wished their respective passengers the very best for the future.

Then they both piled into the Toyota, as Ray was to take Roger out to his plane before turning his vehicle for home, where, after attending to some chores along the way, some tucker and the bunkhouse waited.

While far from luxurious, this place which each of them called home was quite comfortable by outback standards. Together with the owners' extended family and their workmates, these men helped to run one of the largest properties in a part of the country where a station is measured in hundreds of kilometres, not acres or hectares, and where it might take weeks to ride around the boundaries on horseback.

Tammy watched them go a little wistfully, for she realized that she had taken one step closer to that life the others talked incessantly about, and about which she knew absolutely nothing.

Dave looked over to her as he half listened to the conversation going on around him. He promised to tell his friends everything as soon as he could catch a breath, then excused himself and went over to stand by Tammy's side.

They stood there, together, leaning on the verandah rail and watched as the vehicle got smaller and smaller, finally disappearing in the cloud of dust that accompanied anything that moved out here.

"Are you okay, my love?" he asked, as he put a gently arm about her slim shoulders.

"Yes," she answered, softly. "It's just... Oh, I'm alright." she said. "It's just that, well, it seems that one step at a time, I'm getting further away from that which I know and closer to that which I..." Here she stopped for a moment, as she searched for the right words to describe her feelings.

"It's okay, you know." said Dave. "To feel a little strange about it all, I mean. After all, think for a moment what has happened in the last few weeks.

"It seems as if one day, there you were, out in your lonely bush home, and then whammo! Here you are, surrounded by mobs of weird people and stuck with a broken down old bush pilot for the rest of your life. Fair dinkum, it's enough to scare anyone half to death."

Laughing now, Tammy hugged Dave and said, "Thank you."

"For what?" Dave asked. "For rescuing you or for scaring you to death?"

"Oh, for coming out of the sky and for loving me." she said simply. "I do know that everything will be okay. Just promise me that you will be with me through all that I know is coming; things that I'm not sure I'm ready for."

Dave pulled her gently around to face him and, enveloping her in an embrace, he kissed her.

"Just try and prize me away from your side, my love. Please believe me when I say that I will support you all the way. The worst of it will be the press, but once that is over and you are with your family, you'll see that it will be okay."

"Sometimes I wonder if they will know me, or want me." Tammy whispered.

"What? Not want you? For goodness sake, girl, one look at you and they couldn't help but love you!" said Dave. "You are so beautiful, they won't be able to help themselves."

Tammy giggled softly from within Dave's bear hug embrace, and somewhat reassured for the present, she relaxed and allowed his gentle arms to fill her with a real sense of peace and security.

She knew in her heart that Dave was true. She knew that what she felt for him was true. And she knew that God was true. He had always cared for her and was always with her. And, despite her foolish fears, she knew that she had not somehow left God behind in the wilds of central Australia.

So, as they parted briefly, and stood arm in arm watching a tiny speck in the sky waggle it's wings, they waved a final goodbye to Roger as he headed for home.

Then they turned to their hosts and, accepting a freshly filled glass each from the lady of the house, they sat down with the group to continue their story.

"Hey! Guys!" said Dave. "We have to ring the police and make a time to go in and give them a statement about Joe and his friends."

"Yeah!" Was Bob's only comment, as he sipped his cool drink and swirled his glass slightly while he watched the ice cubes clinking softly.

He licked his lips and savoured the moment, remembering how images just like this had tormented him out in the desert.

He recalled how at times he'd wondered if he'd even survive, let alone be sitting here, sipping a drink, sitting in a comfy chair while a gentle breeze stirred the curtains as it wafted through the airy room behind them.

"Sorry, mate," he said, as suddenly he realized that Dave had actually spoken to him. "Yeah, are you gonna do that? Make it any time you like, we'll just tag along. Tammy is the real hero here, and Barda's lot."

Bob stopped suddenly, as he realized he'd spoken out of turn. He looked at Tammy and mouthed the words, "I'm sorry."

However, their hosts were listening to Viv regaling them with the horrors of the desert and apparently did not hear Bob's unguarded comment.

"Whew!" he said softly. "Okay, Dave, our brave and fearless skipper. Lead on, your valiant crew will be behind you all the way. Way behind!" he added with a cackle as he enjoyed his own joke.

"Righto, then." said Dave with a wry grin, and asking his hosts, and occasional employers, if he may use the phone, he went out to offer the services of himself and his friends.

Each of them wanted to play their part in making sure that Joe, Ed and Lenny received the punishment they deserved for their crimes.

He was gone for several minutes and when he returned he informed them that someone was actually patrolling this area, and had been contacted by radio. Two officers would be calling on them tomorrow and would take their statements.

Dave had been told that if they left details of their various addresses with the officers, then they would be contacted if it was thought they could clear up any points later. Or if it was considered necessary for them to give evidence at the trial.

None of them ever wanted to see those three again, but realized that if it meant the difference between them getting off the charges against them, or going to jail, then they knew they'd do whatever it took to see that justice was done, at least for the family of the murdered woman.

Tammy knew too that she would make herself do whatever it took to see

Joe, Ed and Lenny locked up for a very long time.

A meal of gigantic proportions was put in front of the group later that evening, and then, once more Tammy put herself into the hands of a kindly hostess, who took her to a comfortable room, not unlike the one she'd slept in the night before. As she settled into the big bed, luxuriating in the feel of the cool sheets, she lay there for a while thinking over the last couple of days. Riverside was, as Dave had said, very much like Tumberrumba, but, there was something different. What was it, she asked herself. Then, as she tried to remember some of the things she'd seen as they approached the homestead, she had a sudden sense of déjà vu. Had she been here before? Was this the station property from which her family had begun their adventure? As sleep overtook her, she determined to ask her hostess in the morning.

Morning dawned bright and clear and this time, Tammy was up in time to enjoy it. She had risen early, as was her habit and had been for a walk.

With all the food that had been offered to her and all the unaccustomed conversation, she had felt the need for some solitude and the peaceful balm of an early bush morning.

Taking the opportunity to spend some time in prayer, she had thanked God for all His blessings and with her usual quiet faith, had placed the rest of her life into His capable hands. She did not forget to thank Him for bringing Dave into her life or for delivering her and her new friends from the very real dangers presented by Joe and his partners in crime.

By the time she had returned to the homestead, everybody was up and about and another huge breakfast waited for her in the big dining room. Some had carried plates heaped with food out onto a wide, shaded verandah, and so Tammy served herself a small meal and joined them.

When their hostess came out to check if they were all okay, Tammy took the opportunity to ask, if indeed this was the station property that her father had worked at.

Unfortunately, her hostess could not answer her question, as she and her husband had not been there that long, but she said she would ask one of the hands and if anyone could remember, she'd let her know. Tammy thanked her very kindly, and tucked into her breakfast.

The meal had only just been cleared away, when a vehicle drew up outside the house in a cloud of dust.

A couple of police officers got out and after being welcomed as old friends of the station family and gratefully accepting a cool drink, they settled on the verandah with the castaways and, pens at the ready, began to take notes as one by one each person told their story as they remembered it.

Slowly, a pattern began to form and soon enough the senior of the two officers suggested that they had all they needed.

The three crooks had left a trail that a blind man could follow, according to the younger of the two police, and neither of them anticipated any difficulty in gaining convictions that would see each of the miscreants out of circulation for what they hoped would be a very long time.

Then they turned their thoughts to Tammy.

"So what do we do with you, young lady?" asked the Sergeant. "We'll need some particulars, so that the record can be set straight. Your parents are dead, I believe?"

"Yes, a number of years ago," replied Tammy. Then, recalling all the details she could and then checking her mother's little book for names, addresses and dates of birth, she watched as the officer jotted it all down in his notebook.

"Well, that should do it, I reckon," he commented. "I'll see to it that the good people at Births, Deaths and Marriages get all this, so they can list you among the living. Can't have a bride-to-be listed as dead, now can we?" he joked.

Tammy smiled. She still wasn't used to the way men joked about things. And she especially wasn't used to the appreciative way they looked at her.

To be fair, a man would have had to be dead, not to notice her beauty. And the inner peace that glowed from deep inside her, gave her a serenity and added beauty that most women could only hope to gain from a jar on the shelf.

Eventually, satisfied that they had done all they could for the time being, the officers got to their feet and prepared for the journey back to base.

It would be long past midday before they saw their lunch, possibly at a neighbouring homestead, and that would be at least half a day's travel from Riverside.

Goodbyes were said and after a brief wave, they climbed into their car. Then, followed by the ever-present, all pervading cloud of dust, soon disappeared into the shimmering distance.

Early though it was, the heat was already beginning to build so it seemed good to the travellers to retreat indoors, to the comparative cool of the interior of the house.

At which time, even before anyone could turn their attention to the rest of the day, another car arrived at the door. On board were some reporters and a photographer.

Two days ago they had heard the news of the 'lost child' being found by a group of stranded adventurers and, not known for letting a good story get away, had immediately commandeered a four wheel drive vehicle and headed out to see for themselves.

They were hot, tired and thirsty, for their trip had taken them first to Tumberrumba, their informant having been unaware that the group had moved on to Riverside.

This was the moment that Tammy had dreaded and she had fervently hoped that it would not happen until she had arrived back east and found her 'land legs', so to speak. However, here they were and not to be deterred. Bush hospitality prevented her hosts from packing them off to whence they had come, without at least providing their basic needs, so once again, all sat down on the verandah and the story was told.

With Dave by her side, suddenly it didn't seem as bad as she'd feared, and apart from a tear or two as she spoke, yet again of her beloved parents, she quietly told these reporters about her life in the wilds of central Australia – although she was really amazed that her simple existence could evoke such interest.

She was oblivious to the fact that she was an extremely beautiful girl, and that her survival in itself, was some sort of miracle - and a story with great public appeal.

Simply, and without any sense of drama, on her part at least, she told the reporters about her father's dreams and aspirations, how he had guided and prepared her for her life, and how she had managed to survive in such a harsh and unforgiving environment for so many years.

The story of yet another plane crash and how that had resulted in meeting her new friends, not to mention their adventures with three very unsavoury characters, was met with great amazement and the two of them scribbled furiously to get it all down - reluctant to miss a single word.

In their haste to get out to the station before anyone else got wind of the story, they had rushed off without tape-recorder or laptop computer, so it all had to be written down in long forgotten shorthand. One of them remarked that he hoped he could transcribe it all when he got back to the office.

Soon, Tammy felt that she had told them everything that she could think of and asked to be excused. The rest of the group added a thought or two and then they too suggested that there was nothing to be added to the story.

All had very carefully left Barda and his people out of their stories. Finally, after another photograph or two, these guests too were on their way, with a final toot of the horn and a cloud of dust.

As the vehicle, swallowed up in its red dust cloud, vanished from their sight, Dave remarked that as they would all be heading back to 'civilization' the following day, they should all check if there was anything they needed to do. If so, then perhaps they had better go and see to it. An early start was advisable, the days heated up quite soon enough. Each agreed and so the rest of the day was spent in sorting through meager possessions, washing clothes and effecting running repairs where necessary, and writing their memories down for the folk back home.

Home! The word had a strange feel to it and each wondered what it would be like to finally set foot back in the houses they'd left behind - was it only three or so months ago? It felt like a lifetime.

Lunch had been a hurried affair, squeezed in between the myriad tasks that had presented themselves. Then, a short nap in the heat of the afternoon, before some took a gentle stroll around the shady garden as an evening breeze brought a breath of fresh air and a renewing of energy.

An early night seemed like a good idea, so, after a light evening meal and a few last minute preparations, all were soon in their beds and sound asleep.

The next day dawned with the customary crisp coolness, but by the time the travellers were ready to leave, the heat had begun to build. The air conditioner in the vehicle would get a good workout as they traversed the many miles back to Queensland.

There would be several days of driving ahead of them, and they knew that family members would be waiting anxiously to receive them back into the fold.

Gary, Bob and the sisters had driven out to their outback farm-stay holiday – the journey an integral part of the adventure, so the trip home would be made in tandem with Dave's somewhat older workhorse of a vehicle.

Tammy had packed a small suitcase, given to her by her hostess.

Her luggage consisted of the few mementos she had brought from her home in the bush – those she had managed to hold onto after the willy-willy, and a couple of sets of clothing bequeathed to her by her kind hostesses, from both Tumberrumba and Riverside.

Expressing her gratitude to these generous ladies had been difficult and Tammy felt that her fumbling words had been inadequate. But the truth of it was that both ladies had been very touched by her simple thanks, and had they been asked, both would have remarked that Tammy's thanks had been most eloquent.

Clothes, for their own sake had no real appeal for Tammy although she was most grateful for those she had been given. But it was the treasures from her bush-land home that she packed securely away – the aging photos and the addresses of the people she had been told were her family, and the few mementos of her parents.

As she had placed them carefully among her few possessions, she had felt a pang of apprehension as she wondered again how these people, strangers to her, would receive her.

Dave too had packed meagre possessions into a battered old rucksack. He was also heading back to a life long forgotten.

While he constantly maintained a confident demeanor for Tammy's sake, he couldn't help but feel some uncertainty as he wondered what lay ahead.

The only thing he knew for certain was that whatever the future held, Tammy and his newfound faith in God, would be the biggest part of it.

As Tammy packed the last few things into her bag, the lady of the house knocked softly at her door.

"I went in search of old Barney. He's been here forever so the men say. I asked him whether he remembered your family and he said that he did. Reckoned they all spent weeks searching for you and months more hoping that they'd find some trace of you out there when they went mustering. But, no, obviously they never did.

He said to tell you that he's really sorry about your folks. Said he really liked your dad – 'a real bushman, that one', he said."

Tammy thanked her warmly for finding out for her, and asked if she could show her where they had lived. Glad to oblige, she took Tammy out the back door of the homestead and showed her a small cottage some hundred or so metres behind the main house.

"Barney said that's where you all lived," she said. "He told me that your mum had started a vegetable garden growing out the back there, and she kept that house neat as a new pin, he reckoned."

"May I go over and have a look?" Tammy asked.

"Of course, dear," her hostess replied. "Take all the time you need. It hasn't been lived in all the time we've been here. We just use it for storage. So be careful, dear," she added. "I would say that most of your parents' belongings would have been disposed of long ago, but if you find anything, please feel free to take it with you."

Thanking her warmly, Tammy went to find Dave and the others, and told them what she'd discovered. Dave was fascinated to discover that they had both started from the same property, and had in fact lived at the same place, albeit some years apart.

So, before heading off on their homeward journey, Tammy made another journey. One back in time – to a time barely remembered. As she wandered around the small cottage, she tried in vain to see her family living here. But it didn't happen. She peaked into each small room, but could evoke no memories. The cottage was in reasonable condition, but the paintwork was tired and grubby and dust lay everywhere.

Then as she looked out the back door she saw a swing hanging by one rotted rope, from the branch of a large tree in the yard.

Suddenly, she saw herself swinging there, yelling for her father to push her higher and higher.

Glad that at last she had some memory of this home, she was then able to turn back to the interior of the house and see it with new eyes. Then she saw a few boxes in a corner of the living room. When she went over to it and opened it, she realized that the contents may possibly have been things that had belonged to her parents.

Jane, their kind hostess, had followed them down to the cottage and as she stood watching Tammy, she told her that she could take those things if she wanted, as they belonged to her anyway. So Tammy sifted quickly through the things, but found nothing to prompt her memory. So assuming these were not her parents' things at all, with a little sigh she brushed away a tear and was about to tell Jane that she could throw them away, when she spotted another box. This one, tucked in a dark corner, contained books and toys. It seemed that the station hands who had been charged with disposing of Dan's and Betty's personal effects, had not been able to throw away a child's belongings.

These tough men of the outback simply couldn't bring themselves to do it, so sticking the box in a corner they went and told their boss that they had done as requested, and took themselves off to finish their other chores. No doubt trying to block the image of teddy bears and dolls from their memory.

As soon as Tammy saw the books she immediately recognized the covers. These were the ones that her mother had read to her when she was tiny, and held the stories that she had tried to remember for her daughter out in their desert home. Clutching them to her, with tears blurring her eyes, she carried them back to the main house. Slowly she sorted through them, selected a few remembered items and packed them away in her bag with the other mementoes.

She thanked her hosts once again for everything, as at last they took their leave of Riverside Station. This was a place that now held some ties for Tammy as well as for Dave and somehow this connection made their newfound love for each other even more special.

Ahead lay a life that would be vastly different to anything she could remember, and as the car pulled away from the house where her hosts stood waving goodbye, she couldn't help but wonder what the future would hold.

For Tammy, arrival back east would mean meeting new people, adjusting to a life that was completely foreign and trying through it all to keep trusting in God.

For Dave, arrival would mean trying to adjust to a new life also; one he could share with Tammy. But it also meant finding his daughter. He and Tammy had talked about that, and she had insisted, that whatever else they did, that was to be a priority. So the butterflies in his stomach were becoming more active, the closer he came to Brisbane.

How different it all looked. It had been not much more than a big country town when he had left it so many years ago. The city he returned to was big and brash and bustling. And both he and Tammy felt certain that when all the formalities of their return were over, they would be trying to find an oasis of peace, somewhere far from the maddening crowd.

During an overnight stop, somewhere along the way, discussions had been held as to where they should go first. Each of them would need to go in quite different directions.

Over coffee and a meal in a cabin at a roadside Caravan Park, they had talked again of the plans each had for the future.

Chapter 14
FINDING FAMILY

Quiet descended on the group as they realized that in the next couple of days it would be goodbye, for now at least. As the coffee cups and empty plates were pushed to one side, notebooks were taken from handbags that had finally been retrieved from luggage, and Dave's mobile number was jotted down. Someone gave him a piece of paper with contact numbers and addresses on it and he and Tammy promised to let everybody know when they'd found somewhere to settle. Then, after clearing away the clutter of their light meal, they had all headed for bed, ready for another early start.

Another day on the road, and suddenly it had been time to part company. They stood by the cars early that morning, and just looked at each other for a moment.

Then, there were hugs all round and a few tears. This group of people had been through such a lot together.

Four people, who had gone up north for a bush holiday, realized that here, standing beside them was a man who, at first had been just a pilot taking four people on a joy flight – a man who had now become closer than a brother – and a slip of a girl, to whom each of the four holiday makers truly believed they owed their lives. These two were heading off to a new life together. Viv and Marian knew how busy life could get and they wondered, a little tearfully, if indeed they'd ever see them again. It suddenly seemed so final after the weeks of sharing every part of their lives together. The less emotional menfolk felt sure that, somehow, they'd manage to keep in touch.

Finally, after several rounds of hugs, and promises to keep in touch, Bob, Gary and the girls, got back into Bob's car and with much tooting of the horn and vigorous waving out the windows, drove away.

They would spend a day or so looking around Brisbane, before turning their vehicle south, back to Sydney, where family and a new business venture waited.

Tammy and Dave stood side by side in the sun, holding hands for a few moments as they watched the vehicle slide out of view. Then they turned to each other and just held on tight for a moment, before getting back into the dusty old 4x4. This vehicle had seen many a rugged mile and traversed some of the most difficult country imaginable. Slightly battered in its appearance, it still offered a reasonably comfortable ride, despite the worn upholstery – and the air-conditioning worked!

"Well, where to, my love?"

"Lead on, darling. I don't really care. Although I suppose I'd better try and track down some of my family."

So, out came the little book of addresses from a secret place, and Dave's battered street directory. It had lived under the seat for many a year, sliding around as the vehicle had travelled its many dusty kilometers.

And thus began an interesting attempt to find suburbs that had changed, along roads that hadn't even been there last time he'd looked, until, finally Dave admitted defeat and pulled into a service station to buy a new directory.

Tammy laughed till tears poured down her cheeks at Dave's antics, as he ceremoniously committed the tattered old book to its final resting place – in the service station's rubbish bin!

With a book that actually showed the streets they needed to travel, they eventually found the first suburb on Tammy's list, and the right street. Unfortunately, the house didn't reveal anybody they were looking for, the current occupants being renters who had absolutely no idea where they should start looking.

No, the owners were not the people that Tammy and Dave were looking for. The young woman, a harassed mother of three small children, all of which were demanding her attention, told them between ear-shattering screams from the one on her hip and much skirt-pulling from the one at her side, that her landlords had bought the house only recently; approximately six months before she and her family had moved in.

She knew this, she told them, because the owner constantly talked about, and promised her that his renovation plans were on the drawing board. He kept telling her, so she said, that 'Rome was not built in a day'. She commented that she sincerely hoped he'd fix some plumbing problems, really soon, before she went completely mad trying to cope with a mountain of laundry each day.

Dave and Tammy bade a sympathetic farewell offering hopes that the problems would all soon be fixed. Then they took their departure, beating rather hasty retreat to their vehicle, hoping they were not too obvious about their relief to be away from there. Glad, Tammy commented, to have escaped with their ear-drums reasonably intact.

Not to be outdone by the failure of their first attempt, they headed for the next suburb on the list. And in a leafy street, in a quiet part of town, they struck pay dirt!

As soon as the door opened, Tammy gasped. For standing right in front of her was her mother! Well, at least a younger, carbon copy of her.

The young woman who had come to the door, looked at Tammy for a moment, and then yelled for her mother!

"Mum, come quick!" she yelled.

Footsteps sounded at the back of the house, and then a tall, blonde woman stood beside her daughter and gazed in amazement at the slip of a girl standing on her doorstep.

"Betty's girl," she whispered.

"Yes," stammered Tammy.

"Betty's and Dan's little Tammy," she said again, as tears began to fill her eyes. "O, my child," she said, reaching out her hand as if she feared Tammy might disappear if she made any sudden moves. "We were so sure you were dead. My goodness, you look so like your mother. How did you survive? Where on earth have you been?"

Suddenly, she pulled up short. "O, my dear, I'm so sorry, here I am, babbling away like a fool. Come in, come in."

Then as if suddenly remembering her manners, she smiled at Dave and put out her hand.

"How do you do?' she asked politely. "I'm Tammy's aunt Susan. Her mum, Betty, is my sister. Oh dear!" she cried, and suddenly crumpled into a nearby chair. "She's dead, isn't she?"

"Yes," answered Tammy softly, "Many years ago, I'm afraid. Both Mum and Dad died out in the bush."

Drying her tears and attempting to compose herself, their hostess stood up and ushered her guests into the lounge room.

It was a comfortable room, light and airy, after the fashion of the 'Queenslander', a style of home popular in Brisbane and other Queensland towns and cities for more than a century.

High set, on timber – or more recently, concrete or steel stumps, these homes had been designed to catch every available breeze, in a climate totally foreign to migrants from the cooler countries of Europe. European style homes had soon proved inadequate for living comfort in a climate so vastly different to that of their homelands. Susan's home was large and well maintained. Caring for it had been a labour of love for her and her husband, Donald.

A ceiling fan offered a little more breeze than the day provided, and as they sat in cane lounge chairs and sipped the cool drinks that Becky had brought, memories came flooding back to Tammy.

"You've always lived here, haven't you?" she asked her aunt.

"Yes," answered Susan. "Donald and I bought this place when we got married. We've renovated it gradually over the years – it was always a dream, to own one of these old homes and do it up. We own it now, and have been able to afford to do a little more to it."

"I remember coming here sometimes," said Tammy. "Becky was a baby when we went out to stay at the station with Dad for a while."

"That's right, love," said her aunt. "You went off to stay where your dad was based for some contract he had out there. "Your mother felt that it was best for the family to be together. That's when your dad got the idea of the 'round Australia' trip. We... never heard anything about you after that.

"I remember the big search, of course." she continued, as she fought back the tears that had suddenly welled up in her eyes. "That went on for weeks. But eventually, they decided that you must all be dead, and gradually they called off the search.

"But, you weren't dead, were you?" she asked wistfully.

"No, but we knew that we wouldn't be found. A huge storm had hit us, just a few days out, and it blew us around like a leaf. We didn't have a hope of knowing where it was taking us, or where we ended up. Dad made a home for us in a huge cavern that he found, and we lived there.

"Mum died when I was fifteen. She seemed to die slowly, as if the life just went out of her a bit at a time. She tried so hard and was so brave, but eventually, it just seemed as if her body couldn't keep going. She just went to sleep one afternoon and never woke up."

"Oh, you poor dear," said Aunt Susan, reaching out her hand and stroking Tammy's arm. "You poor dear." she said again.

"Dad got bitten by a snake one day, when I was eighteen. I tried everything I knew, but nothing worked. So I buried him next to Mum and just tried to carry on, as I knew he would have wanted me to. Both of them had taught me so much and it seemed wrong somehow to just give up. So I made a life for myself.

"Then, one day, out of the blue, a plane crash-landed right where ours had – so many years before. And there was Dave.

He had four people with him on a joy flight from one of the stations out there, when a storm blew up and tossed them about, just like the one that hit us. It had been so long since I'd seen anyone or spoken to anyone, and I was terrified. But Dave was so kind and gentle and they all needed me so badly, that I took them to my home. We decided together, to try and walk out. So, here we are."

"Goodness, what a story! How on the earth did you manage that? How far did you walk?" asked Becky.

"We don't know. We walked for days. We came across three criminals who tried to kill us and a willy-willy that blew away all our stuff... But, we made it somehow.

"We'd begun to wonder how much longer we could go on, when we saw a car in the distance. We tried to catch their attention, but the vehicle was too far away and travelling too fast. By the time we got to the road all that was left were the tyre tracks, and the dust-cloud. Then as we continued walking a plane flew overhead, from a nearby station. He was heading back home after looking for stray cattle, and found us. He said the fact that we were all running around and waving frantically attracted his attention.

"Anyway, he alerted the people at the homestead and eventually got us all to safety. The crooks are in jail. The police suspect that one of them murdered a lady out on a station property, somewhere in Queensland."

Tammy suddenly yawned, as the heat and all the rushing about suddenly caught up with her. Her aunt looked at the time and realized how late it was and apologized profusely for keeping her talking when she was obviously all done in.

"Where are you staying, dear? Do you have somewhere organized?" she asked as she got up from her chair.

"No, we have been driving around looking up these addresses," said Tammy, indicating her mother's little book.

"Oh dear, that's Betty's address book. She kept everybody in there." Tears sprang into Susan's eyes. The realization that her sister really was dead, suddenly hit her and she fell back into her chair.

Deep sobs wracked her body as years of pent up anxiety suddenly overwhelmed her.

These were indeed, long overdue tears, and a long overdue release from the grief of an unfulfilled sense of loss; the pain of 'not knowing' where a loved one was – if they were alive or dead.

Gradually, the sobs subsided and she managed to compose herself a little.

Apologizing profusely for her sudden show of emotion, she dried her eyes and tried a shaky little smile.

Tammy, who had rushed to her side instantly and placed an arm about her shoulders, reassured her that she had no reason to apologize, that she and Dave understood completely.

"I cannot imagine how hard it must have been for you," she said. "You must rest assured that although both died much too young, they were never in pain and completely at peace in their love for the Lord. Mother knew that she was dying and although she was sad at leaving us, she was at peace. The Lord kept her right up until He came and took her home. Dad knew too, when his time came. I tried to save him, but... Finally, he lapsed into a coma and simply didn't wake again. We had prayed together, and he too was peaceful.

"I was a bit of a mess for a while, but I knew that both of them had given everything to ensure I had the best that could be arranged out there so far from anywhere. So I went to our 'special' place, where we used to pray each day and hold church every week.

"I spent a long time there, talking to God – I don't know how long I was there, but finally, I knew I was ready to carry on. So I sang a couple of praise songs that Mum had taught me, ones we used to sing along to in the car when we went on trips, then I thanked Jesus for looking after me and simply went on with my life.

"Hey! I suddenly remembered being in a car. I'd forgotten that. When the car from the station picked us up, I thought then that I'd never been in a car before. How silly."

"I certainly don't think that was silly," said her aunt. "You were so young when you left us to go out there. How brave you've been, my child."

"Not really, Aunt Susan," said Tammy quietly. "I really didn't have much choice. It was either go find a place, lay down to die too, or get up and get on with it." This with a shy smile and a gentle shrug of her shoulders.

Just then a car drove into the yard and doors slammed as the man of the house came in from work.

"Hello, what's this? Visitors?" said a big, burly fellow as he came into the room. A giant of a man, he filled the doorway. He looked as though he should have been a construction worker or something of that nature, and looked rather incongruous in a business suit.

Tammy looked up as he stood there... And suddenly it seemed as if the years simply melted away. This giant, this gentle giant of a man was suddenly clear in her memory. She remembered how they had played when she was little, how she'd ride around on his back - him bucking and swaying from side to side, and her squealing with delight and hanging on for dear life.

Her eyes were suddenly full of tears as precious memories of two families, as close as one, came flooding back.

"Donald!" Susan was saying, "This is Betty's girl - our Tammy! She's come back to us after all these years!"

"Wha...!" Donald tried to think of something to say, but he just made funny little noises as he sort of laughed and cried together. Flinging out his great big arms, he finally got out...

"Tammy! Oh Tammy. Come to your Unka' Dona'. Oh, little one, we thought you were dead! Mum and Dad...?" He sort of looked around as he wrapped Tammy in the biggest hug she'd had since she'd been the littlest thing.

"Are they...?" He couldn't finish, for suddenly he knew the answer. He pulled back from the hug and holding Tammy's shoulders gently, he looked into her eyes.

She didn't need to speak, for he knew. Nodding slowly, he enveloped her once more in his big arms, this time more gently, as if she were a little child and might break. He patted her shoulder softly as he held her. Tears filled his own eyes and eventually he had to break away and reach for a hanky to wipe away the tears that came unbidden.

"Oh dear. Such a joy to see you, Tammy. Sue, what's happening about these two?" This to his wife, who had been watching all this with tears streaming down her face too.

"I was just about to make some arrangements when Tammy showed me Betty's little address book, and I sort of went to pieces. I was just getting myself back together when you came home.

"Tammy, you and Dave must stay here with us until you find a place of your own. Um-m, what are the sleeping arrangements with you two kids?"

"Oh heavens, Aunt Susan!" Tammy laughed. "My poor mother would turn in her grave! Dave and I have fallen very much in love and he has asked me to marry him.

But we haven't even talked about – 'that'. I hoped that Dave understood that I could never..." She kind of petered out, embarrassed.

Dave stepped quickly to her side and took up the story, without missing even a heartbeat.

"Aunt Susan, is it okay if I call you that? Tammy and I will be married as soon as we can arrange things. But for now, separate bedrooms are the go. I totally respect Tammy's faith and her beliefs – in fact thanks to her sweet faith and trust in God, she has led me to make my own commitment to God. So it would be a complete betrayal of all I've embraced to... well... you know."

"Well, thank you, Dave. Yes, you may call me Aunt Susan. You must consider this your family now. Tammy, do I get to arrange your wedding? We'd consider it the biggest honour, wouldn't we Donald?"

Donald's face broke into his big expansive smile and with a great big "Yippee!!" he said, "You bet! It will be the best wedding this old town has seen in years!"

"I do not expect you to pay for our wedding, Sir," said Dave. "I intended to organize that myself."

"Well, we can sort out that side of it together, you and I, at our leisure. In the meantime, I'm sure we can leave it to the girls to organize the rest. Becky, darling, are you okay with all this? You know that when you find 'Mr Right', we'll put on the best 'do' for you, don't you?"

Becky was still wiping tears from her eyes. She was completely overwhelmed by the sudden appearance of Tammy and her handsome companion. She had been so little when Auntie Bet-Bet and Uncle Dan had left to go north. But she knew, from many stories told over many years, how close her mother had been to Aunt Betty. Over the years since the disappearance, she had watched her mother's pain, as she had hoped and prayed for the safe return of her beloved sister.

If she'd had any misgivings about her parents' love for this beautiful girl; the cousin she remembered only from photographs, they were swept aside by the joy of the occasion. This young woman looked so much like her mother, the Aunt that even as a toddler, Becky had loved almost as much as her own mother, and who she knew had also loved her.

Though she had been so small, she thought she remembered the goodbyes and the promises to 'see you soon.' Although, perhaps it was just that she had been told so many times about the hugs and the words Aunt Bet-Bet had whispered in her ear. "Look after your mother for me, won't you," she had said. "She's very special, just like you. I love you, precious one."

Those were to be the last words she was ever to hear from her beloved Aunt and sometimes the ache in her heart matched the pain she saw in her mother's face, each time she had asked her, "When are Tammy and Aunt Bet-Bet and Uncle Dan coming home, Mummy?"

"Oh Daddy, of course I'm okay. I think this is marvelous. I only wish that Aunt Bet-B... Aunt Betty and Uncle Dan could be here..." her words petered out.

"I knew who Tammy was the moment I saw her at the door and I just screamed for Mum." Becky continued, sort of rushing her words, as if trying to hide the sense of loss that they all felt so keenly.

"It's like having the sister I never had. Tammy, will you be my sister?" she asked at last.

"Becky, it is my joy and delight to be here with you all. I will be whatever you want me to be. I feel as if I've come home."

Suddenly, it was Tammy crying, and the next little while was a bit messy, with all three women hugging and crying and laughing as they jumped around the room in a big group hug. The cat which had been lazily watching all the proceedings from the comfort of a corner chair, suddenly decided that this was all too much on a sultry afternoon and took off for quieter parts of the house.

Dave and Donald looked on, both trying their best to keep some sort of manly composure. But closer inspection would have shown that both had very shiny eyes as they watched the emotional women.

Order was restored after a few moments and then Susan became all business.

"Okay, Tammy, you'll go in the spare room at the end of the hall, and Dave, there's a sleep-out on the back verandah. I hope you'll be comfortable out there." she said.

"Aunt Susan, I have slept in some very odd places in my life, none odder than over the past few weeks. I'm quite sure that your sleep-out will be a palace, compared to what I've been coping with. Thank you very much."

The next little while was taken up with organizing sleeping arrangements, bed linen etc. Susan was horrified to see Tammy's scant wardrobe and made plans to take her shopping at the very first opportunity. This niece, who had returned from the dead, was going to be her daughter and both she and Donald knew that if they had any say in it, she would want for nothing.

As soon as sleeping arrangements had been organized, Susan turned her attention to the kitchen and began cooking a meal for her suddenly extended family. Tammy, who had never been waited on, was keen to help, but Susan hustled her out of the kitchen.

"Not tonight, my sweet, you and Becky go off together and get acquainted while I attend to things here.

And you boys," this to Don and Dave, "You can sit there and have a cool drink while you get to know each other. There's Cola or Ginger Beer in the fridge on the verandah."

Dinner was a simple meal, tastefully prepared, and the family soon sat down to enjoy it. Conversation over dinner was animated, with much laughter and banter, as Tammy and her aunt and uncle discovered that the easy relationship they'd had so many years ago, was still very much in evidence.

When the meal was finally cleared away, late evening found them all draped in easy chairs on the front porch, catching a cool breeze and holding icy cold drinks as stories were exchanged. Tammy had a great deal to tell her family, and she needed as well, to know where the rest of her family was.

"Your Dad's family has all moved away, love," said her aunt. "His brother, Uncle Kevin, became very ill some years back and so they moved to Sydney, to be near their son and his doctors. Dorothy, his sister, has moved several times and now she lives up the north coast. She never married, you know.

"I can give you their addresses. Kevin needs a lot of specialist care. I think he had a stroke, after a heart by-pass operation. Amy has a computer, so we can email them and let them know you've come home. Dorothy has email too, so I'll get one off to both of them before I head off to bed tonight. They both check them regularly, so they'll get them tomorrow."

"What on earth is 'Email' and what's a 'Computer'?" asked a puzzled Tammy.

Everybody laughed, but then they suddenly realized that here was a young woman who had lost touch with the world, and who knew nothing of the things that they all took for granted as a part of everyday life.

"Come with me, Tammy," said Becky. "I'll show you."

So everybody trooped into the study, Don turned on the light and an overhead fan and Becky went to the desk, where all the trappings common to the computer literate family were spread out. She turned on the power and switched on the computer. Tammy gasped as it started with a small burst of music, followed by some beeps as the screen lit up and a series of images flashed by one after the other.

"My goodness, what on earth is this?" asked a stunned Tammy.

"This, dear girl, is a computer," said her cousin. "Welcome to the 21st Century. See? Now it's ready. Why don't we send those emails now, Mum?" asked Becky.

"Okay, love, you can do that if you like. The addresses are there in the Address Book. Just tell them Tammy has come home and that we'll write later with all the details."

"Okay." said Becky as she logged onto the internet. Tammy was fascinated by the weird noises coming from the strange-looking box on the desk.

"Is it okay?" she asked. "It sounds like as if something is wrong with it."

"No, Tammy, there's nothing wrong, that's just the sounds it makes while its dialing. It's kind of like a long distance telephone call,' explained her aunt. "But soon, hopefully, those noises will be gone for good. They are talking now of switching us over to something called Broadband – just when that will be, we aren't sure, but we hope it's soon."

"Broadband! What's broadband?' Tammy asked, more puzzled than ever.

Becky tried to explain, "In the world of computers, we can be connected to what is known as the World Wide Web, or the internet. Computers anywhere in the world can be connected to each other, sort of like telephones, only cheaper and more efficient. Broadband simply means that the computer is connected all the time. And that means no more dialing up and waiting in queues if lines are busy. You just click on it like opening any other program. Simple! Or at least that's what they promise. Ah yes indeed, the marvels of technology eh?"

"Yes, of course," said Tammy hesitantly, although it was obvious to everybody that she had no idea at all.

"You wait, Hon," said her cousin, "you'll get the hang of it in no time, won't she Mum?"

"Of course you will, Tammy darling," her aunt said, as she put an arm around Tammy's shoulder. "There must be a lot of things you'll need to learn, but that's what we're here for, sweetheart. We'll guide you through the maze and you'll be confidently facing life in no time. Won't she Dave?'

"I'll make sure of it," he said. "Although I must confess, this computer business is a bit beyond an old bushie like me.

But, anything else, I'll certainly be doing the best I can to help her figure it all out.

"I learned a whole lot about a very different kind of life out there in Tammy's world, so now it's my turn to help her come to terms with the world we know and... um-m-m... love?"

Laughter filled the room again. "Love?" said Don. "Tolerate, more like," he said with a groan. "Still, mustn't scare our Tammy. It really isn't that bad sweetie," he reassured her. "We are just joking, because sometimes it really seems like a bit of a rat-race."

"Yes, I remember hearing Dad say life was like that. He said that was why he wanted to go up north – to get away from it."

"Yes, I remember him saying that too," said her aunt. "He and Betty were very happy out there, so we can't have too many regrets, can we? Not everybody gets to live their dream, do they?"

"No, that's very true," said Tammy. "And we were. Happy, I mean. Even in our new home, in the cavern, we were happy – happy just being together. It was peaceful.

"It was just... well, Mum, she missed being able to contact the home folks, you know? If she'd been able to phone, even, it would have made all the difference."

Tammy brushed a little tear from her cheek and smiled at her aunt. "I'm okay," she said. "Really, I'm okay. I know that she's truly 'home' now."

Meanwhile, Becky had finished the letters and Tammy watched in amazement as her cousin put the finishing touches to them, then pointed the little arrow at a word 'send' and said, "There you go, they've gone. They'll find those tomorrow when they check their mail."

"Does everybody have one of these," asked Tammy.

"Pretty much," answered her cousin. "Most households have at least one of these; some have several, especially if they've got kids."

"Wow!" whispered Tammy. It all was really very strange and she realized again, that coming back to the world after all these years was going to take a lot of learning. She hadn't even guessed that such things as these even existed. Sure, they were around when she was little, but not everybody had one and she couldn't remember ever having seen such a thing before.

Then, suddenly, tiredness overwhelmed her and she swayed a little as she stood behind Becky's chair.

"For goodness' sake, my child," cried her aunt, "You must be done in. Such a day you've had. What on earth were we thinking, keeping you up all hours of the night? Come on, little one, you are going to bed."

So her aunt led her to her room, showed her where she'd placed some personal items then took her to the bathroom.

"You can shower now, or in the morning, whichever you prefer, darling." She said.

"I'd like a bit of a splash before I turn in, if that's okay," she said. "It's been a hot and sticky day."

"Yes, indeed it has, and a busy one for you, driving all over the place. I'll leave you to it and you can settle in." said her aunt, as she hugged her niece before leaving the room with a final smile.

Susan needed to sort out her feelings. She was so excited to have Tammy home, and they'd all been so busy since she and Dave had arrived on the doorstep, that she'd had no time to digest the fact that her beloved sister was really dead. She needed time to grieve, she realized.

Later that night, as she and Donald lay in their big bed under the fan, she suggested to him that they might consider a funeral, well, a memorial service, for Dan and Betty. All these years they had not been able to lay them to rest and now, at least they knew.

Don agreed. "It's a very good idea, honey," he said. "You need closure. It's an important part of the grief process. I know that it's been very hard for you all this time - knowing in your heart, but, not knowing.

How hard it must have been out there for our Tammy. She is indeed a very brave girl. Surely, it's a miracle that's brought her home to us."

"Oh yes, Don, a miracle indeed. I'm not sure whether I want to laugh and rejoice, or simply cry until I can't cry any more. I was so sure I'd cried all the tears I had."

She laughed as she said that, but tears came readily to her eyes and she buried her head in Don's big shoulder and wept for some time, until finally, exhausted, she dropped off to sleep.

Whispering a prayer of thanks for Tammy, Donald reached over, turned out the light and drifted off to sleep, dreaming of a little girl, riding on his back, squealing with the joy of playing 'horsy' with her 'Unka Dona'.

In his sleep-out room, tucked away on the back verandah, Dave looked about him and smiled.

He recalled his childhood in this sub-tropical city, a city that in those days, had barely rated as an overgrown country town. How it had grown in the years since he'd lived here in his youth. Brief visits over the years hadn't prepared him for the way it had changed since last he'd been here.

He remembered how, as the oldest of three boys, he'd been relegated to the sleep-out of the rambling Queenslander they'd called home when he was a lad of about twelve. He'd loved it out there, where he could sleep with his old blue cattle dog. There'd always been a breeze out there, even as there was, here, tonight. And he'd been lord of all he surveyed, as his room overlooked the long back yard. From his vantage point at the rear of the high-set home, he could see a vista of rambling back yards and other homes just like their own, as, set atop a hill, neighbouring yards dropped away below him. His parents, sadly, were long gone.

He experienced a moment's regret, as he realized that like so many people the world over, they had probably died without knowing the Lord. That would have been him, he supposed, if not for meeting Tammy.

He realized that he must contact his younger brothers again soon. It had been too many years. One was Stateside, he knew, following a dream to be a Texas cowboy. And the other had a high-powered job somewhere in Sydney. Neither had married. Seemed bachelor-hood ran in the family.

As his 'new' family settled for the night in the big house behind him, he stretched out on the bed, which surprisingly was quite comfy, and thought about the happenings of the day.

They'd driven most of the previous night. He tried to remember just how long ago he'd actually slept, recalling a brief hour or so, sometime during the long journey. They'd stopped, he recalled, at a roadhouse for a comfort stop and a midnight snack. So he'd suggested to Tammy that they should grab a few minutes shut-eye before they continued.

He had woken all too soon and had sneaked off to the loo. Nature's needs satisfied, he'd grabbed a quick drink and then decided to head off again, while Tammy continued to sleep. She had woken at some stage, smiled up at him, and reassured that he was still there, had drifted off again for another hour or so.

Suddenly very tired, he realized he'd been on the go for days, with hardly a break. Bob and Gary had been more fortunate, having two of them to share the driving.

Dreaming he was on his little cot at home with 'Bluey', Dave finally drifted off to sleep.

Tammy had gone for a quick shower, accustomed now to modern plumbing, and had returned to the pretty room that after a few moments, she remembered as the one she's shared with her parents when they first came to live in Brisbane.

They had lived there with Susan and Donald for a week, until her father had found a place to rent. After that, she'd used this room sometimes for a sleepover, when her parents had gone out for dinner and a show, or later, if her mother, a nurse, had to work a late shift.

She remembered how often her dad was missing – off flying planes for someone or other, ferrying people and goods all over the outback. She'd loved hearing his stories of far away places and loved going out to the station properties for holidays.

They'd never owned a home, but she'd loved the rented home they'd lived in. Her room was pink, and all frilly, she recalled. But she couldn't for the life of her remember where that house had been. And she knew she'd never find it in the big, busy and thoroughly modern city that Brisbane had become.

As Tammy drifted off to sleep, she thought how strange it was that she remembered this room and the pink room from the rented house, but had no real memory of the cottage at Riverside. She could not even remember which room had been hers, or what it looked like. How strange, she thought...

Then, dreaming dreams of childhood; of games with her uncle, riding horses on outback properties and that fateful trip, she drifted away as sleep overtook her.

The house was quiet as the family slept and the cat prowled about, ever watchful for anything that moved.

But finally, having done his rounds, and satisfied that all was in order, he too found a comfy spot and soon dozed off.

It had been a long time since this fellow had been a night rambler. As he slept, he dreamed of chasing night creatures through the back yards of his neighbourhood – but that had been when he was young... back in the days before responsible people realized that native fauna were in danger from the nocturnal activities of their feline pets.

Morning dawned bright and clear. Don and Susan were up and around early, as Don had to go to work. Becky surfaced a little later and after a light breakfast also headed off to work in the city.

She had a nice, well-paid job in the public service and was saving for a trip overseas, before finally settling down, hopefully, one day to find the right man and marry.

However, for now, it was off to work, just like every other day. But today wasn't really like any other day, so she left strict instructions for her mother to tell Tammy she'd see her that afternoon as she climbed into her little car and waved goodbye.

Dave had been out of bed for quite a while and had been for a walk around the nearby streets. He marveled that once you got out of the busy parts of the city, the rows of Queenslanders were still much the same as he remembered.

Many, he noticed, had been lovingly restored to their original glory and Dave was impressed with the landscaped gardens and the obvious pride these people had in their homes. Every now and then an old home, tucked away in its overgrown garden, would look slightly out of place; but it reminded him of many of the homes near where he'd lived. So many folk simply hadn't been able to afford to paint their large homes, and gardening was a luxury for those who didn't have to work eighteen hours a day.

He returned to the house in time to join his hosts for breakfast and was enjoying a cup of coffee when Tammy came out, yawning and stretching like a young cat.

She smiled sheepishly as she joined the others at the kitchen table.

"I'm sorry," she said. "Someone should have woken me. I didn't mean to sleep so late."

"Nonsense, my child," said her aunt. "We intended to let you sleep as long as you needed. You were exhausted last night. Did you sleep well?"

"Oh yes, I went almost straight off to sleep and never moved all night. I remember now, that's the room we used – Mum, Dad and me. Wasn't it?"

"Yes, dear, it was," answered Susan. "You and your parents used that room when your father first brought you here from the little farm out west.

"You probably don't remember that place. It's where your folks were when you were born. Dad was working for some city bloke, trying to keep his hobby farm from collapsing. It was never going to work, what with the drought and all.

"The property simply wasn't big enough to support enough stock. Eventually it all came to naught, so the owner sold it and your parents came to Brisbane.

"We thought that your dad would get a job and settle down for a while, but, no, soon enough he was off out west again, flying planes for some property owner. As his reputation as a capable flyer spread, he got more and more jobs, flying further and further afield. We never knew where he was or when to expect his return.

"Your poor mother, it's just as well he left her here, close to us most of the time, where we could keep an eye on the both of you.

"Not that your Dad wanted to leave you, but that kind of work was all he knew and he'd have died cooped up in an office somewhere like Don.

"Then, one day he came home and told us that he had a job on a station property in the Northern Territory and he wanted his family with him. So, off you all went, and..., we... never saw any of you again..." Susan's story faltered there, as she remembered how much she had missed her sister. "Well,

135

darling not till you came knocking at our door," she added at last with a smile.

"When that story was in all the news, about a family lost in a big storm, Donald had made phone calls to the station where Dan had worked – River something, was it? Anyway he was told that, yes, it was your family that had gone missing.

"He was told that people were out searching and that they'd let us know if they had news, but the days had become weeks and the weeks, months, until years had gone by until finally, I suppose I said goodbye to all of you in my heart.

"And now, here you are darling, back home at last. Oh dear, I can hardly believe it. It is such a miracle."

Susan jumped up from her chair and rushed around the table to wrap Tammy in a big hug. They clung to each other for a moment or two before Susan went to sit down, as both of them wiped their tear-filled eyes.

"Well, what are you two going to do today?" she asked finally.

Dave looked at Tammy and Tammy looked at Dave, and they both shrugged.

"We don't know." Tammy finally said with a laugh. "Perhaps we need to find a place to stay."

"Nonsense, both of you can stay here for as long as you need to," said Susan. "I won't hear of you living anywhere else. Dave, are you okay out there in the sleep-out?" she asked as a sort of after thought.

"Yes, I'm absolutely fine," answered Dave. "And you are too kind. I don't want to impose in any way, not being family, you know."

"Dave, you are going to marry our Tammy, and that makes you family.

"I insist that you both stay here until after the wedding. Meantime, we'll make all the arrangements, maybe find you some work and in between times, we can go house hunting. You'll need a place of your own once you get married, won't you?"

Dave couldn't help but be amused by Susan's enthusiasm, and touched by her warm-hearted hospitality. He graciously accepted her offer to stay and agreed that, indeed, he needed to put his mind to finding some work, or he'd be running out of money before too long. He had a good bit put aside from years of earning good wages and not spending too much of it but it wouldn't last forever.

Of course there was the fiasco of the wrecked plane, but he hoped there'd be some insurance on that. Not enough to buy another one, but he reasoned that he didn't want to do that anymore. No repeats of Tammy's childhood for them.

He intended to find some settled work, wherever he could, so that he and Tammy could buy a home and, oh boy, maybe even start a family. Wow! That was something he'd never even thought about, until just this very moment.

"I guess I'd better see the insurance company about the plane," Dave said. "And if we don't have to look for digs, I suppose I'd best look for some sort of work. What's available, any idea?"

"Depends what sort of work you want to do, love," said Susan. "Let's look in the paper and see if there are any jobs offering. You can always go to Centrelink (that used to be Social Security). You don't have to be on the dole to put your name down for work. We have this thing called Job Network now, and there's lots of places where you can put your name down and they find you a job."

"Okay, sounds fine. Let's look in the paper first and see if anything is offering. Goodness only knows if I've got any qualifications for anything these days. I'm a bit of a jack of all trades, master of none."

So they poured over the wanted ads in the paper, but nothing seemed suitable. So after the breakfast dishes had been cleared away, Dave and Tammy said goodbye to Susan and headed off for the city. Dave had rung the insurance people and they had said to bring in any paperwork he had on the plane. He'd need to fill in a claim form and then they'd take it from there.

Chapter 15

NEW JOB - NEW DRAMAS

The day was spent filling in forms, and job hunting - both of which proved to be exhausting and not very productive. So by the time they headed their noses for home, they were hot and tired and more than a little frustrated.

But Susan met them with good news. She'd remembered about a man she'd known for some years, who owned a big farm out in the Lockyer Valley.

About lunch time, she'd called him, hoping to catch him when he came in for a bite to eat, and was lucky enough to find him at home.

His wife had answered the phone and said, yes, he had just come in and was washing up. So after a moment of exchanging pleasantries, her husband had come into the room and she had put him on the phone.

Susan, in her usually direct manner, had come right out and told him what she needed. A job for an honest, hardworking young man who was about to marry her long lost niece. She added, as an afterthought, that they'd probably need a home too, as they were to be married very soon.

Her friend said that he was astounded that she should ring, because his foreman had walked out on him that very day and he was shorthanded and desperate.

"What does this fellow know about farming?" he'd asked.

"To tell you the truth, I'm not too sure," Susan had answered. "He's been flying planes up in the Territory for years, and as far as I know, he can turn his hand to just about anything on a property. "I'll get him to ring you when he gets back tonight. They are out job hunting at present. Thank you, Pete, I owe you," Susan had told him as she hung up the phone.

"So, there you are, Dave, our conversation in a nutshell," she said. "Does that appeal to you?"

"Indeed it does, Aunt Susan," Dave answered.

He took the number from her and went straight to the phone. Tammy and her aunt sat at the table and talked about the day, while they drank a cuppa that Susan had made the moment she'd heard their car in the driveway.

Dave was gone some time and Tammy wondered what was going on in the other room. Then finally Dave came back, with a grin as wide as all outdoors on his face.

"It looks like I've got a foreman's job," he said. "Pete wants me to go out there tomorrow, so we can talk about it.

He wants you to come too, Tammy, because the Foreman's job comes with a house. He says you should come out and inspect it and Aunt Susan, he said you should come too and give it the 'once over' with your critical eye," Dave added with a laugh.

The three of them were talking it all over and enjoying their tea or coffee, when Donald came in from work. Becky was just a little behind him, having been delayed by some shopping after work. As well as buying some things for herself she had also bought a couple of blouses and a pair of shorts for Tammy, that she was sure would fit.

Tammy took them with a small word of protest, which was quickly brushed away, and then with her customary shy smile and a hug of thanks. She held them up against her and agreed with Becky, that she was sure they'd fit.

The two of them then gratefully accepted a cup of coffee and were keen to hear the news of the day.

Becky was sad at the thought of losing Tammy so soon after finding her again, but was reassured when she was told that Tammy wouldn't be going anywhere until after the wedding, and in any case the Lockyer was only an hour away, down the highway.

Dinner was organized and an early night planned, as Dave and Tammy and Susan would need to be up and gone very early the next day.

"You and Becky will have to get yourselves off to work in the morning," said Susan. "I'm sure you can both manage that. I've spoilt you both for far too long as it is," she said with a laugh.

Becky stuck her tongue out at her mother as she scooted out of the room, and Donald just smiled. It obviously didn't matter what this woman said to him. He adored her and would do absolutely anything for her.

Tammy smiled a sad little smile. She remembered how loving her parents had been to each other too, and she hoped that she and Dave would share the same kind of love. She looked up in time to see him looking at her across the table. There was that look again.

How often she had caught that look out on their wild trek across the desert. She remembered how her heart had fluttered each time, aware that it was skipping about even now. Yes, she thought. Our love will be just like theirs. I know it in my heart.

The next morning proved to be more than a little hectic, with all of them trying to get ready together. Tammy, her aunt and Dave were a bit ahead of the other two, but with each of them trooping in and out of the bathroom, and dodging around each other in the kitchen it was a traffic jam at times.

Becky was rushing in and out of her room, dodging anyone who happened to be in the hall, insisting that her mother must have lost her favourite blouse in the wash, because it wasn't 'anywhere'.

Her mother calmly walked into her room, turned over one or two items that had been residing on the floor for some time and with a sweet smile, produced the offending blouse.

"You can wear it if you like, dear," said her mother. "But," she held it up to her face and wrinkled her nose a little, "I'd probably go for a different one, if I were you. Looks like this one missed the wash, love."

Tammy turned away quickly, before Becky saw the smile that lit up her face, suddenly finding something of far greater interest to attract her attention. No way was she buying into that one. Her uncle caught her eye as she turned away and with a small cough, carried on quickly down the hall, before he gave the game away completely. Becky gave a small grunt as she snatched the offending blouse, following her mother's exit from the room with a resoundingly slammed door.

"There goes the picture in the hall again," said Susan, "I must straighten that every other day. Our Becky runs on adrenalin and emotion, bless her."

Back in the kitchen, some order had been restored. Dave was washed, dressed, fed and had cleared the dishes from the table. Susan said that there was no point in doing the dishes, because Don and Becky still had to eat. However, Dave had already washed most of those already used.

"Wow! Look how organized this man is, Tammy? What a catch!" marveled Susan.

Tammy simply smiled. She knew already how handy Dave was in any kind of situation.

A completely self-sufficient man, who it seemed, could cope with almost anything.

Finally, the three were ready to leave and Donald and his daughter, well over her huff by now, were sitting down to breakfast.

Goodbyes were said, and then Dave led the way out to his car. A quick check to make sure it had enough of all the essentials, and a once over of the windscreen – somehow they always need cleaning – and they were ready to leave.

"Lockyer Valley, here we come," said Dave, as he started the big vehicle and backed down the sloping driveway.

The trip was uneventful, as city driving goes. They were slightly ahead of the peak hour stuff, but it was still much heavier than Dave had been accustomed to for many a year. However, his skill as a driver had not deserted him and he managed to circumvent most situations as they arose, with a minimum of fuss.

Soon enough they were out of the city and heading down the highway. Most of the traffic was inbound to the city and they pretty much had the road to themselves. Tammy was delighted as they drove along.

"It's so pretty out here," she said. As they drew nearer to their destination,

Tammy was fascinated with the rows of crops and the dark chocolate colour of the soil. It all looked so fertile and beautiful, compared to the dry and barren landscapes she had lived with for most of her life.

Susan was sure she knew where her friends lived, as she and Don had visited a couple of times since they had first met them several years ago, at a seminar in town.

But it took a few minutes to get her bearings, as it had been a while – and eventually, she had to admit that they'd better ask for some directions – then, at last they were driving down a long entrance road, between paddocks of healthy looking crops. The house came into view around a bend in the driveway and Dave pulled his big Toyota up alongside another one that could almost have been its twin. It's just as dirty too, thought Dave with a wry smile. And he made a mental note to wash the old girl that evening.

As the vehicle pulled up and they got out, a tall man came out of the house and started down the stairs.

He jammed a battered old hat on his head as he came out into the sunlight, but pulled it off again as he greeted the ladies.

He was long and lanky in appearance, with weathered features. Dave knew he was looking at a man who had spent the best part of his life on the land, his eyes accustomed to looking into the distance, mostly through the glare of the sun so many crinkles around his eyes told their own story. They also told of the ready smile that came to his face at the slightest opportunity.

Quiet-spoken and gentlemanly, despite his rough, work-hardened handshake and his soiled overalls, he greeted his guests with what they would come to recognize as his trademark smile, and quickly invited them into the house.

"No point in staying out in this sun any longer than you need to, ladies," he said, "Mother's got the kettle on in there, so come up and have a cuppa while we get acquainted."

Dave liked this man immediately, guessing him to be a straight-shooter.

His guess that he'd grown up on this very property, helping his father from a young age and taking over once the old man had passed on soon proved to be correct.

This was the kind of man that Dave had worked with all his life. And it soon became obvious to the ladies that the two men had a great deal in common, even though the type of farming had been vastly different.

Introductions were made and Pete's wife, Gayle, soon made Tammy and Susan feel welcome. A comfort stop was on Sue's mind and once that was out of the way, a cup of tea was most welcome. Tammy, who had acquired quite a taste for coffee, gladly accepted a cup as she sat down at the big kitchen table.

Dave and Pete got right down to business, and after their coffee, left the house to go and look at crops and machinery and to discuss the finer points of the job Dave was considering.

Pete introduced him to a couple of guys working in the machinery shed. They were repairing a tractor that had inconveniently decided to quit doing what it was meant to do, and they were obviously having some difficulty.

Muttering about having to go into town for a part, one of them briefly shook Dave's hand as he headed off to a Ute parked nearby.

"Hang on, Mate," called Dave. "Can I have a quick squiz at that before you go?" he asked.

"Why not," said the farmhand. "Good luck to you if you can get it to go, darned if we can fix it. Reckon we'll need to replace some bits and wouldn't you know it, we've got everything but the one thing we need."

Dave went over to the machine and stuck his hand out to greet the second farmhand as he pulled his head out of the tractors nether regions. He wiped his hand on a rag hanging from his back pocket and shook Dave's hand.

Within minutes, Dave was buried in the working parts of the machine and after a bit of mysterious tinkering, stepped aside and suggested that they try it and see if it worked.

Much to the surprise of everybody, the tractor roared into life and the offending levers did just what they were supposed to do.

"How did you do that?" asked Pete, impressed to say the least.

"Comes from living and working a long way from any town," he said. "You get to know how to fix things in ways that aren't always conventional, or you do without," he added with a chuckle.

"You'll need to get that replaced of course, but it should get you through till you need to go to town for other things."

The farmhands were impressed, and not offended, because Dave's manner had been casual and in no way implying that they didn't know what they were doing. Pete was impressed, because the tractor and his hands were heading back out to the job with a minimum of wasted time.

"That job is definitely yours, young fella, if you want it," said Pete. "Let's get the ladies and go look at that house."

So they went back to the house, where Pete announced to the ladies that Dave was going to be his new foreman.

"This young fella just got the old Ferguson going. The lads were having a bit of trouble and he just fixed it. No idea what he did, but it worked. Gayle, I'll give you a list of things we'll need, if you're going to town later."

"I'm going first thing in the morning, Pete," his wife answered. "Will that be soon enough?"

"Yep, that should do it okay, I reckon," said her husband. "Thanks to Dave here, we won't have to make a special trip. Anyway ladies, come and look at this house. It's just down the road a ways. I hope you'll like it, little lady," he said to Tammy. "Brad's wife was happy enough there. They only left because Brad got sick.

"Seems he's got some allergy and the doctor said he couldn't work on the land anymore. Not too sure what it was, but he'd been sick for such a long time and no one knew why. Apparently it was the job making him sick all the time. Dunno, never heard of anything like it before. You never can tell, though, can you?"

His listeners agreed that there were, indeed, some strange things that happen from time to time and Susan added that sometimes constant use of certain chemicals etc., could cause the body to set up a resistance to it. Then, suddenly, one day, an allergy develops for no apparent reason.

"It can happen with something as simple as laundry powder," she added.

Pete nodded wisely and agreed with her, even though he'd never heard of it happening to anyone before. But he was sure that his friend would know far more about these things than a simple old farmer like himself.

They all piled into Pete's 4x4 and set off down the driveway towards the main road. Just before the gate, they pulled into a side-track, and there, hidden among the crops was a neat little home.

Obviously well cared-for, as were all the buildings as far as Dave could tell, this looked like it would be more than suitable for his needs.

He hoped that it would suit Tammy too, for he intended that she would be joining him here as soon as it could be arranged. Pete stopped the car in front of the house and they all got out. Tammy was at once entranced by the pretty little gardens around the house.

"Brad's missus was a keen gardener," he told her. "She took a real pride in her little garden, as you can see. She was not at all happy about leaving it either. Still, they had no choice. Brad had to go. I think they've gone to the coast, somewhere.

The doc seemed to think that the sea air would help clear up Brad's skin. I've never seen anyone itch and wheeze like that fella did – poor guy."

Tammy ran up the little path to the door of the house and peered in through the front window. She liked what she'd seen in the garden, but was keen to see what the house looked like inside. If she came here with Dave, this would be her home for some time and she wanted it to be something special.

Of course, it didn't really matter, she supposed. She'd been happy sleeping out in the desert with Dave. A house, any kind of house would be a luxury after what they'd been through.

Pete came up behind her and stuck a key in the door. He opened the door and then stepped aside so the ladies could go in and have a look about.

"Let the ladies check it out, eh mate," he said to Dave. "Us blokes don't worry too much about that side of things, do we?"

"If you could see where I've been tossing my swag for the last umpteen years..." Dave mused softly.

For him, this little house was a palace. If it suited Tammy, he'd be happy.

"Oh, Dave, it's gorgeous!" said Tammy excitedly. "It's so neat and clean. Brad's wife was certainly a good housekeeper," she added to Pete.

"Yep, took great pride in cookin' and cleanin', that one," declared Pete. "Guess she could make a home anywhere for her man."

"Well, I'll make a home here for us, Dave," Tammy said softly. "If you're happy to live here, I'll be happy here. If this job is what you want, then, you and me together... this will be great!"

Dave turned to Pete and held out his hand.

"Looks like the deal is set, Boss," he said, laughing. "I accept the job if you want me. My future wife is happy with the home and that's good enough for me. Does all this furniture go with the house?" he asked.

"Yep, I figured that some folks wouldn't have much, so over the years we've put in a few bits and pieces. If you've got your own stuff, we can always put this in storage," Pete added.

"Oh, goodness, no." said Dave. "What we've got is pretty much what we stand up in.

I've got a vehicle and a swag and Tammy, well... suffice to say, we appreciate you providing this for us," said Dave, as he stood in the centre of the living room, with his arm around Tammy's slender shoulders.

"Well, that about wraps it up, I reckon. If you good folks will excuse me, I think I'd better get back to work. Times a' wasting. You good folks go on up to the house and rest awhile if you like, but I'd better get back to the chores. Dave, welcome aboard. When can we expect you to start?"

"Could you give me a day or two to sort some things out? I've got some insurance matters to take care of. I crashed my plane up there in the Territory. When we leave here, we are going back to the insurance office to see if we can sort it out. We didn't have too much joy yesterday, so I want to have another go today. Can I call you tomorrow?" asked Dave.

"That'll do it, okay, I reckon," said Pete. "I'll appreciate it if you can start as soon as possible. But I understand you need a bit of time to get sorted. Call as soon as you know, okay?"

"I certainly will, Pete, thanks. And thank you for the job. I hope I'll turn out to be all you hope for."

Then with a final wave of his battered hat, Pete left and went off back to his farm. Dave and the ladies wandered about the little house for a bit more, checking out all the little details, and then they sauntered back up the long driveway to the main house.

After a short time socializing with the lady of the house, they said their goodbyes, promising to be in touch real soon, and took their leave.

Tammy was very excited for Dave and for the future that they planned together. She was also a little sad too, because she realized that Dave would need to come out here to start work, while she would need to stay in the city with her aunt and uncle. It simply would not be right for her to come out here with him until she and Dave were married, as much as she longed to.

As they drove back towards the city, they talked excitedly about the future. Susan was pleased for them both that Dave had found a good job. Something he'd enjoy in the outdoors. She had known that it would never have worked to try and find a job in an office – or any kind of job indoors, for that matter.

This was a man whose life had been lived in a place where the horizons went on forever. To shut him up in a confined place would slowly but surely kill him.

On arriving in the city, they went directly to the insurance office – well, after driving around for almost half an hour, looking for a place to park.

Dave was determined to be a little more assertive this time and insist that some action be taken. He had a policy and he intended that the company would honour it, and that was that.

So, he demanded to speak with the manager and when they'd been shown into his office, Dave produced his paperwork, once again, and laid it on the line.

"I have a current, paid-up policy here, and I absolutely insist that your company honours it," he said.

The manager looked at the man standing before him and did not miss the no-nonsense attitude. He coughed a little, slightly embarrassed, before he spoke.

"Well... Look, I'll see what I can do." He said, finally. "Leave it with me and I'll ring you later today with an answer. I'll need to talk to the board and see what we can work out for you."

Dave was not happy with his smarmy manner, but he consented to waiting till that afternoon for an answer.

"I'll expect to hear from you before closing, today," he insisted. "If I don't hear from you, I'll be taking this further. I'm sure that I have some sort of legal recourse here," he said firmly.

"You'll hear from me, I promise," said the manager. It was obvious that this fellow was not going to go away, so he made the decision that he'd best get on with it and find a solution. He wasn't happy, but could see no way out of it.

So, not over-the-moon happy, but satisfied that at least something was happening this time, the little group went and found the car and headed home.

They stopped at a café on the way home and had a coffee and a snack, realizing that lunch time had come and gone unnoticed, and so it was some time after three in the afternoon before they arrived at the house. The phone was ringing as they went up the front stairs, so Susan quickly opened the door and rushed in to answer it before the answering machine picked it up.

Dave and Tammy followed her in and had only just fallen into a chair when Susan came into the kitchen and told Dave that it was the insurance fellow on the phone.

"Well, that was quick," said Dave as he went into the hall to the phone.

"Hello, Dave Wilson, speaking," he said.

"Mr. Wilson, its Mr. Thompson here. Look, Head Office is insisting on seeing the wreck of this plane of yours. They're saying it could be anywhere, you know.

I mean what guarantee do we have that it really is wrecked, you know?"

"Because I've told you that it is, that's how," said Dave, angrily. "My word is my bond and if I say it crashed, then it crashed!"

"I'm sure that's the truth, but they won't move on this. Look, the assessor is on his way out to see you as we speak. He should be there any moment; he left here nearly an hour ago. I'm sorry; my hands are tied on this. Talk to him, he'll sort it out, I'm sure." And with that he hung up before Dave could argue further.

Dave slowly walked back into the kitchen and Susan and Tammy could see that he was very angry.

He was such a gentle, laid-back kind of guy it was very unusual to see him upset.

"An assessor is on his way here," he said. "They are insisting on seeing the plane. They don't believe it crashed. I think they reckon I've sold it or something."

The girls looked at him, horrified. What a suggestion! As if Dave would do such a thing. It didn't seem fair, especially after all that he'd been through.

However, they didn't get much time to discuss it, for no sooner had he said that than there was a knock at the front door.

Susan went through to answer it. There was the sound of voices from the front of the house, and then Susan came back into the kitchen with a young man in tow.

Chapter 16
THE TROY AND A TRIP OUTBACK

"Dave, this is Troy Fisher, he's apparently an insurance assessor." The way Susan said that, you'd have thought she'd picked up some derelict from somewhere, and she wasn't too sure if he should sit on her clean furniture.

"Hi!" said the assessor. "Seems that we have a small problem here, eh?"

"The only problem here is with a bunch of bureaucrats who don't know their right hand from their left," said Dave impatiently. "How on earth are you going to see this plane? It's in a million pieces on the desert floor somewhere in the Northern Territory, for goodness's sake!" said an exasperated Dave.

"Look, I know it's tricky, but let's look at this logically. There must be some way to find it, surely. I've brought maps and charts and we can work out a grid system from your last known position and then we'll have a ballpark idea of where it is." The young man drew a breath and went on. "I've organized a helicopter to pick us up at Tumberrumba Station tomorrow. We can fly out there first thing in the morning, I've booked a flight."

"What!" said Dave in amazement? "You've booked plane tickets to take us to the Territory tomorrow? How do you expect me to just pick up and head off out there at the drop of a hat?"

"Well, you want this settled quickly, don't you?" asked the assessor.

"So, let's get it done. Soon as I see this wreck, it'll all be taken care of. Bit of paperwork and you'll have your dough." He shrugged his shoulders and took a drink from the coffee that Susan had reluctantly offered him.

"I'm starting a new job," said Dave. "I can't just head off up north again, just like that."

"Look, it will only take a couple of days. We're not talking weeks, here. We'll fly out there, get in the chopper, and locate the plane - then hey presto! Job's done!"

"Have you any idea how vast that territory is?" he asked the young man. "It could take weeks just to find it."

"Nonsense! We'll work out a grid pattern, using landmarks you recognize and we'll find it a piece of cake," said Troy, confidently.

"Well, if you are dead set on this madness, then Tammy must come too. She lived out there most of her life and will recognize her home territory quicker than I will. And that's not negotiable," he added quickly, as Troy went to speak.

"Okay, if you insist. Just give me a moment to verify that with the boss. Can I use the phone, please, lady?" he asked Susan.

Still stunned by all that had occurred, Susan simply waved her hand in the direction of the hallway. Let him find the darned thing by himself, she reasoned. If he hopes to find a plane wreck in the middle of the Australian bush, then he can find a phone in a hallway without too much trouble.

They sat at the table in silence, sipping their coffees and listening to their visitor talking in the hallway. In no time he was back in the kitchen.

"Well, that's all fixed," he said. "I'll pick the two of you up here at six o'clock in the morning. I'll take you to the airport; we'll board the plane and be at Tumberrumba Station by mid afternoon. The chopper will be waiting."

"How do you propose that a commercial airliner is going to land on a Station airstrip?" asked Dave slowly. He had begun to wonder if this young man had any idea what he was doing.

"Not a problem," said Troy with a little smile. "We are not going on a commercial flight we're going in the company's corporate jet. Nifty little machine, the pilot can land it anywhere."

Dave and the girls looked at him stunned. This was all going far too fast for them - a corporate jet, for goodness' sake? What next?

Troy grinned, and suddenly a boyish charm was apparent that they hadn't noticed before.

"It'll be okay, honest. I do this kind of stuff all the time. There ain't nuthin' that the Troy can't do!"

With that, he shook a stunned Dave by the hand, waved goodbye to the ladies, and with a "See you all in the morning," he took his leave, quietly closing the front door behind him. They could hear his cheerful whistle as he took the front stairs two at a time on the way to his car. He backed out of the drive and they heard him accelerate away down the quiet street. Susan briefly wondered what her neighbours would think.

"Goodness me!" said Susan. "What a whirlwind!"

The three of them were still sitting there moments later, when the phone rang again. Susan went out to the hall to answer it. It was Donald, wanting to know if Dave had got the job.

Telling him that she'd have to tell him all about it when he got home, that something had come up and she simply couldn't explain it all over the phone, she told him that she loved him and hung up the phone.

"That was Donald," she told the others when she came back into the kitchen.

"Dave," she said, "Pete... You must ring him at once and tell him what's happening. Then, we'd best see about organizing you two for another big day, tomorrow."

Dave threw his hands up in the air.

"What on earth am I going to tell Pete. He needs me to start now, not in a week's time. I'll be lucky if he holds the job for me."

Dave headed out to the phone, wondering how he could explain this mess to his new boss. But he needn't have worried, Pete understood completely.

"Look, mate, it can't be helped. These kinds of things happen. We'll just carry on here as usual. Thankfully its all just maintenance stuff going on at the moment. We'll manage. You just get this mess sorted out. Your job will be here when you get back. You keep in touch, okay?"

Dave couldn't believe it. What a guy! He thanked him most profusely, and promised to let him know the moment he had anything to tell. Pete brushed aside his thanks, saying that he knew a straight-shooter when he saw one, and no matter what happened he knew he had the right man for the job.

"You just get yourself sorted out, mate, she'll be right, you wait and see." said Pete. "See you when you get back, eh?"

"You certainly will, Pete, thanks. Goodbye."

Dave hung up the phone and came back to tell the girls the good news.

"Pete says its okay. He's holding the job and says not to worry. He's a very special fellow, that."

"Yes, he is, Donald and I knew that the first time we met. We were all at a church seminar. He and Gayle had made the trip in from the Lockyer. Somehow, the four of us just clicked. We've been friends ever since.

We talk on the phone a lot and write some, even get to visit occasionally. They are really good folks. Salt of the earth, as they say," said Susan.

"Well, there's no point in sitting around here," she continued. "You two had better go and get organized for tomorrow. Dave, do you still have those maps you said you used out there?"

"Yes, I do. I'll get them shortly and we can see if we can narrow the search area down a bit. The sooner this gets sorted, the better," he said as he went out to his sleep-out.

Dave and Tammy didn't have a lot of packing to do. Tammy still didn't have much in the way of clothes. All she really had were the few things that her hostesses at Tumberrumba and Riverside stations had given to her and the few things that Becky had bought for her. Susan had found a couple of bits and pieces that she thought might fit, things she'd... grown out of a little. Well... she'd been slim once too.

Dave took only moments to throw his gear into his battered old rucksack. He'd always traveled light. He wondered briefly what on earth he would find to put in all the cupboards in his new home. He smiled wryly. This was going to be a whole new adventure, he realized.

With his packing done, he picked up the maps and charts he'd kept from the plane and made his way back to the kitchen. He was poring over the maps when the girls finally came back into the kitchen.

He wondered what they'd found to do, as Tammy had only a few things to pack. But he knew better than to ask. Who knew what mysteries women got up to, he mused. A wise man knows when to keep his peace, he thought as he smiled to himself.

All three of them were searching the vast reaches of the outback, trying to make some sense of maps that covered an area too huge to grasp, when Donald and Becky both came in from work. Their questions about, 'how was your day?' were fielded quick smart, as Susan proceeded to tell Donald all that had transpired.

He sat, bewildered as she tried to tell him all that had happened that day. Beginning with the good news about the job and then on to the fiasco with the plane, almost without drawing breath.

But, finally, after slowing her down, and asking a few judicious questions, he got to the bottom of it all.

"You mean that they want to go trooping off to the wilds of Central Australia, to search for a plane that's lost out in the boondocks?" he asked.

"That's exactly what they want," said Dave. "I've argued till I'm blue in the face, but all to no avail. They've made up their minds, and that's that! This young fella, Troy, is picking us up here, Tammy and me, at six in the morning, and we're all heading off up north in a corporate jet, no less. Going straight to Tumberrumba, where he's apparently got a chopper all organized. Then he's got some idea that we'll work a grid pattern and then, voila! A plane wreck – there she'll be! Don't ask!" he added.

Donald could not believe his ears and he sat there shaking his head in amazement. Becky thought it was all terribly exciting and wanted to go too.

"Sorry, dear girl," said Dave. "No can do. This trip is crazy enough. It's not going to be easy. I think this fellow reckons he's going to fly up there, go right to the wreck, land this 'copter, check serial numbers or some such, then simply fly away home – all in a day's work!" Dave shook his head.

154

"Anyway, enough of that for now," said Susan. "Let's get dinner over. We will have an early start again in the morning. Come on you lot, let's get organized here!"

Donald knew better than to argue with his wife when she was in 'go' mode, so he complied. All hands together soon had a meal on the table. They gave thanks to God for the food, for each other, and then took a few moments to ask for His provision on the morrow. They sought an answer to this problem that confronted Dave, and asked the Lord to lead them to the plane, to sort out the insurance and to bring them all back safely once again.

Having committed it all to God, each one felt a measure of peace. So they tucked into the meal with gusto, suddenly realizing how hungry they were. Conversation turned to other matters as they put the issue of the plane out of their minds for the time being.

Susan broached the subject of a memorial service for Tammy's parents. Everybody seemed to think it was the right thing to do – a way for all of them to say goodbye to Betty and Dan and to put the past behind them, so they could fully plan the future.

So it was that a tentative date was set, for sometime before the wedding.

As Susan dried her tears, for the umpteenth time since Tammy had landed on her doorstep, she suddenly felt an easing of the tension that she knew she'd been holding since that awful day when Donald had come in from his phone-call, to tell her that it was indeed her sister and family that had gone missing, out in the wilds of the Northern Territory.

So with planning for the service under way, Susan felt lighter somehow and as she got up from the table and carried dishes to the sink, she found herself singing a little song.

All hands were on deck to clear the meal away and chatter around the kitchen sink was lighthearted and full of laughter.

An early night was in order after all the excitement of the day, but sleep did not come easily. Dave lay on his bed long into the night, trying to see in his mind's eye, what the countryside looked like in the place where his little plane lay all in pieces on the desert floor.

He remembered the sparse vegetation, the large rock that had taken one of the wings off his plane, and the stones and rocks that lay about on the ground, some of which had put paid to any hope of the landing gear ever operating again.

He remembered the slip of a girl, who had appeared out of nowhere, to scramble his brain and turn his life upside down. He wondered if he'd recognize the rocky outcrop that housed Tammy's incredible underground home. He struggled to recall any of the landmark features that he'd tried to embed in his memory, as he'd circled uselessly, looking for a safe place to put the plane down; a place that would ensure the safety of his four passengers.

He wondered again how they were, making a promise to himself that he'd call them up as soon as he could and tell them all about the way things had turned out.

So much was going on in his head that he was getting dizzy. So he scolded himself and decided to put it all out of his head. Then he realized that the best way to do that was to spend some time in prayer.

So he took a few moments to thank God for Tammy, for her family, so welcoming and so willing to take him in as a part of their close-knit circle. He gave thanks for Pete and Gayle, for their kindness in allowing this crazy diversion to their plans to give him a job, and for the home they were giving Tammy and him.

Then, as he still found himself trying to sort through stuff, he remembered how Tammy had always handed everything over to God and so he did that. Almost instantly, he felt the peace of God flow through him, and in no time was sound asleep.

Tammy had knelt by her bed for a few moments, and given it all to God. She asked Him to find the plane for them and look after them – and then, with her usual trust and faith, climbed into bed and instantly fell asleep.

She was awake early the next morning. Instantly wide awake, like a cat, even though it was hardly light. Dave too was up and about. As quietly as they could, they set about getting a light breakfast – and a coffee, whispered Tammy, with a little giggle.

Susan soon joined them, for she had set an alarm, not wanting to miss helping the kids get off okay.

She fussed about them, making sure that all was in order, even though they had it all in hand.

Soon enough, there was the sound of a vehicle outside and then a knock at the door.

Donald and Becky came out, rubbing sleep from their eyes, to bid farewell and wish them a successful endeavour, and then Dave and Tammy headed off down the stairs, to Troy's company vehicle.

They rode to the airport in silence, letting Troy handle the early morning traffic. The car, a late model Falcon, was comfortable. Automatic, with power steering, cruise control, climate control and all the latest gadgets and gizmos, the car whisked them along. In no time, they had arrived. Troy arranged to put the car into long-term parking and then they headed off for the jet.

Dave had to admit to being impressed with the plane. Small, it looked sleek and fast and he smiled a little as he mentally compared it to his own little craft. Not too much future in worrying about that, he thought.

The flight north was accomplished without fuss. The plane was, as she looked, fast. In-flight service was efficient. Dave was more than a little stunned that a hostess had been part of the deal.

Food and drink were available at the lift of a finger, but Dave and Tammy needed only the basics.

Mid afternoon saw them, as promised, nearing their destination. When they landed on the outback airstrip, they alighted from the plane to be greeted by their hosts.

Apologizing for the fact that they could not stay to chat, they were hustled to the waiting helicopter. A quick wave to the people who had been so kind, just a short time ago, and they were in the air again.

The pilot was experienced in outback flying, and seemed to know what he was about. He gave headphones to Dave and a pair to Tammy as well, to enable them to talk without shouting at each other over the racket of the helicopter.

Troy contented himself with being lookout. Completely untroubled, he had absolute confidence that they would achieve their objective, either this day, or the next, if it should be necessary.

In the jet, flying north from Brisbane, Dave and Troy had pored over the maps and charts, both those that Dave had brought along and those that Troy had organized.

So once they were in the air again, it was, according to Troy, a simple matter of working the grids and keeping a sharp eye out for familiar landmarks.

Once in the air and heading for the country that the group had traversed in their bid for rescue, Tammy began to experience feelings that she could not immediately describe. After a while, she began to realize that what she was feeling may have been homesickness.

She tried hard to dismiss these sensations as being fanciful and quite ridiculous, but despite her best efforts the feelings remained. So she determined that when they found the wreck, she would go to her home and maybe bring a few more keepsakes back with her – things to remind her – memories to take into her new life.

When she'd left her cavern on that fateful day, she had intended never to return. In many ways she found it difficult to comprehend that before this day was over, she may once again walk down that path.

In her mind's eye she saw herself entering that crevice, walking the dark corridor, climbing the stairs her father had painstakingly carved into the rock, and stepping over the threshold into the only home she had known for seventeen years.

The helicopter roared on. Deaf to all but the voices of the pilot and Dave in her earphones, Tammy tried to concentrate and to follow the grid pattern that they were flying.

So far nothing had appeared to be even remotely familiar; but then again, would she recognize anything from this perspective? Tammy didn't know. She fervently hoped that she would, because a lot rode on this for Dave and she longed to see this issue dealt with and put away once and for all.

Back and forth they flew, covering the squares of a grid pattern that had been carefully worked out and plotted. The pilot remarked that they were over the area, beneath which lay the most western part of the Great Artesian Basin. This vast underwater system is the largest of its type in the world and covers about 20% of the continent.

It lies beneath most of Queensland, the South East corner of the Northern Territory, the North East of South Australia and part of Northern New South Wales.

Environmentalists continually fight both governments and big business, to preserve the integrity of this precious source of underground water.

Tammy sat up straighter, looking out the window, sure that now, she would see something, anything at all that would give her a clue as to where they had come from.

Time wore on and the constant noise of the helicopter was beginning to have a numbing effect. Tammy's eyelids began to flutter and she feared that she'd drop off to sleep and miss something. So she sat up straighter, stretched a little, as much as one was able in this confined space, and took a few deep breaths. Dave handed her a bottle of water and she gratefully took a sip.

Mentally shaking herself, she turned her attention to the window once more and continued scanning the endless horizon for any recognizable landmark. Then, she saw it.

"Dave!" she cried. "Over there! See it? That's the oasis where we captured Joe and his friends! It is, isn't it? I'm sure of it! Look, I don't think they've capped the bore yet, because you can see steam rising, even from here."

The pilot brought his machine a little lower to the ground and circled a little more slowly.

"We can't stay up here much longer, folks," he said. "We'll need to be heading back in, oh, half an hour, three-quarters, tops, I'd reckon."

"Thank you, mate," said Dave. "But I think we are minutes from finding the wreck."

Checking the maps again, they located the artesian spring. As one of very few major springs in the vast landscape, it had rated a mention on the map as a waterhole of some significance. Dave noticed that the map called it a bore, which meant that someone, probably Tumberrumba's early pioneers had been there, a long time before them.

There was no way of knowing how long ago that might have been, but Dave was very grateful to those old bushmen, for without the lifesaving provision of that water they might never have made it home. He remembered how thankful they had all been to find such a perfect oasis, despite the dramas that were to follow.

Dave and Tammy both had a pretty good idea of the direction they had traveled on their way to the oasis, and so the pilot headed his chopper north-west from there, remarking that he hoped it wasn't far.

It seemed, however, that only minutes had passed and there it was, right beneath them. Not only that, but the series of strange little rocky hillocks that had led Dan to the cavern where he and his family had made their home, was off to the west of the wreck, the jagged little peaks sticking up out of the sparse bush-land surrounding them.

The trees that Tammy and her father had planted could be clearly seen, surrounding the fertilized ground near the entrance to the cavern. The vegetables had continued to grow. Tammy hoped that Barda's people would make good use of them.

The pilot swung his little machine around and settled her down on the dusty ground adjacent to the plane wreck. No one moved for some time. It seemed prudent to wait until the rotors stopped spinning and the dust settled. But that was not the main reason. It was as if, after all that had happened, it was almost surreal, to be here, where so much had ended and so much had begun.

Finally the rotors were still and the silence hung for a moment or two, as each wondered if in fact the sudden silence meant that they'd gone deaf. Then Dave roused himself from his almost trance like state and began to remove his headphones and undo his seatbelt.

The others followed suit and the pilot jumped out and ran around to open the door for his passengers.

"Okay folks. This is it, I guess – welcome to Miss Tammy's Centralian Resort," he joked, adding, "Golly, it sure is hot out here."

Soon all four of them were standing on the ground, looking around them.

For Dave, it was as if the weeks had simply vanished and he was standing there in the searing heat, looking in disbelief at the wreck of his plane, the end of his dreams. And for all he had known at the time, possibly his life. That was, until a vision had appeared before his eyes and things took a very different turn.

"Well, come on," he said to the insurance assessor. "Let's get this over with."

Together, they walked over to what was left of a small plane.

The assessor checked numbers and details against the paperwork he had in his possession, quickly verifying that this was indeed the machine that belonged to Dave. It was a simple matter to verify that it was lying in the empty spaces of the Australian bush and that it would never fly.

He was curious about a few pieces of scrap metal lying on the ground a few hundred yards away from the position of the wreck.

"What's that lot over there?" he asked.

"That's my dad's plane," Tammy replied softly. "That's pretty much all that's left of it. We used most of it to build our lives here. Strange as it may seem, we both crashed in almost exactly the same place, at almost exactly the same time of year, for the same reason – only, so many years apart," she added wistfully.

The pilot tipped his hat back off his head and said, simply, "Whew!"

Troy seemed to be a million miles away, then he turned to Tammy, "Was your dad's plane insured?" he asked.

"Why, yes, I think so," Tammy said hesitantly. "I think I recall hearing him and Mother speaking about that. Not that it mattered, in the long run. There hasn't been anyone to claim on it."

"Well, if you can find out who it was insured with, I'd be willing to vouch for it being here. Perhaps if I filled out a Statuary Declaration to the effect, then you could file a claim. The money might come in handy," he added.

"Well, come with me, and see my home," Tammy invited the pilot and the assessor. "Its just a little way up this pathway, toward that funny little jumble of rocks you can see there over there through the trees. Most of those Dad and I planted to give us some shade for the veggie garden," she said. "I'm surprised they still look so healthy. Anyway, come on, I can look through my father's papers. Maybe I'll find something useful," she said as she led the way.

Locking the chopper, although this more from habit, for he had no idea what could possibly happen to it way out here, the pilot and his fellow first-time visitor to this wild place, followed Tammy and Dave down a path that both had thought they'd seen for the last time.

The entrance to the cavern was exactly as Tammy remembered. The dark tunnel was negotiated easily with the aid of the pilot's torch, the steps, each cut out by hand with a small spade that her father had carried in the plane's tool kit, still there, just as they'd been when she had climbed them for the last time. And the sudden breathtaking beauty of the huge cavern with its bubbling stream still caused first-time viewers to gasp in amazement.

"Wow!" was the general consensus. "This is totally astounding," said the pilot. "Who would have imagined such a place even existed?"

Tammy led her guests down into her home and settled them into a comfy seat while she prepared refreshments. It seemed as if she'd been no further away than a hunting trip with her aboriginal friends. She wondered how they were, sure that if they were anywhere nearby, the sound of the helicopter would have sent them into hiding. She breathed a soft prayer for them, and asked God to continue to keep them in His care.

While her guests rested and enjoyed a cool drink, Tammy busied herself sorting and choosing which things she'd take back with her.

Though a priority now was to search among her parent's things, looking for papers that she may not even recognize.

"Dave," she called softly, "Will you come and look through these? I'm not sure I know what I'm looking for."

So Dave hurried into the room that Tammy's parents had made their own private space, and, trying to bury the feeling that he was somehow intruding on something very special and private, nevertheless set about searching through the remains of a man's life.

At the bottom of a box, that Tammy had needed to find a key for, Dave found a long, burgundy-coloured wallet, with official-looking documents in it. Sure enough, there were the registration papers, Dan's license to fly and a set of papers that looked very familiar to Dave.

"I don't believe this," he exclaimed. "You wouldn't credit it in a million years! Tammy, your Dad had his plane insured with the same lot that I did. Were you guys the only one's insuring light planes in those days?" he asked Troy, who had wandered in to see what the excitement was about.

"Let me see those," Troy said quickly. "Well, I'll be darned, will you look at that? Well, folks, I guess this will be a double-header. I can't see any reason why the company won't pay up on this one either," he said with his cheeky grin.

"Any hope of finding a serial number of any sort, miss?"

Tammy frowned for a moment as she searched her memory. "What sorts of parts would have the numbers on them?" she asked. Troy answered that any piece of mainframe, the engine, even the undercarriage should bear some sort of number, even if it was only a spare part number. "And hopefully that can be traced and verified," he added.

Well that information sent Tammy in search of a strange piece of equipment, set aside from the main household part of the cavern, to a corner, not so well lit, over the other side of the small creek that ran through the centre of the cave.

There she pulled a trolley out of the gloomy corner, to reveal what was obviously, to the aviators at least, the undercarriage of a light plane, albeit one that had undergone some modifications. Dave realized that Tammy's Dad must have been a pretty handy guy to have around, particularly in a tight spot. And, he mused, few spots were tighter than that which both he, and Dave himself, had found themselves and their unfortunate passengers.

"Dad took the undercarriage off the plane and made this out of it. We used it to carry stuff back and forth," Tammy said. "It seemed easier than carrying everything by hand, and made fewer trips necessary."

Leaping across the creek, with the energy and enthusiasm that they had come to recognize was Troy's way of doing everything, the young man ran over to Tammy.

"Let's see," he muttered to himself. "Somewhere here, there ought to be... Yep! Here it is! Terrific! Reckon that's all I'll need."

He turned to Tammy with his beaming smile. "Are you prepared to sign a Stat. Dec. to declare that this is indeed, you father's plane, or what's left of it?" he asked her.

"What's this Stat..., whatever you called it?" she asked.

"It's a legal document that people fill out and sign, to declare that something they can't prove any other way, is true," he explained.

"Well, yes, okay," said Tammy. "I'm happy to do that. There's no way it could be anything else. I don't see a hardware store anywhere near, do you?"

"No, I certainly do not," said Troy, laughing at the very idea. "Righto then, let's sit down at this amazing table of yours and do some paperwork. That okay with you?"

"Okay," said Tammy. She cleared away the few things that she had placed there, earlier, and sat down with Troy to fill out the necessary document.

He led her, with what each assumed was unusual patience, through the whole procedure, and she put down everything he told her to, in her neat, unhurried handwriting.

"Well, that's that," Troy said at last, beaming from ear to ear. "We'll have this wrapped up in no time at all," he added.

"I'll climb all over the boss until he Okays this. No one's going to mess with the old Troy on this one," he declared emphatically. "Both of you," he said, including Dave in his sweeping gesture, "Will benefit from this. I've no idea how much they'll cough up, but, hey, anything's better than what you've got now, I reckon."

Laughing at his enthusiasm, Tammy went back to packing. She suddenly felt a little lighter in her spirit and wondered how her Dad would have reacted to this energetic young insurance assessor.

Aware that space was a premium, Tammy finally selected only a few items, this time including one or two of her mother's keepsakes for Aunt Susan, placing them into a small bag that she found among her belongings. For a moment she fondled the bag, remembering the many times she had used it to bring home seeds for her garden, or the occasional bird's egg.

Finally, she indicated to Dave that she was ready to say goodbye for the last time, and they turned once more to the stairs. Everybody felt that something really good had been accomplished; even the chopper pilot felt the atmosphere.

As they headed to the entrance of the cavern, he came up behind Dave and gently laid a hand on his shoulder.

"This is good news, mate," he said. "I'm happy for you and the little lady. I reckon you two have a pretty good future in front of you. I wish you both the very best." At which he grinned a bit self-consciously, not used to expressing his feelings in that way.

Dave turned to him and looked into an open, honest face – the face of a brother pilot, who if anyone could, might understand the loss he had endured.

"Thanks mate," Dave said, lightly. "I appreciate that. And yes, I agree. I think the future that Tammy and I will have together will be all we could hope for. We wish you all the best too. Thanks for getting us here," he added.

Chapter 17

A SURPRISE FOR TAMMY

In single file, they found their way through the dark tunnel. Then, as they emerged from the crevice, into the fast fading sunshine, they discovered something that none of them had expected – to be greeted by a crowd.

"Stone the crows!" exclaimed the pilot. "What's this?"

"Barda!" screamed Tammy in delight. She ran to the slender figure at the head of the group and throwing caution and discretion to the wind, dropped her bags and flung her arms around him. She wept and laughed and then simply held him.

"Why did you come?" she asked him at last. He had patiently held her in his thin arms until her wave of emotion had passed.

"We saw you," he answered, in his simple and straightforward way. "We watched and we talked and we decided – it was time. We could not...," he paused... "You came back... to speak with you is a good thing," he finished.

Tammy smiled through the tears that still clouded her eyes.

"Shall I introduce you?" she asked him softly.

"This would be right," Barda answered in his formal way. So, Tammy turned to her companions and introduced her friend to them.

"This is Barda," she said. "He is tribal elder and chief to these people. They are nomadic aborigines, possibly one of the last such tribes still to be found out here.

Until my family arrived here, they had seen only glimpses of white people, from a distance, when their wanderings took them too close to civilization.

"It was their wish that we not reveal their presence when we were rescued. And I have kept that promise, Barda," she said, turning to her old friend. "None of us have told anyone about you and your people."

Tammy continued her story... "If it had not been for these gentle and noble people, my family may well have perished out here. My father knew the bush as well as any white man, but no one knows this land like these people do. They taught us so much, and when my parents died, they became like family to me. I love them dearly."

"Tammy has been like a child to us," Barda said. "It was sad to say goodbye. I have known for some time that our young people wanted to see 'out there'," he waved his hand in the direction from which the planes had come. "Now, it is time," this, with a slightly uncertain smile and a sigh.

Tammy hugged him again and smiled happily.

"Oh, Barda," she said softly, then, as she remembered something she added, "There is a young girl at Tumberrumba station, who overheard a couple of us speaking among ourselves. She said to me that she believes she is related to you. Apparently, her great-grandfather became separated from the tribe at some stage and, lost, he had wandered for days. He was found, half dead, by a stockman and taken to the station, where it seems he stayed and worked, and married a local girl. The family is still at the station. All of them work there, apparently there are quite a few. So if you went there, you'd find family."

"A-h-h, yes! Family is good," Barda said. "We will go. We will follow the way we travelled – we know where the road leads," this with a twinkle in his eye at Tammy's look of amazement. "When you left, we followed. It seemed good to know that you were safe. We saw the machine that carried you away. We went too, and saw the big hut – we remembered you spoke of a house, this is what you lived in, before you came to us?"

"Yes, Barda, a house," said Tammy. "You mean to say, you followed us all the way and never let us see you?"

"You were not looking back," he replied simply with a shrug of his thin shoulders.

"Hey, are these guys gonna be okay to walk all that distance?" asked the pilot. "It's a fair way."

Tammy and Dave laughed gaily and then apologized for their bad manners, explaining that Barda and his people walked everywhere, miles and miles out here in the bush. It was their home and they had roamed this vast area for many, many years.

"Thy will find their way. It may take a while as they travel only as fast as the smallest child can walk. But they will get there and we must prepare for them somehow."

Tammy could not figure out at this stage how this was going to work, but she felt that she needed to make sure that they would be okay before she could settle into her own new life.

"Dave...?"

"Its okay, Tammy," said Dave. "I understand. I will go on back to Brisbane, fix up about the planes and get our new home ready. When you feel that Barda and his people are settled, come on back and we'll get married; when you feel that the time is right. Just promise me that you'll come back to me?" he beseeched her.

"Oh, Dave, how could I not? You are everything to me. And this is so much a part of why I love you. You are such a good man. I love you and I will come to you, just as soon as I know that my dear, dear friends are okay."

Tammy explained to Barda that she would be waiting for them at Tumberrumba station. She told him that she would tell the station folk all about him and his people and that she would make sure they made the integration as easy as possible.

"I found it so hard, at first," she told Barda. "But, I know that you will be okay. Even though it will be very different," she added.

"Yes, this I know," said the old man. "But it is the right time. The young ones need to begin their new lives, just like you have." He smiled at Tammy, and she saw a small glimpse of uncertainty and even a tiny spark fear in his dark eyes.

But she knew that his gentle nature and kindness would endear him to everyone he met and that his quiet courage and willingness to do this for the sake of his tribe, would carry him through. She fervently hoped that people would treat him with the dignity that he deserved.

Finally, goodbyes were said, the pilot added the extra fuel he'd carried on board, and then the four of them boarded the noisy machine once more. As they lifted off, in the cloud of dust they left behind, Tammy saw the tribe watching them as they swung away from the crash site and headed for Tumberrumba. She watched until they were just a collection of tiny black specks in the distance and when she turned to Dave, he gently wiped a tear from her cheek.

"It's okay," he said softly. "They'll be fine, and so will you."

With no need now to search or navigate, they left the business of flying to the pilot and spent the return journey planning how this new development would fit into their own plans.

Tammy was more than a little concerned about getting back to Brisbane without Dave by her side, but he insisted that he would make sure she didn't have to do it alone, even if he had to come back and get her himself.

"You are going to be my wife, just as soon as it can be arranged," he said laughingly. "Don't think for a moment that I am going to leave the future Mrs Dave Wilson out here all alone.

I'll be waiting anxiously for word from you that all is well, and then I'll either be up here to fetch you or, if I can't get away from work, I'll arrange someone to accompany you.

I know that this big wide world is still pretty scary for you too," he finished as he drew her close to him and kissed her tenderly.

So, it was arranged. The helicopter delivered them all safely back to Tumberrumba station. The chopper pilot bid his passengers farewell, with a final warm hand-shake with Dave, before arranging to refuel and return to his base.

His weary passengers adjourned to the homestead for a good dose of country hospitality, before facing the flight back to the city.

Their hosts were pleased and more than a little surprised to see them both back in the area so soon, but understood the problem that Dave had faced with the insurance. They thought it all a little crazy that they should have to fly all the way out here, just to find a wreck, but who understands the workings of the mind of big business?

"Spend a fortune, chasing after rainbows, just to save a few lousy dollars, I reckon," commented their host.

His wife shushed him, saying it wasn't polite to speak this way in front of a guest.

The insurance assessor smiled his easy smile and told her not worry.

"You soon get a thick skin in this business, ma'am," he said. "Don't worry about it. Actually, I agree with you. Still, it's not my money, is it? Anyway, I reckon I've got all I need to see that Dave gets his money. And the lady too," he added. "I think I've got enough information to get the insurance on her Dad's plane too."

Dave mused that, somehow, being out here, and sharing the outback experience, changed people. Even he could hardly remember the hard-nosed, cocky and self-opinionated young man who had bull-dozed them with lightening fast arrangements, before they'd hardly had time to breathe.

What a difference just being out here and seeing all this, and sharing something of Tammy's story had made to him. He fervently hoped that when he got back to the rough and tumble of his business world, he would remember that people are real, and not numbers and they need to be treated with dignity.

Although he reckoned that most of Troy's brashness was more to do with youth, and that underneath it all, a pretty big heart just waited for a good cause to fight for.

And speaking of dignity, his thoughts turned to Barda and his people. So, once they'd all settled down with a drink and a meal, he and Tammy approached the subject with their hosts.

Amazed and fascinated, they promised to take very good care of these people. They had known that they were out there, of course, but no one had seen them for a very long time, and then only the briefest glimpse in the distance. The lady of the house called her little servant girl to her side and gently informed her of the turn of events.

With a little squeal of delight, she ran off to tell the other members of their family – just as quickly running back to apologize to her employer, with a 'beggin' your pardon ma'am'.

Her boss smiled indulgently and sent her off with a, "Quick, off you go."

In a few moments she was back, keen to know if it was going to be alright for them all to live around here.

Her employers assured her that, yes, it was fine. They were sure that the young men would make themselves useful, and one never turned away someone in need, anyway.

They didn't say too much to the girl, but both of them were pretty sure, that once they found their way, some of the younger ones would be venturing into the more civilized parts of the country.

They hoped to be able to teach them enough to keep them from falling into the traps that so many young aborigines fell into in the towns.

This was Tammy's greatest fear. Even in the short time that she had been in the city, and even in the small townships, she had seen the young men hanging about. Dave had explained to her how they seemed to have lost their way, saying that Barda's young ones were so much better off. Now, it seemed, they too were going to have to find their way in a very different place.

All too soon, so it seemed to Tammy, it was time for Dave and the young insurance fellow to board their plane and fly back to Brisbane. Dave really had to get back.

The final details of both insurance claims had to be settled and Dave had a new boss, patiently waiting for his new foreman.

Besides, he had a home to get ready for his bride-to-be.

A last long, lingering kiss, a desperate hug as Tammy clung to him, and then they were gone.

Over the next few days, Tammy kept herself busy around the homestead. Unable to sit still and be waited on, she insisted on sharing the chores with her hosts. So it was that the time went fairly quickly, although each morning and night she spent time in prayer, asking God to watch over her man. And also to watch over Barda and his people, as they travelled through that harsh country, toward an uncertain future. Then, after several days, a young aboriginal stockman came running up to the homestead.

"Missus! Missus!" he called. "They's comin'! They's comin'!"

Everybody dropped whatever it was they'd been doing, and headed for a vantage point to see the new arrivals. Tammy was first out the door, and it was she who ran out into the heat of the day, to greet her friends.

They had stopped some distance from the homestead, unsure of what they should do next, and so Tammy went out to greet them. Barda, ahead of his people, as always, greeted her warmly, and it was obvious that he was very relieved to see her there.

She had promised that she would be, but he had wondered if love for Dave would have overcome her. But, here she was, as promised, and it was good to see this little white girl who had become so much a part of his family.

While the tribe hung back, shy and uncertain, Tammy took Barda up to meet the Tumberrumba family. Introductions were made and everybody was so polite, in a way it was really quite amusing.

Then long lost members of the tribal families shyly came forward to meet their elder. They greeted him with great deference and respect, which pleased the old man, who had wondered if they might have forgotten the old ways.

Soon, everybody was milling around, language difficulties were being sorted out and stories of family were being shared.

The station owners had made living arrangements for the incoming tribe and their family members took them off to help them settle in. Barda was taken to the homestead, where he was welcomed as an honoured guest. He thanked his hosts simply and politely for their hospitality and promised that he and his people would not be a burden to them.

Arrangements for all sorts of things would need to be worked out over the next few days, but for now, it was sufficient that there was somewhere to sleep, somewhere to put their few belongings and food enough for all. Tammy had explained all she knew of the tribe and their habits in great detail.

She informed her hosts that she and her parents had taught these people many things about their culture. Also that they had taught them about God and His great love for all His people.

"Barda has given his life to the Lord," Tammy informed her hosts. "He and many of his people are Christians now, so please make sure they are included when you have worship services of any kind."

Her hosts promised to do that, and also promised Tammy that they would look after these wanderers from a past era.

"Please don't worry about them, dear," the lady of the house assured her. "We will make sure that they are provided for. There is work enough for willing hands, especially those who can be a little self-sufficient.

We will organize some schooling, too, so that when the day finally comes that they venture off into town for the first time, they will be prepared for what they'll find. We don't want the young ones going off the rails, either," she added.

Tammy stayed for a week after Barda and his family arrived at Tumberrumba station, but the day eventually arrived when she knew it was time to leave.

A phone call to Dave soon had travel arrangements organized and then all that remained was for Tammy to say goodbye. Dave had promised to come out and collect Tammy, so she went and packed the few belongings that she'd brought with her, and leaving the room clean and tidy, just the way she'd found it, made her way out to the bunkhouses to find her wilderness family.

Barda came out to meet her as she approached proof that even in these protected surroundings, the old chief was still keeping watch.

Smiling with obvious pleasure at seeing her again, he led her around to the rear of the two long buildings that housed both the regular station hands and the itinerant workers that arrived at various times.

As Tammy and Barda rounded the end of the longer building, the campsite came into view. Like everything else on this immaculate property, the camps were neat, and well placed beneath the shade of spreading trees. While the accommodation was very basic, it served the needs of people who had never acquired a taste for the luxuries of modern living.

Happy to live in the ways of their forebears, they cooked on fires outside their camps, using only the amenities in the bunkhouse.

Barda and his people had soon found where they fitted in best. Some had opted for trying one of the bunkhouses, while others had settled for one of the simpler, more familiar camps that had been constructed when the news came of their impending arrival.

As Tammy approached, a ring of smiling faces greeted her. Many of the children came running up to her, throwing their arms around her. Delighted, she assured Barda that it was really quite okay, for he had immediately attempted to reprimand the little ones for taking liberties.

But Tammy was honoured that the children remembered her and she hugged each one. Finally, they drifted off as their mothers called them away, and Tammy reluctantly relinquished them to their parents. Side by side, she and Barda toured each little camp, as Tammy sadly bid farewell to the people who had been such a big part of her life. There were a few little tears as the women each shyly came forward and received their hug. Hugging was not the way of their people, but they had learned enough from Tammy and her parents over the years, to know it was quite normal for them. So if it made Tammy happy, it made them happy too.

Finally, all the goodbyes were said, until only Barda remained.

"This will not be good-bye, Barda, my friend," Tammy said, as tears glistened in her eyes.

"I will see you again, I promise. I don't know when, or how. But, somehow, I feel in my heart, that this is not the end."

In the days that she had spent, helping out around the house, Tammy's mind had been full of thoughts about these people. She was afraid that, once they moved away to parts far from here, that they would lose their roots and fall prey to excesses of a society that, she had soon learned, ate up the unwary in a moment.

Slowly, an idea had been forming in her mind. She had no idea how she would bring it all to pass, but, with the quiet determination that had secured her survival after her father's death, she was certain, that one day, somehow, she would be back here. And her being here would be 'coming home'.

Oh yes, she knew that family were far away, in Brisbane. She knew how much they loved her, and how much she loved them. But, still, her heart belonged out here, in this wide, brown land. And she knew, as surely as day followed night, that one day she would return.

Another brief hug, another assurance that, one day they'd meet again, and Tammy turned toward the homestead.

A familiar figure was standing on the verandah, and she ran towards him with love in her heart and joy on her face for all the world to see.

The journey home with Dave was uneventful. Their hosts had driven them to the airstrip, where a light plane waited. When she saw it, Tammy looked at Dave, with a little frown on her face, and he smiled at her, reassuringly.

"It's okay, love," he said gently. "I hired her. We'll station-hop to Rockhampton, and then we'll fly home in something just a bit bigger. I can still fly, you know. And the weather is fine this time of the year," he added.

So, more than a little apprehensively, Tammy allowed Dave to guide her up the steps into the small plane. She wasn't too happy about it, but didn't want Dave to see how badly her heart and her stomach were flip-flopping about. She was quite sure they changed places more than once.

Dave settled in behind the controls and after the necessary pre-flight checks, soon had the little craft in the air. The take-off had been smooth and seemingly effortless, and the plane appeared almost to fly itself.

Dave explained that it was much more modern than his old one and much easier to fly.

"It's a breeze," he said, as he looked across at her. "No worries, sweetheart. Honest."

Tammy had thought she'd never want to go up in one those flimsy little gadgets, ever again, but Dave's capable handling of the plane, and the comforting sound of its powerful engine, soon lulled her fears. She began to relax and enjoy the scenery.

This was country she had never seen before, and the nearer they drew to the coast of Queensland, the more beautiful that scenery became. Each of the stations and then the smaller properties they called into, welcomed them warmly and provided for their needs.

Tammy never failed to appreciate the open-handed generosity of people, who were often not as well off as the general populace might imagine. Yes, they were asset rich, but then, who can eat a big homestead and a few thousand acres of arid land?

Nevertheless, it was the way of outback folk to welcome visitors and to make sure that guests had all they could need.

A few hours later, and Dave had parked the little plane that had carried them so capably across one state and a fair slab of another. He quickly dealt with the necessary paper-work, handed over the keys, shook the hand of the agent, and then, dragging their bags out of the plane, found a trolley to carry them to the terminal.

Here, Tammy's mind went into yet another whirl, as she saw the size of the plane that would take them to Brisbane. Dave already had the tickets, and their baggage was only of the carry on variety, so all that remained was to board this enormous machine.

Tammy was glad that Dave had taken most of the things she had brought from the cave, with him, when he and the insurance guy had flown home, several weeks earlier.

As the plane covered the miles to home, Dave brought her up to date on all that had happened since they had parted.

He had started work at the farm and was enjoying it immensely. Pete and his wife were good folks to work for and appreciated all that he did.

The house was proving to be comfortable, but missed, he insisted, a woman's touch.

"Soon, my darling," he said as he held her hand and looked into her eyes, "Soon we'll be together, man and wife, in our new home."

Tammy remembered well, the tell-tale flutter of her heart, from the very first time he had looked at her in that way. So when her heart took flight, it was not a new feeling, but rather, familiar. And not only that, she realized, it was welcome. Finally, she thought, finally, all the interruptions and nonsense were over, and she and this man she loved, could begin their lives together.

Refreshments were served on this big plane, but Tammy secretly thought that they were not a patch on that which they had enjoyed on the insurance company's corporate jet. Still, she smiled to herself, they could afford it. After all, they were certainly not quick to hand over a claim.

Maybe that wasn't fair, she chided herself. And so she asked Dave what had happened with regard to the planes.

'Well, darling," he said with a smile. "It looks like it's going to be okay. The manager was a little more obliging when I went to see him. I guess he didn't want to risk having me climb all over his desk.

"We have to go and see them when we get back. I've got to come into town on some errands for Pete next week, so I'll come to the house and pick you up. Then we can go and sign whatever it is they want, and hopefully, that will be it. The cheques, as they say, should be in the mail."

Tammy hadn't heard that expression, so she missed the irony in Dave's voice. But her small frown, so familiar and so dear, that always came to her face when modern life puzzled her, soon had him explaining that it was one of those things that had become a bit of a joke around the business world.

"Most people recognize it as a way to fob someone off, if you haven't paid a bill. It buys some time. When times are tough, sometimes businesses have to wait for someone to pay them, before they can pay the things that they owe. It can be hard."

"Yes, I think I understand that. Running a business would be difficult, wouldn't it? I do hope that Bob, Viv, Gary and Marian don't have to tell someone that 'the cheque's in the mail', too often," she said, looking at Dave and smiling with a twinkle in her eye.

"I'm sure they'll be fine," Dave said, laughing and giving her a hug. "Gary's been sort of running a backyard business for a number of years, so he told me one day. It had always been his dream to give up his dead-end job and give his little business a go full-time. I'm sure he will be very good at it. And Bob seems like the kind who could turn his hand to pretty much anything."

The plane landed in Brisbane, and Tammy marveled at how much flying she had done in the last few weeks. First a small jet, then a helicopter, then a light plane and now an airliner. Wow! It was enough to make a desert-dweller like herself, positively giddy.

Because they had no luggage to collect, Dave and Tammy were through the queue and out of the airport in no time. Brisbane had turned on its usual muggy heat, so when they found Dave's battered old wagon, they were glad to get the air-conditioning cranked up.

Tammy was amused to see that the vehicle was unusually clean and realized that Dave had been busy.

As she climbed up into the passenger seat, she noticed that not only had the car been washed, but Dave had obviously cleaned the inside too. The somewhat threadbare carpet was spotlessly clean, and the accumulated rubbish from years bashing around the outback, had all mysteriously disappeared.

With a little smile she remembered the mock-serious disposal of the battered and obsolete street directory, at a service station, somewhere in the suburbs of a city that was nothing like Dave had remembered.

Susan and Becky were waiting on the front porch for them when, stiff and sore from sitting so long, they pulled themselves wearily out of the car.

Tammy stretched and flexed her back and legs, before running quickly and lightly up the stairs to greet them.

"Oh, it's so good to be back," she cried. "I've missed you all so much."

"As we have missed you too, darling," her aunt said, as she wrapped her in a welcoming hug.

"How did it all go? We were surprised when Dave told us what happened. Are your friends settling in okay? Fancy you not saying a word about people who had been such a big part of your life."

"I'm sorry, Aunt Susan, but I had made a promise to Barda that I would never mention them. It was never meant to be any sort of insult to you. Of course I know you never would have given them away. But the more people who know, the easier it is to let something slip."

"Yes, of course. I do understand. You had to honour your promise. Just like your parents, aren't you? True and straight as a dye," her aunt said, kissing the top of her head.

Tammy looked up at her and saw the tell-tale tears in her eyes. "Oh Aunt Susan, I love you," she said. "I brought some of Mum's things for you to keep. I thought that you might like them. I had to leave them when we left to walk out, because we simply couldn't carry anything that wasn't absolutely necessary for our survival. But this time..." Running to her room for the bag that Dave had brought back earlier, she began digging around inside it.

He smiled as he watched her go, and turning to Susan, gave her a wink. She smiled back at him, and her heart was glad.

She was happy for both of them, that they had found the same kind of love that her sister had found with her Dan, and that which she had found with Donald. She sighed softly.

With a small cry of satisfaction, Tammy finally found the small pouch she'd been searching for, and hurrying back into the room, carried it across to her aunt.

"Aunt Susan, I want you to have these. I have other things to keep," she added quickly, as she sensed her aunt about to protest. "I want you to have these," she insisted. "Mum would have wanted you to have them."

Susan took them, and with a quick hug for her niece, went to a chair, sat down, and gently began to open the pouch. Inside she found brooches and a pendant and some rings. She looked up enquiringly at Tammy, who smiled and reassured her that she had her mother's wedding and engagement rings.

"These are dress rings that she wore on special occasions, she told me," Tammy said.

"I'm sure I'll never use them, and I really want you to have them, okay? You can wear them for the memorial service, and my wedding!" she added.

"Okay," said her aunt. "Bless you, my dear girl. How sweet of you to think of this. You are so like your mother, it is almost like having her back in this house."

Susan sat there for a moment, as tears fell unchecked. But soon, she regained her composure and insisted on being brought up to date with all the news.

So over a cuppa, and later, over the evening meal and beyond, Dave and Tammy talked of all that had transpired since they had left to find a plane wreck in the desert.

The next morning, Dave said his farewells to his beautiful fiancé, as she was officially now, because amid great squeals of delight, he had presented her with a ring the night before. The station family had watched it all and smiled at their joy before leaving them alone to savour the moment.

Tammy knew, that when the time was right, she'd wear her mother's rings too; but not yet. Time enough for that when she and Dave were man and wife.

She waved him off from the front porch of the house, as he backed the big 4x4 out of the driveway and rumbled off down the street. As if transfixed, she stood there a moment, until she could no longer hear the car, then, with a little sigh she turned and went back into the house.

The next morning dawned bright and clear, and after a hearty breakfast, aunt Susan was full of plans for the day.

"Dave is coming in to town later, on some business for Pete," she told her niece, "So that will give us time to go and do some shopping before we meet him for some lunch and then go to this wretched insurance company. The sooner this is all settled the better, if you ask me," she added impatiently. "So what's this about your Dad's plane?" she asked.

"Well, Troy saw the last of the wreckage, and asked what it was. So when I told him it was our plane, he reckoned that we should be able to claim insurance for that one too, if I had some proof that it was insured.

"He said he would vouch for us to whatever company it was insured with. But, amazingly, it was insured with his company. I was able to find the papers, with Dave's help. So Troy was quite sure that he would be able to push it through and get me a payout for it. He's really quite nice, when you get to know him," she added.

"Well, that's great," her aunt said. "Now darling, drink up," this concerning the coffee that Tammy had learned to linger over and savour. "We must be off if I'm going to fit you out with a complete new wardrobe. We can't have the wife of a foreman going around in borrowed clothes, now can we?

"And," she added with a smile, "you can't get married in that thing," she said, indicating the simple frock that one of her outback hostesses had given her, which, possessing very little else, Tammy had worn almost continuously since her rescue.

So, without too much time to think, Tammy had been packed off to finish getting ready, and then bundled into the car for a trip to one of the big shopping complexes that were now scattered about this busy sprawling sub-tropical city.

What was left of the morning, was enough to leave even Tammy exhausted. Her aunt was a veritable whirlwind when she was on a mission.

She whisked Tammy from store to store, until she had fitted her out with a wardrobe of clothes, suitable for a young woman just starting out in life. Very much aware that Becky would heap scorn on her choices if she wasn't very careful, Susan had been mindful of the advice of the youthful shop assistants. And, of course, she had managed to curb her enthusiasm long enough to let Tammy decide what she liked and disliked. Consequently, two tired but happy ladies, met Dave at the appointed café for a late lunch. Tammy regaled him with tales of all the beautiful clothes that her aunt had insisted on buying for her. She commented that she did not know how she would ever repay her, but her aunt insisted that they were a gift for the child of her beloved sister, and she would not even hear of ever being paid back.

Leaning across the corner of the table, dodging the remains of their lunch, Tammy gave her aunt a great big hug, telling her again, how much she loved her.

This aunt was very different to her mother in many ways. But there were glimpses of Betty, now and then. Sometimes they came unexpectedly, and Tammy found them poignant and she would feel a little catch in the back of her throat.

Yet, in the same instant, she welcomed them, for they made her feel as if she really did belong in this family that had absorbed both her and Dave.

After lunch the three of them headed for the insurance company offices. Dave had finished his business for his new employer, calling him on the mobile phone he had given him as part of the equipment he would need to run the property.

Pete told him to take whatever time he needed to finalize the issue, declaring loudly enough that the ladies could hear him, 'not to take any nonsense from that lot and to make sure that he got all that they owed him.' Covering their mouths to prevent the laughter that bubbled up, they struggled to remain quiet until Dave had finished his phone-call.

"Bless his big heart," said Susan. "He's such a dear. I expect that he's had more than one run-in with an insurance company in his day.

"Big business seems to want to put it over on the man on the land. As if they don't do it tough enough as it is," she finished angrily.

Dave agreed, and was retelling a tale of woe that Pete had shared with him, about another insurance company – something to do with some farming machinery that had been vandalized, as they arrived at the front of the insurance building. An imposing façade fronted the street and a bank of lifts offered an easy ride up the many floors to the offices occupied by the company.

The three of them exited the lift and headed down the now-familiar hallway, to the glass doors at the end. An efficient-looking receptionist greeted them with a formal smile and reached for a phone to let the manager know they had arrived. Dave had insisted on speaking with no one else but the manager. He wanted this finalized, and he wanted it done soon. He'd had just about enough of the carry-on.

The manager was a little hesitant about meeting Dave again, and greeted him cautiously. Despite herself, there was something about the man that Tammy did not like, and she guessed that discovering yet another claim on his desk did little to improve his demeanor.

However, despite any misgivings that the trio might have had, the manager had good news. The board had looked over the claims and decided, reluctantly, Tammy felt, that they must be honoured.

"Of course, you realize that the age of the planes, especially your father's, young lady," this to Tammy, "Must mean that any payout will not represent the value of such a plane on today's market," he began.

"We are well aware of that, sir,' Dave said quietly, "We only want a fair and equitable return on the investments made into purchasing them. What do you have for us, and can we finalize it today? I have a new job to get back to, and a very patient new employer who has done all he can and more to assist me in this matter. I really need to be able to go back and tell him that it is all finally settled."

"Yes, um, of course." muttered the manager. He stood up from his chair and came around the desk. "If you'll come with me, I'll take you to the claims department. I understand that they have cheques drawn for the two of you. All that should be required is your signatures."

He quickly ducked his head and headed out the office door. Dave, Tammy and Susan quickly got up and followed him, somewhat confused.

"What's up with him?" whispered Susan. "You must have him thoroughly rattled, Dave," she giggled, quickly stifling her laughter, lest someone hear her. Tammy really didn't know what was happening. She was thoroughly confused by the whole process and simply followed Dave and her aunt, hoping that this wouldn't take too long. She'd had quite enough of the city for one day.

The manager pulled open a door at the end of another long corridor, and ushered his clients into another office. This was a large room, where, it seemed to Tammy dozens of people, mostly women, sat at computers – all in horrid little cubicles that she would have found most oppressive and claustrophobic.

One of these girls came up to the front desk and with a questioning look at her boss, requested how she might be of assistance. The manager told her who these people were and said that she was to see to it that their claim was finalized immediately.

Sensing that there seemed to be a measure of urgency about this, she assured the manager that she would deal with it straight away. Seemingly satisfied, he nodded to the three of them, excused himself with a muttered, "Cherie will see to everything, I'm sure you'll find it all satisfactory," and hastened out the door without a backwards glance.

Cherie, for that was the name on the girl's uniform, smiled at Dave and Tammy and with a conspiratorial air, whispered that he really needed to learn some people skills.

"Now," she said all business like. "Let's see what the computer tells me." She busied herself with a keyboard on the counter, clicking away busily for a few moments. With a 'mmm' now and then and a frown or two. Finally, she looked up and smiled.

"Right!" she said, with the satisfied air of one who has solved a major problem entirely on her own. "If you'll excuse me for just a minute or two more," she said sweetly, "I'll be right back."

She hurried off, leaving them standing there, wondering what was happening. But, to their obvious relief, she was true to her word and gone only a moment. When she returned to the counter, she was beaming and carrying with her a couple of folders. Laying them down on the counter, she opened them up and took a paper off the top of each.

"This one is for you," she said to Dave. "And this one is yours, love," she said to Tammy. "Sign these for me, if you'll be so kind. Sign here," she said, indicating a dotted line, "and here, here, here and here. And, likewise for you, miss. Here, here, here and here." She then took another piece of paper from each file and got them to sign again; just the once each this time.

Then, with a flourish, worthy of a showman or magician, she produced two cheques, one each of which she gave to Dave and to Tammy.

Taking a book from the counter, she turned a page or two then swung the book around to face her clients.

"Just sign here," this to Dave. "And here," (this to Tammy) "That's just to say that you received the cheque," she explained.

"Well, that should be it, I think." Cherie said with a smile. "I hope that you will both be satisfied with the settlement. I'm sure it's the best they could do. Umm, difficult circumstances, I'm sure you understand."

Dave looked at his cheque and raised one eyebrow a little. He said nothing, however, except to thank Cherie for her help, before ushering his two ladies out of the office. Once in the hallway, he allowed himself a little smile and no more, until they were out in the street.

At which time he allowed himself a huge "Yippee!" of delight, and little jig.

Conservative city folk, not usually given to such outbursts, looked in amusement as they jostled past. But Dave did not care. The payout for his poor misshapen plane was far more than he could have hoped, and he didn't care if it was 'fair and equitable' or anything else. Suffice to say that it would be quite enough to start him and Tammy off with a modicum of comfort.

Tammy, meanwhile, was looking at her cheque, trying to figure out how many zeros there were, and what they all meant. It had never occurred to her that her father's plane might yield some money, and she really had very little idea of the value of things.

To her knowledge, she had never purchased anything in her life. It is possible that her mother had allowed her to buy an ice-cream or lolly for herself as a child, but no memory of this had survived the intervening years.

Slowly, she handed the cheque to Dave, and looked up at him with that so familiar little frown. Smiling, he took it from her, read it, and nodded in satisfaction.

The amount was only marginally less than his own and he was pleased for Tammy.

Obviously, receiving an insurance pay-out for the wrecked plane would never compensate Tammy for the loss of her parents – or for the life she might have shared with them, had they survived. But at least it would help take some immediate pressure off their plans for a new beginning. And with a little care and some careful investment, a nice little nest-egg should grow.

"That is a very fair amount," he said to her with a smile. "You should be able to put that away and save something for our future. There are ways to invest money safely and to let it grow, until it becomes a larger amount.

"Life in the civilized world needs quite a bit of money, and this will help us get started in our lives together. We've done well."

With that, Dave looked at his watch and, with a start, commented that he'd better get going.

"I've wasted enough of Pete's time," he said. "I must head back to the farm. You two ladies take care, now. I'll call you tonight, darling," he called to Tammy as he pulled reluctantly out of her grasp and ran off down the street.

Tammy watched with a smile as he dashed off. Every few steps he would give a little skip, and her heart was glad that he was so happy. She had very little idea of what had just transpired. But, if it made Dave happy, then it was good, and that was all that mattered.

Aunt Susan suggested that they had better start for home, too. We can put that in our local bank for now," she said. "We'll open an account for you, in your own name, and you can make your very first bank deposit. What you and Dave decide to do with it later is your business, but for now, it will be safer tucked away in the bank."

That all seemed to make sense to Tammy, so she gladly allowed herself to be shepherded back to the car for the journey home.

A visit to the bank at their local shopping centre, soon had Tammy's account open, and the cheque safely deposited. Then, picking up some milk and bread from the corner store, they headed for home.

Shopping for the approaching wedding would have to wait for another day. Neither Susan nor Tammy had any energy left for such an important task and Tammy was happy when they turned into the street and the house finally came into view. Don and Becky were home already and wondering when they'd arrive, so they were glad to see them.

Both were pleased too, when Susan explained that Tammy and Dave had received decent pay-outs for the planes, and that Tammy's was safely in the bank, in a brand new account bearing her name.

It seemed like an appropriate time for a small celebration, so Susan prepared a special meal and Don opened a bottle of non-alcoholic wine, the only kind they kept in the house, and they toasted Tammy's and Dave's future together.

So much had been happening that wedding plans had been pushed to the back of everybody's minds. But with the drama surrounding the insurance, now out of the way, Susan's mind was very much back on track.

She and Tammy spent hours over the next few weeks, planning everything. Dave came home each weekend – time Pete insisted he take, until he and the little lady were married – and would take part in the discussions. Not too much though. He was wise enough to know that this was very much women's business, and contributed only when he was asked. He and Don had come to some sort of arrangement regarding who paid for what and neither troubled the girls with the details.

"Sufficient for you to know that all is taken care of, my dear." said an emphatic Uncle Don.

So it was that the household was consumed with dresses, suits, invitations, place names, a cake, a venue, music, and all the myriad details that weddings involve.

Family members had responded to emails and visits were arranged. It seemed to Tammy that she met someone new almost every day, and sometimes her head swam with it all.

But one Friday, all the busyness stopped as the family gathered in the small church that the family had always attended, to say goodbye to Dan and to Betty.

The service, conducted by their kind and gentle minister, was moving and beautiful. The lives of two very special people were remembered, reminisced over, and enjoyed again as memories of the funny little things were shared and laughed over. Tears were shed, songs were sung and love was celebrated.

A family, joined together as one, said their last goodbyes to loved ones that most of them knew they'd meet again some day.

On the way home, all agreed that it had been well worth doing, and although a bucket of tears had been cried, it had been the beginning of real healing for each of them, but especially for Susan, who – never knowing for certain – had never really been able to say goodbye. At last she felt that she could move on with her life. And she had a wedding to plan.

Chapter 18
WEDDING PLANS

One weekend, Dave arrived home from the farm with some news.

"I've tracked down my daughter," he announced to the family at dinner.

"Oh, Dave, I'm so happy for you," cried Tammy joyfully. "Are we going to be able to meet her?

"Well, yes, actually I have met her already," he added with a funny little smile. "Donna, that's my ex-wife, seems to have forgiven me for everything, although I'm not too sure why," he commented, half to himself.

"Anyway, the upshot of it all was that she came out to the farm during the week to see me, and she brought Marlene with her.

"She's eight now and quite the young lady, who, it seems has managed quite well without me. Although," Dave added, "She hasn't been without a father. Donna re-married a year or so after Marlene was born and it appears they are all very happy."

"I've, um-m, invited her, Marlene, that is, to the wedding. Is that okay?" he asked a little hesitantly.

"Oh darling, of course it's okay. It's more than okay, it's wonderful. I can't wait to meet her." said Tammy.

"Well, this is just absolutely marvelous," The whole family is going to be there. I'm so happy for you, Dave. What's she like, is she like you?" asked Susan.

"Thankfully, no." said Dave. "She's pretty, like her mother, but I think she's got a bit of an adventurous spirit. Her mum says she's anxious to be old enough to go orienteering and abseiling and stuff like that. Says she wants to learn to fly when she's old enough, and has declared to all and sundry that she intends to join the Air Cadets as soon as she's fifteen."

"Like father, like daughter, sounds like," commented Susan.

Dave then dug a photo out of his wallet and showed it around. Each of them looked at a young girl looking back at them, with a clear, direct expression. She was pretty, and if that was her mother in the photo, almost exactly like her.

"She has a sister and a brother now, so with three lively kids in the house, Donna's pretty busy. I'm so happy for her, I could never have given her all she has now." said Dave.

He walked over to Tammy and took her in his arms, holding her close for a moment, as if to reassure himself that she was real.

"Are you really okay with this, darling?" he asked. "I sort of jumped the gun a bit, I was so excited to meet her, and all," he finished lamely.

"Dave," reassured Tammy, softly. "Of course it's okay. I'm fine, really. I'm just so happy for you. It is good to have the matter settled once and for all. And I'm really looking forward to meeting her."

So it was settled and Becky hurried off to make another place card, rushing back in only a moment to make sure she had the spelling right.

Bob, Viv, Gary and Marian had been sent invites and had responded with great glee. They descended on the household one weekend, quite unannounced, much to Tammy's delight. There was so much to talk about, even though phone calls had not been infrequent, but it seemed so much better face to face.

Introductions were made to the family and it seemed like everyone had to talk at once, to share all that had happened since they'd parted. Dave decided that this was an appropriate time to refund these dear people their fares for their eventful ride in his plane.

But each of them flatly refused to take anything, declaring as one voice, that it had turned out to be the most momentous occasion of their whole lives, turning them completely around.

"If we hadn't gone on that flight, we wouldn't have met you, Dave, or Tammy. And we wouldn't have found the Lord, and we wouldn't have our little business going."

Marian stopped finally for a breath, and Viv took up the tale. "My goodness, Dave," she said. "If we hadn't gone with you, I don't know where we'd be now. As far as I'm concerned, it's the best day's work we ever did. Right guys?" she demanded of the other three. Each one nodded energetically, murmuring their agreement.

"Under no circumstances are we going to take money off you," said Gary. "Right, Bob?" he asked his brother-in-law.

"Absolutely!" agreed Bob. "And that, my good man is absolutely final!" he finished.

Dave got a bit choked up at that point, and found it hard to find his tongue. But eventually he managed to compose himself and thanked them all most profusely. But they would not hear of that either and declared the subject closed. It was the four of them, not Dave, who needed to say thank-you, they insisted.

So, finally, conversation turned to other matters and questions about the new business venture were fired thick and fast. Amid much laughter as each one tried to tell their own story, Tammy and Dave finally found out, that after a few teething problems getting it all off the ground, it was now going like a house on fire and the whole family were involved.

"In fact," declared Marian. "The kids are all going to keep the work happening while we are here for the wedding. They have been really enthusiastic from the beginning, and have pitched right in to help get it going. It hasn't even taken them long to learn the ropes," she added proudly.

"None of us can quite believe how well it's going. I never would have imagined there would be such a demand for things made by hand, in wood," said Bob.

"We are making toys, puzzles, games, nick-knacks, ornaments and small pieces of furniture. The boys have learned to use a lathe and have designed some really nice, ornamental legs for coffee tables and stools. The girls varnish and polish and paint designs on things. We design, print and cut stencils out of special adhesive material to stick on some of the surfaces. And people just love them. We are busy all the time," he said.

"We've had to remodel the front of our house, and add a shop-front, to display the stock," added Marian. "We've got an almost constant stream of people coming to look, order and buy stuff. It's really very exciting."

"We've even got some local churches buying from us," Viv put in. "We make offering plates, crosses, chalices and communion trays. It's quite a little business on its own," she finished.

Tammy and Dave were thrilled and explained to Susan and Don how, after finally being rescued, the two families had decided to change their complete lifestyle, throw in jobs they hated and start a family business together.

"We are so happy for all of you,' said Dave. "It seems like it was just the right time. And it's absolutely marvelous that you'll be available for the wedding."

"Yes, that's right," cut in Tammy. "Because, my dears we want to ask you a huge favour."

"Viv, Marian, will you both be Matrons-of-honour, for me?"

Amid squeals of delight, both of them jumped out of their chairs and ran to Tammy, hugging her till she thought she'd break. Pandemonium reigned for several moments as the three women, locked together in a group hug, danced around the room.

Susan, Becky and the men-folk looked on with smiles as wide as all outdoors on their faces. Susan was so happy for Tammy. And she could see so clearly the bond that had been forged between these people who had all experienced so much together.

Her own heart was filled with a special joy, because Tammy had come to her one day, and taking her aside from yet another task, had said to her,

"Aunt Susan, I want you to understand something. When I walk down that aisle, I want Uncle Don on my arm, to give me away, and I want you to stand with him, as Mother of the Bride. And when the minister asks who gives this woman...? I want both of you to answer."

With tears of love, Susan had looked into the beautiful eyes of her niece, seeing her sister's eyes, and had taken her in her arms and held her gently for several moments before answering.

With tears of joy and emotion making it difficult to speak, she somehow managed to say how very, very proud she would be and how happy she would be to take that role.

"You will never know how much joy you have brought to my tired and weary heart, dearest child," she finally managed. "I had thought that the sadness in my soul would never heal, but your love has been like healing balm. May God bless you, darling, and may He bring you many, many years of happiness and fulfillment, in you new life with Dave."

Finally, when order was restored, Tammy had grabbed Susan, Viv, Marian and Becky and had taken them aside to look at designs for dresses that she had drawn. When the others exclaimed in wonder at the beautiful designs, she explained that her mother had taught her to draw.

"She would tell me stories from the books back home. But because she didn't have them, I think she made up most of the stories. She said that as we didn't have pictures, like in a regular book, we'd have to make our own. So we'd sit for hours and draw pictures to go with the stories.

"I learned to love drawing, and together we'd design dresses for fairy princesses and wedding gowns for the heroines, and we made books."

"Where did you get paper?" someone asked. "We made it," Tammy replied. "We soon found that Mum's and Dad's little notebooks didn't go far," she giggled. "So we found a way to make paper out of all sorts of leaves and grasses. It isn't really all that hard," she added.

"I did bring one or two, when we went back to find the plane," Tammy said shyly. "Remind me some time to show you."

Everybody immediately clamoured to see them right then, so giving in to her family she went off to find them.

She came back into the room with two little books, neatly bound in vinyl from a plane seat, with the pages tied in with what looked like plaited grass. Flowers had been pressed and then stuck on to the covers, with, as Tammy explained a glue they made from a variety of ingredients they'd found out there. It seemed that sap from a particular tree was part of it.

The family passed them gently from hand to hand and in stunned silence, took in the intricate drawings and the neat hand-writing.

The stories were mostly familiar, with a few additions that her mother had put in when memory failed her. The drawings were beautiful.

"These are precious, Tammy," said her aunt. "You must keep these somewhere safe for your own children. They will be a priceless heirloom in years to come."

"Do you really think so?" asked Tammy in surprise. The last thing she had thought of was that they had any real value, except as something to remember those precious times with her mother.

"I'll find a box for you to keep them in, darling," said Susan. "These are too beautiful to have them damaged in any way. What are they drawn with?" she asked.

"Mostly in pen," Tammy said. ""But when the ink finally ran out of all the pens Mum and Dad had with them, we made pens out of sticks and ink out of all the different things that Barda and his people used for their ceremonial body paint. It worked quite well. I hope it doesn't fade," she added.

"Perhaps we should think about taking them to someone and having some lacquer painted over them, to preserve them," said Susan.

"Well, look no further," said Marian. "We can do that for you. We have all the gear at home and we would consider it a privilege to help preserve such beautiful little books. Will you let us take them home and bring them back when we come to the wedding?" she asked.

"Yes, of course," replied Tammy. "I would trust you all with my life," she added simply.

And so it was decided. Susan went off to find a suitable box, returning without much delay with just the thing. She fetched some tissue paper and tenderly wrapped the two little books before placing them in the box. Then she taped the box closed and gave it to Marian.

"Guard this with great care, won't you?" she asked.

"I will treat it as I would one of my most precious possessions," she promised.

"Now, speaking of Barda," piped up Viv. "I thought we weren't supposed to say anything?"

Tammy apologized profusely, that she had not had the opportunity to bring them up to date on all that had happened. So she immediately began to tell them how Barda and his people had been there to meet them as they came out of the cavern.

"They have decided it is time to come out of the bush," she said. "So they are all at Tumberrumba Station, now. That is why I was gone so long," she explained. "I waited for them to walk in. Dave said I could wait for them, so there would be a familiar face among all the strangers.

"I hated to leave them again. But I know they are in good hands, and I will get back to see them one day, I know that in my heart," she added.

"You mean we don't have to keep quiet about them anymore?" asked Bob.

"No, it's fine now." said Tammy. "But, don't make too much of a song and dance about it. We really don't want the press involved." suggested Tammy.

Everybody agreed that made perfect sense, but were anxious to know all the latest regarding their welfare. Tammy had been keeping pretty close tabs on the happenings out at Tumberrumba, and sometimes she fairly ached to be out there, helping them all find their way. But with so much going on in her life, such a thing was quite out of the question, so saying nothing more about it she had tucked it into the back of her mind, getting on with all she had to attend to. And with a wedding in the very near future, there was certainly plenty to occupy her. But the thought of going back there some day would never leave her. She knew, deep in her heart, that one day...

The four friends could stay only a day or so, and all too soon were heading back to Sydney, with promises to see everybody soon.

"We'll be back here with bells on," said Viv. "There's no way we are going to miss the occasion of a lifetime. And we'll have your little books all fixed up, you wait and see."

So with last hugs and kisses and last waves as the taxi whizzed them off to the airport, they were gone. The house seemed strangely quiet after all the excitement.

But there were still lots of things to do, so no one really had much time to dwell on anything except the particular task at hand.

Life went on, and bit by bit, each job was ticked off Aunt Susan's list. Until, at last everything was ready. And the day was drawing near.

At last the wedding day dawned bright and clear. It was a beautiful autumn day; just perfect for a wedding.

The church was decorated and looked wonderful. Distant members of both families, which until recently had been only names in a book to Tammy, were all there to help them celebrate. Becky made a truly beautiful bridesmaid, while Viv and Marian, made elegant Matrons-of-honour.

To Dave's absolute joy, his two brothers had made the journey to be with him and so Bob and Gary were only too pleased to hand over the reigns to real family. They tossed a coin to see who would fill the one vacant position, and Gary won the toss – or lost, depending on a man's point of view about such things.

So, Becky, Viv and Marian attended Tammy, while Dave's two brothers, Jimmy and Tony, and Gary attended him.

Tammy was a vision in a soft off-white gown that floated about her like the gown of the fairy princess in one of the books she and her mother had made.

Her attendants wore dresses of soft pink or mauve, Tammy's favourite colours, and the guys all looked dreamy in suits of dove grey, with just a touch of mauve – not enough to insult real men, just enough to blend with bow-ties and cummerbunds of a shade a little deeper than that of the girls' dresses.

Dave's daughter was there and she was even more beautiful in real life than her photo had suggested. She was introduced to everybody at the reception and instantly made to feel part of this big and open-hearted family.

In no time at all any awkwardness that she may have felt, had disappeared and by the end of the day, really felt that she belonged here too.

Of course, Susan insisted that she should make their home her own and call in any time at all.

"You make sure that you are not a stranger, little one," Susan said. "You are a part of this family and you always will be. In fact, you and your folks must come one night for a meal. Bring everybody and we'll have a good time getting to know each other. Family can't be strangers from each other, can they?" she added with a laugh.

"That's okay, Dave, isn't it?" she finally thought to ask Dave. "I wouldn't want it to be awkward for you."

"No, it won't be awkward, Aunt Susan," Dave said. "Donna and I have talked and it's just as if we are old friends. I'm happy for her that she found the life she wanted and she's over the moon happy for me, that I've found my soul mate too. You ask away, dear lady. Tammy and I will try and be there too, if that's okay," he added.

"I was hoping that you would be," said Susan. "I won't make it too soon though. You two will need some time to settle down first."

All in all, it was a most attractive wedding. The reception was held in one of the finest places in the city and went off without a hitch. Pete, Dave's patient and long-suffering boss, and his wife, Gayle, had been invited to the wedding and, somewhat surprised but delighted, had attended.

They owned a holiday house on the Sunshine Coast, and had insisted that Dave and Tammy use it for their honeymoon – brooking absolutely no argument on the matter. As if that wasn't enough, when the happy couple arrived that night, tired but happy, they found the house open, and furnished with food and all essentials.

A friend, who unknown to Dave or Tammy, had been commissioned to get it ready, greeted them at the door, handed them each a glass of wine (non-alcoholic, of course) and the key to the door. He smilingly wished them blessings and joy, and without another word of introduction or anything else, bade them farewell and disappeared into the night.

Tammy made a mental note to find out who he was and include him in the many thank-you cards that were yet to be written.

A dreamy week passed by, as they explored each other and the beautiful Sunshine Coast. But, time, as it must, passed by and all too soon the week was over.

The honeymooners began to pack up their bags and prepare to head back to the farm-house in the Lockyer. But as the last memento and the last souvenir was crammed into bulging ports, they looked at each other across the big bed they'd shared for the last few days and suddenly they realized that the adventure wasn't ending, it was just beginning. Dave reached across the bed with his hand and Tammy leaned forward to touch his hand with hers. Together, they looked deep into each other's eyes and smiled.

"To our wonderful life," Dave said.

"To the best years which are still to come," Tammy responded.

Holding hands across the bed, they walked to the end and as they came together and held each other at the foot of the honeymoon bed, they prayed for God to bless their union. Then with one more quick hug and a lingering kiss, they parted and went back to pick up the luggage and carry it out to the car.

As they packed the last things in the car, they wondered what they were to do with the key. But right on cue, their mysterious friend from a week ago, turned up in the driveway. He took the key and sent them on their way with the ever-present smile, assuring them that he would take care of all the details of locking up the house.

"Share a blessed and fruitful marriage," he said to them. "Drive safely, and tell Pete that everything is under control here."

And with that he waved and turned to go into the house.

Chapter 19

A NEW LIFE BEGINS

Dave backed the car out of the driveway, and turned its nose for home. 'Home' now, was to be a simple weatherboard farm-house, in the Lockyer Valley, where Tammy would learn to be a wife, and begin a whole new life.

The years passed quickly for them. Somehow they kept in touch with people who had come to mean so much to them.

The days were busy but fulfilling and they soon became involved in the small community in which they lived.

A lovely church family welcomed them in and Tammy discovered the joy of worshipping with a church full of people other than immediate family. Yes, they had attended church with her aunt and uncle, but this seemed different. Here she and Dave got to really know the people and they got to know them.

She was often asked to speak at functions; to share her amazing tale, for people found it uplifting and her faith never failed to inspire, even as it had inspired Dave, while they had struggled just to survive, in their wilderness wanderings.

The minister often drew parallels with the wilderness wanderings of the Israelites, declaring that if God's people had shown a fraction of Tammy's faith in adversity, they could have saved themselves a great deal of grief. At such times Tammy hid her face in embarrassment, sure that what she had done was not remarkable – simply that which any person in her position would have done. Not so, others commented.

The time came when Tammy discovered that her body was changing. And she shared with her husband her joy, on learning of the imminent arrival of their first child. A healthy son was born to Tammy and she was so full of joy she felt sure that she must burst.

She cradled her baby son close to her breast and sang softly to him, as their heartbeats joined as one. Joshua would always be a special child.

They were to have two more children, both healthy, another boy, whom they named Benji and a little girl, named Libby. The small farmhouse was soon filled with the laughter and endless chatter of children and Tammy's days were full and satisfying.

She loved her husband and her children and delighted above all to serve and care for them. Her family, with the exception of the time she still kept for sharing with the Lord, consumed her time and her energies.

Without fail, Tammy made sure that she spent time each day with her Lord, before her family rose to begin their busy days.

And then, last thing at night, before she fell into bed beside the man she loved, she would find a quiet place, read a passage from her well-worn Bible and whisper a word of prayer to the One who had sustained her throughout her life.

The busy years flew by and Dave continued to work for Pete and Gayle. There had never been any desire to move on. This was a good job, working for honest folk. And Dave and Tammy had no need for all the trappings of modern life.

Such as the Lord provided for them each day was more than sufficient.

However, as the years went by, difficult times came on the Valley. Drought had taken its toll and with Pete nearing retirement, he no longer had the energy to continue fighting to stay on the land.

His sons, who had long ago left the farm to pursue other careers, wanted their father to sell the farm, hoping he would consider putting the money into a business venture that they had been looking into for some time. So it was that one day he called Dave into his office and broached the very difficult subject of the farm's, and by extension, Dave's future.

Dave had known it was coming, however, and had realized that his time in the Lockyer was coming to an end. He did not feel unduly worried by Pete's news for he felt sure that the Lord would provide for his family's future. He told Pete not to concern himself, but rather to consider what his own plans would be.

If selling the farm was what Pete wanted to do, then that was what he must do, and so he tried to reassure Pete as best he could. Still, as he left Pete's house and headed for the little home he shared with his family, he felt that it would be hard to tell Tammy that their time in the comfortable little cottage was over.

Surprisingly, she was neither surprised nor upset. Quietly, she sat Dave down, put a cup of coffee in front of him, as was her daily practice, and told him that she had known about the situation for quite a while. Gayle had spoken to her a couple of times, and had suggested as gently as she could that, perhaps, she and Dave should think about what they'd do 'when Pete finally retired'.

Tammy was no longer the innocent child of the bush, and even before Gayle had first mentioned it to her, she had read the signs. It had become increasingly obvious to her, that their time in this charming little house was drawing to a close.

Chapter 20
DREAMS FULFILLED

Tammy smiled at her husband across the table, and reaching over to take his hand she took a big breath and began to speak.

"Now Dave, is the time to speak with you about something that has been on my heart for years – a pull on my heart that has become more and more powerful. I must go back to Tumberrumba."

As Dave looked at her in amazement, she explained. "When I said goodbye to Barda, I felt very strongly in my spirit, that I would go back there, at a time appointed by God.

"I have learned much over the years – including how to use a computer, and the internet. I have always kept in touch with Natalie and Danny, as you well know, and together we have talked much about a dream that has been locked in my heart for many a year.

"I would never have spoken of it until you were ready to move on, for I knew that this was where we would stay until God said we should go. But, I believe that the time has come – the time is now.

"My dream is to set up a mission-cum-life training facility, on Tumberrumba. This facility would teach young aborigine people how to equip themselves for life in a white man's world.

"We would teach them how much God loves them, how to integrate into society, and hopefully, fill in the blanks that a sketchy, station school-room education may have left. Perhaps in this way, if we can teach them some discipline and some real life-skills, we might save some from going down the terribly destructive path of so many young ones. We would of course take any young people, regardless of colour or creed – any one in need of a hand-up in these difficult times.

"Natalie has spoken with Barda's people too, and they have talked a great deal about it over the years. In fact, so determined are they to see this happen that they have already given it a name.

"The young ones came to Barda one day and told him that they had decided that this place, when it is built, will be called 'Future Dreaming'.

"The folk at Tumberrumba, Natalie, Danny their whole family, and Barda's people, all want us to go back to live there, and Danny wants you to manage the property.

"He tells me that everybody has a job to do out there, but it has all grown so big in recent years, that it is no longer possible for him to take care of all that demands his attention, and give adequate oversight to the whole property at the same time. 'We must have Dave back here to manage this place,' he told me once. And he said, just the other day, that the sooner he could get you out there, the better, he reckoned.

"They're even building a house especially for us to live in, and land has already been set aside for extending the school.

"More bunk-houses had to be built after we left, as the number of folk grew. So there is plenty of accommodation to start with for the young people who will come to our school.

"Barda has agreed to allow us to use his story as a way to publicize 'Future Dreaming' and in that way to raise sponsorship to bring the dream into being. He is very old now, but still strong and alert. He knows, however, that his time is not long – he has already outlived many of the younger men, and lived far longer than his father or grandfather before him. He would love to see this come to pass before he goes to the Lord.

"Natalie, never one to let the grass grow beneath her feet, has already been busy, talking to some of their biggest suppliers and also with the buyers of their beef. I understand she has managed to secure some very interesting pledges. And the owners of neighbouring properties all seem keen to have something like this to offer the young ones on their places too.

So there have been all sorts of offers of help. The teachers at the school have been talking among themselves and also to colleagues down south and here in Queensland, and I understand that there are teachers who are just longing to get out there and be a part of something this radical and new."

"I must apologize to you, my beloved husband. For all of this has happened without your knowledge or input. Of course, if you hate the idea, I will never speak of it again. I'll simply tell Natalie that she'll have to do this without us. But, if this could be your dream too, then I believe that we will know it is of the Lord."

Having told Dave all that had been on her heart for so long, she then stopped pouring out the words and sat quietly, waiting. Never would she hurry him for a response. And despite all that was in her heart, she knew that now it rested with Dave and with God.

Slowly Dave got up from his seat. The coffee had gone cold in front of him as he had listened to his wife. As she had been speaking, he had felt his heart leap, and he knew a sudden yearning. Oh, yes, it had been buried for many a year, but he too had known that one day he would return once more to the land of his youth. Certainly, he had never entertained such an amazing plan... but... to manage Tumberrumba...?

He walked slowly to the window of their small kitchen, and looked out over the property he had loved and worked for the last twelve years.

Yes, it had been good and the years had been kind to both of them. But he knew that it was time. It was God's time; time to go back.

He turned to face his wife as she sat at the table, watching him. He took three large steps across the room, took her hands in his and stood her to her feet.

"Yes!" he said. "Yes, it is time. Yes it is God's time. Yes, we will go back."

Tammy melted into the arms of her husband, and they were still standing there, holding each other, when three children stormed into the house, with all the clamour and enthusiasm of the young. It was time to prepare a meal, help with homework, and cope with all the confusion and busyness of the end of the day.

Finally, all was done. The homework, the dishes, the washing folded and put away. Then Tammy and Dave drew their children into the lounge-room, said, 'no TV for a moment', and sitting them all down and getting them quiet, began to explain what was about to take place.

The plan was met with stunned silence at first, and then they all began to talk at once.

Yes, the whole idea sounded very exciting, but what about school, footy teams, scouts, church, friends. What about the lives they had here?

Dave then tried to explain to them all as best he could, that they couldn't stay here anyway. Pete was retiring and the property was to be sold. There would be no job. The farm was to go to developers, as no one wanted to operate a small farm anymore. The family would have no home, no job and therefore no money, to do all the things they loved to do.

So, a bit at a time, each child began to digest the information. Well, lots of people move away. It's hard, but... to go so far? Why?

Once everybody had quieted down and the first barrage of questions had stopped, Tammy began, in her soft and persuasive way, to tell of her dream. The children knew of her early life, and they knew of the adventures that their parents had shared. They had been told about Barda and his people and had often expressed the wish that one day they might go out there and see all the places that they'd heard so much about, and meet the people that their parents often spoke of.

Bit by bit, they began to see what their mother was on about. Each of them had come to a point in their lives when, one by one, they had committed their way to Jesus, so they understood that if God was leading their parents, then it would be right.

"Will we go to see your house in the cavern?" asked the youngest child. Libby, who had actually been named Elizabeth, after her grandmother, was six. For her the move would be exciting. She had started school only that very year and although she had made a friend, her mother knew she would soon make new friends.

She was beguiling; a totally lovable child. Her father doted on her, as she was a miniature copy of her mother. Tammy saw only her own dear mother, but then except for a very old photo, Dave had never known the beautiful lady who had given birth to his precious Tammy.

The boys warmed more and more to the whole idea, as they talked more fully about the huge property they would live on. There would be horses to ride and acres of virgin bush-land to explore. What boy could ask for more? So their plans were made.

The wider family thought at first that they'd all gone completely crazy. But gradually began to realize that this was real, and it was going to happen, like it or not.

Becky, who for one reason or another, had never married, declared to all and sundry that she would go too.

"I've no life worth worrying about here, except for my parents, and I bet you anything you like, they'll come to visit, and may even stay. I'm sure that I have skills that will prove very useful, and I'll bet Tammy will be glad of another pair of hands with all she'll be taking on."

Tammy had squealed with joy at the news and thrown her arms around Becky.

Aunt Susan was less than overjoyed at the thought of losing both of them at once, but was wise enough to know that her daughter was quite old enough to make her own decisions about the rest of her life, and as for Tammy, well, she had her husband and family and they must do what they believed was the Lord's will for them.

"At least these days we can keep in touch by the internet. Not like the old days with dreadfully slow mail and horrendously expensive phone bills. And I'll expect updated photos of the kids, regularly," she insisted.

Tammy had held her close and whispered her love in Susan's ear.

"You know that I love you as much as if you were my own dear mother," she said. "Of course we'll keep in touch. And you and Uncle Don must come and visit as often as you can. There will always be room for you. And I promise that we will not fly away on some madcap adventure and disappear forever."

Her aunt had held her tight, and the two had stood together for several moments, each with their own memories of years long gone. And so, it was arranged.

Chapter 21

TUMBERRUMBA

Dave and Tammy Wilson, their three children, Joshua 10, Benji 8 and Libby 6, and Becky, packed all their possessions and began their journey to a new life. A life sure to be filled with adventure.

The several family groups that made up the Tumberrumba family were waiting to receive them, including lots of children of varying ages, to the obvious delight of Tammy's three. The new house had been completed by the time they got there, and all made ready, so it did not take the family long to settle in.

The owners of Tumberrumba Station had taken a great deal of care selecting and ordering simple pieces of furniture to put in the house.

They knew enough of Tammy's ways to know that expensive, flashy things were of no interest to her, so each piece was simple and functional, many pieces having been made right there on the property, in one or the other of the workshops that supplied a great many of the station's varied needs.

The moment that Tammy saw it all, her eyes shone and she clapped her hands for joy, turning to her hosts to offer her thanks.

"This is so absolutely lovely," she exclaimed. "Nothing could be nicer. Thank you both, so much."

There were old friends to greet and new ones to meet and many, many plans to make.

Tammy had such a peace in her heart, for she knew that, at last, her dream – now with a name – 'Future Dreaming', would happen.

But, dreaming aside, in the meantime, there was a house to organize and a station property to run. Dave slipped into that role as easily as putting on an old shoe. Danny and his brothers took him under their collective wing, and had him fully up to speed in no time. He knew, even before the first 'grand tour' was over, that this was where God had been leading him, and this was where he belonged.

Tammy, never one to fuss too much about whether the house was a fashion-plate, so long as everything was clean and tidy, soon had things ship-shape. The new house was big and airy, with lots of cupboard space, so a place for everything was found in short order. So with that all squared away, she left her children happily sorting out their own rooms and lost no time in organizing her first classes for the aborigine youth, many of whom had already begun drifting into nearby townships and into trouble.

The young ones from Barda's original group had long grown. Those who had stayed – and Tammy was thrilled to see that most of them were still there – had children of their own.

Even these were all too quickly grown, already being exposed to the pull of modern life via the TV set in the bunkhouse and the computers they used in school. Their parents were struggling to maintain their culture and their ways.

Quick to see the problems, Tammy immediately set about her 'life-classes'. Somehow, she knew, she must strike a balance for these youngsters – a balance between the old and the new, both of which had much to offer. Of course the day must come when the children embraced modern life with all its complexities. Tammy's challenge was to show them the possibilities and warn them of the traps – giving them real alternatives to aim for.

At first some of the youngsters thought it was all a bit of a giggle, but soon came to realize that this gentle but determined white lady, who knew their language and their ways so well, really did know what she was on about. She knew more about the ways of their past than most of them had had the patience to glean from their harassed parents, and she knew a great deal about that big, wide world out there too.

And besides all that old Barda, whom all the kids revered, obviously loved and respected Tammy.

So, gradually they began to realize that she just might have something to teach them after all, and bit by bit, they began to give her their attention, and, in the process, found themselves learning amazing things.

'Future Dreaming' was born.

The next couple of years were the busiest that Tammy could ever remember. Sponsorships were not slow in coming and before she knew it, she was watching a building grow out of the barren earth.

"This will prove to be more fertile than anything this land has yielded in a very long time," commented Natalie prophetically one day. "I have the highest hopes for this place. You mark my words generations of people will bless you for this, my dear."

Uncomfortable with such praise, Tammy simply smiled. Certainly it was her dearest hope that generations to come would profit from her efforts, but she was not one to consider her own part in it to be anything remarkable.

"Many wonderful people have been a part of this, Natalie," she said softly. "You included. I have simply been obedient. God is the one who will bring this place to be what He wants it to be."

"Yes, indeed," agreed Natalie. "Oh, by the way," she remembered, "The Flying Padre will be here on Sunday, so why not get him to bless this place while he is here?"

"That sounds like an absolutely marvelous idea," said Tammy. "What better start could we hope for, than to dedicate it all to God?"

So it was that on a bright and sunshiny, Sunday morning, everybody was up early, dressed neatly in their finest, ready to assemble at the airfield to receive the Padre when he arrived. Visits from clergy were few and far between in their part of the world, so all but those with urgent tasks were gathered for the occasion. White and black alike, all clothes were clean and faces scrubbed till they shone.

Most station folk in Australia's outback, even those rugged souls who have no 'religion', bless Frontier Services for the dedicated people who provide an umbrella of care over outback dwellers.

Long gone are the days of the peddle radio and now even the old 'school of the air', as so many knew it, has gone. For these days, the internet serves everybody's needs so much more efficiently. But sometimes, one missed the noisy, crackly, group chats among neighbours.

No one missed the sound of the Padre's plane as he had buzzed the house to alert the family to his arrival. This had immediately caused a mad scramble to get to cars, trucks or bikes, anything with wheels, that would get a person to the airstrip to greet him. He had been a favourite with local folk ever since his arrival in the area some years before, and was always a welcome guest.

Soon enough the cavalcade of vehicles was escorting him back to the house, where refreshments were waiting. And in the midst of the excitement, Natalie made sure that the Padre was also given a chance to freshen up before a simple church service would be held in the small chapel. These chapel services with the Padre were an important part of station life.

All the babies who had been born since his last visit were presented for baptism and some of the older children, who, in the weeks leading up to his visit, had been busy learning all their lessons so they would be ready for the big occasion, would be keen to take their first communion. As well, a small choir had been practicing a song that they were to sing during the service. Each hoped that they weren't the only one with butterflies in the tummy. The Padre also knew that on many of his visits he was called on to perform the occasional marriage too.

It took some time to work through all the backlog of duties that Tumberrumba folk had lined up for him, but eventually, all was completed, a joyous time of worship had been shared, and the family were finally back at the house sharing a meal. Following the meal, as they all sat around talking and sharing all that had happened since his last visit, the subject of the blessing of 'Future Dreaming' was broached.

Tammy, Dave, Natalie and Danny had enthusiastically brought him up to date on all that had happened since Tammy and Dave had arrived, and had told him too of the plans they all held for the future.

Blessing the project, so early in its development, they said, had seemed like the right thing to do.

The Padre was delighted, declaring it to be 'an absolutely marvelous idea'.

All the planning had already been organized by Tammy and Natalie, so the Padre looked over what they'd done, agreed that it was perfect and said that they might as well hold another service the very next day.

It was such a happy time, and Tammy felt a joy and peace in her heart that she had great difficulty in putting into words. She just enjoyed the feelings that washed over her and silently blessed her Lord for all the wonder of His great love and provision.

The days following the Padre's visit and the blessing of the new school, were busy, happy ones. It seemed that there was always something to do or a new plan to implement and the time seemed to go so quickly.

As she watched her children thriving – learning new things every day, and developing into well-rounded young people, Tammy found it hard sometimes to realize how quickly they were growing up. It seemed they had sprouted like weeds since coming out there, spending so much time in the fresh, clean air.

Schooling had not proved to be a problem. Her three simply went to the school-room with the station family's youngsters and lessons came clearly via the computers. Also, because the Tumberrumba family had grown so much, three teachers had been employed to guide the youngsters through their lessons.

Tammy was relieved to discover that all her children were quick learners; each of them with a hunger to absorb every bit of information about everything. Their teachers were hard pressed at times to keep up with them, and found the internet a great resource in assisting them to feed these keen young minds.

So Tammy took it upon herself to find more and more creative ways to keep their hungry young minds fed.

Out of school hours, they roamed the countryside with whole groups of kids of all ages, both black and white. Sometimes it was on foot; sometimes on horse-back. It had not taken very long before each of Tammy's children had learned how to ride and they were quickly becoming skilled riders. Each child on the station knew that there were certain boundaries beyond which they were forbidden to wander, and apart from the occasional lapse, were pretty good about staying reasonably close to home.

The strictly enforced rule of always informing a responsible adult of their intentions was adhered to with little complaint.

One day, the three Wilson children tumbled into the house with their usual boisterous energy, but this time, they were all trying to talk at once.

"Mum! Mum! Come quick!" yelled one of her offspring.

Tammy's heart missed a beat as she ran through the house, for she immediately supposed that one of her children was hurt. But thankfully, this was not the cause for the excitement.

When Tammy came out to the front of the house, she was confronted with a sight that touched her heart. Sitting on her front step was a young aborigine, who was barely skin and bone.

"We found him out by the west dam," one her sons stated. All too soon remembering that he was not supposed to have been anywhere near the west dam.

"Oops!" he said. "Sorry Mum, "We just sort of followed this trail, and then, there we were. And then we found him, Mum, lying there all crumpled up like he was dead or something.

"He jumped up when he saw us, and tried to run, but he was too weak and he fell over. So we helped him up and half carried him home. We knew you'd want us to," he finished triumphantly, hoping, no doubt, to deflect his mother's inevitable wrath for his infringement of the rules.

Tammy quickly had the children help her get him into the house, and then shooed them all away, except for her eldest, whom she dispatched, posthaste, to fetch Becky and Natalie.

"Oh, and if you can find your father, you'd best tell him too," she added. "And we'll be talking later about you taking the younger ones near that dam."

"Mum, I'm all but grown now. I'm not gonna drown in any dumb old dam."

"Maybe, maybe not," said his mother, "But there are still the younger children to consider. However, never mind that now, just go and fetch me some help. Oh, and send someone for Barda," she added as her son ran out the door.

"Yes, Mum," he said, and quickly took off, hoping that by the time he got back she'd have forgotten his little lapse of obedience to her rules.

No one messed with Josh's mother's rules. And every kid on the station knew that.

Meantime, Tammy busied herself with trying to help her unexpected guest. She knew it was too early to be plying him with questions, but she longed to know how he had come to be out there and what had brought him to Tumberrumba Station.

Help soon arrived in the shape of Becky and Natalie, both having left cleaning up the school-room to come at Joshua's earnest bidding.

So together, the three ladies did what they could to help him. Soon, Dave and Barda arrived, and so the ladies were able to surrender his care to the men, who could better help him bathe and dress in some clean clothes.

While they attended to those details, Tammy and the others set about preparing something for him to eat. This would have to be simple fare, as he had the look of someone who had not eaten much for some time.

Eventually, he was cleaned up, and was enjoying a cool drink, which he obviously relished after sampling the muddy water of the dam.

He managed a few bites of food, then with a smile on his face, took a deep breath, and right before their eyes, dropped off into a sound sleep, sitting upright in his chair.

Dave and Barda stepped forward to catch him as he almost toppled from the chair, and Tammy quickly checked to make sure he was indeed only asleep and not unconscious. Then, smiling at each other, they carried him gently to a day-bed, tiptoed softly out of the room, left him to it.

Although why they tiptoed was a mystery for had they danced the Highland fling in hob-nailed boots, it was highly unlikely that they would have disturbed this exhausted young man. Finding out who he was and where he had come from, would have to wait.

As evening wore on, the family tended to their normal routine, each trying their best to contain their curiosity. Joshua was chagrined to discover that his mother had not forgotten his abuse of her trust, and had to endure a brisk talking-to.

However, Tammy was not unreasonable, so after she had got it all off her chest, she and Dave sat down with him and, together, they thrashed out a new set of rules for a boy who was fast approaching his teens.

Reluctantly accepting that her son was a capable bushman in his own right, with a sensible head on his shoulders, she agreed that perhaps he was entitled to a greater measure of freedom – 'within limits', she insisted. So, between them, they worked out a few more freedoms for her oldest child, and after he had done his chores and scrubbed off a layer of red dust, he happily went off to bed.

Benji was not quite so delighted, insisting that he too deserved more freedom.

"I'm a big kid too," he insisted.

"Not big enough, yet," his parents insisted. And sadly, Benji had to be satisfied with that for a time. He knew his mum and dad well enough to know that once they'd set a rule, that was it, and no arguing would be tolerated. So, he too took himself off to bed. It seemed as if their mysterious guest would sleep till morning anyway.

Tammy checked on her house-guest before she and Dave turned in for the night, but he was sleeping the sleep of the just, as they say, so she spread a cover over him and after a final check of each child, as was her habit, she found her quiet spot, spent her time with Jesus, and fell into bed with the man she loved.

The morning dawned bright and clear, as most mornings in that part of the world did. Tammy, according to her long established routine, has risen early and had most things on the go before her family surfaced.

No sooner was breakfast cleared away, than Barda was standing on the verandah, waiting quietly for Tammy to notice him.

Smiling to herself that even after so many years, he still showed the shy reticence that was so typical of his people.

"Come in, Barda, my dear friend," she called to him.

And so he stepped across the threshold, still, Tammy noticed, with the air of a man unused to such things as a house with steps and doorways.

Then they went into the family room, where Tammy's mysterious guest was sitting on the edge of the bed, unsure where he was or why.

Barda approached him and spoke to him softly, in the language of his people. The young man answered him in the same tongue – a small matter that solved one problem at least – he belonged to the same language group as Barda.

Soon, after what Tammy knew to be formalities necessary to such a meeting, the two men began to speak with each other about the issue to hand. Who this young man was and where had he come from. After some moments in conversation with the lad, Barda walked out of the room and onto the verandah. Tammy followed him. Together they stood there in the morning sun and Barda spoke softly about the trials that Tammy's house-guest had endured.

It seemed that there were other people out where no one ever went. Barda was puzzled that he had never known of them.

"It is strange," he said, "That we never found each other. Apparently there are several families of our people still out there," he added, waving his hand vaguely in the direction from which his own people had come.

"From what he says they have lived further south and much further to the west, where the land is truly hard and many have died. He said he was sent on ahead to scout for food and water, but I think that he is too young to do that. I think he felt the need to prove himself to be a man, and set this task for himself.

"He said that most of their leaders have died and his father has taken over as the elder. He is apparently one of the few men left; the tribe is mostly women and children. They had sat down for a council and decided to leave their tribal lands and try to walk towards the east. They hoped that perhaps they would find food and water. But because some people are weak from hunger and the little ones can't walk far, this young man decided to go on ahead and scout. He is very brave, but very foolish, and he almost died. Yet, he is here, and I must send some men to find his people and bring them home." Barda said.

Tammy thought it interesting and heart-warming, that this man, who for so many years had considered the desert to be his home, should now refer to Tumberrumba as home.

With a final nod, as though the decision was now made, Barda walked away. Tammy watched him as, back still ram-rod straight, this elder statesman went off to make plans to find a group of people, who were most likely in dire straits.

Several days passed, stretching into weeks, during which life at 'Future Dreaming' went on in much the same way as always.

The new buildings and facilities that Tammy had planned for, were nearing completion and soon, all lessons would be held under the same roof. The invitation would then go out to the surrounding districts, that any who wished, were welcome to come.

Then, early one morning, as the clear air began to give way to the shimmer and haze of the building heat, Tammy noticed a group of people walking towards the camps beyond the bunkhouses.

She watched as a slight figure came out from beneath the trees and walk towards the incoming group.

She went to meet him, and the two stood side by side as the men Barda had sent on the mission of mercy, came up to them, accompanied by nearly a dozen very tired, dirty and painfully thin people.

Barda went over to them, and with the air of competent leadership that typified him, greeted each one with a word and then turned towards the campsites where many of their own people were preparing their morning meal and getting ready for the day.

When all were settled and were being welcomed by their hosts, Barda and Tammy went to Natalie and Danny, to inform them how their station 'family' had grown.

Tammy then went to her house and, finding her guest fully recovered now and more than ready to leave, told him, in the language she had never forgotten, that his family had arrived and that he could go now to meet them.

"There will be a place there for you to live, as there is for all your family too," she told him.

He smiled a little uncertainly. It was very unusual for a white woman to speak so fluently in the tongue of his tribe. But he understood her and willingly followed her out to the aboriginal camps.

Tammy witnessed as his parents first welcomed him, then berated him for his foolishness. They had believed him lost to them, and in the way of people long used to the harshness of wilderness life, had needed to move on. Finding their son alive was a joy that such people had rarely experienced.

It seemed to Tammy that the Tumberrumba family just kept growing, and she knew, again, deep in her heart, that her job here had only begun – that there would be many young people, and some older ones, who would need all that 'Future Dreaming' would offer in the years to come.

She was aware of a huge sense of responsibility, but at the same time aware of a great sense of peace and 'rightness'. This was, indeed, the place where God had brought her. The future was here.

As the months flew by, 'Future Dreaming' became a present reality at Tumberrumba Station. Word of this place spread far and wide throughout the outback, as station folk from three states heard of all that it offered. Folk in need, as well as those with gifts and talents or monetary support to offer, came from near and far.

Chapter 22
THE FUTURE BECOMING A REALITY

An enormous complex of buildings had risen from the dry ground, and the necessary infrastructure had turned the station property into a small metropolis. It had fast become one of the busiest places for miles around, and it seemed that people came and went at all times of the day.

A new hostel was now home to around thirty young people, most of whom were aborigines, but some of whom were youngsters from neighbouring station families.

These were the offspring of desperate parents – outback families, who had long understood that a sense of responsibility and an awareness of belonging to this wide and beautiful land was an integral part of life in this part of the world. It seemed that, in the case of these particular youngsters at least, busy parents had tried, but failed, to instill these values into their children.

So while most bush children love the freedom of the wide open spaces, some grow up longing for bright city lights. As a result, some of the local youths had become bored and dissatisfied with the rich life that was their heritage. Wanting something more and believing it to found in the towns and cities that they visited occasionally, they had lost sight of the quality of life on offer right here, in their own beautiful neighbourhood. In Tammy's mind at least this was a place which had no equal – anywhere in the world, she was quite sure.

As a last resort these young boys, not quite men, and some girls too, had been packed off to Tammy, in the hopes that she could somehow infuse into these teenagers, something of the peace and joy that bubbled out of her, in a seemingly endless stream.

The success stories that began to flow from 'Future Dreaming' soon became local legend. And Tammy was replete with joy. For her to see even one child 'get it' – to grasp something of the wonder of life, was all the incentive that Tammy needed to keep going.

She loved to watch the transition as a young person, who may have come to her with lacklustre eyes and bored expression, would suddenly light up one day, as a timeless truth dawned in his or her mind and heart. The challenges and the joys were food and drink to her and all those around her were infected too.

Tammy had also watched her own brood grow and develop in this environment. Never had there been a moment when they had looked back to life as they thought they'd known it. There always seemed to be something exciting to do and for them every day was a new adventure.

Eventually, however, the time came when Josh reached an age when Tammy and Dave wondered if he might need to go south and get some schooling beyond that which could be provided at Tumberrumba. Although the school had grown and would they hoped, soon outstrip any city school, they felt that he needed some exposure to the wider learning possibilities on offer in the city.

A really good school was chosen and of course Susan and Don were ready to open their home to him. So it was that the subject was brought up at the table one night. At first Josh rejected the idea totally. He wanted nothing to do with heading off to a city and attending a big city school. He earnestly believed that the school at Tumberrumba could offer him all he'd ever need. But gradually, he warmed to the idea, as his parents explained some of the things that were on offer at the school.

"Of course, you'd come home for holidays," said his mother. "And Aunt Susan will look after you even better than I do," she added, laughing.

So it was that all the arrangements were made, and Tammy's oldest son, now almost a man, was to go off to Brisbane, to live with his great-aunt and uncle and attend a private school.

As the holiday season, and the time when he would have to pack and leave, drew near, he came to his mother early one morning and confronted her as she stood at the sink washing dishes.

"Mum, I've been thinking," he said. "There is one thing that I must do before I go away."

"What's that, my son?" asked his mother.

"I must go and see your house in the cave. Do you realize that, even though you promised, we've never been there?" he told her.

"Yes, that's right," Tammy said softly. "Somehow, there just never seemed to be a time to do that. And I know that I did promise," she said with a smile.

"I'll talk to your father later, and maybe we can work something out during the holidays, before you have to leave for Brisbane. So, later that day, Tammy found a moment to take her husband aside, and tell him about her conversation earlier that day with their son.

Dave smiled at her and agreed, yes, they had promised the kids they'd do that.

"Looks like we are going back, sweetheart," he said. "There's no way we can put it off again. And Libby is always going on about it - she's never forgotten," he added.

So when the family all came in that evening, and they were all finally sitting down to the evening meal, Tammy brought up the subject that had long been put on hold.

"As you kids know," she said to Benji and Libby, "Josh is going off to school in Brisbane next year. He came to me this morning and asked me if he could go and see my cavern home before he goes away.

We are aware that we did promise to do this sometime, and that all of you have been keen to go. So your father and I have talked about it and agreed that it would be a good thing for us all to do this holiday."

"So," added their father, breaking in on the sudden babble of excitement, "We will be organizing a trip as soon as school finishes for the holidays. Natalie and Danny have told me I can take my holidays too, and of course the school here will be in recess.

"Natalie has said that she has plenty of help to take

care of the live-in students while we are away, so your mother will also have a holiday – the first one she's had since our honeymoon, and that's a while ago."

The rest of dinner time was filled with excited chatter as the three children fired a myriad of questions at their mother – each one trying to outdo the other with their memories of the stories they'd been told. Then as soon as the meal was finished and all cleared away, they ran off to plan what they'd need to take with them, and to discuss the coming adventure together.

Dave turned to Tammy, as they walked into the lounge to sit and talk over the day, and taking her hand he looked into her eyes.

"Are you okay with this, darling? I mean, really okay?"

"Yes Dave, I am. In fact, I'm quite excited too," she added. "I was wondering as well, that maybe we could manage to bring some things back – if they are still okay, I mean. I left an awful lot of stuff behind, and I've been thinking lately that it might be good if I had some of them here."

Dave took her hands, and then pulling her towards him, hugged her tight.

"Do you know that you are so beautiful?" he asked her.

She looked up at him and saw a strong, handsome man. The years sat easily on him, she realized, and he was still as youthful and vigorous as the man she had married, many years before.

She had never really thought of herself as beautiful, in fact never really thought much about herself at all, except to recognize how blessed she was. She never failed to appreciate the love of such a good man, or the love of three precious children. And of course, the love of God, which she valued above all.

With a contented sigh, she leaned her head against her husband's broad shoulder, and turned her face towards him, to receive his gentle kiss on her forehead.

The busy days hurried by and soon the pace of life at the school began to slow. A few at a time, those students with homes to go to for the holidays, said their goodbyes and left; either with parents who had arrived to collect them, or in the planes that would carry them across the miles to the station properties from which they came.

Some would return in the New Year, others were going on to school in bigger towns or cities, or to jobs or apprenticeships.

Tammy was sad to see these go, yet at the same time overjoyed at the enthusiasm with which they now faced their futures. She loved them all as if they were her own and sent each one off with her love and a prayer. Not one child ever left her care without hearing about the love of God, and it was a testimony to her own love for them that most responded by discovering the truth of the gospel for themselves.

She laughed before the Lord some days, when she saw how long her prayer list had become. It had come to the point, that at times it seemed, if she was to get anything done in a day, she must lay the list out before Him and offer them up in a block. Oh yes, some days there were certain ones that needed special thoughts for the day, but she relied on God's Holy Spirit to prompt her when He needed her to pray for a particular person.

For some reason, Dave's daughter had been on her heart for a while, too. Tammy believed that the Lord had prompted her to pray a lot lately for this young lady.

So as she and Dave sat together one evening, talking over their plans for this upcoming holiday, she brought up the subject of Marlene.

"Have you heard from Donna how Marlene is getting on?" she asked him.

"Nothing much lately," he responded. "I can't say I've heard anything much since her birthday in August. Perhaps I should ring Donna and see how they are all getting on." he said.

"I was wondering if that might be a good idea," said Tammy. "And, while you're at it, why don't you ask if she'd like to come out to the cavern with us? She's what, twenty-two, now? She might be off about her own life, with a job and that boyfriend that Donna doesn't like, I suppose. But you could ask anyway. She can only say no if she isn't interested."

So Dave went off to the phone and was gone for quite a while. Tammy had some material that she wanted to read and so she spent some time with that while she waited for Dave to come back.

When he came back, he was looking a little worried, so she asked him what the problem was.

"I'm not too sure," he replied to her question. "Donna is worried about Marlene. It seems she's been a bit unsettled lately and she's become very moody. Apparently she recently broke up with that fellow she's been going with for about three years and it's hit her pretty hard.

"As we know, Donna has never liked him. Said he tended to be a little wild and wasn't really good for Marlene. She's always had a bit of an independent spirit, so as soon as her mother expressed her concern about him, that seemed to make her more determined to go out with him. Donna said she knew it would come unstuck one day."

"Where is Marlene?" Tammy asked. "She hasn't gone off somewhere, has she?"

"Well, that's just it, you see, Donna isn't too sure."

"What do mean, not sure?" asked Tammy. "Surely she'd know if Marlene wasn't at home?"

"Apparently she's been flatting with a friend for a few months, and this friend has just told Donna that she hasn't seen Marlene for two or three days. She had apparently rung only an hour or so before I did, to ask if she'd gone back home," Dave said worriedly.

"She told Donna that she didn't ring sooner because Marlene often stayed the night with that boyfriend of hers, which her flat-mate wasn't too keen on either so it seems, or with other friends if they'd been out late together."

"We must pray about it," said Tammy firmly.

Dave remembered well, how Tammy had prayed about anything and everything when they were on their trek out of the wilderness. And he knew how often she prayed, every day, for every matter to do with their family or the school, or anything at all.

So they sat together and bent their heads in prayer, offering this young woman, whom both had learned to love, up to the Lord. They realized, and regretted, that because of their very different circumstances, they really hadn't got to know her all that well.

They asked God first of all, to keep her safe, wherever she was, and then to bring her back to her mother's arms.

Then, just as they were finishing, the phone rang. Dave got up and went to answer it. He came back into the room and sat back down with Tammy.

"You will never guess what that was about," he said to her. "That was someone from the police station, in Rockhampton."

"Rockhampton?" said Tammy in amazement. "Why on earth would police from Rocky be ringing us?

"Well, it seems that stories about our school have reached across to the coast. He wanted to ask me a few things about it and whether it was everything that he'd heard. I told him, yes, it was an amazing place and that my wonderful wife had a truly marvelous way with young people. I told him that you had turned dozens of kid's lives around.

"Well, he was most impressed, of course and suggested that we may like to take the occasional troubled kid from over their way, if it could be arranged. I said that I was quite sure that could be arranged if it became necessary.

"Then he blew me away. He said that they'd picked up a young woman, who had been hitchhiking out on the highway. It seems this girl said that she was trying to get to Tumberrumba Station in the Northern Territory.

"She's told them that she didn't have a clue how to get there, just that she'd headed north from Brisbane and hoped that somehow she could work her way across from somewhere up this way. She'd got a ride with a truckie, and had travelled most of the way with him, but he had dropped her off at a roadhouse a few kilometres from where the police found her. Apparently he had put the hard word on her and because she'd knocked him back, he had refused to take her any further.

"When they questioned her some more, she said that her father lived out here and she really wanted to find him. I asked the policeman what her name was and he said, Marlene. But he said that she wouldn't give him any other name except Wilson. He'd heard of the school, as I said, and knew our name was Wilson, so he rang here to find out if she really was my daughter," he finished.

"You mean to say that Marlene is in Rockhampton?" asked Tammy in amazement.

"Well, that's what he said," replied Dave. "I don't think she has much money with her. Anyway, it seems that's where she is. I don't know a whole lot else.

"He asked me what I wanted to do about it, so we decided that they should put her on the first plane heading this way. Apparently that is happening tomorrow. She'll be flown to Winton, where they can organize for her to connect with the Flying Doctor. It seems the sergeant knows, I'm not sure how, that the doctor has a call out this way tomorrow, so they are going to ask if they'll detour and drop her here.

All we'll need to do is to pick her up out at the strip. I told him to make sure to tell the Flying Doctor that we'll reimburse them for their trouble, just to let us know how much it will be. I guess we'll have to pay her airfare from Rocky to Winton too." Dave added with a rueful smile.

"Well," said Tammy. "We can't help that, I'm sure she wouldn't have been hitchhiking if she had any money. And Donna obviously didn't know what the girl was up to.

"Anyway, we'll worry about that later. For now, we'd better get an early night, looks like we've a busy day ahead of us. I just knew that I had to be praying for her lately; there has been a real burden on my heart." Tammy said simply.

Dave remembered reading somewhere about God's 'prevenient grace' – how He goes before His little ones and prepares the way. And shaking his head in wonder and amazement at how immediately the Lord had worked, he went off to pray some more for his daughter. He had always been ready to help out if Donna needed anything, but he had been so busy lately, he realized that he had been content to let her new family watch out for her. He figured he needed to confess his apathy before the Lord and commit to paying a little more attention in the future. He knew that there was nothing to be gained by beating himself up, but he knew that he needed to be, and in fact wanted to be, a little more pro-active about her welfare from now on. It looked like he was to have that chance.

After a while, Tammy came up to him and gently tapped him on the shoulder.

"Sorry to interrupt, darling, but don't you think you'd better ring Donna, and let her know what is happening?

"Yes, of course. I got so caught up with it all, I clean forgot.

"Thank you, as always, darling for being on the ball. You know," he said, as a thought occurred, "Donna has said occasionally that Marlene is really very young for her age.

She seems to be really quite immature. It's a bit of worry, especially as the hormones seem to be working overtime," he added with a frown. "I mean, it's not as if she's a child anymore, but, one can't help worrying, can one?" he finished lamely.

Tammy, however, knew what he was trying not to say and was aware that the same concerns had been on her mind also. So giving him a reassuring smile and a quick hug she left him to finish off his prayer. Then Dave then went straight to the phone and rang Donna for the second time that night.

She was very grateful to hear that her daughter was okay and amid tears of relief made Dave promise he'd ring first thing, as soon as he had Marlene there and knew for sure she was alright. He promised faithfully that he would, as he mentally added up the cost of three phone calls to Brisbane.

But then he immediately committed that to God, who always provided for them, and apologized for worrying about the cost of a phone call when his daughter's future was in the balance. So he simply thanked God for all He had done and once again prayed for Marlene's safety and protection on the morrow.

Finally, at peace about the situation, and exhausted from all the excitement, he offered all of his family up to the Lord, and went to join his wife in their room. She smiled at him as climbed into bed beside her, and gave him a questioning look – one that clearly said, 'are you okay?' He took her in his arms and held her to him.

"In answer to your unspoken question, yes, I am okay," he laughed. "But I am so grateful to God for you, my darling." Then he gave her another big hug and a long, lingering kiss...

Chapter 23
MARLENE

The morning came quickly enough and Dave took a moment or two to collect his thoughts, as he lay watching the brightening sky through the window.

Then, as he remembered what was happening that day, he flew out of bed and headed for the bathroom.

Tammy was up, of course, and had already been for a walk. She was in her quiet corner, doing what she did every day of her life – committing the day, her family and her 'Future Dreaming' kids to the Lord. Today, she was committing Marlene too, as well as the Flying Doctor team that was heading out this way to attend to someone in need. She quietly offered them up too, asking the Lord to make the problem a little one, easily fixed, and to speed any recovery time.

Then she was up and in the kitchen, preparing to meet the onslaught of hungry kids as they piled out of bed, rubbing sleepy eyes and chorusing the words she knew so well – 'I'm hungry, Mum!'

Breakfast was soon over and done with; Tammy never failed to be amazed at how much food her offspring could consume, and how quickly it vanished.

Smiling to herself she hunted them off to get organized for their lessons.

They had been told over breakfast, that Marlene was coming, but very little else. After all, what else could they tell them, except that she had hitchhiked her way out of Brisbane and up the coast? They protested about having to go to school, while their parents went to get their half-sister, but their mother insisted.

"The year isn't over yet, and you still have work to do," she said firmly. "You'll get to see Marlene over lunch," she promised.

Then, with that look, that each knew meant 'no argument' she sent them on their way and went to finish getting ready herself.

Dave was all ready to walk out the door and could hardly contain himself. He had remembered to inform his employers what was happening, and had received immediate permission to do whatever was necessary.

When Dave had spoken to her the previous evening, Natalie had immediately contacted the Flying Doctor Service and asked, as the plane was diverting here, could they bring some supplies for her first-aid kit. They had, as always been happy to oblige.

She had also asked Dave if there was anything she could do to assist in his situation and he thanked her warmly but said, no, it was just a matter of picking her up and bringing her home.

"What will happen from there, well, that's another story. We'll just have to wait and see," he had told her. "We can but hope that there are no unpleasant surprises attached to this unexpected visit," he'd added.

Soon Tammy was ready too, and they headed off for the airstrip. She warned that they were probably early, and may have a bit of a wait, but Dave could not be contained a moment longer.

They went out to the vehicle that Dave had brought around to the front of the house in the early hours. Gone was the old war-horse that had carried him all over the outback in his single years. With all the needs of family and the school to consider, a newer vehicle had become a necessity, much to Tammy's relief. She had begun to wonder how much longer the old one would hold together on some of the tracks out here.

As predicted, they arrived out at the airstrip in plenty of time, and as Tammy had warned, needed to sit and wait for quite a while.

Thankfully, a shelter had been built and a rather scraggly old eucalypt had grown up so that it hung over the shelter a little, providing some scant, but none-the-less welcome shade.

So they sat there, brushing the flies from their faces with the eternal 'Aussie salute', and waited. They spent the time talking together about what they might expect from their young visitor. Dave told Tammy how he had talked with the Lord last evening about how slack he'd been as a father.

But Tammy reassured him. "Darling, you weren't given the opportunity to have a lot of input into her life. If you hadn't made the effort to find her, you may never have even known her at all. And you can't go back now and fix the mistakes of your youth. You've long since given all that to God, so please don't blame yourself for this, or for whatever else may have happened. Marlene's a big girl now and must be a bit responsible for her own decisions and actions.

"I know that it has been difficult, with me dragging you way out here again, after being so sure you'd left the outback for ever. And I know that you did want to spend more time getting to know her.

But they had their lives too, and you couldn't always be there interfering when Phillip had taken her on as his daughter. We always told Donna that if she needed anything to just ask us. You have done all that could have been asked of you, under any circumstances.

"We will just cope with whatever comes. We'll love Marlene, no matter what, and together, we'll work it out," she told him, as she looked up into his face and smiled at him. "I love you," she said, "And I love all that you stand for. You are such a good man, and I think Marlene knows that, and that's why she's come looking for you," she finished with an air of finality.

"Bless you, darling, as always," he said. "Somehow, you always know the right thing to say. What would I do without you?" he asked.

Then, as they hugged each other, they heard a sound break into the silence of the bush. The Flying Doctor was coming, and he was bringing a precious package for Tammy and Dave.

They stood and watched as the sturdy little plane touched down on the dusty strip, and turned their faces away as the wind blew the dust their way. Then, as the plane taxied to a stop, they ran out to meet it.

The door opened and the doctor came down the steps to the ground. He was carrying a parcel in his hands.

"This is for Natalie," he said as he reached out to give Dave the box and shake him by the hand.

"Thank you, Jim," Dave responded to the man known so well to station folk far and wide. "We really appreciate you doing this for us," he added.

"Not a problem," Jim replied. "In this part of the world, we all need to pull together. Now, Dave, I've another package for you," he said with a smile. "I think you know who this is," he said, indicating the young lady standing at the top of the steps.

"Come on down, Marlene," he called to her. "It is okay, honestly. No one's going to bite you."

A little hesitantly, she started down the steps to the hot, red earth. She squinted a little at the sudden glare and reached for the sunglasses in her bag.

Then she came over to Dave and stood in front of him, with a small frown creasing her brow.

"Marlene," said her father. "Are you okay?"

He waited for an answer, as she seemed to hesitate.

Then she smiled a little shyly. "Yes, thank you, um, Dad... I'm okay. Is it alright to call you Dad?"

"Of course, if you want to, I'd be privileged. I just didn't suppose, even for a moment that I'd earned the right," he said.

For a moment, both seemed awkward with each other. Then Marlene took a deep breath and stubbing her toe into the soft dust at her feet, said softly, "I'm really sorry for the mess I've caused."

She looked up at her father from beneath a fringe that all but covered her eyes, causing Dave to smile, as he wondered at the fashions that young people seemed to favour.

"Come on sweetie, let's get you back to the house and settled in. Have you got any luggage?" he asked.

"She's got a whopping great backpack," called Jim, struggling down the plane's steps with it. "Goodness only knows what she's got in here," he said breathlessly. "Carrying bricks, are you young lady?" he asked Marlene.

"Sorry," she said, taking it from him. "I just guess I threw in everything I thought I'd need, and then anything else that might come in useful," she added, laughing a little at last.

When she laughed Tammy noticed that she really was very pretty, and she hoped that soon, the laughter would replace the stressed look on that young face.

Tammy asked Jim if he wished to come back for some refreshment, but he declined with thanks, indicating that he was on a pretty tight schedule. So, with a final word of farewell, he climbed back into the plane. The three of them stood there a moment and watched as the pilot taxied out to the end of the runway, turned and then, trundling back past them, took to the air, heading off to yet another outback family.

Taking Marlene's arm with one hand and her bag with the other, Dave guided her to the car and assisted her to climb in. Then he put the bag in the back and got into the driver's seat.

"Righto then, let's get back to the house where we can get a cool drink. It's hot out here," he said.

They travelled back to the house in silence. Marlene seemed lost in thought as she gazed out the window at the passing scene. And the two in the front seemed content to let her be.

After a while, Dave pulled up in front of the house, and climbing down from the car, went round to help Tammy and Marlene. Then he went to the back and lifted her backpack out.

"Wow!" he said. "This is heavy." He smiled at Marlene and gently cuffed her on the arm, as he shepherded the two of them up the steps into the coolness of the house. Tammy took Marlene to show her the room she'd be using, and as she led the way, she was put in mind of another girl, so many years before, being led to a room, by a woman she would come to love as a dear friend.

History has a way of repeating itself, she thought.

"In here, dear girl," she said to Marlene. "This is your room, for as long as you choose to stay," she added.

"Do you mean that?" asked Marlene, seemingly unsure.

"Indeed I do," said Tammy emphatically. "This is your home, for as long as you desire."

Marlene dropped her bag in the middle of the floor, and sobbing, threw her arms around Tammy. The two of them stood there, locked in an embrace, for quite a while.

Dave came to see what was happening, but Tammy looked at him over Marlene's shoulder and just shook her head ever so slightly. So, leaving her to it, he tiptoed away.

Eventually, Marlene's sobs subsided, and Tammy gently led her to the bed, where they sat down, side by side.

"Do you want to tell me what's happening, dear?" she asked. "Do you want to talk to your father?"

"No, not yet," she whispered, almost in desperation. "But, can I tell you?"

"You can tell me absolutely anything, child," Tammy said, gently laying a hand on her arm.

"I'm pregnant!" she said, and immediately began to cry again.

"Is the boyfriend the father?" Tammy asked softly.

"Yes, and that's why he dumped me," she said, as her face crumpled once more.

So, between the tears and the sniffles, as Tammy proffered endless tissues, the story came out.

She had been persuaded, or bullied more like, to have sex with her boyfriend, Bryan.

She had been taught by her mother that it really was best to wait. But it wasn't easy for her. He was so controlling, and she had become a little afraid of him. So she'd given in. Straight away she'd regretted it, because he changed then. He became more domineering, and was often angry with her for no reason. And then, when she told him she was pregnant, he called her filthy names and told her it was all off, that he never wanted to see her again.

Grief-stricken, she had thought to go home to her parents. But then felt that she couldn't face her mother or Phillip, even though she knew both of them loved her. So while her flat-mate was at work, she'd sneaked into the unit they shared, packed her bag and had taken off. She realized too late, that she should have left a note, at least.

"I'm not sure why I decided to come here. I just knew that this is where I had to be. I'm so sorry," she wailed.

Tammy sat and held her for a while. Then she took her by the shoulders and looking into her eyes, told her that it would be alright.

"You are here with us now," she told her. "We will look after you, and the baby. And if you decide to stay here with us, there will always be a home for both of you. Now, why don't you dry those tears and go wash your face. Then when you've composed yourself you can come out to see your father. I think it would be best if you tell him all that's happened. You'll be surprised how understanding he is."

"Oh I can't, I couldn't!" Marlene cried. "I'd be too embarrassed. And he'll be ashamed of me."

"No, he won't, dear," said Tammy. "Trust me on this."

"Can you tell him for me? Please?" Marlene begged. "I'll talk to him later, but, can you tell him everything first? Please, please, please," she begged.

Tammy looked at her distraught face and tried to imagine herself in the same position. Then, taking the sobbing girl in her arms, told her again that everything would be alright.

"Okay, I will, if that's what you really want. So you go and freshen up, sweetheart while I go and talk to your father. By that time the kids will be coming in for lunch. They were so excited about you coming, that I had my hands full just getting them off to school this morning.

"You can leave talking to your dad until the children go back to class. They don't need to know anything just yet. That can all come a bit later, when you feel more comfortable about it." Tammy added.

All too soon, the house was full of noise, as three hunger machines stampeded in from school. Tammy was interested to note, that instead of, 'I'm starving Mum, what's for lunch?' she got, 'Mum! Is Marlene here yet?' Then, with hardly time for a breath, "What's for lunch? I'm starving!'

Laughing, Tammy got them off to wash their hands, and sat everybody at the table. Salad veggies, some cold meats, bread and butter, made for a satisfying lunch and in no time everybody was tucking in for their fill.

Over lunch, Marlene told her half-siblings that she was here to stay for a while, this with a side-ways look at her father, and that she'd be there to tell them everything when they came home from school.

Before they had all come tumbling through the door, Tammy had managed to speak with Dave, as she'd promised Marlene she would. And just as she'd reassured Marlene, he was sympathetic, stating his intention to support her, through the whole sorry mess.

So after the meal was cleared away and the children had returned to the school, Marlene came to sit with her father and talk to him about all that had happened. While not pretending to be delighted, Dave was none-the-less, gentle and understanding, and he re-affirmed Tammy's invitation to stay for as long as she needed and wanted.

"This is your home for as long as you want," he told her. "You are to feel completely free to stay, or go as you choose. We'd like you to stay," he added, as he pulled her toward him and gently held her in his arms.

"Dad... that is Phillip, was never one to hug," she said. "Mum does a bit, but not like you guys," she said shyly. "You both make me feel so welcome. I'm sorry I was so afraid to tell you everything. I've been so mixed up," she said. And with that, the tears started down her face again.

Dave felt a bit awkward as he held the sobbing girl, but as she clung to him, he realized that he had been given a tremendous gift.

Not only did he have a golden opportunity to get to know his daughter, but he also had the enormous privilege of actually being a real father to her for the first time. If he handled this right they could build a relationship and maybe he could even help this young woman to face the future with some confidence.

Eventually the sobs subsided and as she straightened up and wiped her face with yet another tissue provided by an ever watchful Tammy, she managed a teary smile. Then as she sat there, being comforted by these two kind people she realized that although it was an emotional time, telling Dave had not been all that difficult. And now, she was aware of an unexpected lifting of weight from her shoulders. And, though completely unable to explain why, in the midst of her tears, she felt laughter bubbling out of her. Because now, she suddenly felt as if everything really was going to be alright. And on top of that, she explained to a puzzled Dave... "I'm home, I'm really home."

All three sat there, for several moments, taking in all that had happened. It wasn't as if there weren't still some serious problems to face, they all knew that. But they were all somehow aware that something special had taken place. In the midst of turmoil, peace had come. Love and assurance had bridged a gap built by years of separation, and gentle understanding had overcome fears and feelings of grief and guilt.

Each of them were a little in awe of the fact, that there, in that room, surrounded by a growing pile of soggy tissues, a family had been forged. And somehow, each knew that the bonds would be enduring.

Reluctant to spoil the atmosphere, nobody spoke for quite some time. Then little by little, they began to discuss plans, as easily as if they had always been family.

Then finally, Tammy mentioned the fact that Marlene really needed to tell her mother everything. There was a moment's hesitation as she digested that idea.

"Yes, I do, don't I?" she said at last. "I think I can do that now."

"Well, remember, we'll be right here beside you, supporting you," Tammy told her lovingly.

So, with Tammy and Dave by her side offering some encouragement, the phone-call was made. Donna was pretty upset at first, but was so relieved to know that her daughter was safe and well, that she soon began to be a bit more upbeat. And although she hadn't thought she was ready, the idea of being a grandmother was already beginning to gain a certain appeal.

She said that she would tell Phillip about it that evening when he came in from work, and they would ring her tonight to talk about what they should all do.

So after talking to her mother for a bit more, and being reassured that her mother loved her and, no, she wasn't mad, and wasn't going to disown her, she finally hung up, feeling much better about everything.

Finally, Dave apologized, but explained that he had chores waiting and he really must get back to work. So promising that they'd talk some more that evening, he hugged his daughter, kissed his wife and went back to work.

Tammy made sure that Marlene knew where to find everything she might need, made sure she was definitely okay, and then left her to settle in, as she made her way back to the school, where she devoted so many hours, building hope for a future into young lives. Left in the house alone, Marlene spent some time unpacking her crammed backpack, organizing her room to her liking, and ironing some of the things that had become crushed almost beyond recognition. Then she lay down on the comfy bed to rest awhile.

Worn out from all the emotion and totally at peace with her surroundings, she was soon sound asleep.

Some time later in the afternoon, she awoke suddenly. For a moment or two she stared around at the strange room, wondering where she was.

Then, instantly, memory returned and she smiled to herself as she got up from the bed and went to wash her face. Refreshed she tidied the bed and went on an inspection tour of the house. But then, fully rested and eventually quite bored with her own company, Marlene wandered over to the school, and having enquired as to where Tammy might be, came to sit in on one of her classes. She crept in and found a seat at the back, where she sat quietly for the remainder of the lesson.

As she sat there, she recalled that she had heard her mother mention

Tammy's school a couple of times. And although she really knew very little about the missional goal of 'Future Dreaming', she had told her daughter that she thought Tammy was doing a really good thing, for 'those kids who've lost their way', as she had put it.

So, as Marlene listened to Tammy speaking, and heard the responses and feed-back from the students – young people of all ages and skin colour, she noticed – she became more and more impressed.

At one point, Tammy challenged the kids to stop and think about what the future might hold for them, asking them if they really thought they had choice about what that future might be. What, she asked them, would they like the future to be, if they discovered that they did have a choice.

After listening closely to the various responses, she went on to say to her students,

"If you put all the right things in place now, and set yourself goals – small, achievable, short-term goals – goals that can grow with you into bigger, long-term goals, then you will be surprised how you will actually see those bear fruit," she told them. "But, you must want them, passionately, and be prepared to make whatever sacrifices might be needed to bring them about.

"If you have a dream, don't put it away by telling yourself it can never happen. There is nothing wrong with having a dream – most of the world's high achievers are big dreamers.

"You will, of course, need to focus on the day-to-day needs while you work towards that which you know to be the desire of your heart. But never let go of your dreams.

"And above all, remember how much God loves you. Remember that you serve Him best by following your heart and doing everything you do to His glory. He made you and He is the One who has given you your dreams. Whatever you do in life, do it as if you were doing it just for Jesus, and He will help you see your dreams come true. Remember that Psalm 37:4 says, 'Delight yourself in the LORD and he will give you the desires of your heart.'" she concluded.

Having come into the class towards the end, Marlene was unsure of the exact context of those words, but they struck a chord and she determined to talk to Tammy as soon as she was free, and find out more. So, as the class broke up for the day, she lingered, waiting until all the students had gone. She wondered as they filed past her, why they were made up of so many age ranges, so when the last student had left and Tammy was tidying up her desk, she went forward and stood there, waiting until Tammy was ready.

"Hello, dear," said Tammy as she put the last thing away and looked up. "I saw you come in, all settled at home?"

"Yes, thank you. I had a nice rest, then the house was so quiet, I needed to at least hear another voice, so I came looking for you," she told Tammy.

"Yes, I suppose it can get very quiet in the bush," said Tammy, with a smile. "I guess I'm so used to it that I hardly notice. But then again, around all these youngsters it's hardly what one would call quiet. But, when I can get away by myself, it is the quiet that I love most about being out here," she added.

"Tammy," began Marlene, "How come the kids in this class are from so many age ranges. Don't schools usually divide into classes by age?"

"Well, yes, they do," agreed Tammy. "And most of our classes do of course. But I'm not a school teacher, so I don't teach the regular school lessons," she explained.

"This is what I call a 'Life Class' and it's for those students who have done, or have almost completed, all the regular schooling they intended doing.

"My hope is to teach them those things that ordinary school lessons can't teach – how to make some sense of the endless choices that young people face, especially those that would lead them down some pretty dark paths," she added.

"Sometimes, these kids slot back into the main-stream and finish where they left off with their studies. Some continue on here, others go off to the city. I'm always delighted when a child, who left school without gaining some sort of certificate level, leaves my class all fired up to go back and get some qualifications.

"So many of the kids out here, especially the aborigine children, don't see the need for an education if all they plan is to be a roust-a-bout on a property or to get a job somewhere digging ditches or building roads.

"But I tell them, 'why just be the one pushing the dirt around, when with a little more education, you could be the engineer designing the roads?'

"So I find it particularly satisfying when they suddenly find the urge to study and go on to do something more fulfilling," she said.

"I know that some will only want to work out here and not go on to anything else, and I tell them that really is fine. I just believe that they ought to know what choices they do have, and then to make up their own minds if what they thought they wanted, actually is what they want – what they'll want for the rest of their lives, not just 'today'."

Tammy shrugged and smiled at Marlene. "Sorry, dear, here endeth the lesson, as they say. I'm afraid I got a bit carried away, there."

"Not at all," replied Marlene. "I can certainly see what you meant about wanting things passionately. You are obviously very passionate about these kids," she added. "I must talk with you some more about the rest of that lesson, all the parts I missed," she said, seriously. "I think I've been drifting a bit with my life. I know that Mum was a little upset when I left school so early. Because it's not as if I've done anything marvelous – except work at part-time, dead-end jobs and get tied up with a good-for-nothing guy who dragged me down to his level and landed me in strife.

"Boy, where did all that come from?" she suddenly exclaimed. "All of that, and I only heard the end of your talk. The beginning must be dynamite," Marlene said, laughing.

"Well, I do try to fire 'em up," said Tammy, as she put an arm around Marlene's shoulder.

As they were walking slowly together up towards the house, Tammy explained to Marlene, some more about her 'Life-Classes'.

"I teach some basic cooking, I teach the girls about pregnancy, child-birth, and also how to care for their babies. We get a lot of young girls here in your situation, Marlene," she told her step-daughter gently. "And most of them have no idea how to cope. I try to smooth that path for them a little. And most of them soon learn that they can come to me at any time, for any reason.

"We now have men involved too; capable fellows who can also teach the boys some important points about that side of life," she added laughing.

"They also teach other skills as well, such as woodwork, metal-work, welding, animal care and dozens of other things that men, and some girls are likely to need, not just out here, but anywhere they might choose to live.

"We teach book-keeping, computer programming, budgeting and even just general house-keeping.

We try to teach all the basic skills for living that many of our students simply do not get – either in their poverty-stricken homes, or on the streets of the towns where some of our students hail from. Then of course, there are the ones who have had all the chances caring parents could give them, but just didn't care enough themselves, to take advantage of it." she said.

"Most of our students live in the hostel where they all have responsibilities. They do all the chores themselves and no slacking off is allowed. They even help to cook their own meals. We have a cook to oversee everything, but the kids are encouraged to do as much as they are able. Certainly they do all the cleaning up for themselves.

"But I think the most important thing I teach them is to love and trust God. It is very rare for a young person to leave 'Future Dreaming' without having found the Lord and chosen to receive Him into their lives. That would, without a doubt be my most satisfying experience – to lead a young person to Christ," she said quietly.

As Tammy had been speaking, Marlene had recognized her passion, and in the same way that her father had, so many years before her, she'd begun to feel her heart burning within her. Somehow, she knew, she would need to explore this subject a little closer.

By the time they had reached the house, Tammy had asked Marlene if she'd like to sit in on her classes while she was here.

"We only have a couple of weeks to go until the end of term, and then it will be the holidays. So, if you want to stay with us for a while, then why not?"

"Umm, you know... I think I might just do that," said Marlene thoughtfully.

"I'm beginning to like it here, and my life is in such a mess, maybe I need to spend some time talking with you and working things through," she continued.

Tammy was pleased and she gave her shoulder a little squeeze.

"That would be wonderful," she said. "But we must talk it through with you mother and make quite sure that it's okay with her. Oh I know that you are old enough to decide for yourself, but your mother loves you and worries about you, so it is the right thing to do, isn't it?" she added.

"Yes, of course. I guess that it's not so much about 'asking permission', but rather considering her needs too, right?"

"That is exactly right, dear, I'm proud of you. And I am sure your mother will be too," Tammy said, as they stopped for a moment. As they stood there, on the path up to the house, they looked at each other, then laughing, hugged, and continued on their walk home.

"There is something else that I'd like to ask you," continued Tammy.

"Go ahead," Marlene responded, "Ask away."

"Well, as I mentioned earlier, we are going for a trip, out into the bush during the holiday," Tammy began.

"I am not too sure how much you know about my childhood years, but, out there," and Tammy waved her hand in the vague direction of the aborigine camp and beyond. "Out there," she continued, "Is where I lived for seventeen years of my life.

"I was with my parents on a flying trip around Australia, when we crashed," she told Marlene. "We never got rescued, didn't know where we were, and Dad believed that Mum and I would not survive trying to walk out. So we stayed there.

"Both of them died out there; Mum, when I was fifteen, and Dad, when I was eighteen. So I was out there, on my own, until I was twenty-three, when your father, with four joy-flight passengers on board his small plane, crashed almost on my doorstep, so to speak – almost exactly in the same place that we had crashed, so many years earlier.

"It was rather uncanny, really. But, that's what happened. I remember that I was terrified. But somehow, your father managed to encourage me and reassure me, and gradually, I began to believe that everything would be alright.

"The five of them insisted that, come what may, they were going to walk out of there, and refused to go without me." Tammy paused a moment, reflecting, and Marlene could see that the memories were still vivid in her mind.

"I knew in my heart," she began again, "That they would never manage it without me. I'd learned so much from my father and from a tribe of aborigines – Barda's people," she added, pointing toward where the camps were spread out behind the bunkhouses. "And I knew how to survive out there – I was sure that they did not."

"So, the upshot of it is, that we did walk out. We certainly had some adventures along the way, but eventually we made it to here – when Roger, the pilot from this station found us as he was flying home from hunting stray cattle. Needless to say, after all we'd gone through together, your father and I were very much in love by then. Anyway, we finally went back to my mother's family – who had thought me lost forever. We married some months after arriving in Brisbane. Your dad got a job on a farm out in the country and we lived there quite some years. We had the three kids there. The rest you know, I think," she finished.

"You must remind us to tell you sometime about the dramas we went through to get the insurance company to pay up on your father's plane."

"Yes, that sounds like a story all on its own," laughed Marlene. "As to the rest of it, Mum did bring me pretty much up to date when Dad found me, at least as much as she knew herself," she said. "I had known since I was quite young that Phillip wasn't my natural father, even though he's always been good to me. But it kind of blew me away when my real father turned up like he did.

"Mum explained to me that it was her fault, not his that he hadn't come to see me sooner. She apologized and told me that she really regretted that dumb decision. But, of course, there's no going back, so all of us just chose to move forward. Funny, isn't it?" she asked suddenly. "How life turns out sometimes," she added.

"Yes, dear, it certainly is," Tammy agreed. "Well, here we are," she said, as they came to the steps of the house. "Let's go on in and get a cool drink. Then we can sit and chat for a while before I need to start getting dinner."

"I don't want you to lift a finger, Tammy," Marlene insisted. "I'm cooking tea tonight. One thing I have learned to do, is cook. Mum's a really good cook, and she made sure that I learned when I was just a kid," she said proudly. "And it was the one thing I excelled in at school," she finished with a giggle.

"So, it's my treat tonight, and you are going to sit down with Dad, and be waited on. And that's an order," she added laughingly, as Tammy began to argue.

Tammy smiled with pleasure, at how easily Marlene had begun using the title of 'Dad', for Dave. She knew that it pleased him and helped to ease the sense of loss that he had known for so many years; lost years. Of course he also knew that there was no going back, and as Marlene herself had said just a few moments ago, it is always best to just move on, and not dwell on the past.

Still, she hoped that over the next few days, these two very dear people would find time to get to know each other better and really forge a relationship that would be able to take them through the rest of their lives.

As the two women sat together, sipping a cool drink and chatting together, Tammy brought up the subject of the trip out bush, once more.

"I promised my children, years ago, that we would go out there again and visit the cavern home, where I spent so many years," she told Marlene.

"I've been back once, many years ago, because of that insurance drama I mentioned before. The insurance company sent an assessor to see us and he arranged for us to fly here to Tumberrumba, in a corporate jet no less, and then out there in a helicopter, to find your Dad's wrecked plane. So, now we know how to find my home, at least.

"Josh has asked me, again, to keep my promise to take him there, and he wants to go before he leaves for school in Brisbane next year. So we talked about it and decided we'd make it a family trip and go for the holiday. My question is, do you want to go with us?"

Marlene grinned from ear to ear.

"Are you kidding? What an adventure!" she said excitedly. "I'd love to. In fact I wouldn't miss it for the world."

"Well, that's settled then," said Tammy.

Then just as she was about to get up from her chair, the three kids came in through the door with their usual dignity, putting an abrupt end to peaceful conversation.

The next few hours were the usual family confusion of homework, telling of the day's adventures, (all trying to talk at once, of course) getting a meal on the table – getting kids showered and ready for bed.

Marlene was true to her word and after sharing some time with the children, headed for the kitchen, where she proceeded to cook up a most enjoyable meal. She had fossicked around in the kitchen, refusing all assistance, as she brought together a bewildering array of ingredients.

Perhaps not surprisingly on a cattle property, the freezer was always well stocked with choice cuts of meat, so with all sorts of gleeful comments and exclamations, she had made her choice from the copious quantity stored there, all of which were neatly packed and labeled for ease of selection.

She took a small beef roast, and when it was cooked her special way, she sliced and arranged it with the several varieties of fresh vegetables she had also found in Tammy's well-stocked refrigerator.

All family members had been banned from the kitchen, as she busily went about her tasks, and Tammy could hear her humming away to herself as she worked.

With Marlene in charge of the evening meal and the children finally busy with their own endeavours for a short time, Tammy and Dave had an almost unheard of opportunity to just sit together and talk. It was an unexpected and most welcome interlude of peace for this busy couple.

Marlene was delighted with Tammy's kitchen, for this dedicated homemaker had made it her business to keep her cupboards well-stocked. She had seen to it that her family had never acquired a taste for junk food. Everything that they ate was fresh and prepared at home except for the occasional special treat on rare trips to the city. At such times she was prepared to let each child choose their own meal from the menu of a carefully selected restaurant, and had always been pleased with their healthy choices.

Naturally, since coming back out to Tumberrumba there had been no restaurant meals, but with fresh meat always available and Tammy's well tended garden ever ready to supply all they would ever need, the family never had cause to complain about the food on their table.

Marlene's meal went over a treat. She had made a most delectable sauce for the veggies and the gravy she made for the meat was delicious. Tammy was most impressed and suggested that perhaps she could pursue a career as a chef.

This idea pleased Marlene, and glowing with happiness as she watched the family gobble down her cooking, she commented that maybe she'd look into it.

"If I'm not too old already," she added a little doubtfully.

"I was looking on the internet for something the other evening," Dave put in, "And I came across a web site for a job training network. Seems they specialize in mature-age students. Apparently they cater for just about every trade, including hospitality," he said.

Keen to find out more, Marlene asked if she could go on the computer later and have a look. Dave said that of course she could, and offered to help her find the site.

Over the meal, the family discussed their coming holiday arrangements. Tammy told Dave that she and Marlene had talked about it earlier that day, and that she would love to go with them.

"That's wonderful, kiddo," her father said. "We are actually looking forward to it ourselves. It's been a very long time, and perhaps it's time for Tammy to bring back some more of her belongings. She left so much stuff out there, because, of course, it was impossible to bring it back.

"You kids will be fascinated by the ingenious gadgets that your grandfather invented to make their lives workable out there," Dave said to his children. "He must have been a truly amazing man, and my one regret in life, apart from not knowing you as a baby," he said as an aside to Marlene, "Is never knowing him," he added.

"I think I would have loved your Mum too, Tammy darling," he said as he reached out and touched her hand. "She certainly bequeathed me an astoundingly beautiful and wonderful wife," he said.

"Ooh Dad, mushy stuff. Yuk!" said his younger son, as he pulled a face.

Benji turned to Marlene and said, "You wouldn't believe how much these two kiss and cuddle. They go on with real mushy stuff all the time. It's disgusting!" he said, pretending to make heaving noises. Then he ducked as his father went to cuff him gently about the ear, and ran off laughing.

"Can't catch me!" he yelled, as Dave got up from his chair and chased him out of the room.

"As you can see," said Tammy to Marlene, "I actually have four children. It's just that one is a little bigger than the other three."

Marlene laughed delightedly. This was a truly wonderful family, and she was aware of a joyous sense of belonging and an inner peace that she hadn't felt for a long time.

The evening meal was soon cleared away, as Tammy had insisted on all hands on deck.

"This is our thanks to Marlene for the scrumptious meal," she told them.

A beautiful dessert had followed the main course. Marlene had put together a marvelous concoction of fresh fruit, whipped cream with a flavouring in it, and some interesting ice-confection that she had made from crushing home-made ice-blocks that she had found in the freezer, and whipping them together with some other ingredients to make a colourful and tasty mixture. This she had then piped through an icing bag to decorate each plate with a pattern – a different one for each family member, of course.

All in all the meal had proved to be a huge success and the family were generous with their praise.

No sooner had they sat down after the meal, however, than the phone rang. Dave went to answer it and it was Donna, ringing to speak with Marlene, as she had promised earlier in the day.

Dave called his daughter to the phone, and patting her on the shoulder, left her to talk with her mother.

After a bit, she came back into the lounge-room and told her father that her mother wanted to speak with him. So Dave went out to the phone.

He was gone for a while, but when he came back, he was smiling.

"Donna says you can stay as long as you like," he said.

"Of course I did, gently I hope, point out that you were

old enough to decide for yourself where you stayed. And she agreed, although somewhat reluctantly at first.

Anyway, the upshot of it all is that she is now resigned, not too unhappily I hope, to you staying here for the time being at least."

He looked at his wife with one eyebrow raised in query and received a nod of approval from her. Then he looked at his daughter, who jumped up from her chair and threw her arms around him.

"I love you, Dad," she said simply. And Tammy watched as her husband positively glowed.

"What did your mother say to you, dear?" Tammy asked.

"She was anxious for me to go back home, but I told her that I really want to stay out here, for a while anyway," she told them a little hesitantly. "I think I'd like to stay, at least until the baby's due... if that's alright?" she asked.

"It's more than alright," said Tammy. "We want you to stay, for as long as you want to stay. And I think that it would be good for you to be out here in this clear, fresh air, while you are carrying the little one," she commented with the practical air of one who knows what is best.

So, even though each knew that there was some sadness for Donna, it seemed that things were settled, for now at least. Marlene would stay here until her baby was due, at which time she would go to the city for proper medical supervision. After that, well – time would tell.

The next couple of weeks were busy and full of new experiences for Marlene. She attended Tammy's Life Classes every day, helped around the house and began to take on lots of little tasks around the school, including helping Tammy with some of her cooking classes.

At the weekend, when she wasn't helping with the chores or the holiday arrangements, she would go off with Dave on an errand, or off with the kids on one of their many adventures. She got to know Barda, who rarely ventured far from his camp these days, and also got to know some of his people.

They were shy by nature, as was Marlene too, but they soon seemed to find a common ground and in no time had formed some strong bonds of friendship.

This was something that Tammy treasured in her heart. Her own children were always at the camps and played endlessly with the children.

Since coming back to Tumberrumba, it had been Tammy's daily routine to visit the camps and to spend as much time as she could with these people from her childhood. She was saddened to see her old friend failing in health, but she realized that he was very old – how old, she had no way of really knowing – but one of the men, who had been a lad when she had known him all those years ago, told her that his father had known Barda as a young man, and with his new-found mathematical skills, had worked out that Barda must be well into his mid to late eighties at least, maybe even into his nineties. So she made it her business to spend whatever time she could spare, with him. Especially as it had become more difficult for him to seek her out and speak with her as she went about her day.

The days flew by, with seemingly increasing speed, as the time for the family to go on their trip drew nearer. Tammy was sure that the days grew shorter in direct correlation to the amount of tasks still waiting to be attended to.

"The more I have to do, the less time I have to do it," she muttered one day, to anyone who was in hearing range at the time. But all she got for her trouble was giggles from her kids and a pseudo-sympathetic 'tut-tut' from her loving hubby.

Declaring that they were all most unkind, she simply got on with whatever it was she was doing, and with a wide smile, commented that they would all 'get theirs' when she caught them.

Christmas was on them before anyone had time to think. This proved to be a joyous time with the whole Tumberrumba family joining in.

There were gifts to prepare and wrap, little surprises for loved ones to devise and arrange, endless meals to prepare and enjoy, and of course a beautiful Christmas morning church service, where everybody, both black and white came to celebrate the happy occasion of the birth of the Christ Child.

Christmas was always a big affair on Tumberrumba and they always did everything with great enthusiasm and much style.

Chapter 24

HOLIDAY IN THE CAVERN HOME

At last the big day arrived, when Tammy and the family were to go on their holiday. Natalie and Danny came up to the house to farewell them and wish them a wonderful, safe and happy trip. Danny had insisted that they should take a trailer and a generator, as well as all the other necessary equipment for travelling in the outback.

So by the time they were ready to leave, the vehicle and trailer were well loaded. They said their good-byes and all climbed into the car.

As they drove away they turned to wave, discovering a sea of black faces behind them, all jumping up and down and waving furiously. They waved back, just as enthusiastically. The odyssey had begun.

For a while, Tammy found it difficult to adjust to how much faster they covered the distance than they had during the days when they had slogged wearily over the endless miles of emptiness.

The journey took three days of pretty solid driving even so, and they were relieved that there were no untoward misadventures. There was a punctured tyre at one stage, as the vehicle ran over some of the spiky grass that covered much of the terrain. But this was soon changed and at the evening stop Dave set about patching it, in case they needed it for an emergency spare.

They stopped briefly at each of the main waterholes where the group had camped, so that the children could get the feel of their parents' experience. And at the big oasis, where Joe and his cohorts had been captured, the children insisted on a blow by blow description of the whole episode.

Joshua declared to all and sundry that he thought his parents were the bravest people in the world.

Tammy was glad to see that the pond was still there, but relieved to see that it had finally been capped – to preserve the water.

A notice on a steel post informed any travellers that a large handle in the shape of a wheel, could be turned anti-clockwise, allowing water to flow from a pipe connected to the one in the centre of the pool.

A steel rod, attached by a chain, could be used as a lever if the wheel had tightened. The sign also warned that the water would be under some pressure and VERY hot.

She and Dave were relieved that the water was being preserved, for they now knew that the Artesian water, contrary to popular belief was not a renewable resource and it seemed wasteful to have it bubbling up endlessly, just going to waste.

She was glad too that a way was provided for any stranded travellers, such as she and Dave had been, to access the water if needed.

Such a beautiful spot was a rarity out in this stark landscape and looking at it through less stressed eyes, she could truly appreciate what a miracle it was. She thought that the trees had grown a little since she'd last seen them, but couldn't be sure after such a long time.

Eventually they arrived at their destination, weary but excited. The crash-site had been surprisingly easy to locate. What was left of the wreckage was, somewhat surprisingly, still visible. Although much of it had been covered with sand, enough of it was exposed to allow immediate identification.

The boys wanted to examine it all in minute detail, while the girls were more interested in how anyone could have survived out here, with no water and no shelter.

"Grandpa must have been amazing," said Libby. "He must have known just what to do. Did he Mum?" she asked.

"Yes, darling, I think he must have, because in no time he had a lean-to constructed and had gone off to find water. I never did ask just where he got that, but I suppose I've always assumed it was from the waterhole where Barda's people always camped."

"Where was that, Mum?" asked Libby.

So, Tammy directed them to the oasis at the foot of an interesting rock formation, where her dear friends had spent a great deal of their time. She was fascinated to discover that remnants of their camps were still visible after so many years, even though Barda had made sure there was no rubbish left lying around.

Memories flooded her mind and she sat for some time on a flat rock by the water.

She allowed her mind to travel back over the years, to the times, when as a child, she would sit here, right on this very rock she recalled, and learn a language, that for a while was so strange to her ears, and now was as familiar as her own.

She remembered watching the mothers caring for their babies and preparing food for their families. She could see in her mind's eye, the children playing and laughing – a carefree people, sharing all they had with each other and opening their hearts to three stranded 'white-folks' who were as foreign to them, as they were to this child from another world and way of life.

Finally, she stood up and informed her family that they must go to the cavern, unload the car and get settled for the night, or they'd be caught trying to work in the dark.

So, shaking off the lingering memories for the moment, she led the way back to the car. Driving up to the cavern was something new for Tammy, and she wasn't sure how far they'd get.

"We wouldn't want to damage any of the trees we planted," she insisted. "So, if we can't get close, we'll just have to carry stuff. Did we pack the powerful torches, Dave?" she asked.

"Sure did, my love," he said. "I'm pretty certain that we didn't forget anything," he reassured her.

Eventually, the track they were following narrowed and they were unable to take the vehicle any further. So they parked, each grabbing as much as they could carry, and walked the remaining distance.

Tammy led them unerringly, as despite the years that had passed, the memories came one on top of the other, and she knew, as surely as she knew her own home, every step of the way. She was amazed to discover that, although it had gone a bit wild, it was still possible to see where her vegetable garden had been. There were even a few straggly plants still producing, she noticed. Not that she imagined they'd be very tasty. Still, if one should be starving...

Taking the torch from her husband's outstretched hand, she led the way into the dark corridor behind the tangle of branches and vines that still covered it, exactly as they had when, as a terrified young woman of a mere twenty-three years, she had led five uncertain guests into her home – the first visitors ever to enter behind the vines.

Making weird noises, hopefully to scare his sister, Benji followed his mother. She was almost certain that most of it was to cover up his fear of dark and scary places so with a simple 'Benj,' she shushed him and informed the family that it was quite safe.

"Unless someone has been here, which I doubt, or there's been a rock fall, there should be nothing to fall over," she assured them. "Just be aware that the path slopes down quite a bit. We actually finish up quite a way underground."

With the bright light of the torch to guide them, they discovered no objects or obstacles to prevent safe access, and in no time they were over the big rock and standing at the top of the stairs.

They stood there for a moment, and took it all in. All were absolutely silent. Then Josh broke the silence with a simple "Wow!" an expression that really summed up the feeling of all of them – even Tammy herself.

For there it was, just as she had left it more than sixteen years ago. As she descended the stairs cut out by her father so long ago, she listened to the once familiar music of the water, as it bubbled out of the cliff wall at the back of the cavern.

It was not as bright as it usually was inside, because the sun was lowering and no longer pouring its welcome light down through the holes in the roof. But enough light still showed for the family to see the spectacular beauty of the cavern their mother had called home for nearly half of her life.

"It's beautiful, Mum," said Libby, almost reverently – obviously in awe. "It's like Aladdin's cave," she said as she wandered about, looking at everything.

Benji went straight to the water and splashed his hand through the water gurgling out of the wall.

"This is wonderful," he commented. "Did you bathe in here?"

"Yes, we did," his mother told him. "We worked out a system, whereby each of us was able to bathe in private. We were very strict about that. Absolutely no peeking was to be tolerated," she said, laughing.

Then, like a child again, she ran to each alcove and touched everything. She was surprised how little dust had settled, although she'd need to wipe things over before they could be used. But it seemed that time had preserved, rather than destroyed her home, and her heart was glad.

Then, suddenly all business, she snapped out of her reverie and rallied the family to get organized and bring all they'd need for the evening, back from the car.

"Bring only what you'll need," she instructed. "We can get the rest tomorrow. We'll have plenty of time then to do it safely in the daylight."

So, while the rest of them fetched and carried, she set about cleaning.

Like a dynamo she scuttled about, wiping surfaces. She took the bedding over to the far side of the cave and shook and bashed the dust out of them, before bringing them back and to remake the beds.

They had brought sleeping bags and a ton of modern camping gear, but these old beds would serve again, as they had served her family so well.

By the time Dave had declared that all necessary items had been unloaded, she had the place reasonably shipshape. Then all that remained was to get some food together. She had packed a meal in the freezer section of the car fridge before leaving home. At the lunch-time stop she had taken it out so that it would thaw and be ready to eat at the end of the day's travel. So all that was necessary, was to wash some plates and other utensils, and heat the food and serve it. Dave had brought in the generator so he soon had more light going than the cavern had ever seen.

The car fridge was set up and the gas re-connected. It was great the way it had kept things cold as they travelled, even while disconnected. Dave had decided to bring gas for the fridge; to save the generator fuel only for lighting and emergencies.

As soon as the meal was eaten, each one set about organizing their sleeping places.

Dave and Tammy were to use her parent's room of course, even though each found the thought a wee bit strange. And because beds had been manufactured to accommodate Tammy's five visitors, there was still plenty of bedding for the two boys, Libby and Marlene.

Becky had wanted so badly to come, but there simply had not been enough room. Tammy had promised faithfully, that next time, and there would be a next time, that they'd make sure she could come.

Meantime, she had agreed to stay behind and help look after the students who needed to stay at the school over the holiday break.

She had waved goodbye with all the rest of them, after a tearful hug for Tammy and a whispered word of love and best wishes for a safe and happy journey.

By the time all beds were made up and each family member had taken their turn for a wash in the stream, it was definitely time for a travel-weary bunch to hit the sack.

Morning, with its new adventures and discoveries, would be upon them soon enough.

The next two weeks were busy and full of adventure. Tammy led her family to all the places she'd explored as a child, sat them down in shady places and told them stories about her life and how her father had taught her to survive in this wild and beautiful place.

She took them to Barda's camp several times, and they all played and splashed around in the deep pool. Then she'd sit them down and teach them some of the things that Barda had taught her. She began to teach Marlene some of the language, which her own three already spoke like natives. They'd been learning since early childhood, at Tammy's gentle insistence.

All too soon, after a marvelous two weeks, it was time to load up the car and head for home. Tammy did a last whip round to make sure she had all that she wanted to take with her, and that the family hadn't left anything behind, and then, once again, for the third time in her life, she walked away from her childhood home.

But this time it was different. This time, she knew that she would be back.

And she knew too, that as soon as possible, she must encourage her dear aunt and uncle to come and see the place where she and her parents had lived for so long. She realized that arranging such a visit was long overdue, and resolved to correct that situation at the earliest possible time.

The family had all voted, unanimously, that this was where they would come for their holidays, as often as they could, even perhaps before they would head south to spend time with Aunt Susan and Uncle Don, where they'd get to see all the other relatives as well. Perhaps, next time they came here, instead of going to Don and Susan, they should come here and experience some outback hospitality.

Now that the ice was broken, and the family had actually come to this place – a place, that Tammy knew, had an atmosphere unlike anywhere else, she also knew that others would want to come here too, and deep in her heart, she began to dream again. And Tammy had learned from what she continually taught her students, and her own children, every day...

'Don't squash a dream, follow your heart, and do it as if for the Lord!'

So the trip home began. Along the way more stories were told, landmarks were pointed out and if a story was connected to it in any way, a full re-telling of the adventure was demanded. In this way, four days later, tired, dusty but happy, the family arrived back at Tumberrumba.

They had spent nearly half an hour on the dusty track where the five weary travelers had first seen a vehicle – their first sign of civilization. They had all climbed down from the car and had stood there in the dust and the heat, trying to imagine themselves there on that day.

The three young ones stood there for a while, trying to see, in their mind, the dust from the vehicle still hanging in the still air, the only sign of its recent passing. To try and get the feel of the mixture of excitement and desperation, that their parents had felt as they had stood there so long ago.

Once again, they were realizing just how much these two people had endured and young as they may be, were beginning to appreciate how these experiences had contributed towards making them the wonderful people – the wonderful parents that they were.

A crowd had gathered to welcome them when they arrived home. Someone had seen their accompanying dust-cloud, long before they actually drove up to the house, and the word had passed quickly around.

It was with great excitement, that the children began to tell everyone what a wonderful time they'd had, and in no time had run off to share their experiences with their friends.

Tammy, Dave and Marlene, a little more sedately, were glad to climb down from the car and stretch a little, before going inside.

A cool drink had been prepared by their hosts/employers, although more like dear friends. So, resisting the urge to rush about unpacking, they sat for a while, resting and telling Natalie and Danny all about their trip.

At last, the unpacking called for their attention, so promising that another trip would happen and that this time, they must go too, they let them go back to their chores and turned their hand to the somewhat tedious task of putting everything back in place, getting some laundry started and generally finding their feet again, after four weeks away.

Dave asked Marlene if she'd go and fetch the children so they could help unpack, so she willingly went to do that, returning in not too long a time, with the three of them in tow.

So, with all hands on deck, whether willing or reluctant, the job was done in plenty of time to prepare a light evening meal and relax a while before heading to bed. It was the end of a very big day.

In the days that followed, all sorts of issues were waiting for Tammy and Dave to deal with, so in no time it seemed as if they had never been away. But deep in their memories, were treasures to keep.

During the remainder of the holidays, Tammy and Marlene made endless plans, and the children enjoyed the freedom of their lives, playing with their friends, rambling through the bush, riding their favourite horses and doing all the myriad things that bush children find to do when school lessons are not occupying their time.

Dave, still managing this massive property, had his hands well and truly full. The holiday was definitely over for him.

The last couple of weeks of the holiday were also busy ones for Tammy and Joshua, as all the arrangements needed to be made to get him ready for his journey to Brisbane. At first, they had thought he would go to boarding school, but Susan and Donald had insisted that he live with them.

They had given him the choice, and he had decided, in the short-term at least to stay with his aunt and uncle. So he packed all the things he thought he'd be likely to need and was as ready as possible when the time came.

It was agreed that he and Tammy would fly to Brisbane. Dave would not be able to get away again so soon, so he would stay behind and look after the other two. Marlene, who at first said she'd go too, changed her mind and decided to stay behind and look after the family.

"Dad will be busy, so he'll need someone on the home-front," she'd insisted. Tammy and Dave had finally agreed, and gratefully accepted her offer.

Chapter 25
A NEW SCHOOL FOR JOSHUA

So the day arrived. Dave drove his wife and son out to the strip, where the Tumberrumba plane was waiting, and waved them goodbye, as they flew away. Roger was still flying for the station that had been his home for so many years. But these days he and Tammy had an easy, friendly relationship. He was no longer so brash, and she was no longer a skittish waif, afraid of everything and everyone.

The plan was that Roger would fly them to Rocky, from where they would travel by one of the major airlines to Brisbane.

The trip was long and tiring, but uneventful. Susan was at Brisbane airport to meet them and was overjoyed to see them again. There were hugs and kisses galore and not a few tears, but eventually, things had settled down enough for them to gather their luggage, get out to the car and begin the trip back to the house.

Aunt Susan told Tammy how quiet the house had been without Becky, "And without you too, darling," she had said. "I'm sure you have no idea how much I miss not having you around," she said. "It's so good to see you."

The next little while was busy, getting Josh settled in his new school, and Tammy stayed for a couple of weeks, just to make sure that he was happy and able to join in.

She tried not to worry, as she knew that her oldest child had grown into a fine young man. As a senior, he would have plenty of responsibility in his new school and she knew that he would fit right in and prove to be capable in whatever he turned his hand to.

Then, finally, she knew that the time had come and she must get back to the rest of her family. So she reluctantly said goodbye to her first-born, and hugged her precious aunt and uncle, reassuring them once more that Becky was fine and would be in touch.

Susan and Don had both agreed that they must make the effort to get out to Tumberrumba and promised to arrange it for Josh's trip home for the next long school holiday.

A taxi arrived to take her to the airport, so after a final hug each, and after securing a promise from them both that they would indeed come to visit next time Josh came home, she descended the stairs, bag in hand, and waving goodbye once more, got into the cab and drove away.

Her flights back home were without incident and she marveled at the way she had become so used to flying, after once believing that she'd never go near a plane again.

On the flight home she had time to pray and read her Bible, and to reflect on the future directions of 'Future Dreaming'.

Dave was waiting for her when the Tumberrumba plane touched down on the station's airstrip, and she fell into his arms, hungry for the feel of his strong arms around her.

As they drove back to the house, she told him how well Josh had adapted in the couple of weeks she had been there, and that she really felt they would have no need to worry about him. He was really enjoying his new school and had already made a friend.

"Well, that's the first one to fly the coop," said his father. "I guess we'll have to get used to that, as each one reaches that age," he finished.

"Yes, I know," said Tammy sadly, "But please, don't remind me of that right now." She sighed and a little tear escaped.

"I just know I'm going to miss him terribly," she added. The words were a little muffled through her hands and the tissue with which she was wiping her face.

Dave grinned and reaching out a free hand, touched her gently.

"He'll be fine, just you wait and see. In no time at all that boy will be setting the world on fire," his proud Dad said. And Tammy smiled through her tears, cheering up a little as she recounted to Dave the promise she had extracted from her aunt and uncle to come visit when Josh came home for the holidays.

Dave was very pleased and agreed with Tammy that such a visit was indeed long overdue.

Becky and Marlene were there to greet them when they reached the house. Marlene had a meal all ready just to sit down and eat. So Tammy gratefully went off to freshen up and after hugging Marlene in thanks, sat down to enjoy the food put in front of her.

"I could really get used to this, you know," she told Marlene, with a smile. "I rather like having someone cook for me."

Marlene glowed with happiness. Of course, glowing was something that Marlene was doing a lot of at the moment. Her pregnancy and the fresh air were really agreeing with her and she had been keeping very good health. The flying doctor made regular stops to check up on her and was thrilled with her progress and the health of her baby.

As they ate, they talked over the things that had been happening on the home front. The live-in students were all well and happy. But Becky reported that a visit from Tammy was mandatory.

"They are missing you, my dear," she told her cousin. "If you don't go to see them, there'll be a mutiny, or something," she added, laughing.

So after dinner, as the evening shadows were stretching out across the sun-kissed landscape, Tammy wandered over to the dormitory building.

She found the young folk all going about their own interests, and was pleased to see that they all had hobbies and were happily pursuing them. However, all activity ceased when someone called out that Tammy was coming. So as she walked into the Common Room, she was instantly surrounded.

Amid the clamour, she gleaned questions such as, 'how's Josh?' 'How did your trip go?' 'We thought you were never coming home.' 'We missed you so.'

A hug for each one was called for, then they all sat down in the easy chairs scattered about the room, and she told them all she could think of about her trip south.

They wanted detailed descriptions of Josh's school, so she took out some photos to show them. They wanted to know what Brisbane looked like, so she was able to show them some photos of that too. Finally, exhausted, she excused herself and with a promise to see them tomorrow, she made her escape and took herself over to the camps.

Barda was resting, and Tammy was told that he didn't go anywhere much these days.

"He has become very weak while you were away," one of the young women told her. "We are afraid that soon we will lose him," she added, with tears in her eyes.

Tammy was saddened to hear that, even though she had known for some time that it was coming. She went over to sit beside him, as he reclined on a bed.

"Can I have you brought to the house, Barda?" she asked, longing to make him more comfortable for his last days.

But smiling in his gentle way, he refused her offer.

"I am better here, where I am surrounded by my people," he said softly. "I am thankful for your offer, I know that my dear Tammy speaks with love in her heart. But I am happy here," he added. "Please do not worry about me. Soon I will go to meet with your father and your mother," he said. "And I will see this God you introduced me to, face to face. This I am very much longing to do."

So, with a smile and the gentlest of hugs, she left him in the care of his own, and returned to the house, wiping the tears from her eyes.

Chapter 26
THE END OF AN ERA, AND NEW BIRTH

Later that night, a gentle knock on the door, revealed a small aborigine girl, with a message for Missy Tammy.

"Barda would see you, if that is alright," she said politely. "He is so weak, but he said to me, 'Leya, go ask if Missy Tammy can come'. I could hardly hear him, he whispered so soft," she said. Tammy could see how sad she was.

So excusing herself from her family, Tammy made her way to the camps, for the second time that day.

Barda welcomed her with a touch on her hand and a weak smile.

"I would bid you farewell, little one," he whispered as Tammy bent close to him. His voice was so frail, she could barely hear him. "Please do not be sad, this is the way of life and it is good that I go to such a good place."

His whispers were so soft, but his will was still strong, and he still had one more thing to say. So, with stops each little while, to catch his breath, he spoke the words that were on his heart.

"I want to thank you that I will go now to my Saviour, and... not to the place of demons that I would have gone to... if your father's plane had not crashed. I owe my eternity to each of you, as well as to our Jesus," he whispered. "To Jesus, because He died for me – to you, because you were faithful to Him... I am at peace." And with those final words, he simply closed his eyes, and with a final, gentle breath, he was gone.

The keening sound of a tribe in mourning accompanied Tammy, as she tearfully made her way back to the house.

There was no need for her to tell the family what had happened, they could hear the women as they let their grief be known to any who were in range.

As she sat with her husband and children, they listened to the sound of weeping, but as they listened, the wailing turned to singing, as someone remembered a hymn they had been taught. For the next hour, the family sang too, as familiar song after familiar song came wafting across from the camp.

When silence finally fell, Tammy went to bed, worn out by her big day and by her grief. Tomorrow, arrangements would be made to finally farewell this elder statesman, a regal leader of a noble people.

In the days that followed, Tammy went about in a bit of a daze. She was glad that it was a quiet time at the school, with some students still not back from visiting their families. She found it difficult to concentrate on tasks and was increasingly grateful to Becky and to Marlene for the competent way they simply took over, leaving her to attend to Barda's funeral and to help his family to grieve.

It truly was the passing of an era.

Eventually, Tammy began to see things clearly again. Ashamed that she had left so much to the others to do, she apologized to them. But they would hear none of it.

"You have done so much for all of us, Tammy," they insisted. "What makes you think that we would not be glad to give you a helping hand at a time like this?" Becky scolded gently. "We are here for you, darling girl, just as you always have been for us."

Gradually life began to get back into rhythm. Overdue students began to filter back to the school, some with apologies, others... well... Tammy just smiled. They were learning, but some still had a way to go.

Marlene's time drew near and all knew that, soon, she too would be leaving them. Tammy knew that if she left it too late, the airline wouldn't take her, so she began to make arrangements.

Donna was anxious to see her daughter, and was thrilled when Tammy rang her to tell her that a ticket had been bought and Marlene would be arriving very soon.

The flight number was duly written down and Donna was given strict instructions that she must let them know immediately that Marlene was safely home.

"And we must have a photo of the baby as soon as possible," Tammy instructed, laughing. "How I wish I could be there for the birth," she added wistfully.

The day for Marlene's departure duly arrived and there were many tearful farewells. The girls at the school had grown to love her and she was leaving behind some incredible young cooks. She had been teaching them to find their way about a kitchen for months and many of them had been really keen learners. So on the day she left, practically the whole school turned out to wave her goodbye.

As the Tumberrumba plane lifted off the tiny airstrip, taking Marlene home to her mother, Tammy wept openly and prayed earnestly for her safety, her well-being, the safe delivery of her baby, and a wonderful life for both of them.

She knew that Marlene was not coming back, at least not for a while. She had confided to Tammy that she had plans.

"Mum has said she'll mind the baby for me if I go back to school," she had said. "I hope to train as a chef," she had told Tammy.

Tammy had been delighted, but sad too, for she knew that if Marlene was going to pursue a career, she may never see her again.

In the months that followed, 'Future Dreaming' continued to grow. Children and young people came from all around to learn from the team of dedicated and highly qualified people who taught there and who counseled and cared for the students.

Courses were expanded as willing hands came on deck to support the various subjects and soon the school was as big as a city school.

It never failed to amaze Tammy, how the idea had caught on from its raw beginnings. It had not been that long ago, when Tammy would take small groups and teach them to stretch their minds. She had been determined to somehow assist outback youngsters to look beyond a primary school education – encouraging them to see themselves as people of worth, with the potential to be anything they were willing to work towards.

She had, from the beginning, refused to admit that it was inevitable, that youth from the camps particularly, would end up in the towns, following scores of their predecessors into the spiral of unemployment, hopelessness, drug addiction and alcohol abuse.

With what had soon become her trademark 'can-do' attitude, she had set about changing the status quo, working with ones and twos, until eventually a class of young people reluctantly decided to give it a go and see what the lady was on about.

History would reveal that her efforts had been hugely successful, and largely responsible for rescuing dozens and dozens of children from eventual darkness and despair.

"If we keep expanding this way we'll have to request the government to take us up to university standard," Dave said, laughingly one day. "Although, that may not be as silly as it sounds," he added. "Much of our curriculum is TAFE level already, and with a bit of a kick along, could soon reach university level," he said.

"Something to think about for the future, I suppose," Tammy had said. And she wondered where it could go from here, the potential seemed endless.

The time passed in a busy whirl and the school continued to grow. Students from all over the place began pouring in. And it seemed to Tammy that they always seemed to be building something, as the needs of the school grew.

So it was, that after a series of discussions with the decision-makers back east, the first tentative explorations began – with a view to investigating whether there would be any hope of upgrading the Tumberrumba TAFE College, as the 'Future Dreaming' part of the station school had become known in education circles.

Somehow, although it had started more as a joke than with any hope of reality, it had reached the point where it seemed more and more to be the next direction for 'Future Dreaming.'

Meantime, word had filtered back to them that Marlene's baby had been born. She had given birth to a girl, just as she'd hoped and both were well. Photos followed and everybody had to look and 'ooh' and 'aah' over this beautiful child.

Donna, it seemed, was reveling in her role of grandmother, and willingly took over the day to day care, when Marlene finally went off to college.

Chapter 27
A WEDDING, A REUNION, STILL DREAMING

The years went swiftly by. Marlene excelled in her studies, and as a qualified chef began a career that soon took her to some interesting places.

Photos and letters and emails came regularly, as she kept her outback family up to date with her successes.

She met a fine young man, another chef that she had first met at college, but met again when, a number of years later, they worked together at a large restaurant in Melbourne. It seemed like no time at all to Dave and Tammy before she announced her engagement.

So a trip south was planned for a wedding. Much joy and happiness was shared with both families and Marlene made a beautiful bride. Her new husband, Tony, was very nice. He was a gifted chef, and a dedicated Christian, so Marlene, who had given her life to Jesus amid tears and laughter of the purest joy, one evening in the lounge-room of Dave's and Tammy's home, was at peace about her future with this man.

She had confided to Tammy, that he was her life's soul-mate – "Just like Dad is to you," she had whispered.

Tammy and her soul-mate, finally turned their faces towards home, and saying goodbye to all the relatives once more, drove away for the long journey home.

Every year, Tammy made her pilgrimage to her cavern home. It had become the family's holiday house and anybody who was free at the time would tag along.

Susan and Don did make their long-awaited journey to the outback, the very next year, bringing an excited Josh home to spend his holiday with his family. The plan was that on the way home, they would take the time to tour and see all those places they had promised themselves they'd see 'one day'.

Tammy was so excited when they finally pulled up outside her door that she could hardly contain herself. Of course, Josh was there – safely delivered to his anxious mother's arms. And although she had known that her aunt would look after him well, she was almost surprised at how well he looked. Not to mention how much he had grown in a year!

After the joyful reunions and the settling-in process was over, the family sat down together for a meal prepared for them by Becky, who was also thrilled to see her parents after such a lengthy separation. Yet even though she missed them terribly, she was still sure in her heart that this was where she was supposed to be, and so had no plans to go back down south with them when they left to go home.

It was, of course, holiday time again, so Tammy, Dave and an assortment of people were planning their annual excursion to the cavern. Becky had insisted that this was her time too and because some past students were available to live-in and care for the boarders who had no place to go for the holidays, she was free to do so.

And so the trip was planned. This time it involved taking more than one car, because of the number of people who wanted to go. Dan had insisted that Natalie should also take a break and go with them, declaring that he'd manage – maybe not as well as she did, but well enough to get by. So, laughingly she agreed and seemed as excited as a kid at the prospect.

The trip out was uneventful, although slow, as Tammy and Dave discovered that they needed, again, to stop at all the places where significant events had taken place, just as they had on their first journey out here with the children.

But eventually, they had arrived, and once more Tammy was struck by how simply magical the place was. It seemed that no matter how often she stepped over that threshold and looked down at the golden glow of the rock and the glitter of the little stream as it bubbled cheerfully out of its rocky prison and made its way across the sandy floor of the cave, somehow that little thrill was always there.

Susan and Don were amazed, as were all those who followed Tammy down the tunnel-way to the large rock that separated the tunnel from the wide expanse of the cavern below – struck, as was every visitor, by its sheer beauty and the wonder of finding such a place in the centre of a vast and barren land.

Seemingly so hostile to the casual visitor, it was quite a revelation to find such a place deep beneath the rocky ground.

Having descended to the cavern floor, Tammy oversaw the putting away of all the food and equipment and baggage that each person had brought, and then set about finding somewhere for each one to sleep. Since the first visit, more sleeping places had needed to be arranged, so there was somewhere for everyone to lay their head.

Then, before setting about sorting out the evening meal, Tammy took her aunt and uncle into the room where her parents had slept for so many years.

Tenderly, and with tears in her eyes, Susan wandered about the room, touching little things and trying to imagine her beloved sister using them – trying to see, in her mind's eye, how her sister had coped in this strange and wild place.

Yet, she realized, as she looked about her, that there really was something about this cavern that seemed safe and substantial, and somehow comforting. And she began to understand Tammy's deep connection to this place she had called home for such a large part of her life.

Over the next few days, Tammy had taken her visitors to each of the special places around her home. The pool where Barda and his people had camped for a good part of each year, sitting again on the flat rock where she had sat so often absorbing the language and culture of one of the last groups of truly tribal aborigines.

She took her guests to her vegetable garden, still growing after all these years, although in serious need of some weeding she noticed. They wandered along the paths where Tammy had daily strolled in search of food, and walked with her along the path that had taken her to a time and place that would be forever etched into her memory.

The walk that had taken her to the place where the planes had crashed

– her father's, so many years before, and then Dave's – an incident that had set in motion a set of circumstances that no one could ever have imagined or planned. Only the hand of God could have orchestrated such an outcome.

As time passed, visiting the cavern was to be cemented into Tammy's routine, as surely as her daily rituals of visiting Barda's camp at Tumberrumba, and each time she came reinforced the certainty in her heart that there was more..., that somehow this beautiful place was wasted just on the few.

Still a dreamer, she began to conceive a plan, whereby she would bring students, in small groups, out to the cavern. As the idea began to grow in her mind, she felt the now familiar stirring within her spirit, and knew that God was leading her yet again, in yet another part of the amazing adventure that her life had become under His mighty, guiding hand.

Here she would teach them the skills she had learned as a child. She would take them to all the places she had wandered to, she would teach them how to cook and prepare meals from those things they would find in the bush. Here they would learn how to find water in the barren wastelands of central Australia, and she would tell them how God had provided for her family and how He had guarded their way.

When the children had first begun to nag her about keeping her promise to take them to her home in the desert, she had applied for, and was granted, permission to visit the area, which was deep within country marked on the map as 'aboriginal reserve – permit required to travel in this area'.

She had, much to her great relief and pleasure, been granted the right to go there at any time, 'due to her long tenure – the result of circumstances beyond her control'.

Of course, there was also her many years of close association with Barda's people, the traditional owners, even though, at the time they had lived there, they were completely unaware that the land had already been claimed on their behalf. Other tribal groups, who had found their way to the east and become assimilated into the white man's ways, had long ago claimed the area as their tribal lands and their ancestral home.

Once the idea had been born in her mind and her heart, there was to be no looking back for Tammy. So she had gone to see Barda, to try and explain to him all that she hoped to accomplish. With his usual wisdom and quick grasp of issues both large and small, Barda slowly nodded his wise old head and promised Tammy that he would support her in seeing her dream come to fruition. And so it was that one by one, with Barda's help, she was able to persuade his descendants to put aside their ancient fears and accompany her on her trips.

Word was soon to get around, via the 'bush telegraph' that works so well out here, and it seemed that in no time at all schools from the towns and cities to the east began asking if they could bring groups out for bush-craft, orienteering and adventure camps.

When Tammy saw the way that her idea was growing, she was unsure at first – surely it was becoming too big too fast. But as she was never the one to turn her back on a good idea, she soon agreed, while realizing that special care would need to be taken to protect the fragile environment.

And added to that concern, was the reality of dealing once more with bureaucracy. This situation would be somewhat different to that which was covered by her existing permit arrangement. New permits for this somewhat unusual extension to the original agreement would need to be negotiated.

There was a certain amount of bureaucracy to deal with of course, however despite the very different circumstances to the run-of-the-mill requests, and because Tammy's connection to Barda's tribal group was such a well-established fact, permission was eventually granted, on the understanding that certain conditions would be met and strictly adhered to.

Tammy had, of course, undertaken to respect sacred sites and to protect the pristine nature of the environment. What the greater majority of its aboriginal owners did not realize, was that the area was as precious to her as it was to them, in fact, in many ways, more so as she had lived with its various moods, struggled against its intractable hostility to the maintenance of human life, and through it all, learned to love it with every fibre of her being.

Eventually, the place was to become so busy, that at times she could hardly remember how quiet and lonely it had been. And with so many organizations asking to send groups to visit, it eventually came to the point where it seemed appropriate to give the place a name. Simply referring to it as 'the cavern' explained nothing. In fact it detracted from the totally amazing experiences that visitors discovered there.

Much thought was given to this, and many and varied were the suggestions. The students at the school made dozens of suggestions, Barda and his people were consulted, and the family all had ideas too. But finally, Tammy made the final choice by combining a piece each of the best suggestions that she had received.

She ran the idea past each group who had helped and found that all of them thought her decision was excellent. And so it was that the cavern became known as 'New Beginnings – Place of Hope and Refuge'.

A great many trips had been made to the cavern since Tammy's first trip back there with her family, and as a result many children and young people had gained a new understanding of the bush and a new appreciation for the courage of those who had struggled to survive in one of the harshest environments on earth.

For the aborigine children it was a way to revisit their cultural heritage – to gain a new respect for the old ways; to understand how hard it had been for their ancestors to survive in the wilderness. And to realize that if you knew how, you could survive where shops were unheard of and food and water were hard fought for. As Barda's people knew all too well, and as Tammy and her family had discovered – if you found water, the life-giving nectar, you lived another day, if you didn't... well for some that had meant death, in a very lonely and unforgiving land.

For the European and Asian youth who came from towns and cities all over Australia, the experience was eye-opening to say the least.

Tammy had made it her personal goal to see to it that no young person would leave her 'Place of Hope and Refuge' without coming to terms with the wild beauty of the place, or without finding a new realization of who they were and who they could become.

Tammy had grown to believe with all her heart that an experience in the wild and wonderful place of her childhood would allow every person who came to seek deep within themselves – to find strengths that they had never realized were there – strengths, she would tell them that can only come from faith in God.

She always told her young visitors about the faith that her parents had held so strongly and how, even in the desperate extremity of being marooned far from civilization, they had held on to that faith, passing it on to their little daughter.

"God is faithful," she would tell her young charges.

"Even in the most desperate times, He never leaves you, and come-what-may, will always see you through. All that is needed to see a miracle of God are the eyes of faith," she would tell them, paraphrasing an old saying that her father had taught her. "Out here, away from all the distractions of life, a person can meet God. And here, in this peaceful place, you can begin again, and find a new strength, a strength that comes from God."

The pilgrimages to her old home had become a comfortable and familiar pattern to Tammy. Gone forever were her old fears. She had learned that she could rise above her fears and that, once those fears were faced head on, they ceased to have the power she'd thought they had over her. These days, Tammy was a mature and confident woman, respected, loved and even revered by all who met her and knew her.

One day, as she was walking back to the house, having cleared up her classroom and helped close the school for the day, she heard the phone ringing. Running the last few yards and taking stairs in a couple of leaps, she ran to the hall and grabbed the phone. To her joy, it was Marlene's voice on the other end.

"I'm coming home, Tammy," she said, after the usual greetings. "Tony and I and our two children, have decided to come back to Tumberrumba and work with you."

Amazed, Tammy could hardly think of what to say, but she finally stammered, "Why, that's wonderful, Marlene, dearest. But what about the careers you've worked so hard to establish, and the children's education?"

Marlene laughed lovingly. "You run a school, you darling goose," she said. "The children will be fine. In fact they'll be better than fine at 'Future Dreaming', just like the hundreds that you've sent successfully on their way," she added.

"Yes, of course, how silly of me," laughed Tammy. "But you and Tony, you have busy lives and successful careers, what about them?"

"We have made a lot of money in the last few years, Tammy, and we have, just lately, been convicted by the Lord, to put it all to some good use. So, we are coming out to 'Future Dreaming', to help teach, and to do any other chores that may be needed.

"Don't worry about living quarters," she quickly added as Tammy went to ask yet another worried question. "We will all live in the bunkhouse until we build our house. Yes, we intend to build our own house. You didn't know this, but Tony has been training under a builder for a couple of years now. He felt that if God was calling him out bush, he'd better have some handy skills to use.

"So that's what we're doing," she finished breathlessly. "We'll see you in about a month, as soon as things here are finalized," she added. "We have put our home on the market and we've been told that it will bring a good price. So pray that it sells quickly," she finished.

With great excitement, Tammy flew to tell Dave, whose heart was so full at the news, he could hardly speak. Who would have thought that the child he thought he would never get to even know, would become such a vital part of his family.

He blessed God for Tammy that she had so unreservedly taken Marlene to her heart. Sometimes he reflected on the years that had flown by.

He remembered the lonely, slightly cynical young man he had allowed himself to become, all those years ago, and how that had changed in the twinkling of an eye, when a vision with white-gold hair had stunned him, captured his heart and filled his whole life with more joy than he reckoned a man ever had the right to hope for.

As for Tammy, well, she was so busy with her life, she hardly ever reflected, unless she was up at the cavern. But, nevertheless, she never failed, each day, to thank her Lord and God for the richness of the gifts he had bestowed on her.

As she walked away from telling her husband that his daughter was coming home, she almost skipped like a girl, there was such lightness of heart. With a whispered prayer of thanks, and a song on her lips, she went happily about her tasks. Marlene was coming home!

What a day of rejoicing it would be, when the family finally arrived. Of course Tammy had refused to entertain any idea of them living in a bunkhouse, so she had immediately set about making room in the house.

Benji and Libby had both gone off to do senior at a school in Brisbane. It probably wasn't really necessary these days, with the school providing as good an education as any city school, but she and Dave felt that it would broaden their horizons. If they were to come back here in later years, then both their parents wanted it to be for the right reasons, not simply because it was all they knew.

They had excelled in their studies and university had followed almost as a matter of course. Both nurtured the hope of pursuing careers that would eventually bring them home to work with their mother, as Joshua had done. The outback was in their blood and even though they were temporarily far away from it all, somehow all they longed for was to go home. But each knew that useful qualifications were an important part of that plan.

So, for now, their rooms were vacant. And although Tammy often stood in the doorways and wistfully gazed in as if she could somehow conjure them up, she was practical enough to realize that the rooms would be suitable, if temporary, accommodation for Marlene and her family.

Chapter 28

HOMECOMINGS

Josh had only quite recently come home to work on Tumberrumba, and although he had been thrilled to move back into his old room, he nevertheless insisted that it should be him who would move into the bunkhouse, so that Marlene's children could use his room.

And although Marlene argued with him over the phone, that her children could quite easily manage together in one room, or in the bunkhouse, he would not hear of it.

"It makes much more sense for a single guy to move over there, than a whole family," he argued. "I won't hear of my sister and her children living over there, and that is final," he had said emphatically.

When Josh had left school in Brisbane, having passed all his subjects with flying colours, he had gone on to university and now, with well-earned degrees and post-graduate honours in engineering and teaching, both done simultaneously despite his mother's reservations, had come back to pass on his skills to the students at the school.

Tammy had been delirious with joy when she'd heard that he was coming back, and had waited impatiently for his arrival. Sometimes since his return, she would often find herself just watching him, as she marveled at the fine, mature young man her eldest son had grown into.

Just lately, she'd noticed that her grown-up son was making frequent trips to the bunkhouses and one evening she noticed that it was not the men's house that he went to.

Further investigation revealed that there was a certain jillaroo, with long golden hair, that he seemed to spend a lot of time talking to. And with a slight pang of something she could not quite identify, she realized that her eldest child was growing up – no, had grown up and that, soon, he would be thinking about a family of his own.

The day of Marlene's and Tony's return finally arrived. They had told the family that they would be driving up from down south, taking several days to enjoy a good look around on the way. A new Four Wheel Drive vehicle had been purchased for their trip 'outback', along with a self-contained off-road caravan.

A phone-call one evening from a truck-stop somewhere along the way, had heralded their expected arrival within the next day or so, most probably in the early evening, if all went to plan.

So, as the sun was sliding down towards the horizon at the end of a timeless, outback day, their dusty vehicle had pulled up in front of the house, amid a great deal of excitement.

Finally, after hugs all round and with essential bags unloaded, the family were gathered on the front verandah of the big house that had been home to Tammy, Dave and their children for so many years. It seemed to Tammy as she sat quietly looking around her, amidst the excited conversation, that rather than getting smaller, her family was getting bigger, and she thought that for sure her heart would burst with joy.

Not only was her adopted daughter home again, a young woman that Tammy had come to love as if she were her own, but along with her, a husband, who she had it on the best authority, was a good man – a provider of some means and a wonderful husband and father. Also, there were two new grandchildren to get to know.

To further add to Tammy's happiness was news from Benji and Libby, who had emailed their mother, only that day, to say that they were both flying home for a holiday break. A break, she understood, that they intended should be a working holiday – insisting that Tammy should find plenty for them to do. It would be, they had informed her, good training for when they came home to live and work with her. And, they had promised her, the time for that would not be too far away, if they had anything to do with it.

How she was longing to hold them again. The time for their permanent return to the fold could not come soon enough for this clucky mother hen. Her children were so dear to her heart and it filled her with joy to know that all three of her own children, and Marlene too, each shared her passion for the school. And each of them had come to trust the Lord with their hearts, something that made Tammy's heart sing for joy.

She remembered the day that Dave and their good friends from their trip across the trackless waste of the outback had each committed themselves to the Lord.

What a celebration that had been. Friends forever, Bob, Gary, Marian and Viv, had all come to visit a few times, making, as so many before them, the pilgrimage to the wilderness home of Tammy's childhood. How good it was to have such wonderful friends. It was so wonderful too, that all of them shared the same love for the God who had carried each of them safely across a trackless waste to the sanctuary of Tumberrumba Station.

Tammy's dream, to teach life skills to outback youngsters – to somehow give young people the tools to navigate a world that sometimes seemed determined to destroy them – had become so much bigger than even she had ever thought possible. And as the conversation, and the happy voices of her loves ones flowed all round her, she paused for a moment, smiled her soft little smile, and whispered her heartfelt thanks to God.

Chapter 29

STILL GROWING – STILL DREAMING

As evening fell and a cool breeze drifted in from the bush, the family sat together on the wide verandah, sharing news and swapping their stories of all that had happened since last they'd seen each other.

The sun had begun to set when Tammy noticed Natalie wandering over from the homestead with the mail for the school.

"Come on up here and join us for a drink," Tammy invited. "Surely it's time for a break. You've been hard at it all day. And look, Marlene is home, and her family with her," she told her friend.

Natalie gratefully accepted the drink that Tammy handed her and sat, insisting that she really only had a moment as she too had a house full, all of whom would be clamouring for a meal before she could say 'Jack Robertson', as the saying goes.

Among the mail that she had handed to Tammy was an official-looking envelope, bearing the emblem of the Queensland Government. Tammy ripped it open with trembling fingers.

"Dear Mrs Wilson, Your application to upgrade the TAFE College, known as 'Future Dreaming', attached to the Tumberrumba Station school to university status, has been duly considered," the letter read. "Although your request would appear to be somewhat unusual, the department has decided not to discard your application.

"We have taken note of the many letters of recommendation we have received on your behalf – most, it seems, unsolicited by yourself – and the scholastic achievements, which, it appears are quite spectacular and numerous, occurring across a wide range of students, regardless of age, ethnicity, gender, social background or previous schooling. The department considers these results to be most unusual and in fact exceptional, so although your situation is quite different to the main stream, after due consideration and consultations at the highest levels, provisional approval is hereby granted.

"Please expect a visit from representatives of this department, soonest. They will bring the necessary documentation, to be signed only if final approval is to be granted, should it be found that your campus does in reality, meet our standards. And that, of course, will depend on the results of their inspection of your campus facilities. You should expect this inspection to be extremely thorough, covering all aspects of your operation."

There followed an extensive list of the areas that would need to meet the approval of the inspection team, and a brief summary of the minimum standards for each. These included staff numbers and their various qualifications, the curriculum, building and infra-structure, equipment, including computing, medical, engineering and mechanical equipment, student accommodation, catering facilities, student quarters, hygiene... and so the list went on.

Following all that, came the caution that, should approval be granted, they would still have to undergo an accreditation process – something they should expect to be stringent and to occur on a regular basis, if university standard was to be granted to, and maintained by 'Future Dreaming'.

The letter continued... "Of course, we do hope you fully understand that your situation is extremely unusual and you need to be aware that in practical terms no actual criteria exist by which to judge your facility. Also please be aware that funding for such a venture will be limited, and dependent entirely upon the reports we receive from the inspection team."

There was a paragraph or two which contained some bureaucratic mumbo-jumbo and what passed for an explanation of legal requirements.

The rather full envelope also contained several sheets of documentation that were to be completed and ready for the inspection team when they arrived.

A brief statement was added almost as an afterthought, that perhaps if they sought some 'legal advice' they might find that 'advantageous', particularly if they found the forms 'a little confusing'.

Tammy thought, Confusing? Were they kidding? Raising her eyes heavenwards, she sighed.

The letter concluded with...

"We thank you for your dedication to the education and well being of the young people of the outback and wish you continued success as you bring quality tertiary education to the children of isolated families.

Yours truly,

Director."

Beneath this official salutation was a scrawled signature that Tammy found impossible to decipher.

She simply sat there for a moment, with a stunned look on her face. Then, as if it had all suddenly hit her, she jumped out of her chair and screamed with delight.

Conversation on the verandah came to an abrupt halt as each pair of eyes turned towards her.

"What's happened?" her husband started to ask. But Tammy was twirling and dancing around and simply did not hear him.

"We made it! We made it!" she cried, jumping up and down with joy. "Our school is, provisionally... well – almost, a university – 'The University of Tumberrumba District', serving Western Queensland, and the southern half of the Northern Territory, known locally as 'Future Dreaming'" she recited proudly.

There was great excitement on the homestead verandah that evening. The normally quiet, late-afternoon peace was quite shattered by all the laughter and celebrating. It was some little time before things settled down again. Offering her sincerest congratulations, and receiving Tammy's heartfelt thanks for everything she had contributed, an excited Natalie finally headed off home to share the good news with her family. She knew that they would be overjoyed, as each had put their whole heart and soul into the project too. Somehow, from nothing, it seemed as if there was to be no stopping it.

'Future Dreaming' had almost taken on a life of its own and just seemed to grow and grow. Natalie realized that from its earliest beginnings, it had never really looked back, and as she ran towards her home, she offered up her thanks to God for blessing them, overshadowing them and guiding their every move.

Tammy's heart too, was full. It seemed, as she sat on the now quiet verandah watching the sun retreat behind a row of trees, that everything she had ever hoped for had come to be, or was promised. Of course, ever practical, she was very aware of all the work that lay ahead of her and at the end of that, no real certainty that it would come to pass. But her faith in all that God had led her to was as strong as ever, and in the quietness of her heart, she knew.

She knew that 'Future Dreaming' would become a university. And she knew too, that it would go from strength to strength, bringing a new way of life to outback kids, hopefully for generations to come.

As she sat there, quietly reflecting on all that happened to her, from the moment she had seen Dave's plane crash in the desert, to this wonderful moment of fulfillment –

the fulfillment of the dreams and hopes of so many, she marveled again, at the future planning of the amazing Creator God, who had never left her, and had never let her down.

She thought of all that had transpired, from the days when she had lived with her parents in their home in the outback, the cavern of her isolated childhood. She marveled at how it had become a favourite place of learning and adventure for dozens of children and young adults alike. And she realized with an intense gratitude, how her dream of bringing life and hope to outback children had become such a reality, a reality beyond her wildest dreams. And then there was her beautiful, growing family, for which she gave daily thanks to God. Each one of them was a constant source of joy and pride and there, in the half-dark, before rising to go inside, Tammy gave a gentle sigh of pure joy, and gave herself a little moment to enjoy watching them as they too celebrated all that had occurred.

Rising to her feet, she smiled to herself, as she recalled once more, the words that she had quoted to her students so many times, and in her heart she rejoiced again at how the words of Scripture always seemed to be so appropriate. 'Colossians 3:23-24,' she murmured softly to herself:

'Whatever you do, work at it with all your heart, as working for the Lord, not for men, since you know that you will receive an inheritance from the Lord as a reward. It is the Lord Christ you are serving.' "Amen," she whispered.

With the words of Scripture on her heart, she thought of a passage that she knew, from Nehemiah, in the Old Testament – a promise that God had made to the Hebrew people through Nehemiah – echoing words spoken by Moses so many years earlier.

Nehemiah 1:8-9...

"If you are unfaithful, I will scatter you among the nations, but if you return to me and obey my commands, then even if your exiled people are at the farthest horizon, I will gather them from there and bring them to the place I have chosen as a dwelling for my Name.'

"We will be faithful, Lord," she whispered. "We will be faithful."

Then, blinking back sudden tears, that made her eyes shine in the light coming from the open door behind her, she looked around at her family, still celebrating, sighed a happy little sigh and turned to her husband with a smile. What more, she wondered to herself, could anyone ask. How much I love this man, she thought.

Then, reaching out and taking his hand she whispered softly, "I love you," adding simply, "God is good." Dave drew her into his arms, kissed the top of her head, breathing in the soft scent that always seemed to surround her, and reflected that of all men, he was the most blessed.

"Yes," he whispered in return, "God is good!"

THE END

'For it is by grace you have been saved, through faith--and this not from yourselves, it is the gift of God-- not by works, so that no one can boast. For we are God's workmanship, created in Christ Jesus to do good works, which God prepared in advance for us to do.'
Ephesians 2:8-10 (NIV)

"So do not fear, for I am with you;
do not be dismayed, for I am your God.
I will strengthen you and help you;
I will uphold you with my righteous right hand."
Isaiah 41:10

"Trust in me and rest," my Jesus said,
"Your burdens, I will gladly bear.
Do not let your heart be filled with dread;
No matter where you go, I will be near."

My heart can be at rest for this I know –
Your word is true, Your promises are sure.
Each day to me, Your faithfulness You show,
My hope in You, forever is secure.

In this wide land of hazy far horizons,
Beyond where human eye could hope to see,
The eye of God roams free – where no horizon –
Can keep His loving eye from you and me.

© Jenny E Shaw

www.ingramcontent.com/pod-product-compliance
Lightning Source LLC
Chambersburg PA
CBHW030628110726
47901CB00002B/366